Clarence Ford

The Life and Letters of Madame de Krudener

Clarence Ford

The Life and Letters of Madame de Krudener

ISBN/EAN: 9783337319588

Printed in Europe, USA, Canada, Australia, Japan

Cover: Foto ©Raphael Reischuk / pixelio.de

More available books at **www.hansebooks.com**

THE LIFE AND LETTERS

OF

MADAME DE KRUDENER

BY

CLARENCE FORD

LONDON
ADAM AND CHARLES BLACK
1893

PREFACE

It is a somewhat curious fact that no life of Mme. de Krudener has ever yet appeared in the English language. Even in the periodical literature of the century her name occurs but rarely, and the articles which profess to deal with the events of her life are, as a rule, both singularly inaccurate in fact, and amazingly prejudiced in tone. No adequate presentment of one of the most striking feminine personalities of modern times was ever offered to the English reading public, until Mr. William Sharp included the earlier of Sainte-Beuve's delightful portraits of the lady in his recently translated *Essays on Men and Women*. And even this literary masterpiece only deals with the earlier years of our heroine and with the lighter and more graceful sides of her character.

In the French and the German language, on the other hand, there exists an extensive bibliography dealing with every phase of Mme. de Krudener's career. Her prolonged residence in both these countries naturally accounts for this expression of general interest. More than once has the tide of public opinion concerning her ebbed and flowed. We find on the one hand an excess of partisan eulogy, and on the other an excess of cynical misrepresentation. After rising to a pinnacle of celebrity by the side of Alexander I. throughout the stirring year of 1815, Mme. de Krudener passed through a period of bitter hostility and rancorous detraction, which continued for some years after her death in 1824. A revulsion of feeling was inevitable after so much palpable injustice, and the tide of public opinion on the continent was definitely turned once again in her favour by the publication in 1849 of the invaluable life in two volumes by M. Charles Eynard. This work, which displays an immense amount of conscientious research, and which was largely compiled from private letters and diaries to which the author had access, has been adopted as a groundwork for almost all subsequent biographies and critical notices. In tone, however, it is perhaps hyper-laudatory, and it loses in breadth and, in my opinion, in accuracy of judgment by being written from an exclusively evangelistic standpoint. In this respect, however, it may be said to act as an antidote to the views expressed by many of the lady's French biographers, who decline to recognise any religious influence in her life, in spite of the testimony supplied by fifteen long years spent in preaching the Gospel throughout Europe.

There is one author to whose gross mis-statements I should like to draw attention. I refer to the well-known French bibliophil P. L. Jacob in the volume entitled *Mme. de Krudener, ses lettres et ses ouvrages*. On the opening page he states that Mme. de Krudener was at one period of her life (1782) the acknowledged mistress of Suard, the Academician, a statement drawn from the life of Suard by J. D. Garat, who, however, only refers to the lady as "Mme. de Kr——." On what authority Jacob elects to identify this person with Julie de Krudener it would be difficult to say. I will only point out that the *liaison* is described as taking place in Paris in 1782 after the lady had been deserted by her husband. As a matter of fact, in 1782 Mme. de Krudener, aged eighteen, and still unmarried, was living with her parents in Livonia. Nor did she set foot in the French capital before the year 1789. Other inaccuracies of detail serve to yet further discredit this highly improbable legend, of which not the faintest corroboration is forthcoming in any other life of the lady. Unfortunately, it has not always proved so easy to unravel the many mis-statements both intentional and accidental of which our heroine has been the victim.

The Russian authorities concerning Mme. de

Krudener are, unfortunately, singularly meagre and uninstructive. This is not surprising, when it is remembered that the later years of Alexander's reign were marked by a painful revival of all the most stringent press regulations. It would have been high treason to pass criticism on any person who had been received into the intimacy of the reigning sovereign. Even to-day the period is scarcely sufficiently remote, and the parallels that might be drawn between the later policy of Alexander I. and the actual *régime* of Alexander III. are too distasteful to the authorities, to allow of unfettered historical research. Hence, with the exception of an admirable essay by Poupine in one of the Russian historical magazines, there is but little information to be obtained, short of a permission to search through the Imperial Archives at St. Petersburg.

The writer of the present volume can lay claim to no originality of research, to no successful unearthing of hitherto unsuspected documents. The book professes to be no more than the outcome of a careful and conscientious sifting of all material accessible to the historical student in the libraries of London and Paris. The task has been vastly facilitated by the existence of numerous letters of Mme. de Krudener, collected from many sources, letters which reveal the real characteristics of the gifted writer far more vividly than any words of her biographer could hope to do. Hence the letters have been largely drawn upon, the majority indeed being printed in their entirety in the present volume. It is hoped that the result, presented for the first time in the English language, may prove not without interest to the English reading public.

February 1893.

CONTENTS

CHAPTER IX

CHAPTER X

CHAPTER XI

CHAPTER XII

CHAPTER XIII

CHAPTER XIV

CHAPTER XV

CHAPTER XVI

CHAPTER XVII

CHAPTER XVIII

ILLUSTRATIONS

AUTHORITIES CONSULTED

Madame de Krudener, Portraits de Femmes, 1837—Sainte-Beuve.
      ,,   ,,   Derniers Portraits, 1852—   ,,
Vie de Mme. de Krudener, 2 vols., 1849—Charles Eynard.
La Baronne de Krudener et l'Empereur Alexandre, 1866—J. B. H. R. Capefigue.
Mme. de Krudener, ses lettres et ses ouvrages, 1880—P. L. Jacob.
Mémoires sur la Reine Hortense, 1836—Louise Cochelet.
Mémoires' Inédits, 1825—Mme. de Genlis.
Mme. Swetchine, sa Vie et ses Œuvres, 1860—Comte de Falloux.
Mémoires d'Outre-Tombe, 1849—F. R. de Chateaubriand.
Mémoires du Prince de Talleyrand, 1891—Duc de Broglie.
Histoire de la Restauration, 1845—J. B. H. R. Capefigue.
Mémoires Secrets—Comte d'Allonville.
Histoire de France sous Napoléon, 1829—L. P. E. Bignon.
Life of William Allen, 1846.
Life and Times of Alexander I., 1875—C. Joyneville.
Memoirs and Correspondence with Alexander I.—Prince Adam Czartoryski.
Notice sur Alexandre, Empereur de Russie, 1840—H. L. Empaytaz.
Etudes sur l'Empire des Tsars, 1847—J. H. Schnitzler.
Histoire de la Russie, 1846—Alfred Rambaud.
Mme. de Krudener, Biographie Universelle (Michaud)—Parisot.
Histoire de France, vol. v.—M. de Norvins.
Frau von Krüdener, Ein Zeitgemälde, 1867.
Julie von Krüdener, 1864—W. Ziethe.
Gespräch unter vier Augen mit Frau von Krüdener, 1818—Prof. Krug.
Erinnerungen und Bilder aus dem Leben eines Predigers, 1843—J. K. Maurer.
Charakter-Züge und historische Fragmente aus dem Leben Friedrich Wilhelm III., 1843—Bishop Eylert.

Briefe der Königin Luise von Preussen—gesammelt von A. Martin.
Deutschland und die Revolution, 1819—J. J. von Goerres.
Geburt und Wiedergeburt, 1846—F. E. von Hurter-Ammaun.
Kirchengeschichte, 1869—C. R. Hagenbach.
Mme. de Krudener, 1856—Sternberg.
Die Hauptströmungen der Literatur des XIX. Jahrhunderts—Georg
    Brandes.

Valérie, 1804—Mme. de Krudener.
Le Camp des Vertus, 1815—Mme. de Krudener.
Une Lettre de Mme. de Krudener—Documents Lyonnais Inédits.

MAGAZINE ARTICLES

Viestnik Evropie, August and September 1869—Poupine.
Revue Germanique, July 1833—Xavier Marmier.
Revue des deux Mondes, June 1849—Sainte-Beuve.
Mercure de France, 1803—Michaud.
Blackwood's Magazine, vol. iv., 1819.
London Magazine, July 1820.
Gentleman's Magazine, May 1825.
Westminster Review, vol. lvii.
Bentley's Miscellany, vol. l.
Spiritual Magazine, vol. iv., 1869—William Howitt.

MADAME DE KRUDENER

CHAPTER I

1764-1789

IN no country of Europe have women worked out their own emancipation so rapidly as in Russia. During six long centuries, from the day on which the Empress Olga, daughter-in-law of Rurik, received Christian baptism at Constantinople from the head of the Greek Church, the women of Russia were doomed to lives of rigid domestic seclusion, enforced by the combined influence of both early Slav custom and of later Byzantine teaching. It was not till the middle of the 17th century that the Empress Natalie Narischkin, mother of Peter the Great, won a first victory on behalf of her sex, by bravely drawing back the curtains of her litter, and daring to show her face unveiled to her subjects, as she was carried through the streets of Moscow. From that day to this, Russian women have played a foremost part in the political history of their country. The 18th century was the age *par excellence* of Empress rulers. Elizabeth Petrovna, the two Annas, and the two Catherines held in turn the reins of supreme power for a period of well-nigh seventy years, during which Russia advanced by giant strides in territory, in wealth, in civilisation. That Russian women, with their magnetic attractiveness, brilliant linguistic attainments, and characteristically feminine charm, possessed a special aptitude for diplomacy, was brought home to a past generation of Englishmen by the Princess Lieven, the friend and correspondent of Earl Grey and of Guizot. In our own day, the revolutionary party has elaborated as a principle, what previously had only been grasped in a tentative and nebulous fashion, namely, that no great national movement can grow to maturity without the co-operation of the national womanhood. The early leaders of the revolt against despotism appealed in eloquent and impassioned language to the patriotism of their sisters, and the appeal was not made in vain. There has never been any lack of a Vera Sassulitch, a Sophia Gunsberg, or a Mme. Tzebrikova in the Nihilist ranks.

There is an indescribable vividness and intensity about a Russian woman of culture. Although she may outvie her French sister in luxury, in elegance, in fabulous expenditure, she has little or nothing of French flippancy or cynicism in her composition. Her emotions, whether good or bad, ring out more true and natural, and her real self is less frequently disguised under that mask of conventionality which appears to be the inevitable adjunct of centuries of civilisation. The Confessions of Marie Bashkirtseff could never have been written by a daughter of Western Europe. Russian women are gifted with an almost limitless capacity for self-sacrifice. In other words, they are profoundly religious. Millions adhere closely to the National Church, with its sumptuous services, its Catholic doctrine, its tender wailing chants. Others have revolted against the religious atrophy which even the most gorgeous ritual in the world cannot wholly disguise, and have broken away in varying directions. Thus the Nihilist women have replaced the love of Christ by the love of their country. On the other hand, certain *âmes d'élite*—and their number has been not a few—have found in the Catholic Church that intimate sense of union with God which the Church of their baptism failed to supply. Who, in this connection, will not call to mind Mme. Swetchine, whose *salon* in the Rue St. Dominique was for thirty years a centre of spiritual activity for Catholic France? Or again, the girlish figure of Natalie Narischkin, a 19th-century namesake of the 17th-century Empress, who joyfully hid her imperial lineage under the stiff white *cornettes* of a Sister of Charity?

It is in this same group, though with an individuality all her own, that we must class Barbe-Julie de Krudener, the saintly friend of the Emperor Alexander, the prophetess of the downfall of Napoleon, the inspirer of the Holy Alliance, the repentant Magdalen who preached the forgiveness of sins throughout the length and breadth of Europe. True, she never entered the Catholic Church, though, at one moment of her life standing, attracted, yet hesitant, almost on its very threshold ; but she is the outcome, equally with Mme. Swetchine, of that wave of religious enthusiasm which, with vivifying touch, passed over Russia in the first decades of the century, and which forms one of the most attractive chapters in her history. In Mme. de Krudener may be seen, curiously blended, not only all the essential characteristics of Russian womanhood, but also a remarkable development of that religious mysticism which is so profound and fascinating an expression of Christian faith. Thus she is at once a type both of her country and of her age ; and her personality, once so potent both for good and for evil, surely merits to be rescued from the oblivion into which of recent years it seems so strangely to have fallen.

Barbe-Julie de Wietinghoff, known to the world as Mme. de Krudener, was born in her father's mansion at Riga on the 21st of November 1764. The Wietinghoffs, who are of German extraction, trace back their descent to the 14th century, when they claim to have provided the Teutonic Order with two Provincial Masters in the persons of Arnold and Konrad von Wietinghoff. But from that period until the middle of the 18th century, when the family prosperity was resuscitated in the person of Mme. de Krudener's father, the Wietinghoffs existed in complete obscurity in the Baltic province of Livonia. A large proportion of the inhabitants of these so-called Baltic Provinces, lying on the extreme western frontier of the Russian Empire, with which they were only incorporated at a comparatively late date, are of Teutonic or Scandinavian origin ; and at a time when the rest of Russia, with the exception of the great towns, was still sunk in a condition of Eastern barbarism, the nobility of Livonia, Esthonia, and Courland enjoyed considerable material prosperity, and a certain measure of German civilisation and culture.

M. de Wietinghoff, the father of our heroine, was a man of keen business capacity and much determination of character, who, at a very early age, flung himself into commercial enterprises with so marked a success, that by the time he had reached the prime of life, he found himself the proud possessor of a vast fortune, of large properties at Kosse and Marienburg, and of a sumptuous town-house at Riga, besides having attained to the official rank of privy councillor and senator. He enjoyed no title, but would exclaim with pride, "I am Wietinghoff," and behaved with all the arrogance of a great noble. One of his pet extravagances for many years was the maintenance of a private theatre adjoining his town residence, which, however, he ultimately sold to the municipal authorities of Riga.

Mme. de Wietinghoff, the mother of Barbe-Julie—also of German origin—was a daughter of the celebrated Marshal Münnich, the successful commander of many campaigns against Turks and Tartars, who subsequently suffered twenty years of Siberian exile, and was only received back into favour by the Empress Catherine II. Mme. de Wietinghoff appears to have inherited a fair share of her father's capacity and strength of character. We are told that every morning by six o'clock she was to be found looking after her household matters, and directing her servants, whilst later several hours of the day were devoted to her children ; but in the evening, with a handsome presence and dignified manner, she posed as the accomplished *femme du monde*, and did the honours of her house with great brilliancy.

She was the mother of five children—two sons and three daughters ; but the eldest son died in infancy, whilst the eldest girl was a deaf-mute. Barbe-Julie, the subject of this biography, was the second daughter.

The early years of Mme. de Krudener were mainly divided between the town of Riga and her father's country-place of Kosse.   Here the summer months were spent in happy, healthy freedom, and here the little Julie, impressionable and poetic from her earliest childhood, cultivated that love of nature and that passionate attachment to the dreamy and somewhat melancholy beauty of her northern home, which remained with her through life as two of the most marked characteristics of her curiously complex personality.   Many years later, in one of the opening pages of *Valérie*, she wrote lovingly and regretfully of "the solitude of the sea, its vast silence and stormy activity, the uncertain flight of the kingfisher, the melancholy cry of the birds that inhabit our northern regions, the sad, tender light of our aurora borealis, all of which encouraged the vague and fascinating aspirations of my youth." And in the intervals of her stormy and eventful career, it was to her old home at Kosse that Mme. de Krudener turned most willingly for the rest and quiet she so greatly needed, but which she seemed incapable of tolerating in any other place.

Of Julie's early education it is difficult to speak with any precision. Some biographers have written of her as though her infantile precocity and learning almost rivalled that of John Stuart Mill himself. The truth seems to be, on the contrary, that her general education was very much neglected, but that like all Russians she possessed a considerable aptitude for languages; hence at an early age she was taught both French and German—the former because it was the language of all good society, and the latter because it was largely spoken in the Baltic provinces. Of her religious teaching nothing definite is known, and the question—interesting in the light of subsequent events—as to whether Julie was reared in the Orthodox or in the Lutheran faith has been generally left undecided. But bearing in mind that her parents were both of German extraction, we are justified in assuming the correctness of a casual statement contained in the *Mémoires Secrets* of the Comte d'Allonville,[1] to the effect that in her childhood Mme. de Krudener was a member of the Reformed

---

[1] Armand-François, Comte d'Allonville, author of *Mémoires Secrets de 1770 à 1830*, married a great-grandchild of Marshal Münnich, and niece of Mme. de Krudener.

Church.   As a matter of fact, however, all that we
know of the family circumstances points to the conclusion that religion was a very neglected quantity
in the Wietinghoff establishment, and that the
newest philosophical ideas, promulgated by Voltaire
and the Encyclopedists, were in all probability
imbibed by the younger members of the household
as forming part of a correct French education.

Early in 1777 the necessity of placing their
afflicted eldest daughter in a suitable asylum, caused
M. and Mme. de Wietinghoff to undertake a journey
to Hamburg, in which they were accompanied by
their younger daughter Julie.   They subsequently
spent some time at the then fashionable baths of
Spa, and here Julie, aged thirteen, made her first
acquaintance with that brilliant cosmopolitan society,
in which a few years later she took such keen delight.
At this time, however, her principal attraction to
strangers lay in the fact that she was reputed to be
one of the richest heiresses of Livonia—for she was
still an overgrown, undeveloped, silent girl, with a
rather large nose and an uncertain complexion, but
with ample promises of future beauty in her big blue
eyes and curling chestnut hair, and in her singularly
well-shaped hands and arms.

The following winter was spent in Paris, where
no doubt many fashionable doors were opened to
the rich Russian family; but of Julie herself all
that we know for certain is that she took dancing-
lessons from Vestris—a solitary fact which seems to
imply that her education was taken hardly more

seriously than that which Mme. de Genlis describes in her entertaining Memoirs as having been her own portion in early youth. After a few months spent in England, during which visit they were accompanied by a French governess, the Wietinghoffs returned home, and Julie was able to take her place as a travelled and accomplished young lady of the world in the rich provincial society of Riga.

The next two years must be passed over in silence. There exists a family tradition that at sixteen, Julie, whose growing beauty and charm combined with her monetary expectations made her the object of many matrimonial proposals, was officially promised in marriage to a certain baron of the neighbourhood, of suitable rank. The young girl's own inclinations were not for an instant consulted, and even when Julie protested with tears against the proposed alliance, her parents remained obdurate. Then, in her despair, for the first time in her life, the future preacher and prophetess turned to God, and implored Him to rescue her from her fate. Shortly afterwards she was seized with a severe attack of measles, which affected both her health and her looks for a considerable period; and whether from that reason, or because in her delirium she expressed such unequivocal horror of the proposed marriage, certain it is that her betrothed voluntarily withdrew all claim to her hand, and Julie herself believed that her deliverance was due to the merciful hand of Providence in response to her own ardent prayers.

She felt no such aversion, when, two years later, she was sought in marriage by Baron Bourkhardt-Alexis - Constantine Krudener, who had already achieved a high position for himself in the Russian diplomatic world. Born in 1744, and of Livonian origin, Baron Krudener had distinguished himself in his youth at the University of Leipsic, had travelled through Europe, entered the diplomatic service, and had earned the gratitude of Catherine II. by the successful manner in which, as Minister at the little Court of Mitau, he had prepared the annexation of the Duchy of Courland to Russia. He had been already twice married and twice divorced, and by his first wife was father to one little girl, Sophie, at that time nine years of age. These matrimonial experiences do not appear, however, to have been regarded in the light of a drawback either by Julie or by her parents, who warmly welcomed the advances of the Baron. It is true he was twenty years older than his bride, and that she, on her side, did not profess to feel any romantic devotion to her future husband ; but, on the other hand, his high position, his talents, his undoubted integrity, and the brilliant future he was able to offer, satisfied the ambition and flattered the vanity of the young girl, and induced her to enter willingly into the bonds of wedlock. Such, indeed, is the explanation of her marriage that she herself gives at a later date, in a letter to her friend Bernardin de St. Pierre, and it must be admitted that a brilliant *mariage de convenance* was the most natural consummation of her whole education.   Fashionable society towards the close of the 18th century did not strive after soul-satisfying unions in lawful matrimony. A husband, who, having given his wife a certain position, treated her subsequently with every mark of outward respect, was held to have amply fulfilled his marital functions ; and a wife who presided over a brilliant *salon*, and thereby gratified her own vanity whilst serving her husband's political interests, was all that a wife should be in the eyes of the world. More than that neither side was called upon to furnish, and Mme. de Krudener's earliest griefs arose from the fact, that, in her youthful inexperience, having chosen with her head, she expected at the same time to satisfy the longings of a singularly romantic heart.

The marriage ceremony took place in the spring of 1783, at the Castle of Ramkau, near Mitau, the residence of Baron Krudener's mother, and here the first months of Mme. de Krudener's married life were spent under the chaperonage of Mme. de Mayendorff, her husband's eldest sister, and her own godmother.   With music, dancing, and private theatricals (in which husband and wife undertook the principal *rôles*), the days slipped pleasantly by ; something, too, was accomplished towards filling up the blanks left by Julie's early education. M. de Krudener, who, during a residence in Paris, had enjoyed the friendship of Jean-Jacques Rousseau, was anxious to encourage a taste for literature in his wife, and the reading aloud of selected French fiction became one of the regular occupations of the family circle. A passing visit from the Comte and Comtesse du Nord, afterwards the Emperor Paul I., and the Empress Marie, during the winter of 1783, brought the castle festivities to a brilliant climax. A few weeks later (30th January 1784) the young wife gave birth to her eldest and only son, Baron Paul de Krudener, to whom the Emperor Paul stood as godfather. A further proof of imperial favour—the appointment of Baron Krudener as Ambassador to the Republic of Venice—necessitated a temporary visit to St. Petersburg, where the youthful ambassadress, barely out of her teens, naturally took part in all the festivities of the Court of Catherine II. In the following autumn the whole Krudener household undertook the long and wearisome journey in post-chaises across Poland and Austria, arriving on the shores of the Adriatic before the winter set in.

It is impossible to describe the life led by Mme. de Krudener at Venice, in all the exuberance of her youthful enthusiasms, without anticipating somewhat, and referring to her novel *Valérie*, published indeed some twenty years later, but which we are only following the example of Sainte-Beuve in accepting as a trustworthy picture of her Italian experiences. The graceful, tender, capricious, girlish figure which is evoked before our eyes by a perusal of Gustave's passionate love-letters, is none other than the authoress herself, a little embellished perhaps, a little poeticised, and yet instinct with life and reality, and in harmony with all the descriptions furnished us by contemporary writers. It is true that it was by *Valérie* rather than by Mme. de Krudener herself in later years that M. de Sainte-Beuve was inspired when he penned his first incomparable sketch of the lady;[1] and when the stern facts of her later life were brought into prominence by M. Charles Eynard in his valuable and conscientious biography, the great critic half petulantly complains[2] that his modern St. Elizabeth, with her mystic aureole, should have been dragged "from the dim white radiance out of which she smiles on us," into the fierce uncompromising light of grave historical criticism. In his second essay M. de Sainte-Beuve openly regrets the sympathetic enthusiasm with which he had at first approached the authoress of *Valérie*. *Désillusionné* on several points, he allows her no other virtues than those of a singularly attractive *femme du monde*. Judging of Mme. de Krudener's agitated existence as a whole, this first "Portrait" gives, indeed, but one side of her many-sided character. But it remains none the less a true and vivid presentment of the Julie de Krudener of those early innocent days in Venice, ere her married life had ended in disaster, and when the dreamy mysticism of her nature had already cast a halo of poetry over her gay, luxurious existence.

In spite of her large expressive eyes and delicate complexion, Julie de Krudener could never be classed as a strictly beautiful woman. Her features

---

[1] See his *Portraits de Femmes*; also *Essays on Men and Women*, translated into English, with a Memoir, by William Sharp.

[2] See *Derniers Portraits*.

were wanting in regularity; but she possessed to a singular degree that charm of manner and personal fascination, which may exist independently of actual beauty, and which seems to be the birthright of so many Russian women of noble birth. They possess something of the exquisite fragrance of a hothouse blossom, reared, as they are, in the midst of almost inconceivable luxury, tempered by all the refinements of French civilisation, and artificially sheltered from every contact with the inclement rigours of their northern climate.

Mme. de Krudener, as we shall see, preserved a certain magnetic attraction up to the very last years of her life. Added to this she possessed an extreme gracefulness of carriage and lightness of motion, which, together with her fair curling hair that fell in soft ringlets round her face, lent an air of unusual youthfulness to her appearance. At Venice, the young wife and mother of twenty-one still looked like a girl of sixteen. But we must let Julie speak for herself, for the best portrait of her is that contained in a letter from Gustave to his friend Ernest:—

I cannot describe Valérie to you better than by reminding you of your cousin, the youthful Ida. They are strangely alike, and yet she possesses something special that I have never yet seen in any other woman. It would be easy to possess as much grace, and much more beauty, and yet to be far inferior to her. People do not perhaps admire her, but she possesses something ideal and fascinating which forces one to be struck by her. She is so refined, so slight, she might almost be a fleeting thought. Nevertheless, the first time I saw her I did not think her pretty.

She is very pale, and the contrast between her gaiety, I might even say her wild spirits, and her face, which is meant to be serious and sensible, had a curious effect upon me. I have since discovered that the moments in which she appears to be simply a happy child are very rare. Her habitual temperament is, on the contrary, somewhat sad, and she flings herself at times into an exaggerated gaiety, just as highly sensitive people, with very delicate nerves, may behave in a manner quite contrary to their habits.[1]

It is easy to conceive what an *épanouissement* of beauty, of grace, of exuberant romantic sentimentality, must have taken place in this daughter of the North on her first experience of southern sunshine and colour and fulness of life. She herself has left a record of the intense impressions of those early Italian days—a record which shows us how keenly sensitive she was to all the beauties that surrounded her. As a description of life in Venice, nothing could be more vivid than the following passage :—

Venice is the chosen home of languor and indolence. You recline in your gondola, which glides through the imprisoned waters; you recline in your box at the opera, where you listen to the enchanting tones of the most exquisite voices in Italy. You sleep during part of the day, and you spend the evening either at the opera or in what are known here as "casinos." The square of St. Mark's is the capital of Venice—the *salon* of good society by night, and by day the general meeting-place of the people. There you may enjoy a succession of sights; the cafés constantly open and shut; the shops display their wares; the Armenian smokes his cigar in silence; whilst veiled, and with a light step, the wife of the Venetian noble, half concealing her beauty, and yet displaying it with art, crosses the square, which serves her as a promenade during the day, whilst at night, glittering with diamonds, she may be seen visiting theatres and cafés,

---

[1] See *Valérie*, Letter III.

and finally taking refuge in her casino in order to await the morning sun. Add to all this the tumult on the quay that runs close to St. Mark's, the groups of Slavonians and Dalmatians, the boats which bring to shore all the fruits of the islands, the public buildings in all their majesty, the columns on which the horses seem to be alive, proud of their strength and of their classic beauty. See how the Italian sky harmonises its delicate tones with the sombre antiquity of the monuments; listen to the sound of the bells mingled with the songs of the gondoliers; watch all this crowd of people: in a single instant every knee is bent, every head is reverently bowed; it is a procession that is passing. Note the magic distance: it is the Alps of the Tyrol which form that curtain, gilded by the sun. What a glorious belt tenderly encircles Venice! It is the Adriatic; but her imprisoned waves are none the less the daughters of the ocean; and if they play around these exquisite islands, from which dark cypresses spring up, they can also roar and rage, and threaten to submerge these delightful retreats.[1]

As at Mitau, private theatricals—for which there was a craze in smart society towards the end of the last century—were the chief amusement of the Krudener household; the diplomatic body, foremost amongst whom was the Countess Brenner, wife of the Austrian ambassador, joined in heartily, and various representations were given before a select Venetian audience. The opera also and the theatre filled up many evenings, and were a source of intense delight to the youthful ambassadress. She even attempted herself at this time to learn to play on the harp, but with little success. In the Italian language, however, she proved a proficient scholar; and it is worth noting that she was able in later years to read and speak fluently no less than five

---

[1] See *Valérie*, Letter XXI.

languages—Russian, French, German, Italian, and English—whilst of her remarkable talent for French prose composition we have abundant proof both in her novel and in her letters.

In spite of all the admiration lavished upon her by others, Julie's only ambition at this time was to please her husband. With an ardent and romantic nature, she imperatively required some object on which to lavish her affections, and during the first years of her marriage she made a persistent and honest attempt to regard her husband as the hero of her life. The glowing description of the Count in *Valérie* represents Baron Krudener more as his wife's ardent imagination loved to picture him, than as he really was. The truth is, he did not lend himself readily to the *rôle* of a hero of romance. Julie's love was of the exacting sort, that craves for recognition. She herself, we are told by M. Eynard, spent her days in attempting to prove her affection by ceaseless attentions. She would undertake lengthy and fatiguing expeditions in order to obtain some special fruit or flowers for her husband's table. If he appeared preoccupied or worried, she would attempt to amuse him, and from the moment he entered her presence she would follow him closely with her eyes, eager for some smile or glance of recognition. Intensely timid on the water, she would yet hide her fears in order to accompany him in a gondola on the lagoon. All these delicate attentions were simply wasted on the ambassador. Twenty years older than his wife, of a naturally serious disposition, and absorbed in his diplomatic duties, he had no time for those *petits soins* which women value so highly. Devotedly attached as he was to his charming Julie, he was utterly incapable of understanding the fanciful, romantic side of her nature ; he would try, gently and gravely, to check her impetuosity and train her character, and was least responsive at the very times when she craved most for his sympathy. In the spring-time the family moved out of Venice to a charming villa on the banks of the Brenta, and here there occurred a little incident, graphically described by M. Eynard, which is worth repeating as curiously characteristic of the relations between the husband and wife.

One evening when the Baron had gone to pay a visit to some friends, and when Julie was sitting alone in the villa, a sudden thunderstorm burst over the country, accompanied by torrents of rain. Under the influence of the electric-laden atmosphere, Mme. de Krudener's nerves were more than usually susceptible ; her vivid imagination easily conjured up visions of all the misfortunes that might overtake her husband on his way home, and the hours passed in an agony of suspense. Sending the servants to bed, she determined to sit up alone and await his return ; but towards two in the morning she could bear the anxiety no longer, and started off by herself along the road to Padua. Meeting an empty carriage on its way home, she drove back to the villa, called up her maid, and started off to meet M. de

Krudener. They encountered the ambassador not far from the house, and he was not unnaturally filled with amazement at finding his wife, half beside herself with terror, driving about at such an hour. " But, my dear child, how could you be so foolish ?" he exclaimed; "what possible harm could have happened to me ? You ought to have gone to bed !" These affectionate words pierced the heart of Mme. de Krudener like a dagger. "Alas !" she thought, "in my place he would have gone to bed, and to sleep !"

It was the old story of fundamental incompatibility of temperament. The Krudener household at this period presents the spectacle of a domestic drama which in its main elements is painfully trite and commonplace. Almost as a matter of course further complications arose in the presence of one, who was pining to offer all that M. de Krudener was incapable of supplying. Alexandre de Stakieff, the Gustave of Mme. de Krudener's *Valérie*, and private secretary to the ambassador, of an intensely romantic and imaginative temperament, early fell a victim to the charms of the young wife, with whom he was fated to live in close daily intercourse. An ardent devotion to his diplomatic chief, combined with an unusual sense of honour, enabled the young man so far to conquer his infatuation as to keep it a secret from the object of his love, though it is difficult to believe that Julie, with all her keen sensibilities, should have remained for months in ignorance of the passion that was burning beside her. It is certain, however, that she was not fully enlightened as to the nature of M. de Stakieff's devotion until some time subsequently to her residence in Venice.

In the spring of 1786 Baron Krudener received orders from St. Petersburg to transfer his ambassadorial functions to the Court of Copenhagen. Before proceeding northwards, he and his wife undertook a short journey through Italy, visiting Bologna, Florence, Rome, Naples, etc. It was at Rome that Angelica Kauffmann, then at the height of her fame, painted the portrait of Mme. de Krudener which now hangs in the galleries of the Louvre, representing her sitting under a tree with her little son Paul, as Cupid, beside her. It is the most pleasing of all the original portraits of the lady ; but the artist has entirely failed to render that slenderness and lightness of form which was one of the chief charms of her sitter. This is the picture that is referred to in *Valérie*, and which the heroine sends back to Gustave at Venice, that it may hang in her *petit salon jaune*, to console him for her absence.

Life at the Copenhagen Embassy was necessarily one constant succession of dinners and fêtes. Count Skavronski, M. de Krudener's predecessor in office, had kept open house with almost regal splendour, and his successor was obliged to incur enormous expenses in order to keep up worthily the hospitable traditions of the Embassy. Moreover, he was obliged to entertain at his table all the officers of the Russian fleet, which, owing to the recently declared war with Sweden, was then anchored in the Sound.

In the meanwhile Julie, who was daily learning to realise the extent of her own fascinations, and who, perhaps, had grown a little weary of confining her attentions to the middle-aged ambassador, flung herself with characteristic ardour into all the dissipations of the Danish capital, exciting the envy of the women, and courting the admiration of the men. Then it was that Alexandre de Stakieff, who was still acting as secretary to the Embassy, felt that his heroic Platonism would give way, and that the only course open to him as a man of honour was to take his departure. It was one thing to hide his feelings when the betrayal of them would have ruffled the conjugal peace of the life at Venice; it was quite another to allow himself to be supplanted by half the young officers of the Danish Court.

M. de Stakieff accordingly left the capital, and wrote a letter to his chief explaining the true reason of his departure, in which the following words occur: "What I cannot explain, but what is nevertheless true, is that I worship her because she loves you. If ever she were to love you less, she would be no more to me than any other woman, and I should love her no more." Touched by this pathetic revelation of an unsuspected passion, and apparently possessed by a complete confidence in his wife's affection, the worthy ambassador was guilty of the almost incredible folly of showing the letter to

Mme. de Krudener. The result was the very reverse of what he had intended. All her life Julie had been filled with a desire to inspire a *grande passion*, and this sudden revelation of the extent of her power over the hearts of men, merely excited her to fresh conquests. To awaken in others a passion which her husband had shown himself incapable of supplying, appeared to her distorted moral sense as the legitimate satisfaction of a sensitive heart. By revealing the contents of M. de Stakieff's letter, M. de Krudener drove the first nail into the coffin of his domestic happiness.

After several months of this festive and frivolous existence, during which all her aspirations were drowned in mere amusement, Julie became for a second time *enceinte*, and as a natural result of the exciting atmosphere in which she lived, her nerves, and indeed her whole health, suffered. The little girl, Juliette, was but a puny infant at her birth, whilst her mother remained in extremely delicate health. She was not only subject to fits of hysteria, but her lungs became affected, and she began to spit blood. Continued residence at Copenhagen seemed out of the question, and Mme. de Krudener herself, always eager for fresh experiences, no doubt energetically supported the doctors' opinion that she should spend some months in a warmer climate. Her departure possessed the further advantage of allowing her husband to reduce his establishment at Copenhagen, and effect some very necessary economies. Accordingly, in May 1789, Mme. de Krudener, accompanied by her step-daughter Sophie, then a girl of about sixteen, her governess, Mdlle. Piozet, of Geneva, and her two little children, Paul and Juliette, started for the South of France, with the intention of remaining some time in Paris on her way.

CHAPTER II

1789-1793

"STILL a child at Mitau, Mme. de Krudener only sought for amusement. At Venice, her heart speaks. At Copenhagen her vanity is roused. But it is in Paris that her intellect appears to claim its rights." [1]

These few lines summarise with accuracy the early life of our heroine. Her visit to Paris, occurring simultaneously with her first separation from her husband, forms an epoch in her life. Her childish yearning search after happiness had never yet been fully satisfied. Marriage had proved a failure; mere frivolous dissipation had proved a failure (for she had grown honestly weary of the never-ceasing round of festivities at Copenhagen); religion, which at a later date was to transform her whole existence, as yet only affected her at intervals as some mystical and poetic dream ; now, at five-and-twenty, Mme. de Krudener was about to fling herself with her usual impetuosity into literature and art, in the hope of satisfying the undefined longings of her romantic nature. Fully conscious of her educational

[1] See *Vie de Mme. de Krüdener*, by C. Eynard, vol. i. ch. ii. p. 30.

shortcomings, from the date of her arrival in Paris she devoted much time and trouble to her own self-improvement, reading, studying, visiting museums, and frequenting as much as possible the society of contemporary *hommes de lettres*. The Abbé Barthélemy had published a few months previously his *Voyage du Jeune Anacharsis en Grèce*, a work which had been received with immense applause both by the fashionable and literary world of Paris. Mme. de Krudener, with a ready capacity for hero-worship, went into raptures over both the author and his book, and it is said that she not only read and re-read the adventures of the youthful Anacharsis, but copied out whole passages in order to learn them by heart. When the Abbé was elected a member of the French Academy, she insisted on being present at the ceremony of his reception.

First and foremost amongst her literary friends, however, must be placed the author of *Paul et Virginie*, who, years before at St. Petersburg, had lived on terms of intimacy with her grandfather, Marshal Münnich. Before long his little retreat in the Rue de la Reine Blanche, Faubourg St. Marceau, had become as a second home to her, where she could always be sure of the warmest of welcomes. Bernardin de St. Pierre and Mme. de Krudener were at one in their intense love of nature, and, as a writer, he was gifted with just that natural sentimentality with which at this period of her life she was enamoured. Moreover, Julie was possessed by a very genuine appreciation of the simple joys of life, and escaping from the conventional entertainments of Parisian society, she would take her children, and accompany St. Pierre on his long country rambles beyond the city. On these occasions she would appear at her best, full of unaffected gaiety and girlish enjoyment; and possessing the curious faculty of being only conscious at any given moment of one side of her many-sided character—a faculty which explains many of her seeming inconsistencies —she was convinced whilst enjoying the society of St. Pierre, that she had never cared for anything but nature and the simple joys of life. Thus, writing of her past life to her friend, she says: " I experienced a longing to be felt, and in the midst of all the luxury and senseless pleasures of Copenhagen I remained simple and true, and always in harmony with nature." And again : " I am possessed of a soul of which the unalterable desire is to be true and just." In the light of these assertions it is somewhat of a shock to learn that, in spite of this overwhelming love of simplicity, and in spite too of a very positive necessity for economy, Mme. de Krudener incurred in the course of a few months a bill for £800 to Mdlle. Bertin, the celebrated dressmaker of Marie Antoinette!

Although this visit to Paris was made in the fateful year 1789, and although Bernardin de St. Pierre himself was an enthusiastic disciple of the early principles of the Revolution, there is no trace that public affairs exercised any influence over the mind of one, who, in later life, was credited with the

power of directing the fate of nations.   Neither is
there any reason to believe, on M. Capefigue's
authority,[1] that Mme. de Krudener devoted her
whole time to a study of magic lore and the occult
sciences.   After six months of social and literary
pleasures, the Krudener household, accompanied by
an old professor of botany, the Abbé Famin, travelled
southwards (December 1789) to Montpellier, where
several months were spent.   In the spring-time a
move was made to Nîmes, and from thence Mme.
de Krudener wrote a few descriptive lines, inspired
by that under-current of melancholy which was only
partially disguised by her fits of youthful gaiety.

With the abbé we explored the mountains covered with
thyme and sweet marjoram, and I clambered up to the most
inaccessible heights.   One of my greatest pleasures was to watch
the wonderful effects of light, and the vivid red of the evening
sky, against which in the distance there stood out the dark green
of the cypresses, whose spiral shapes have so melancholy an
effect.   At times I used to remain absorbed in silent reflections ;
sometimes, too, the abbé used to discourse to me on science. . . .
My soul, deeply moved, was also stirred by passionate longings,
and even in these enchanted regions I used to shed hot tears of
misery. . . . I went to Avignon, absorbed, owing to certain
circumstances, in the most gloomy reflections, and as usual I
tried to forget my troubles in nature and in country pursuits.
I hastened to visit Vaucluse.   The dismal appearance of the
rugged rocks, the dark tints of the moss, the occasional song of
solitary birds, all was in harmony with my soul and made me
cling to the spot, whilst the accents of Petrarch added to the
picture something of that passionate fanaticism, which engraves
our emotions in the deepest recesses of the heart.

Midsummer found Mme. de Krudener at Barèges

[1] See *La Baronne de Krüdener et l'Emp. Alexandre*, par M. Capefigue.

surrounded by a host of friends, which included Mme. de Lobkoff, Count Poushkin, the Duc de Fleury, and the Comte Adrien de Lezay-Marnésia, who will reappear in Mme. de Krudener's later life under very different circumstances. The whole party appear to have indulged in the gayest of pranks and the wildest of spirits, Mme. de Krudener being the recognised queen of the season, and setting the fashion in all things. On one occasion she happened to purchase from a pedlar a fancy handkerchief, which she tied round her head, and immediately the whole stock was bought up by the ladies of the town, who all appeared with their heads decked with handkerchiefs. Excursions were made almost daily to neighbouring places of interest. One evening after tea somebody proposed a moonlight drive to Luz, and the suggestion was received with rapturous applause. A start was made, but the way was long, and the roads bad, and it was midnight before the joyous party with shrieks of laughter rattled noisily into the little town of Luz, awakening the startled inhabitants from their sleep. The landlord of the inn took them for emigrants, anxious to cross the Spanish frontier—a mistake which added to the general hilarity. Sleep was of course out of the question, and at sunrise the whole party re-entered Barèges as excitedly as they had started. Local society was much scandalised at the escapade, and Mme. de Krudener, from the fact of her being always *en évidence*, received the largest share of the blame. Reproof, however, fell on unheeding ears, for Julie was determined by this time to set the laws of conventionality at defiance, according to her own good pleasure, and she regarded any form of restraint as an unwarrantable interference with her liberty.

The following winter was again spent at Montpellier, and it was whilst residing outside the town, in a solitary little villa. which had captivated her fancy, that Mme. de Krudener made the acquaintance of the Comte de Frégeville, a handsome and fascinating young officer in the hussars. He fell passionately in love with her almost at first sight, and devoted himself to the task of winning her love. M. Eynard has told us in detail the whole story of her resistance, vacillation, and final self-abandonment: how week by week on one flimsy pretext or another she delayed her projected journey northwards; how she lost the protection of Mdlle. Piozet by the marriage of that lady with a M. Armand; how at length realising her own weakness she made all her arrangements for leaving Montpellier; and how, when the moment came for bidding a last farewell to her adorer, her courage failed her, and, vanquished by his passionate entreaties, she consented to allow him to act as her escort through France.

It is not easy to follow in detail the life of Mme. de Krudener through the months that follow—months which were spent for the most part in Paris, by the side of her lover, in spite of the urgent and repeated requests of her husband that she should rejoin him at the Embassy at Copenhagen. We have glimpses

of her frame of mind from her letters to her friend
Mme. Armand, with whom she commenced at this
period a correspondence which was to extend over
many years, and which forms one of the most valuable
sources of information at our disposal as regards
both the inner and outer life of the writer.   The first
raptures of passion being spent, Julie de Krudener
was not of a nature to find either peace or happiness
in the new tie into which she had entered.   Conscience declined to be stifled, even when least
consulted.   Her children, her husband, her own
spasmodic sense of duty, on the one hand, and, on
the other, the overwhelming claims of M. de Frégeville, kept her in a constant state of agitation and
melancholy.   "You ask me whether I am happy?"
she had written to her friend in the early days of the
liaison.   "Yes indeed, I am, and as though I had
never been happy in my life before."   But a little
later she has to admit that "a few light clouds,
inseparable from human existence, from time to
time cast shadows over our life."   And again, in
a pathetic and quite futile attempt to reconcile her
sense of duty with the desires of her heart, she
writes (June 1791):—

I am more and more confirmed in my idea of renouncing
all society and of retiring into my domestic circle : wherever I
may be to bring up my children, to retain if possible that heart
without which I can enjoy no peace, to comfort the afflicted, to
instil virtue into the minds of my children, to watch over the
fortunes of M. de Krudener, and to surround him with my care.
Such is my plan, in order to counterbalance the evil of a passion
which has been the fate of my life.

In other words, the idea of a discreetly managed *ménage à trois* began to take shape in her demoralised mind, as the only tolerable solution of her actual matrimonial dilemma.

Public affairs came to the rescue of Mme. de Krudener in the midst of her vacillations, and her departure from Paris was finally hastened by the flight of Louis XVI. to Varennes. She was on terms of friendship with Mme. Korff, of whose passport the King had made use, and fearing thereby to have incurred the suspicions of the authorities, she deemed it advisable to beat an immediate and hasty retreat. Once more the Comte de Frégeville acted as her escort, though on this occasion disguised *en laquais*—his position as a nobleman and an officer making it impossible for him to leave the country openly.

The difficulties and dangers of travelling at this juncture, joined to a very natural disinclination on the part of the lady to arrive at the end of her journey, resulted in many weeks being spent on the road northwards. Halts were made at Brussels, at Cassel, at Hanover, and at Hamburg, at which latter town the ambassador had decreed that M. de Frégeville, who had been represented to him by his wife as a quite unexceptionable escort, should be left behind. Nevertheless the disguised count continued to accompany the baroness as far as Copenhagen, where the inevitable explanation between husband and wife at length took place. For weeks past Mme. de Krudener had been hardening her heart

to make an unabashed confession to her husband
of her conjugal infidelity—a communication the
ambassador appears to have received with as much
dignity as circumstances would permit.   In spite of
his express commands, however, his wife continued
to receive the visits of M. de Frégeville.   A
miserable two months followed, during which society
looked askance at the lady, whilst the natural agitations of her mind were rendered still more acute by
the severe illness of her lover.   Worn out with her
emotions, Julie was driven into making a pathetic
appeal to her husband to sue for a divorce ; this he
declined to do, but suggested that a prolonged visit
to her mother at Riga might prove an effective
means of escape from a situation that had grown
intolerable to either side.   The ambassador proposed
that his son Paul should remain with him, but that
the little Juliette should accompany her mother.
Julie gratefully accepted the proposition, although it
necessitated a final separation from her lover, for
M. de Frégeville after escorting her as far as Berlin
was bound in honour to return to his military duties
in France.[1]   No doubt the *grande passion* had well-
nigh burnt itself out on either side, for Mme. de
Krudener's letters to her friend are filled with the
peace and rest of her new life.   " I spent two months
in Denmark as in hell," she writes with graphic terse-
ness.   " Thank God I am rid of that awful country."
From which we may fairly conclude that the *ménage*

---

[1] The Comte de Frégeville proved himself a very distinguished soldier, and
earned rapid promotion ; he was appointed general of division in 1800.

à trois she had sketched so light-heartedly on paper had appeared to her in its true light when reduced to practice.

Up to this time the religious side of Mme. de Krudener's character had been quite undeveloped; indeed, the only symptoms she had shown of future religious possibilities lay in her dreamy aspirations after the beautiful, and in the very real dissatisfaction she habitually felt for the frivolous life, which, at the same time, exercised so great a fascination over her. From the date of her visit to her mother's house in 1792 the tone of her mind underwent a very definite change. She lived in comparative seclusion, in delicate health, and with shattered nerves, and it was only natural that she should reflect on the terrible moral crisis through which she had been passing. Her letters to Mme. Armand, written with complete candour and without the possibility of any thought of future publicity, are filled with a sentimental religious fervour. She grows ecstatic over the beauty of the divine love, and laments in fluent and graceful terms over her own shortcomings; but the true note of humility is somehow absent from these effusions :—

I have deserved several of my misfortunes (she writes), and the remainder have been inflicted by a merciful God whose hand prepares a hundredfold reward. Alas! having enjoyed the sweetness of passion, I must now experience some of the thorns! . . . I have suffered much, but I thank God for it; I have gained much and learnt much for my future happiness.

And again—

I have spent nearly the whole of my visit here plunged in

the deepest melancholy. My head was so affected by my disordered nerves, that at first I could not even think of France without shedding tears, and even now I cannot bear to go into society. Absorbed by a passion which has been surrounded by misfortune, a martyr to nervous attacks, and with my brain seriously affected—thus I have spent the whole time of my visit here ; but a merciful God has enabled me to draw many useful lessons from the past.

In truth Mme. de Krudener's religion was then—what her detractors declare it never ceased to be—an outlet for the romantic imaginings of her heart, and an excuse for her favourite habit of self-contemplation. There is a refined complacency in her self-analysis, which is curiously characteristic of the authoress of *Valérie*. Her sincerity—both now and later—is beyond a doubt, but her powers of self-deception are occasionally stupendous. She is honestly convinced at this time that she is cured of all her previous faults, and she indulges once more in raptures over nature, and the simple joys of life, oblivious of the fact that for months past she has not bestowed upon nature a single thought.

Making excuses for weakness—and weakness is inherent in humanity—my soul is at peace, and my wishes are moderate. They are restricted to a simple life, spent in harmony with nature. When my health is once re-established, or at least improved, I shall live for my children and also for M. de Krudener, so as to relieve him of his troubles and brighten his life. . . . No more useless intercourse, no more superfluous vanity or exhausted coquetry, no more intense longing to succeed ! I have shone, and I wish neither for the successes nor the anxieties of that brilliant society.

On 11th May 1792 she writes :—

I often reproach myself for my caprices, and you will find

me very much changed for the better. Suffering purifies, and I thank God that He has enabled me to learn a salutary lesson from the events of this winter. Oh! my dear friend, I am indeed cured of my faults of vanity! How I pine after a useful and pleasant life far removed from the agitations of society.

It is satisfactory to know from Mme. de Krudener's own letters, that Mme. de Wietinghoff received back her wayward daughter with every mark of maternal devotion. M. de Wietinghoff, who had always been regarded by his family with great affection, tempered by awe, was spending the winter at St. Petersburg, and it was the month of June (1792) before his daughter had sufficiently recovered her health to be able to rejoin him. The meeting was destined to be of short duration, for a few days later M. de Wietinghoff was attacked by a sudden illness, and in spite of all the care lavished upon him by his daughter, he shortly afterwards died in her arms. This sudden sorrow seems to have had a very sobering effect on Julie: it brought home to her with renewed force all the loneliness of her own life, and we find her clinging still more closely to her friend Mme. Armand, and making endless plans for a speedy meeting. From St. Petersburg, where she had been rejoined by her widowed mother, she writes (16th July 1792), with reminiscences of Bernardin de St. Pierre in her scheme :—

I am writing to you from a little garden belonging to my brother, where I never come without praying to God to grant me some little retreat with you, either in Switzerland or elsewhere. A few chickens, some flowers and fruit, a cow, a little table at which I could watch you drinking your coffee, our children, and then some needlework, some books, the Lake of Geneva, and a droshki, for which you always had a liking. There is a picture of our life: we would work like farmers' wives, doing good, bearing the ills of life with resignation, and always blessing the beneficent Creator of all things for what He sent us. . . .

If you only knew what benefits I have derived from my troubles. The craving for conquests, the delirium of vanity, has all become fused in a calm tranquillity of soul!

M. de Krudener, relieved of his diplomatic duties at Copenhagen, was also at St. Petersburg at this time, and it was inevitable that husband and wife, though living apart, should hear news of each other from common friends. One day a certain Mme. de Krock, a friend of both parties, in answer to Julie's inquiries, admitted that the ex-ambassador was in low spirits, and much worried over financial difficulties—the result of his Copenhagen hospitality. All that was generous and true in Mme. de Krudener's nature was stirred by this sudden discovery of her husband's need, and without a word to any one, carried away by the intensity of her feelings, she hurried into his presence, and flinging herself on her knees, implored him to forgive her past misdeeds, and to receive her back into his house. Her only stipulation was that Copenhagen should not be their place of residence. Touched by her evident sincerity, the Baron gladly granted her request, conjugal peace was once more restored, and it was arranged that Mme. de Krudener should proceed with her husband to Berlin, where her health could receive proper attention. Her happiness was made complete when she was once more united to her son Paul.

One little incident of this time must not be omitted — a meeting between Julie and her old lover, Alexandre de Stakieff. He was in mourning for his mother, and came to offer his condolences on the death of M. de Wietinghoff. "Le pauvre Stakieff," writes thè lady to her friend, "looks very ill and unhappy." One can only speculate on the frame of mind in which the originals of Valérie and of Gustave met again after years of separation, and wonder whether M. de Stakieff had indeed kept his word, and been cured of his love by Julie's desertion of her husband. Unkind gossip in later years was wont to declare that Mme. de Krudener, having killed off her lover of a broken heart in her novel, greatly resented being reminded of the fact that he had in reality happily survived his unrequited passion.

For various reasons the journey to Berlin was delayed for some weeks — a delay all the more trying to Mme. de Krudener's nerves, as her friend, Mme. Armand, had promised to meet her in the Prussian capital. It was February, 1793, before Berlin was reached ; and then, in spite of all her good resolutions to devote her life to her husband's happiness, at the end of two short weeks Mme. de Krudener insisted on taking her departure for Leipsic. She pleaded, and her devoted biographer, M. Eynard, has pleaded for her, that the exigencies of Berlin Court life were utterly repulsive to her, and that late hours and crowded ball-rooms worked havoc on her delicate health. But one cannot help suspecting that the overwhelming *ennui* to which she fell a victim the moment she had to reside under her husband's roof, was far more the result of hopeless incompatibility of temperament between her and the ambassador than of any outside circumstances. Be that as it may, it is difficult to accept in all seriousness her rapturous allusions to the love and mercy of the Almighty, when we find her on the next page persistently neglecting the plainest duties of life. Mme. de Krudener had many and varied experiences to go through, before the time came, when her daily life, inspired by the spirit of self-sacrifice, was to be a practical demonstration of the doctrines that she preached.

CHAPTER III

THE next five years of Mme. de Krudener's life
offer but few points of interest to the reader. They
were spent for the most part in a wandering existence through Germany and Switzerland, during
which time her meetings with her husband seem
to have been rare, and of short duration. Few
ladies of her time travelled as persistently as our
heroine, but she was possessed of a nervous, restless
temperament which forbade her being happy for
long in any given spot. Even after her conversion
this characteristic is still noticeable. There is
plenty of evidence to show that wherever she
elected to take up her temporary residence, she
enjoyed a gay and frivolous existence; and that
if the ceremonious entertainments of Berlin and
Copenhagen filled her with repulsion, she was
nevertheless in possession of sufficient health, to
fling herself with zest into the impromptu fêtes and
dances of the more Bohemian society in which she
felt at home. For the most part M. and Mme.
Armand, her step-daughter Sophie, and her own

little Juliette were her companions in these wanderings, whilst Paul de Krudener, after a first winter
spent at school at Leipsic, seems to have rejoined
his father.

At Leipsic the whole party lived in a large
pleasant house surrounded by a garden, and amongst
the little colony of French emigrants who had
taken refuge in the town, Mme. de Krudener found
many of her old Parisian acquaintances.   The most
noteworthy amongst her new friends appears to
have been Jean Paul Richter, with whom she subsequently corresponded for many years, although but
a single meeting of an hour's duration took place.
Even in so short a period Jean Paul seems to have
been vividly impressed by the lady's fascinations.
He wrote to a friend " that unlike as Mme. de
Krudener was to all other women, so was the
impression she had made upon him different from
that of all other women "; whilst to the lady herself
he declares rapturously that " The hour in which I
saw you floats like the evening glow still lower
beneath the horizon.   You came like a dream, and
fled like a dream, and I still live in a dream!"   It
was also from Leipsic that Mme. de Krudener
renewed her long - interrupted friendship with
Bernardin de St. Pierre, in a letter which we reproduce in its entirety.   Though written in an
artificial strain, and with a view to possible
publicity, revealing just so much of her private
history, as she herself felt it advisable to give to
the world, it is yet of interest as being the earliest

example we possess of Mme. de Krudener's writing, which has any claim to literary merit. It also throws a light on the warm friendship of the author of *Paul et Virginie* for the authoress of *Valérie*— a friendship which, in the case of the lady, was not without influence on her literary career.

MME. DE KRUDENER TO BERNARDIN DE SAINT-PIERRE.

LEIPSIC, *26th February* 1793.

After fourteen months spent for the most part in such intense nervous suffering that my reason almost gave way, and my health was reduced to a most wretched condition, I am at last enjoying a period of comparative peace; the fever which burnt in my blood has disappeared, my brain is no longer affected as formerly, and hope and nature once more penetrate into my soul, which has been agitated by bitter sorrows and by terrible storms. Yes, nature once more offers me her gentle and soothing distractions! She is no longer shrouded in a funeral veil. Once more I am a mother, and I live once again in the friends who were dear to me, and whom I love as tenderly as before. With the return of my faculties and my memory, my thoughts have flown out towards you. I feel the most intense longing to know what you are doing, dear and venerable friend, and I feel the necessity of assuring you that I shall continue to love you as long as I retain any faculties of affection. I am tormented by terrible anxiety on your behalf. What life are you leading in the midst of such universal troubles? You, who are so devoted to peace and solitude, are you in a position to enjoy these precious gifts? On the strength of my great friendship for you, let me beg of you to send me news at the earliest opportunity. Oh, if we could only spend a few moments together as in the old days! Why can I not join you in the little garden in which you forget the world and all its tormenting agitations, and where you live quietly in simple moderation, so as to find myself once more surrounded by peace and happiness? Why can I not listen once more to the noble teaching with which your conversation was filled? It was as pleasant to me as the perfume of the surrounding flowers.

Those who are acquainted with grief, those who suffer, interest us doubly. I feel that with the confidence you always inspire, and which I have long felt in you, I should be able to talk to you of my troubles; your friendship, your touching goodness, would soothe them. You yourself have suffered sorrows, you know how to sympathise in those of others. Do tell me, dear and venerable friend, whether you have not some plan of spending a few months in Switzerland in order to see that glorious country? I know you love France too dearly to desert her for long, but a little expedition into Switzerland would be a pleasant holiday. If I dared to hope that some day you would spend the summer on the borders of the Lake of Geneva, the very idea would help to brighten my life, and I would appeal to the friendship that fills your soul to come and live in a little country villa with me. If it were only for a few months of your life, I entreat you to come and live beside a friend who offers you a true and sympathetic heart, who lives far from society, who would surround you with care and with the spectacle of two charming children whom you love, and who, moreover, would know how to respect your solitude instead of disturbing it, who knows of herself how sweet and necessary solitude is, and, finally, whose society would put no restraint upon you. I make you this offer straight from a heart that knows how to appreciate you. I add nothing to it, for I am simple and true and not at all eloquent.

I have deserted my own country, the climate of which ruined my nerves; whilst there, after a previous absence of eight years, I was present at the death of my dearly beloved father, the best of men, who died after long sufferings. Terrible pains oppressed my chest and affected my brain; bitter sorrows consumed my soul, whilst physical ills consumed my health.

Oh my dear friend, my eyes fill with tears at the thought, although several months have passed since then. My soul is still crushed down. For the present I am in Saxony, at Leipsic. My husband selected the town as our residence, as it offers exceptional advantages for Paul's education, and I have the satisfaction of being near my son, and of following his progress. Every summer he will go and rejoin his father in Denmark, and spend several months with him, and in the interval I shall be able to make some little excursions into Switzerland. Our means, which have been greatly reduced by the recent war, and by the terrible expenses to which M. de Krudener is condemned in Denmark, do not permit us to live together in so expensive a country, and other reasons too long to go into have also contributed to our resolution. . . . Here I spend very little! The town is inexpensive, I see no one, the climate is pleasant, the fruit good, the neighbourhood charming. Mdlle. Piozet, the friend whom you must remember during my first stay in Paris, is still with me, though she has married since; the good creature, who takes care of me and my children in turn, is quite necessary to my soul, which still suffers so frequently.

My children, thank God, are in excellent health and very good and happy; the little girl, whom you nicknamed the Beatitude, has still the same contented expression, and.my son also fills me with the most encouraging hopes. Keep well and strong, and do not forget me. I beg you to write to me at Leipsic, Poste Restante, as soon as possible. I embrace you in imagination, and am always your best friend,

B. DE KRUDENER.

P.S.—*Paul et Virginie* is translated into German. I should be very glad of an opportunity of sending it to you.

In 1795 we find Mme. de Krudener back again in her mother's house at Riga, terribly bored by the conventionalities and restraints of provincial society. The summer months were spent at what was now her own property of Kosse, when she first began to take an interest in her Esthonian peasantry, building schools for their children, and introducing inoculation into the district. The end of 1796 saw her established at Lausanne, at Les Grottes, the former residence of Gibbon, and this continued to be her head-quarters for over a year.

At this period Lausanne, besides the charm of

the surrounding scenery, possessed a further attraction in its little literary coterie. It is true that Mme. de Staël took her departure about the time of Mme. de Krudener's arrival, thus deferring to a later date the graceful friendship which existed between the rival authoresses; but the cultured traditions of the place were fully maintained in the *salons* of Mesdames de Necker, de Charrière, de Constant, and de Montolieu, whilst a little band of French emigrants, full of gaiety in the midst of all their misfortunes, contributed to the festivities of the neighbourhood. Here Mme. de Krudener was in her element: graceful, piquante, full of *verve* and enthusiasm, and in appearance as youthful as ever, she was received with acclamation by the residents, and soon became the ruling spirit of the little society. With a renewal of health she flung herself into every form of amusement, and we hear of her dancing the celebrated *danse du schall,* as it is described in *Valérie*—the dance which fired the imagination of M. de Sainte - Beuve, and which Mme. de Staël herself immortalised at a later date in the pages of *Delphine.* The passage is worth quoting, not only for its literary interest, but as a pleasant tribute of admiration from one *grande dame* to another.

Never before have grace and beauty produced so extraordinary an impression on so numerous an assembly. This foreign dance possesses a charm which it is impossible to describe: it has a combination of indolence and vivacity, of melancholy and gaiety, quite Asiatic in character. Sometimes when the music became soft, Delphine would take several steps with her head bent down and her arms crossed, as though some memory, some regret, had suddenly obtruded itself in the midst of all the splendour of the ball; but in a few moments recommencing her light and airy dance she would envelop herself in an Indian shawl, which, indicating the lines of her figure, and falling with her long hair to the ground, formed a most fascinating picture.

There is no doubt that the cultured atmosphere of Lausanne had considerable influence in turning the thoughts of Mme. de Krudener towards that literary career, which a few years later became the height of her ambition. Even at this time she began to try her skill by jotting down short "thoughts," after the manner of La Rochefoucauld, which were printed at a later period under the title of *Pensées d'une Dame Étrangère.*

Revolutionary complications, and a threatened invasion by a French army, were the cause of a general dispersion of Lausanne society early in the year 1798. Accompanied by her children, by Mme. Armand, and the Abbé Becker, an aged and learned ecclesiastic, Mme. de Krudener spent the next year or two wandering about Germany, and residing in turn at Lindau, Toeplitz, Munich, and Dresden. A few words must be said here of her two daughters. Sophie de Krudener, who was only ten years younger than her step-mother, and who became the wife of M. Ochando, proved herself through all these wanderings not only a charming and sympathetic companion, but a keen observer, to whose letters and recollections posterity is indebted for

many details of Mme. de Krudener's private life.
Little Juliette, who even after marriage was to remain her mother's inseparable companion, was now
blossoming into early girlhood—a slight, graceful,
bashful figure, with all the charm of intense refinement and delicacy, with a soul as pure as crystal,
and, as later events were to prove, a heroic capacity
for self-sacrifice.   All through her youth she was a
type of the perfect *ingénue*, and it is almost needless
to add that a most passionate attachment united
mother and daughter.   After a short reunion of
husband and wife in 1799, Mme. de Krudener writes
to the ambassador from Dresden (29th December):
"I am very pleased with Sophie; I live in my
domestic circle and avoid society; Juliette causes
me indescribable joy.   Docile, diligent, gentle,
orderly and affectionate: there is her portrait."
Neither the dissipations of Court circles, nor all the
experiences gained in the wandering Bohemian
life that her mother loved, seem to have affected
Juliette de Krudener, or to have rubbed off the
bloom of perfect innocence and simplicity.

In the first months of the new century M. de
Krudener was appointed ambassador at Berlin, and
his wife, then residing at Toeplitz, and deprived of
the companionship of Mme. Armand, who had returned to Geneva, was seized with sudden, if somewhat tardy remorse for her utter neglect of her
conjugal duties, and resolved on taking up her
residence at the Embassy.   M. de Krudener, overjoyed at the prospect of seeing his family once

more around him, procured a charming residence, and made every arrangement for his wife's comfort. Unfortunately the Court of Berlin was ruled by strict etiquette, and of all things in this world, Mme. de Krudener loathed etiquette the most. As ambassadress she was obliged to pay her respects in turn to all the royal households, and long before these ceremonious presentations were completed, her patience was utterly exhausted, her nerves began to give way, and she pined once more for the freedom and happiness of her Swiss home. One endless source of trouble was her hopeless unpunctuality. It was in vain that the ambassador would put forth all his diplomatic art to ensure her punctual appearance at the royal palace on occasions of state. Mme. de Krudener invariably kept the whole diplomatic corps waiting, and her husband was reduced to making what excuses he might to Frederick William III., the most punctual of monarchs.

M. de Krudener's presence by no means consoled his wife for the absence of Mme. Armand, to whom she poured out her various troubles, both real and imaginary, in frequent letters.

BERLIN, 1800.

I went to the baths again this year, and they did me much good. I revisited Toeplitz, which I love from every point of view, as it reminds me of our stay there together, besides the benefit which I derive from its waters, and the liberty which I enjoy there free from all restraint. You know how fatal all conventional restraint is to me. I should always prefer the most ordinary position, with the most limited of pecuniary resources, if accompanied by liberty, to the brilliant slavery of Court life, with all the worry of visits and presentations and social restraints. I have lived through terrible moments of intense regret at having condemned myself to such torture; but religion has come to my assistance, has dried the bitter tears that I shed in secret, and has shown me the hidden charm of painful sacrifice. I have said to myself: Religion will support and will save this feeble body from being utterly crushed. . . . When I said to myself that I had only come here to wear smart clothes, to go into society, to waste my precious time, and to sacrifice all the pleasures of liberty, a sort of dull misery overwhelmed me. My pleasant and useful life, the society of my daughter, the charm of living together, of working, reading, and enjoying the innocent pleasures of life, would all come back to me, and the most bitter regrets and an inexpressible grief filled my soul, especially if I happened to pass by a little house or garden. Although the smile which I forced to my lips used to hide my sorrow, I went so far as to reproach myself secretly with having sacrificed a life in which I could work and do some good, write out my thoughts for others, and educate my daughter—that I should have sacrificed all that, I say, to this miserable world where I am only valued for my rank, while I don't give a farthing's worth of happiness to any one.

From Riga, where she took refuge in the autumn in her mother's house, she wrote again, more than ever in the tone of the *femme incomprise*.

6th October 1800.

Yes, indeed, if Heaven spares my life, I must rest in a beautiful climate, after all the fatigues of travelling. Yet a little while longer in the tumult of Berlin, and after that a visit to you, and a sight of the lovely scenery of Switzerland. It really is a necessity for me, for you will have seen by my letter from Berlin how intolerable to me is the life that I led there. Had I undertaken it a year ago it would have been utterly impossible for me to carry it out, or even to have attempted it. But, thanks to the Almighty, the baths of Toeplitz have made me much stronger, and although at dinner parties I always feel on the point of being ill, still I am able to tolerate society without such terrible nervous prostration, although I still suffer a great deal. You can see that daily, and indeed almost hourly, sacrifices cannot be put up with for very long. I may say that I have borne it heroically, but constant suffering would be impossible, and I hope to put an end to it all. M. de Krudener appreciates no sort of domestic happiness; he is more bent than ever on dinners, visits, theatricals, etc.

The feminine injustice of the last remark will be obvious to every one, for it was Julie herself who had deprived her husband of any possibility of enjoying domestic life. Fortunately, in her more reasonable moments, she gives the ambassador credit for the possession of solid virtues, and after her return to Berlin she writes once more to her friend (1801):—

You ask me whether my husband would not be vexed at your coming? I assure you not; he is too kind and too susceptible to all goodness ever to be indifferent to you. I have described to you his political life, his successes, and the charm that active work has for him. Thirty years of similar labours and all the attractions of high honours may well have affected his character, and may perhaps have rendered him inaccessible to true happiness, which it is very easy to confound with glory and the approval of public opinion, but his kind heart has never changed. He is always loyal, just, high-minded, and thoroughly good.

The mistake has frequently been made of dating Mme. de Krudener's touching friendship with the beautiful and patriotic Queen Louise of Prussia from the time of her first residence at Berlin. As a matter of fact the friendship between these two gifted women arose at a much later date, and under far more sorrowful circumstances, and at this time their intercourse was of a purely official nature. Although bored to excess by Court festivities, the ambassadress knew well how to play the part of a fascinating and graceful hostess in her own house. She amused herself by wearing eccentric and impossible costumes, and surrounded herself with a host of admirers chosen from the most lively and frivolous circles of Berlin society. She particularly affected French acquaintances, and amongst these mention must be made of Comte Alexandre de Tilly,[1] usually known as "le beau Tilly," from his powers of fascination with the fair sex—powers which were not without a certain measure of success in the presence of Mme. de Krudener. On the occasion of an elaborate fête which she organised in honour of the Grand-Duchess Helen of Mecklenburg-Strelitz,[2] Alexandre de Tilly was entrusted with the duty of writing a complimentary ode, which won for him the order of St. John of Jerusalem from the Emperor Paul.

It will be readily believed that Mme. de Krudener, far from being of assistance to her husband in his diplomatic career, as she herself was pleased to imagine, was often a positive hindrance to him by her capricious and thoughtless behaviour. The period was a most critical one in European politics. Paul I. had laid an embargo

---

[1] Count A. de Tilly, courtier and adventurer, was the author of extremely amusing, if not precisely edifying, memoirs on the manners of the last century. He died by his own hand at Brussels in 1816.

[2] A Russian princess, daughter of the Emperor Paul I.

on British vessels, and in his bitterness against
England was almost ready to declare war against
Prussia, for declining to join the Northern Alliance,
by which it was hoped to destroy British commerce.
It required all M. de Krudener's temporising skill
to avert an open rupture.   Fortunately he stood
high in the favour of the Emperor, who loaded him
with favours, whilst Mme. de Krudener, totally
ignorant of international complications, with characteristic self-glorification took to herself all the
credit of the ambassador's good fortune, and wrote
to Mme. Armand :—

I believe God has wished to bless my husband since my
return to him.   He is obtaining every sort of favour.   Why
should I not believe that a pious heart, which prays to God with
simplicity and confidence for grace to contribute to the happiness of another, obtains that for which it asks?

On the 23rd of March, 1801, the Emperor Paul
indited a dispatch to his Berlin representative which
contained instructions to inform the King of Prussia
without delay, that if he did not make up his mind
to immediate action against England, he (the
Emperor) would march 80,000 men across the
frontier.   Count Pahlen, Governor of St. Petersburg, and at that moment the most powerful man
in the Empire, wishing to prevent the ambassador
from acting on these precipitate orders, wrote with
his own hand at the foot of the dispatch : " His
Imperial Majesty is to-day in bad health.   Serious
consequences may ensue." [1]   M. de Krudener

---

[1] See *Histoire du Consulat et de l'Empire*, by Thiers, vol. ii.

accordingly refrained from taking action, and the next courier from St. Petersburg brought the news of the midnight murder of the unhappy Paul in his own palace, on the night of 23rd March, the main instigator of the crime being Count Pahlen himself.

This tragic event, which resounded throughout Europe, came as a special blow to the Krudener household. Deprived of his imperial patron, and uncertain of the future, the ambassador was under the immediate necessity of reducing his expenditure, and attempting to pay his debts. As a first step Mme. de Krudener took her departure for the baths of Toeplitz, accompanied by both her daughters, Sophie and Juliette—husband and wife little imagining that they were never to meet again on earth.

CHAPTER IV

1801-1802

At Toeplitz Mme. de Krudener found herself surrounded by old friends, and she was soon the centre of a gay and brilliant circle, which included Prince Radziwill and his wife, Princess Louise of Prussia, the old Prince de Ligne, Prince Henry, brother of Frederick the Great, Princess Clary, Princess Dolgorouki, and many more. Theatricals furnished as usual the main amusement; and, relieved of her oppressive official duties, and also, one cannot but feel, of her husband's presence, Mme. de Krudener showed herself once more sparkling with wit and brilliancy. No one would have imagined that but a few weeks previously she had written to her friend Mme. Armand of "that society which I detest, and in which I live as a slave." From Toeplitz (3rd July) she indites a friendly little missive to Alexandre de Tilly, in which, after thanking him in her daughter Sophie's name for a gift of flowers, she continues in her characteristic vein :—

I am forbidden to write, as my nerves are not cheerful.

Will you not come and try the waters here? They are excellent. You will find beautiful trees, beautiful scenery, and beautiful mountains, of which one never wearies. You will also find the Prince de Ligne, who is as lively as ever; and besides him a whole host of German nobles, with a following of ridiculous women, who are always amusing. And finally, I trust you will find me, and that you will be very glad to see me, who am always kind and frank to my friends, always at open war with the Germans and their thirty-two quarterings; always devoted to everything that is pleasant, true, simple—requiring nothing, living my own life, and existing on a most convenient reputation for eccentricity, which allows me to do as I like.

As the season drew to its close, Mme. de Krudener felt less and less inclined to take up once more the yoke of her life at Berlin, and more and more drawn towards the mountains of Switzerland and Mme. Armand. In the struggle between duty and inclination, duty once more went to the wall; and making a pretext both of her own health, and of a possible advantageous marriage for her daughter Juliette, she wrote to the ambassador, from whom, it must be remembered, she had parted on the most amicable terms, requesting his permission to winter with her daughters in Switzerland, and begging him to make known his wishes on the subject with the least possible delay. Having satisfied her conscience by the despatch of this epistle, the lady seems to have deemed it quite superfluous to await the receipt of any reply, and started immediately on her southward journey, shedding tears of joy as she crossed the Swiss frontier. Thus it was only at Geneva that she received from M. de Krudener a letter, which it is only fair to the long-suffering husband to reproduce *in extenso*.

CÜSTRIN, *27th August* 1801.

Your letter of 18th August caused me extreme sorrow, *ma chère amie*. After the conversation which took place between us on that subject, I confess I did not anticipate a fresh separation. You cannot disguise from yourself how much it detracts from the interests and happiness of our children; and I must tell you, with all the frankness that my love for you authorises, that duty demanded that you should return to the bosom of your family. You seem to regard your absence as a source of economy, as though there could possibly be any economy in keeping up two establishments, instead of one. My expenses give no pleasure to me, and are of no advantage to my family; they are necessitated by my position, and are but little affected by your presence. Finally, I have repeatedly told you that you are quite at liberty to decide what and how much society you will see, or even to see none at all. You allege the state of your health; that is an objection on which nobody has the right to pronounce. But permit me to observe, that it is difficult to believe, that the mountains of Switzerland will re-establish your health, which has suffered from the salubrious and fairly moderate climate of Berlin. However, your mind is made up, and I know that nothing I can say will influence you. I owe these remarks to myself, and I hold you responsible for any consequences that your determination may have, both on yourself and on the children.

You will have seen by the date of this letter that I am still detained at Cüstrin, which causes me great inconvenience. As you had definitely made up your mind to leave my house, why not have informed me of your intention previous to your departure? How is Sophie to rejoin me? There would have been no lack of suitable opportunities from Toeplitz, but I doubt your finding any for the further distance. In any case she will have to travel with people who are strangers to me, or else cross Germany by herself. I beg you to send her to me by the most direct route, and rather by herself than with people of a doubtful reputation, and also that you engage a well-recommended maid and a man-servant for the journey.

I trust, my dear friend, you may never regret the resolution you have taken, and which will once more make the members of our family, and our own children, strangers to one another. I send you every good wish for your health and your happiness. Kiss Juliette for me, and believe me to be ever your most sincere and devoted friend, ———

Geneva became Mme. de Krudener's head-quarters for the autumn, but much of her time was spent at the chateau of Coppée, where Mme. de Staël resided in the constant society of Mme. Necker de Saussure and Mme. Rilliet Huber, attracting around her all that was most cultured and distinguished from amongst the numerous French exiles, who had taken refuge in Switzerland. Our heroine was gratified by receiving the warmest of welcomes from the celebrated authoress of *Corinne*, whose acquaintance she had long desired to make, and she soon occupied a foremost place amongst the little coterie of friends. "Certain women pass through life like spring breezes, vivifying everything on their passage." Thus wrote Mme. de Krudener about this time,[1] and the "thought" is specially applicable to herself. Philosophy, art, science, but above all, literature, formed the *menu* of the daily conversation at Coppée, and this constant delightful intercourse with the *fine fleur* of contemporary French culture, naturally had the effect of kindling into a clear flame the smouldering embers of Mme. de Krudener's literary ambition. No doubt it was the contrast between

---

[1] See *Pensées d'une Dame Étrangère.*

JULIE KRUDNER

L'Auteur de Valérie a dans un cadre heureux
Peint un Sentiment vif, pur, noble, et généreux;
ce Tableau dut être fidèle,
l'Auteur en était le modèle.

the rapid, graceful interchange of thought, and the freedom of expression, which were habitual in the *salon* of Mme. de Staël, and the more serious provincial conventionality of Geneva society, which prompted a remark by our still worldly heroine that has been preserved by the poet Chênedollé: "Je n'aime point les Génevoises: elles n'ont ni les charmes de l'innocence ni les grâces du péché." It is a criticism to which the authoress of *Valérie* certainly never laid herself open.

It was only to be expected that Mme. de Krudener, whose health was always good when she was amused, and who invariably became ill the instant she was overtaken by *ennui*, should let herself be easily persuaded, at the approach of the winter season, to follow her new friends to Paris, all neglectful of the superior claims of the forsaken ambassador at Berlin. Accordingly in December (1801) we find her, after an absence of ten years, established once again in the French capital, in a little apartment on the Boulevard des Italiens, quite close to the Madeleine. It was a moment of peace, and of a general resurrection of that brilliant social existence, which had been temporarily eclipsed by the horrors of the Revolution. M. de Sainte-Beuve gives a delightful portrait of the lady, as she appeared before the eyes of all that was most distinguished in the literary and aristocratic society of the day :—

She was still young, as beautiful as ever, and fascinatingly graceful; a slight pale blonde with the flaxen hair peculiar to

Valérie, and eyes of a deep blue.   Her voice was low, and her
speech sweet and musical—a charm that is habitual to Livonian
women ; she was an exquisite, intoxicating dancer.   Her toilettes
were in harmony with herself; they were the creations of her own
imagination, and some of their secrets have escaped her.   Witness
the shawl dance, and the ball-dress in the scene in which a wreath
of blue mallows is placed amongst the flaxen curls of Valérie.
Thus I always see her in my fancy, swiftly entering some splendid
soirée in the midst of a song by Garat, all heads turning at the
sound of her airy footfall.   It might have been a vision of Music
herself !

Atala had only recently been given to the world,
and had evoked an outburst of admiration from the
whole of Europe ; the *Génie du Christianisme* was
within a few weeks of publication, and was the subject of the most eager speculation on the part of M.
de Chateaubriand's friends and admirers.   "You
must positively meet Chateaubriand in Paris,"
Mme. de Staël had declared to Mme. de Krudener
one day at Coppée : "I will give you a letter for
him, or will introduce you myself.   One can only
understand a book when one knows the author."
The meeting was not long delayed, for true to her
promise the authoress of *Corinne* invited the future
authoress of *Valérie*, together with Benjamin Constant and M. Adrien de Montmorency, to meet M.
de Chateaubriand at dinner, when he read aloud
two unpublished fragments of the *Génie du Christianisme*, to the rapturous delight of his hearers.

As a result of this first meeting M. de Chateaubriand became a constant visitor in the *salon* of
Mme. de Krudener, who removed about this time
to an apartment in the Rue de Clery.   It is obvious

that this friendship with the most celebrated author of the day helped to bestow on the lady that literary distinction of which she was most covetous. She herself was also a welcome guest in the *salon* of Mme. de Beaumont, the *chère amie* of M. de Chateaubriand, around whose couch—for she was already threatened with lung disease—a little coterie of literary friends, Joubert, de Bonald, de Fontanes, Chênedollé, and others, used to congregate. It would be interesting to know how deep were the feelings of friendship that united the author of *Atala* to the authoress of *Valérie*, and how highly he valued her intellectual gifts. Unfortunately the *Mémoires d'Outre-Tombe*, in which Chateaubriand professed to lay bare his life, contain but two or three references to Mme. de Krudener, and as his acquaintance with her coincided with the period of his devotion to Mme. de Beaumont, probability points to friendly intercourse of the more superficial kind. Nevertheless it is true that on the publication of the *Génie du Christianisme*, in the spring of 1802, Mme. de Krudener was the favoured recipient of the first copy of the book. The gift was conditional on a promise of absolute secrecy, which the lady readily gave, but with characteristic carelessness left the precious volume on her drawing-room table, on going out to pay some afternoon calls.

As ill-luck would have it, Mme. de Staël arrived in her absence, proposed awaiting the return of her friend, entered the *salon*, took up the first book that came to hand, and to her amazement discovered it to be the anxiously expected *Génie du Christianisme.* Oblivious of every other consideration in her curiosity to read the book, she carried it off home with her without a word. The despair of Mme. de Krudener, on returning to find her most treasured possession had mysteriously disappeared, may well be imagined. After a frantic and fruitless search, she was forced to the conclusion that the thief could be no other than Mme. de Staël—a discovery which only intensified her dismay. She hastily despatched Sophie de Krudener to demand the instant restitution of the stolen property, but it was only after three hours of weary waiting, that her step-daughter at length placed the precious volume once more in her hands. It appeared that on arriving at the residence of Mme. de Staël, Mdlle. de Krudener had found the lady in eager and brilliant discussion with the author himself, over the merits and demerits of his work. Fortunately the incident was not allowed to disturb the harmonious relations between the parties concerned. M. de Chateaubriand accorded a gracious pardon to the indiscretion, and Mme. de Staël forbore to bear malice, on discovering that she had been somewhat supplanted by the fascinating Julie.

The following letter, although written at a later date, had best be given here, as being apparently the only one that has been preserved out of the correspondence between M. de Chateaubriand and Mme. de Krudener :—

Mme. de Krudener to M. de Chateaubriand.

Paris, 24th November 1803.

I learnt yesterday, from M. Michaud, who has just returned from Lyons, that Mme. de Beaumont was at Rome, and that she was very, very ill: that was what he told me. I was deeply grieved at the news ; indeed, my nerves were quite affected by it, and I have thought a great deal about that charming person, whom I have only known for a short time, but to whom I was truly attached. How often I have longed for her happiness ! How often I have hoped that she would be able to cross the Alps, and experience under an Italian sky all those deep and tender emotions which I myself have lived through ! Alas ! she may, perhaps, have only reached that fascinating country, in order to suffer pain and be exposed to dangers which I dread for her. I cannot tell you how grieved I am at the mere thought. Forgive me, if I have been so absorbed by it, that I have not yet spoken to you of yourself, my dear Chateaubriand. You must be fully aware of my sincere friendship, and in giving expression to the very real interest with which Mme. de Beaumont inspires me, I feel that I sympathise with you more truly than if I were to talk to you about yourself. This sad vision is ever before my eyes. I possess the secret of grief, and my soul is always harrowed at the sight of fellow-souls, on whom nature has bestowed an unusual power of suffering. I had hoped that Mme. de Beaumont would enjoy the privilege she had received of being happier. I had hoped that she might recover her health under the Italian sun, and in the joy of your presence. I entreat you to reassure me, to write to me ; tell her how truly I love her, what prayers I offer on her behalf. Did she receive my answer to her letter written from Clermont ? Direct your answers to Michaud. I only beg a single word from you, for I know, my dear Chateaubriand, how sensitive you are, and how much you must suffer. I thought her better ; I have not written to her lately. I have been overwhelmed with business ; but I have thought of her happiness at seeing you again, and I have pictured it to myself. Tell me about your own health ; trust in my friendship, in the interest which I shall ever feel in you, and do not forget me.[1]   B. Krudener.

---

[1] This letter is published in the *Mémoires d'Outre-Tombe*, vol. iv. p. 176. Mme. de Beaumont expired at Rome, in the arms of M. de Chateaubriand, 4th November 1803.

To return to the spring of 1802. Mme. de Krudener unfortunately did not devote herself exclusively to intellectual intercourse, but flung herself at the same time into all that was most brilliant and frivolous in Parisian society. Carried away in the first instance by her passionate love of music, she allowed herself to enter into intimate relations with the singer Garat, then at the height of his fame. "The soul suffers from languors which render it so melancholy, that it flings itself into some strong passion, just as a man flings himself into the river in the burning heat of a summer's day." So wrote the lady in her *Pensées d'une Dame Étrangère*. In the present instance the passion was but of short duration — although as long as it lasted Mme. de Krudener had been at no pains to conceal it from the eyes of an over-indulgent world — and it was followed by the inevitable reawakening to a sense of disgust and disappointment. Her own self-commiserating frame of mind at this time, is best indicated by the following letter to Mme. Armand :—

PARIS, 12*th May* 1802.

Yes, dear friend, let us feel more and more convinced that it is not in our power to conquer public opinion, that it is often very unfair, and that it is in the hearts of our friends and in our own consciousness, that we see each other as we really are. How often I have said to you: If we were angels, we should be misjudged; but in the end a general opinion as to our character grows up, if one deserve a favourable one.

Alas! you congratulate me on being in elevated regions, but no, my dear friend, it is not so. It is in vain that I try to return to a peaceful frame of mind, to put away from me all that troubles the soul, and to feel satisfied with the many favours which I know how to appreciate. I feel acutely the words of Scripture, "It is not good for man to live alone." At times an overwhelming melancholy penetrates to the very depths of my heart; pleasures disgust me; my tears flow; I feel I am no longer beloved; I feel that I ought to renounce happiness; I never wake without this sensation of melancholy; I dream of the days which are long past, and I weep bitterly. Tell me, my dearest friend, would the world be worth such a sacrifice? Ah no, for the world never deems you capable of making it. If it is a virtue, if it is a duty, as I believe it to be, it is only to that Being who is infinite, who is so good and so just, that we owe the sacrifice; but let us pity, and not condemn, the ardent souls who are made for love, who are thrilled by, and who find their only happiness in this sentiment of love; let us not condemn them if they fall. I have been now several months in Paris; I have often enjoyed myself very much, but I have also been very miserable. And by this time my curiosity is satisfied. I have had many triumphs; I have seen many interesting things, and I realise the emptiness of it all. It is towards you, *chère amie*, that I stretch out my arms, and come what may, I would rather be living with you. One pleasure only is left to me: that of spending a few weeks with my old friend B. de Saint-Pierre. I hope to carry out that plan, and to devote myself for a bit to my books. I have found an apartment in the house occupied by my old friend, with a splendid garden, and situated in a solitary quarter. I hope to live there very quietly. M. de Saint-Pierre has a charming wife and two children, Paul and Virginia.

In spite of all these agitations of the heart, Mme. de Krudener diligently pursued her schemes of literary ambition. She had gained applause as an ambassadress, as a *mondaine*, as the inventor of the *danse du schall;* and now that youth and mere outward charm were beginning— tardily indeed in her case—to slip from her, she was resolved to win still higher renown in the field of letters. With all her apparent capriciousness and superficial brilliancy, she was gifted with great tenacity of purpose and remarkable powers of perseverance. All through the summer months in Switzerland, and during the winter and spring in Paris, she had been scribbling diligently, though nothing as yet had been given to the world. She had been at work on several stories — *Eliza*, *Alexis*, and the *Cabane des Lataniers* — none of which were destined to win her any renown; but in her desk were also the manuscript pages of *Valérie*, on which from the first her hopes had been mainly centred. Sketched out at Berlin, written at Geneva, and revised in Paris, *Valérie* had already been shown in secret to a few literary friends ; and, encouraged by their praise, the authoress was looking forward to a speedy publication of her cherished work, when all her plans were shattered by the death of M. de Krudener, who died at Berlin, of an apoplectic stroke, on the 14th June, 1802. Two months of strict retreat and seclusion followed, during which Mme. de Krudener, now that it was too late, indulged in bitter self-reproaches for the neglect with which she had treated the ambassador, remembering only his sterling qualities, and oblivious of all that had rendered their matrimonial life so intolerable to her. With her intense emotional nature it was inevitable that it should be so ; but it was equally characteristic of her at this period, that a few months later she should have recovered all her old vivacity of spirits and enjoyment of life. These years, in truth, were a time of spiritual transition for Mme. de Krudener. She was indeed very far from the self-sacrificing heroism of her later years, but she was also very far from the careless capricious *mondaine* of the early days in Venice and Montpellier. Her worldly ambitions had at least changed their object from mere personal, to intellectual, aspirations; and although she was now approaching her fortieth year, she was still in appearance so young and so graceful, that it is unfair to suggest, as her more cynical biographers have done, that this change was the result, not of choice, but of necessity. How many women of the world continue to court mere personal admiration long after their fortieth year? Not only in her actions, but in all the letters and writings of Mme. de Krudener, we can see traces of the internal struggle that was in progress. The spiritual, poetical, mystical side of her character, was at open war with the vain, self-absorbed, pleasure-loving side, and for a long time it seemed as though victory would lie with the latter. She honestly detested the hollowness of her social successes, without possessing the strength of character to renounce them. Perhaps the most formidable enemy of her higher nature was her quite overwhelming vanity. She had posed so deliberately, and for so long, that with the best intentions it seemed as though she could never leave off posing. Hence the curious contradictions between her words and her acts, between the pious moralising sentiments of her letters to Mme. Armand, written in the quiet solitude of her own chamber, and her frequently compromising behaviour in public.

Yet it is unfair to accuse her of insincerity. No one was more completely deceived by her own posing than the charming *poseuse* herself, and she believed implicitly in her own sentiments of the moment. It was her misfortune, at this period, that her sentiments changed so rapidly. Very complex natures usually appear as wilfully hypocritical in the eyes of the majority of men, who, in the face of all experience, persist in expecting human nature to conform to certain well-defined standards. Even M. de Sainte-Beuve was almost ready to denounce his heroine as an *intrigante* when he discovered that the graceful, ethereal figure of his early essay was in reality a very frail and emotional woman, with very human weaknesses and temptations, but also with a quite exceptional gift for triumphing over her own failings, and living that higher life, which in her heart she had craved after, even from her earliest childhood. Had Mme. de Krudener's life come to an end in 1805, her moral detractors would have had the bulk of circumstantial evidence in their favour; but, in the light of later events, and of the personal testimony of nearly all who came into immediate contact with her, any accusation of insincerity must fall to the ground.

In the *Mercure de France* for the month of Vendémiaire, year XI. (September 1802), probably through the good offices of her friend M. Michaud,[1] there appeared several pages of "thoughts," with the following introduction from the editor :—

The following thoughts are culled from the manuscripts of a foreign lady, who has kindly allowed us to publish them in our magazine. Those, who can think with so much refinement, are justified in selecting for their expression the language of Mme. de Sévigné and of La Fayette.

Written at various times in imitation of the Maxims of La Rochefoucauld, these fragments of feminine philosophy give evidence of a certain faculty for delicate observation, combined with much poetic sentimentality of soul. Intensely subjective in tone, they reflect with accuracy the frame of mind of the authoress, during this intermediate stage of moral development.

When we do good, let us first of all remember that we are growing better, and let us expect nothing from others.

Society friendships are like small diamonds ; they glitter but have no value.

Commonplace people regard enthusiasm with suspicion, because they have been told that it may have unfortunate results ; it is, however, a disease to which they themselves are never liable.

It might be said that most men of the world live off small ideas, just as the people live off small coins.

If painters, poets, in a word, men of genius, are to be envied, it is far less for the sake of the glory that awaits them than for the sense of beauty they possess.

---

[1] Joubert writes to Chênedollé (5th July 1803) that Michaud is "obsédé et possédé" by Mme. de Krudener.

Some glances are words, and some voices, music.

In the battle of life, as in the gladiatorial combats, he who falls is not always the weakest. Frequently it is the strongest, and he who has resisted the longest.

In early youth we expect everything from the outside world: we appeal for happiness to all that surrounds us, and little by little we are driven back into our own souls.

The more perfect we are, the more beautiful the world appears to us.

A sense of beauty is not sufficiently cultivated in young and gentle souls; yet we should remember that without enthusiasm there can be no moral spring-time, and that without blossom there can be no fruit.

Cold hearts have only memory: loving hearts have remembrance, and the past for them is not dead, but absent.

Our best friend is the past.

The virtuous impulses of youth should become the principles of middle life.

Often one might resist one's own passions, but one is swept away by those of others.

A lovely woman, of noble carriage, but destitute of the gentle and beneficent virtues of her sex, resembles a beautiful lily on which nature has failed to bestow any scent.

Life resembles the sea, which owes its finest effects to storms.

It is doing an injury to those whom we love, to plan surprises for them; we deprive them of the pleasures of expectation.

The melancholy of tender and virtuous souls is the resting-place between two worlds: they are still sensitive to the pleasures of this world, but they are on the threshold of a more lasting joy.

CHAPTER V

1802–1804

MADAME DE KRUDENER did not in any way suffer in material fortunes by the death of her husband. The Emperor Alexander I., son and successor to the murdered Paul, not only undertook to pay all the debts of the late ambassador, incurred in the discharge of his diplomatic functions, but he also settled a considerable property on Mme. de Krudener for life. Leaving Paris in August, she spent some weeks at Geneva, before finally settling for the winter at Lyons, where she seems to have formed some plan of buying a small estate. Her thoughts at this time, however, ran mainly on the publication of her novel, *Valérie*, and she was determined that the inevitable delay caused by the death of M. de Krudener, should be made to serve for the preparation of a really brilliant success. Although confident in the artistic merit of the book, she was yet fully aware that other qualities besides mere excellence are necessary, in order to carry by storm a *blasé* Parisian public. In her own words, "Nothing can be had in Paris except by charlatanism "; and the revelation of all her preparatory manœuvres forms a most curious chapter in the history of literary wire-pulling.

Her chief agent in the matter was her Parisian physician and confidant, Dr. Gay, a man of some reputation and much ambition, a friend of the Abbé Raynal and of Laharpe. To him we find Mme. de Krudener inditing the following letters :—

Lyons, 3rd January 1803.

. . . I have another request to make : pray have some verses written by a good poet to our friend Sidonie.[1] In these verses, which I need not describe to you and which must be in perfect taste, there must be no other *envoi* but "To Sidonie." The poet will ask her why she resides in the provinces, why we are deprived of her wit and grace? Her triumphs call her to Paris. Her talents and her charms will there be appreciated at their full value. Her enchanting dance has been described ; but who can describe all that distinguishes her? *Mon ami*, I confide in your friendship; I am ashamed on behalf of Sidonie, for I know her modesty, and you know that she is not vain. But I have a reason far more important than mere vanity for begging you to have the verses written, and as soon as possible. Mind you say that she is in retreat, and that it is only in Paris that one is appreciated. Do your best not to be discovered. Have the lines printed in the evening paper. It is quite true that Sidonie's dance has been described in *Delphine ;* do read it, it will give you pleasure. But do not let it be said that she has been described in *Delphine*. Let there be no further heading to the lines than "To Sidonie." Please settle with the newspaper ; I hope to explain my reasons later. Please send me at once the paper in which the poem appears, addressed as usual to Mme. de Pelleport, at Lyons. If the newspaper refuses to insert the poem, or if there is much delay, send me the manuscript, and it can be published in one of the newspapers here. You will

---

[1] Sidonie was the heroine of the *Cabane des Lataniers*, and in many ways a portrait of the authoress herself.

greatly oblige your friend by doing this; she will explain her reasons personally for having troubled you. You know her hatred of civilisation, her love of solitude, and her indifference to praise, but in this case it will be doing her a special service. . . .

Lyons, 6th January 1803.

I wrote to you, my excellent friend, four days ago, and on the same day I received your letter; mine had already been sent off, and so I was unable to tell you how anxiously I desire to assist you in the acquirement of that reputation, which your talents and your virtues deserve. Yes, my worthy and excellent friend, I look forward to advancing your cause. I am impatiently awaiting the moment, when, once more in Paris, my time, my thoughts, and my zeal can all be consecrated to your advancement. You must introduce me to Laharpe, who is already acquainted with one of your friends. I shall use all my influence with Bernardin de St. Pierre, Chateaubriand, and many more of my friends; and we shall succeed, for pure intentions always do succeed.

From which we may conclude that the benefits conferred were to be mutual, though it is difficult for the candid reader to discern much purity of intention, either in the writer, or in the recipient of the foregoing letters.

Delphine, by Mme. de Staël, had been published in the autumn of the previous year, and had raised throughout France quite a storm of mingled applause and censure—applause for the artistic merits of the book, and censure for the boldness and unorthodoxy of the social and religious views expressed. We seem to trace a vein of feminine jealousy through the following letter, written by Mme. de Krudener on the subject of her friend's novel. There is no doubt that in many ways Mme. de

Staël's wayward and *exaltée* heroine recalls to one's mind the Julie de Krudener of early days.

Lyons, *17th January* 1803.

Have you read *Delphine?* Fontanes[1] has utterly crushed the authoress, who no doubt has been guilty of many absurdities, but who does not deserve such injurious criticism. Mme. de Staël has told Sidonie that she meant to describe her dance, and you will find it in the first volume. *Delphine* dances a Polish step at Mme. de Vernon's ball. According to several persons Mme. de Staël has described the figure, the imagination, and the ways of talking of Sidonie, and then she has mixed in with it her own religious and political views, for Sidonie is deeply religious, and never interferes in politics. It is very sad that *Delphine*, who is so good and so generous, should be guilty of so many foolish and unfortunate actions; but there are some beautiful things in the book. I begged you to send me some verses "To Sidonie," and we will have them inserted here. But while saying that her talent for dancing has been described, you must not say "some one " has done so, but simply : A talented pen has sketched thy dance ; thy successes are known, thy graces are as celebrated as thy wit, and yet thou dost hide them from the world; thou dost prefer retreat and solitude. There, with religion, nature and study, etc. etc. etc. . . . This, my dear friend, is what I require of you, and I will tell you why. . . .

The gallant doctor proved himself equal to the task imposed upon him, and in a few days we find Mme. de Krudener writing him a gratified letter of thanks for the " charming Elegy " he has sent. This first attempt was in prose, but a second poetical

---

[1] M. de Fontanes was the original founder and editor of the *Mercure de France*. The article to which Mme. de Krudener refers in her letter contains a most scathing and brutal attack on *Delphine*, which, being signed with an F., was universally attributed to Fontanes. He, however, wrote to disclaim the authorship. (See Mme. de Staël in the *Portraits de Femmes*, by M. de Sainte-Beuve.)

version followed shortly, and the lady, more and more flattered, writes again :—

LYONS, 25th January 1803.

Sidonie has entrusted me with the task of expressing her grateful thanks to the most amiable of friends. The verses are charming, and convey with accuracy all that could interest her; they were published in a newspaper, and it was in that way that she saw them; they have caused a real pleasure to all her friends. The author possesses indeed a happy talent! It is easy to see that he is the friend of Sidonie! How well he expresses his thought! Every stroke of the pen is inspired by his soul, and it is indeed a sublime soul to which Sidonie owes so sincere a gratitude. . . .

A later letter seems to refer to yet another set of verses, sent by the complaisant doctor.

Many thanks for your lines, which are charming. If only you could extract some from the great Delille! Never mind what people say: it will be useful to Sidonie, and you know how I love her! The world is so dense! It is this charlatanism that makes one conspicuous, and that allows one to serve one's friends. I am burning to know your plan, and to work with all my strength in your favour. I am writing about it to Camille Jordan, whom Mme. de Staël prefers to me; for I suspect that the dear lady is possessed by the jealousy of success, especially now that some of the charms and graces of *Delphine* have been recognised in Sidonie. She was fond enough of me in former days to paint the talent which she has described so well, but celebrity and too much success have apparently cooled her reflections. However, Camille will be able to serve your interests with her.

Would it not be a good plan to speak about Sidonie to our Neuilly friend?[1] You understand whom I mean. Chateaubriand, who sees him frequently, has already broached the subject to him. He admires Sidonie very much, and assures her she will have a tremendous success, and that she should return very

---

[1] J. F. Ducis, the poet, and member of the French Academy.

soon. I will soon send you a letter for him. Work at the Neuilly business, and write to me about it. Yes, my venerable friend, you shall have all the glory that your talents and your virtues deserve. . . .

Of Mme. de Krudener's social existence at Lyons during this, her first year of widowhood, we gain a glimpse from the following letter to Mme. Armand :—

LYONS, 1st March 1803.

My health is immensely improved. We have been drawn into eight balls running. I have been up for eight nights without suffering any ill effects. What happiness, my dear friend! I should never finish if I were to try and tell you how I have been fêted ; verses rain down upon me ; homage and admiration struggle for the first place. People snatch at a word from me as at a favour ; every one discusses my reputation for wit, my kindness of heart, my conduct. It is a thousand times more than I deserve, but Providence is often pleased to overwhelm her children even with favours that they do not merit.

Later she feels it necessary to explain to her friend the necessity that exists for her return to Paris—a return on which all her hopes had been set for months past :—

I should consider it cowardice on my part not to produce a book that might be useful, and that is how my visit to Paris has become a necessity, while my heart and my imagination both tempt me to the shores of your lake to which I am longing to come, disgusted with my stay in Paris, indifferent as to her triumphs, and only caring for peace and for quiet friendship. I should be extremely happy if I could spend my summers in Switzerland and my winters here, for Lyons has all the attractions of a large town. . . . Every one likes me, and I am so extolled by every one that it makes me blush.

To Sophie de Krudener, then at Berlin, she writes in the same strain :—

Lyons, 17th April 1803.

With all my old "horripios," as Vallin terms them, I am regarded here as an *élégante.* My Turkish and Persian costumes, my diamonds, and my laces, have obtained for me that sort of consideration which such magnificence can always command. Mme. de Staël's book, the reputation for dancing that I have gained from it, the laudatory notices of the newspapers on behalf of the " Maxims,"[1] the deluge of verses and portraits from Paris, my previous reputation, my friendship with Chateaubriand and with St. Pierre, the character for goodness and generosity with which the emigrants have endowed me, which I have done so little to deserve, and which has been exaggerated, and finally the credit gained from *Valérie,* which has been read here by Bérenger and by others ; all has contributed to procure for your mother much curiosity, a flood of provincial verses, invitations, receptions, etc. : all inspired by much goodness of heart, for the Lyonese are kindness itself. . . .

Paris did not tempt me ; I am pretty well *blasée* as to success, and I only seek for it now on behalf of my *Valérie ;* I expect the book to make a great sensation. . . . Oh how pleased I believe you will be with it ! It leaves Sidonie far behind ! . . . *Valérie* is in two volumes. The plot is simple, the details effective, and the style seems to me good. I have seen sentimental souls shed tears over it, and I have heard clever people say that it was full both of wit and of good taste. I really think the book is a good one : it is pious, moral, and filled with all that appeals to the imagination.

It is the success of *Valérie* that makes me wish to go to Paris. You know how much one is obliged to do oneself amongst journalists, in order to work up the success of a first book, so as to be able to trade lazily on one's reputation later on. I feel sure that St. Pierre, Ducis, Chateaubriand, and Geoffroy will all speak in its favour. Thus launched on the world, the young lady will be received everywhere. You know quite well that

---

[1] No doubt a reference to her *Pensées d'une Dame Étrangère,* published in the preceding autumn.

neither talent nor genius, nor the excellence of one's intentions, are sufficient to ensure a success; everything demands some charlatanism.

Having thus skilfully paved the way, Mme. de Krudener returned to Paris in May (1803) in order to personally superintend the final preliminaries of publication. She writes to her friend Mme. Armand (24th May) :—

Chateaubriand is enchanted with my *Valérie*, and I trust she will be a success, but do not talk about her at all. I see more and more how impossible it is to publish away from Paris. Chateaubriand assures me that the best books published in the provinces have no success. . . . Paris bores me; I pine for the lake and your company and a little quiet. A summer spent without birds seems to me like bankruptcy.

2nd August.—M. de St. Pierre is enthusiastic over *Valérie*, and so are other journalists and authors. They assert that it will be one of the most striking books that have appeared for long, but all are agreed in declaring that I must not publish just now, for the season is quite dead, and nobody is in Paris.

In the end *Valérie* was not published till December 1803, appearing with the date of the following year. M. Eynard gives an entertaining description of the singular manœuvres in which the eager authoress indulged, in order to ensure the final triumph of her book :—

During several days she made the round of the fashionable shops, incognito, asking sometimes for shawls, sometimes for hats, feathers, wreaths, or ribbons, all *à la Valérie*. When they saw this beautiful and elegant stranger step out of her carriage with an air of assurance, and ask for fancy articles which she invented on the spur of the moment, the shopkeepers were seized with a polite desire to satisfy her by any means in their power. Moreover, the lady would soon pretend to recognise the article she had asked for. And if the unfortunate shop girls, taken aback by such unusual demands, looked puzzled, and denied all knowledge of the article, Mme. de Krudener would smile graciously and pity them for their ignorance of the new novel, thus turning them all into eager readers of *Valérie*. Then, laden with her purchases, she would drive off to another shop, pretending to search for that which only existed in her imagination. Thanks to these manœuvres, she 'succeeded in exciting such ardent competition in honour of her heroine, that for at least a week the shops sold everything *à la Valérie*. Her own friends, the innocent accomplices of her stratagem, also visited shops on her recommendation, thus carrying the fame of her book through the Faubourg St. Germain and the Chaussée d'Antin.[1]

And yet, after all these months of journalistic wire-pulling and elaborate self-advertisement, the lady writes complacently to her friend : [2]—

The success of *Valérie* is complete and unheard of, and some one remarked to me just the other day that there is something supernatural in such a success. Yes, my dear friend, it is the will of heaven that the ideas and the purer morality the book contains should be spread throughout France, where such thoughts are little known !

Valérie, or, The Letters of Gustave de Linar to Ernest de G——, is a novel of very simple construction. Gustave, a young Swede of romantic and melancholy temperament, accompanies a certain Count to Italy in the capacity of secretary, and very shortly falls a victim to the fascinations of Valérie, the Count's child-wife. Her extreme youth and inexperience, coupled with her touching devotion to

[1] See C. Eynard's *Vie de Mme. de Krüdener*, vol. i. p. 136.
[2] 15th January 1803.

her serious-minded and paternal husband, save Valérie from all knowledge of the dangerous passion that is growing up beside her; and Gustave, inspired by the loftiest ideals of duty and honour, and an almost filial affection for the Count, resolves never to betray his guilty secret. He falls a prey to all the agitating emotions of a hopeless passion, his only relief consisting in pouring out his despairing soul in letters to his friend Ernest in Sweden. At length, with shattered health, feeling unequal to the strain of this prolonged daily struggle, Gustave retires to a mountain village in the Apennines, and dies of a broken heart, fortified by all the consolations of religion, and attended in his last moments by the Count himself, who hurries to his bedside on learning from Ernest de G—— the tragic plight of his secretary.

It is easy to recognise, even from this brief outline, what we have already pointed out, namely, that Mme. de Krudener's novel is but an idealised version of her own Venetian experiences. Over the whole situation, as it existed between husband and wife and secretary, there is thrown that halo of poetry and romance so dear to the soul of the authoress; but making due allowance for the exigencies of literary composition, the story is practically autobiographical in character. Some biographers have even taken the book *au pied de la lettre*, and Valérie being described as only sixteen, have assumed that Mme. de Krudener herself was married at fifteen, instead of eighteen, and have fixed the date of her birth three

years too late in consequence.   The only part of the
book entirely drawn from the imagination of the
authoress, is the final pathetic scene when the husband watches by the bedside of the dying lover; for,
as is well known, Alexandre de Stakieff outlived his
boyish passion, and came into contact with Mme. de
Krudener more than once in later years.   The
dramatic unity of the work undoubtedly demanded
some such striking episode in conclusion; but the
fact that Mme. de Krudener falsely described an
admirer as dying of love for her, gave rise to the
calumny that she went through life glorying in the
fatal nature of the passions she was able to inspire,
and that, in the exaggerated language of Parisot,[1]
"the tombs of her victims were scattered over
Europe."   For such an accusation there is not a
trace of real evidence, although the undeniable
vanity of the lady, and the tone of naïve complacency that pervades *Valérie*, are some slight
excuse for the invention of the fable.

Like *La Nouvelle Héloise*, like *Delphine*, *Valérie*
is written entirely in the form of letters—a form so
popular a hundred years ago, and so wearisome to
the modern reader.   *Valérie*, however, thanks to the
absence of incident, and to the extreme simplicity of
the plot, is saved from the unrealities and improb-
abilities which the exigencies of this form of novel-
writing render almost unavoidable.   Moreover,
though originally published in two volumes, it is

---

[1] See article on Mme. de Krudener in the *Biographie Universelle*, edited
by Michaud, Paris, 1841.

quite a short book, consisting of but forty-eight letters in all, of which forty-one are written by Gustave, who relates his own sorrows in a perfectly natural manner to his friend in Sweden.

Thus *Valérie* may still be read with pleasure, even by a generation which is privileged to form its standard of fiction on *Anna Karenina* and *Richard Feverel.* In truth, there is a tender pathos, a delicate elevation of tone, and something fresh and genuine even in the exaggerated sentimentality by which the authoress is inspired, which has prevented *Valérie* from growing antiquated and out of date, in company with the works of Mme. Cottin or Mme. de La Fayette. The detractors of the lady—and they have been numerous—give vent to exclamations of horrified surprise when her friends attempt to draw any parallel between her writings and those of her more celebrated contemporary Mme. de Staël; but I venture to think that with less power, less passion, less detailed observation than are to be found either in *Delphine* or in *Corinne, Valérie*, within its own narrower limits, possesses a unity of conception and an artistic completeness of treatment, which give to the reader a truer sense of enjoyment than is often to be obtained from works of a more ambitious character. Mme. de Krudener has infused into her *chérissime Valérie* much of her own indescribable magnetic charm—a charm which no age could dim, and which gave a peculiar quality to the preaching of her later years.

Above all, throughout *Valérie* there breathes an

intense love of nature, and more especially of solitude, of mountain scenery, of summer evenings, of
all that appeals most strongly to the emotional and
melancholy side of human sympathies.   The sub-
dued monotony of the scenery around her northern
home had given an impress to Mme. de Krudener's
susceptible nature, which may be traced through all
her descriptive writing.   Several of the letters
written by Gustave from his mountain retreat read
almost like prose poems.   Nor is the religious element wanting.   Both Gustave and Valérie profess
to be inspired by strong religious feeling, and in
more than one scene, as when Gustave prays before
the altar of the Blessed Virgin during the illness of
Valérie,[1] and later in his visit to the Chartreuse
Monastery,[2] there are unmistakable indications of
that emotional mysticism which was to be the key-
note of Mme. de Krudener's character in the second
period of her life.

Of the character of Valérie herself enough has
already been said.   As is only natural, she is infinitely the most successful impersonation in the book.
The Count, in spite of the almost pathetic efforts of
the authoress to render him a 'sympathetic' figure, is
inevitably somewhat stilted and oppressive, as the
elderly husband of real life, reduced by circumstances
to a subordinate position in his own household, is
apt to be.   Gustave, on the other hand, impresses
the modern English reader as terribly mawkish
and sentimental; it is only the irresistible charm

<hr>

[1] Letter XXIV.   [2] Letter XLIII.

of Valérie which rescues the situation from positive absurdity. His very virtue, and the unimpeachable purity of his intentions, strike at times a conventional and unnatural note. A comparatively recent critic, Georg Brandes, expresses astonishment that Mme. de Krudener, than whom no one was more capable of portraying from her own experience the passionate side of love, should have preferred to paint so seraphic a picture of chaste affection. But in truth it is specially characteristic of the lady, that all through her life the moral sentiments she committed to paper were of an unimpeachable nature, and that her own repeated lapses from morality, though frequently ignored, are never specifically condoned. Hence her *bonâ fide* horror at certain opinions contained in *Delphine* — opinions which are in open defiance of many of the received canons of morality and religion.

Mme. de Krudener in no way exaggerated to herself the applause with which her book was received. Her triumph was complete. Chateaubriand was frankly delighted, and used to speak of Valérie sometimes as "the younger sister of René," and sometimes as "the natural daughter of René and of Delphine." The *Mercure de France*, then an important arbiter of literary taste, and which only a few months previously had dealt out such hard measure to Mme. de Staël, published a most flattering critique of *Valérie* from the pen of M. Michaud. But no one has done so much to place *Valérie* on a footing of permanent literary interest as M. de

Sainte-Beuve. "*Valérie*," he writes, "both by its thoughts and its sentiments, is not inferior to any novel of wider scope; it has maintained without effort a natural proportion, a true unity: like the person of the authoress, it possesses the infinite charm of harmony."[1] The great critic furthermore declares that *Valérie* should be numbered among the books which may be read with pleasure thrice in a lifetime. It is therefore not surprising to discover that *Valérie* was republished in Paris, only a few years ago, amongst the volumes of the *Petite Bibliothèque de Luxe*. Curiously enough, it appears never to have been translated into English. Though the flowing graceful style loses more than half its charm by translation, we venture to render, as a specimen of a work which is wholly unknown on this side of the Channel, one of the most striking scenes in the book, a description of the celebrated *danse du schall*, as written by Gustave himself, an onlooker from outside the ball-room window, to his friend Ernest.

The guests continued to urge Valérie, who repeatedly refused, and pointed to her forehead, as though to imply that she was suffering from a headache. At length the crowd dispersed; the guests went to supper; Valérie remained, and there were only some twenty people in the room. Then I saw the Count, accompanied by a lady covered with rouge and diamonds, advancing towards Valérie; I saw him beg her, implore her to dance; all the men went down on their knees to her, and the ladies surrounded her. At length I saw her give way; I myself, carried away by the general excitement, had joined my entreaties to theirs, as though she could hear me, and when she acceded

<hr>

[1] See "Mme. de Krudener" in the *Portraits de Femmes*.

to their request, I felt a moment of anger. The doors were closed, so that no one else should enter the room; Lord Mery took up a violin; Valérie asked for her dark-blue muslin shawl; she brushed away her hair from off her forehead, and placed her shawl over her head, so that it fell on either side of her temples down over her shoulders; her forehead was outlined in the classic manner; her hair was hidden, her eyes cast down, her head bowed, whilst her shawl fell in soft folds over her arms, which were crossed on her breast, and you might have thought that the blue garment, the pure and gentle face, had been drawn by Correggio in order to express tranquil resignation; and when she lifted her eyes, and her lips attempted to smile, you might have said with Shakspeare, that she was Patience on a monument, smiling at Grief.

These varying attitudes, expressive one moment of terror, and the next of pathos, form an eloquent language drawn from the passions and the sensations of the soul. When they are represented by pure and classic figures, and by faces gifted with the power of expression, the effect is quite indescribable. Lady Hamilton, who was endowed with these precious gifts, was the first to give any idea of this truly dramatic form of dancing. The long scarf, which is at once so classic and so adaptable to varying poses, now drapes and now conceals the figure, and lends itself to the most seductive effects. But it is Valérie you must see; it is she alone who, modest, shy, noble, intensely sensitive, thrills, excites, agitates, brings forth tears, and causes the heart to beat as it only beats when stirred by some strong emotion; it is she who possesses that delicate grace that cannot be taught, but that nature reveals in secret to a few chosen mortals. It is not the result either of lessons or of art; it descends from heaven with the virtues; it is the grace that inspired the brush of Raphael, and the soul of the artist who gave us the chaste Venus. It is very real in Valérie, where it exists side by side with modesty and chastity; it betrays the soul, whilst attempting to veil the beauties of the form. . . .

One moment, in imitation of Niobe, she would draw a stifled cry from my soul torn by her grief; the next she would be flying like Galatea, and my whole being seemed to be drawn along in her airy footsteps. No, I can give you no idea of my agitation, when, a moment before bringing her magic dance to a close, she made the circle of the ball-room, running, or rather flying, over the floor, looking backwards half frightened, half bashful, as though she were pursued by Love. I opened my arms; I called her; I cried in stifled tones: "Valérie, Valérie, come to me! It is here you ought to take refuge; it is on the breast of him who dies for you that you ought to rest." And I clasped my arms with a convulsive movement, and the pain I inflicted on myself roused me, and yet I had only embraced emptiness. What am I saying? Emptiness? Oh no! As long as my eyes were feasting on the vision of Valérie there was joy in the illusion.

The dance came to an end. Valérie, exhausted with fatigue, and pursued by acclamations, came and flung herself down close to the window where I stood. She attempted to open it by pushing it outwards; but I prevented her with all my strength, trembling lest she should take cold. She sat down and leant her head against the window-pane; never had I been so close to her; a mere sheet of glass separated us. I pressed my lips to her arm; it seemed to me that I was breathing torrents of fire; and you, Valérie, you felt nothing, nothing—and more than that you will never feel for me.

CHAPTER VI

1804-1808

THE success of *Valérie* was the last worldly triumph
that Mme. de Krudener was to enjoy. Her departure from Paris for her mother's house at Riga,
in the early spring of 1804, marks the close of this
first period of her life. Never had she appeared
more worldly-minded, more bent on winning the
applause of men, than during the months that preceded the appearance of *Valérie*; never before had
her vanity been so fully gratified as by the chorus
of admiration which greeted the publication of the
book; and yet, unknown to herself, and certainly
unsuspected by the world, she was on the eve of
the great moral crisis of her life—a crisis which was
to transform the brilliant, gifted, pleasure-loving
woman of the world, into the friend and comforter
of the poor, the religious guide of queens and
emperors, and the preacher and founder of one of
the most curious revivalist movements of the
century.

Few details have reached us of the first year
that Mme. de Krudener spent in Livonia after her

return in 1804. We know that, deeply attached as she was to her mother, the society of Riga was nevertheless unbearable to her, and her happiest days were spent at Kosse, where she busied herself with the welfare of the peasantry, and endeared herself to the hearts of all her dependants. The following letter was evidently written in one of her most *exalté* moods :—

MME. DE KRUDENER TO L. P. BÉRENGER.[1]

RIGA, LIVONIA, 10*th June* 1805.

Pray do not think, my dear Bérenger, that I have forgotten you. No indeed! As long as I love tender sympathy and noble sentiments and kindly virtues, and all that gives a charm to life, your memory, that of Ducis, of our good and generous Camille Jordan, and above all of our adorable Bernardin de St. Pierre, will mingle with one another on the much-loved banks of the Seine and the Rhone.

How fascinating they are, those joyous banks of the Seine— those delightful surroundings of the Isle-Barbe! What welcome shade! what mysterious valleys! what romantic vistas! what a country and what friends! I weave it all into tender and touching verse, which sets me dreaming, and sometimes even makes me shed tears. Then I forget that I am far away from you and from Lyons, the town I love most on earth, and which seems to have been built on purpose to gratify both my imagination and my heart!

At Lyons my life, oblivious of all worries, seemed to flow onward with the Saône, tranquil and peaceful, between smooth meadows. With one glance I was in Switzerland; I penetrated to the Valais . . . with another I crossed the Alps and flew towards Italy. I seemed to traverse their snow-clad summits, their calm solitudes and their torrents, so numerous and so pure. . . .

---

[1] L. P. Bérenger, professor at the Lyons University, and author of *La Morale en Action*.

By following the impetuous course of the Rhone I arrived first at Vaucluse, which you have described so successfully in your *Soirées Provençales*, and I saw again in my imagination the pier and harbour of Marseilles. . . . Opposite, the Scipé with its dark pine-trees indicated the religious house of the children of Bruno; I saw once more that Chartreuse which inspired the novel which you asked of me, and which I am sending you corrected, from the shores of the Baltic, writing to you, at eleven at night, in a twilight which resembles the most beautiful dawn. In two hours' time I shall see the sun once more shining both on sea and sky.

Thus, from the far North, Imagination, that glorious faculty, carries me frequently back amongst my friends. Yes, friendship gives back to me the illusions of the land of my heart. . . . Nature has indeed treated you Frenchmen like spoilt children! Are you really conscious of your good fortune? What nation in all the world has such cause to give thanks to that divine Providence, which fools presume to deny in the proud blasphemy of their delirium? . . . No, no! I am not on the shores of the Baltic; I do not dwell amongst our pine forests. I am on other shores, less bare and solitary; I am in that "tant doux pays qu'on ne peut oublier," as Mary Queen of Scots used to say. I am there; I fly thither on the clouds of Ossian: they appear to me as mountains, as squadrons. I call to them; I give them names of which the memory will lie in my heart to all eternity. . . .

Oh, my dear Bérenger, do not think me quite mad; one is not mad when one loves France and the French so passionately. Besides, the former habits of my heart cannot be effaced. How indeed, without ingratitude, could I forget that Providence caused me to regain my health in France? My daughter, my Juliette, who nearly died in Denmark where she was born, was saved in Paris. It was at Lyons that my own convalescence was so prompt and so enchanting. I found there real friends, souls in perfect harmony with my own, cultivated men who encouraged me, foretold my successes, and did not deceive me. Finally, it was at Lyons that I finished *Valérie*. I had begun the work at Geneva, inspired by the melancholy beauty of Lake Leman and of the Grande-Chartreuse. I read half of it to you, and I confided it also to Vallin and to Camille Jordan. I was implored to finish it, and I completed this romantic and most faithful picture of a passion as unprecedented as it was stainless.

It was not the desire of displaying my wit which inspired those pages, which are, I think, touching, and to which your newspapers deign to accord some praise. No indeed; whatever in *Valérie* is of worth, belongs to those religious sentiments with which Heaven has endowed me, and which He wished to foster by causing them to be beloved.

No doubt you have read that other novel [1] in which the good and virtuous heroine so horrifies her sex by committing suicide; in spite of its many striking beauties it ought not to be a success. And religion stands erect ready to strike a fatal blow at such a doctrine—all the more terrible from the power of the talent that attempts to disseminate it. However, an inconsequence is not an intention; and why need we suppose that Mme. de Staël meant to write a dangerous book—she who has made a study of morality, and who believes firmly in the perfectibility of this strange century?

Let us do justice to the many beauties to be found .in the work. I only see in *Delphine* the sad victim of a violent and unhappy passion, and in her last acts nothing but the inconsequences of a brain incapable of reasoning. A good woman, with an ardent soul, surrounded by the perfidy of the great world, falls, in all her innocence, into the meshes of love and misfortune. . . . And if Delphine is so terribly punished, has not the author, by thus exciting fear of the consequences of sin, divined the true secret of morality, and attained the aim of the novelist?

Moreover, I can see by the success of my beloved *Valérie* that piety, pure and resisted love, touching affection, and all that appertains to refinement and virtue, are more appreciated in France than elsewhere, and more at Lyons than in any other town.

It is time to tell you something of myself, as regards my health. . . . I will write on that subject to-morrow, for the traveller who is to take charge of this letter remains here a few days longer. This delay will allow my daughter to send our

---

[1] *Delphine.*

friends a little present of tea and of essence of roses, which come to us by means of the caravans from Kashmir.

No one is more truly devoted to you than the

BARONNE DE KRUDENER, *née* MÜNNICH.

It was a few weeks later that the incident occurred, which was to prove the turning-point in the life of our heroine. Whilst gazing idly one day out of a window of her mother's house at Riga, a young man, one of her most ardent admirers, passed down the road, raising his hat in recognition of the lady. The next instant he fell dead to the ground, the victim of heart-disease. The suddenness of the calamity made a profound impression on Mme. de Krudener. Her eyes were all at once opened to the worldliness of her life, and she was seized with inexpressible terror at the thought that she too might be struck down one day, and hurried before the judgment - seat of her Creator, without a moment for prayer or repentance. The tragic event appeared to her in the light of a solemn warning, and for days and weeks she was haunted by the gloomiest thoughts and forebodings, seeing no way out of her troubles.

Light came to her in her perplexity from an unexpected quarter. She was being measured one day by a local cobbler for a pair of shoes, and glancing casually at the face of the man kneeling before her, she was startled by his expression of peace and happiness, in striking contrast to her own listless misery. With characteristic impetuosity she put the question to him: "My friend, are you happy ? " and received the unhesitating reply : " Oh, I am the happiest of men ! " Nothing more was said, but all night long the words rang in the ears of Mme. de Krudener, depriving her of sleep, and filling her with envy and despair. " He is happy, whilst I am the most wretched of women," she kept repeating to herself, and unable to rest until she had solved the mystery, she hurried off early next morning to the shoemaker's cottage, in order to question him as to the cause of his joy.

It transpired that the shoemaker was a member of a little community of Moravian Brothers,[1] a simple, God - fearing people, meeting together for daily prayer and a diligent study of the Gospels. The happiness on the shoemaker's face was but the reflection of his inward peace of mind. Before long Mme. de Krudener had made friends with other members of the little community, and the happiest hours of her day were spent in their company. She bestowed her confidence more especially on a Mme. Blau, a lady both of birth and education, who cheerfully supported six children by her own personal labour, trusting implicitly for all things to

[1] The Moravian Brothers, or United Brethren, were founded in 1457 by some of the disciples of John Huss. They flourished principally in Moravia and Bohemia during the 16th century, and, though maintaining friendly relations with Luther and Calvin, were never united to the Protestant Churches of Germany. After a short period of religious prosperity the sect was broken up and suppressed ; but under the influence of German pietism and the protection of Count Zinzendorf we find it reviving early in the 18th century at Herrnhut in Saxony, which became later a centre of spiritual activity, sending out missionaries all over Europe. The first Livonian colony was founded in 1730. The Moravians belong to the Protestant evangelical school of thought ; they preach Justification by Faith alone, and profess to found their teaching entirely on the Scriptures.

prayer, and bearing her troubles with such un-ruffled equanimity that Mme. de Krudener, filled with amazement, writes of her as " the happiest woman I have ever met in my life."

It is easy to understand the sense of rest and comfort, which an overstrained emotional tempera-ment would acquire in familiar intercourse with these homely unsophisticated people, to whom the weariness and deceptions of life in a higher social sphere were entirely unknown.   Mme. de Kru-dener learnt from the Moravian Brothers that the God of vengeance whom she dreaded, was in reality a God of love calling her to Him.   She learnt to take mere intellectual cleverness at its true valua-tion, to realise the worse than worthlessness of worldly luxury, and, on the other hand, to appreciate to some extent the beauty of unpretending good-ness, and of a conscientious discharge of small daily duties.   And it is equally easy to picture the in-credulous amazement with which the conventional society of Riga must have regarded the " conver-sion " of their most gifted and brilliant member to the evangelistic teachings of an obscure religious sect.   At no time of her life was Mme. de Krudener tempted to hide her light under a bushel ; and now, filled with a missionary zeal for imparting to others the new faith that was in her, she would attempt to speak in her mother's *salon* of our redemption by the Passion of Jesus Christ, un-daunted by the constrained silence, or the cynical smile, with which her words were invariably greeted.

Her daily life, too, bore witness to the sincerity of
her professions. French novels were replaced by
Bible and hymn-book, and much of her hitherto
wasted time was devoted to visiting the poor and
the sick—a task which was at first a sore trial to her
hypersensitive nature. Of all her old friends, Mme.
Armand was perhaps the only one capable of entering into her new interests and aspirations, and in
her letters to this faithful companion she pours out
the fulness of her spiritual raptures :—

Dear Armand, you have no notion of the happiness which
I gain from this holy and sublime faith. I go like a child to be
enlightened and consoled, to rejoice and confide in my merciful
Saviour. When I am worried I pray to Him, and He takes my
troubles away; when I am misjudged I go to Him, and remembering how He suffered, He consoles me; when I see the
ingratitude of men, I realise that we ought to do good, as the
healthy tree brings forth fruit, without troubling ourselves as to
consequences, or wishing for gratitude. As a child turns to its
mother, so my soul turns to that spring of mercy that heals every
ill. When I feel myself under the influence of sin, of temptations to vanity, of a foolish longing to shine before the eyes of
men, I go to Him, and I beg of Him to cure me : then my
soul is released from all worldly passions. Love, ambition, success, seem to me mere folly; exaggerated affections, even when
lawful, seem to me as nothing compared to the pure and celestial
happiness which comes from on high. Yet I feel that I still love
my child and my mother, and even my friends, more passionately
than I ought.

And again, a few weeks later :—

Oh, my good Armand, pray, pray like a child! If you are
not yet in that blessed state, pray, and implore that divine grace
which God always grants for the love of His Son; you will
receive it, and you will feel that man cannot be happy either in

this world, or in the next, without Jesus Christ, and without the belief that salvation can only be gained through Him.

Nothing could be more simple or more sublime than religious truths, but, rather than humble himself, man's pride leads him to have recourse to reason, and how can man understand everything? Ask, and it shall be given you, said the Saviour; seek, and ye shall find; pray with a simple heart, and everything shall be made manifest to you. Deeply imbued with these great truths, my heart has gone out towards you, and I have longed for you to possess true peace of mind, that most sublime of gifts. My dear Armand, you have not sinned as I have. A thousand rocks have been the cause of my suffering shipwreck. But we all of us are in need of the divine mercy.

Oh, my dear friend, if only men could realise the happiness of religion, how they would fly from the fatigue and trouble to which they submit in their search after hurtful riches!

In the early spring of 1807 Mme. de Krudener appears to have left the shelter of her mother's house, and to have embarked once more on a wandering life through Germany. It is at this period that we must place her much-debated relations with the beautiful and courageous Queen Louise of Prussia.[1] After the terrible disasters of Jena and Auerstädt (16th October 1806), followed by the triumphant entry of Napoleon into Berlin, King Frederick William III. retired with his Court to Königsberg, in the extreme north-eastern corner of his dominions. Here Mme. de Krudener, on her way from Riga, interrupted her journey to pay her respects to the unhappy royal family, and was privileged to become the companion of the Queen

---

[1] Daughter of Duke Charles of Mecklenburg-Strelitz; married, 1793, to the Crown Prince of Prussia, who ascended the throne in 1797 as King Frederick William III.

in her daily visits to the sick and wounded soldiers in the hospitals of Königsberg. On these errands of mercy the two ladies discovered that they were far more in sympathy, than they had ever imagined during the course of their official acquaintance at Berlin, seven years previously. Queen Louise, filled with grief for the fate of her country, and bravely facing all the unhappy consequences of an aggressive policy, which she herself had been amongst the first to urge on her husband, felt herself strengthened and consoled by Mme. de Krudener's ardent faith and mystical raptures. In the simple unceremonious life to which the royal family of Prussia were at that time reduced, the presence of Mme. de Krudener appears to have entirely escaped notice; for at a later date, the Queen's much-loved brother, the Grand-Duke George of Mecklenburg-Strelitz, writes with evident indignation: "Mme. de Krudener has never exercised the smallest influence over my angelic sister of Prussia, nor over the King her husband, who was perfectly capable of judging that unhappily notorious person." The existence, however, of very intimate relations is placed beyond a doubt by the following touching letter written by the Queen to Mme. de Krudener when the Peace of Tilsit had deprived the crown of Prussia of half its possessions, and when the patriotic Louise required all the help that religion could give in order to bear the accumulated weight of her country's misfortunes.

I owe to your kind heart a confession which I know you will receive with tears of joy. It is that you have made me better than I was. Your words of truth, and the conversations we had on religion and Christianity, have left the deepest impression upon me. I have thought more earnestly on subjects, of which I did indeed previously feel the reality and the value, but rather with a sense of vagueness than of certainty. Our meditations have been full of comforting results. I was able to draw nearer to God. My faith became ever stronger, and it is thus that in the midst of misfortunes, humiliations, and sorrows without number, I have never been without consolation, and consequently never entirely miserable.

Add to this the mercy of a loving Father who has not permitted my heart to become embittered, but has left it full of love for my fellow-creatures, and still able to feel the necessity of helping and rescuing them. You will understand that I cannot be utterly unhappy when I possess the sources of the very purest joy. I have seen with the eye of truth the vanity of all earthly grandeur, and its utter worthlessness in comparison with the heavenly gifts. In a word, I have attained to a tranquillity of mind and to an internal peace, which make me hope that I may bear with the resignation and submission of a true Christian, all the decrees of Providence and all the trials that are ordained for my purification—for it is thus that I regard the ills that afflict us in this life.

I find myself once again in all the bustle of the world. Promise me always to speak to me with the voice of *Truth*.[1]

The sentiments of admiration and affection with which the writer of this letter was regarded by Mme. de Krudener will appear later in the course of her correspondence with Mdlle. Cochelet.

From Königsberg Mme. de Krudener travelled through Prussia to Dresden, and from thence made expeditions to the various Moravian centres in Saxony, Kleinwelk, Bethelsdorf, and Herrnhut. Everywhere she was received with the warmest of

---

[1] The original of this letter is in German.

welcomes, endearing herself to the simple German peasantry by the sweet cordiality of her manner, and on her side deriving much spiritual benefit from the unrestrained intercourse with these little communities of ardent Christians. With them she felt happy and at peace ; but the moment she again took her natural place in polite society, whether at Dresden or elsewhere, she was assailed once more by her old temptations to vanity and worldliness, and was torn in two by the conflicting desires of her nature. In her search after spiritual advice and guidance she was attracted to Carlsruhe, the home of Jung-Stilling, then at the height of his fame as a religious writer and teacher.[1] In giving her an introduction to his friend Stilling, Pastor Baumeister of Bethelsdorf, knowing the old man's enthusiastic temperament, entrusted Mme. de Krudener with the following message : "Warn Stilling, that I, Baumeister, request him not to canonise you as a saint." Immediately on her arrival at the capital our heroine presented herself before the doctor, who, with characteristic kindness of heart, invited both her and her daughters to take up their residence in his own family circle. Mme. de Krudener joyfully accepted the offer, and spent the next few months as the

[1] Johann Heinrich Jung-Stilling (1740-1817) was the son of worthy and pious peasant parents. Entirely self-educated, and with an early bent towards mystical religion, Jung spent some years both as a school teacher and a tailor's apprentice, and was ultimately enabled to take his doctor's degree, distinguishing himself subsequently as an oculist. From 1803 until his death he practised at Carlsruhe, in the service of his friend the Grand-Duke Charles Frederic of Baden, and was much sought after by rich and poor alike, both for his scientific skill and for his unwavering faith in God and purity of life. He is the author of many religious writings, mostly of a mystical tendency.

guest of Frau Stilling, dividing her days between her literary labours, and visits to the poor and sick.

During her residence at Carlsruhe Mme. de Krudener was enabled to win a final victory over her old repugnance to coming in close personal contact with squalor and misery. On her errands of mercy no task was too repulsive for her small white hands, once the object of so much admiration, and which were now condemned to rough and unaccustomed labour. There is a pretty story belonging to this period, according to which Mme. de Krudener, on leaving the house one morning, noticed a young servant girl crying bitterly whilst she swept the pavement before the front door. In answer to sympathetic inquiries the little maid admitted that, left an orphan by the sudden death of her parents, she had been unexpectedly reduced to entering domestic service ; it was not the hardness of the work, but the degradation of her position that she felt so keenly. Gently taking the broom from the girl's hand, Mme. de Krudener began herself to sweep the pavement before the house, saying at the same time : " My child, there is no humiliation in doing useful work. It has been done by far greater people than you or I. The Blessed Virgin Mary, who was descended from many kings, swept the floor as you have to do, and the Son of God, God Himself, who became man for our salvation, lived for thirty years in humble circumstances. He also would have taken the broom from the hands of His mother in order to help her; for He was subject to His parents, and was meek and humble of heart."

As we have already stated, literature was not neglected during these months. It must have been at this period that the authoress of *Valérie* completed a novel with the title *Letters of certain Persons of Quality*—a novel which, though much praised by those who were privileged to enjoy a private perusal, was never published, and was in all probability destroyed by the writer. She next turned her attention to an anecdote related to her by the Princess of Solms Braunfels[1] concerning a bracelet found in a castle dungeon, and supposed to have been the property of a countess who had languished seven years as a prisoner in the fortress. This incident became the foundation of a novel named *Othilde* or *The Dungeon*, in which the authoress dwelt lengthily on the Christian joys and consolations, of which even the closest prisoner cannot be deprived. Mme. de Krudener herself seems to have regarded *Othilde* with special approbation, but it was probably too didactic for the general reader, and does not appear to have ever attained to a public success.

It was impossible for Mme. de Krudener to enjoy uninterrupted the pleasures of domestic life for any length of time. In spite of her very ardent wish to lead a simple busy life in the midst of the Stilling family, etiquette compelled her to pay her respects to the Margravine of Baden, the mother of

---

[1] Sister of Queen Louise of Prussia, and later Queen of Hanover.

the Empress Elizabeth of Prussia.   The Queens of
Bavaria and Sweden, both daughters of the Margravine, were present at that time at the Court of
Carlsruhe, and were naturally curious to make the
acquaintance of the much‑talked‑of authoress of
Valérie, so that Mme. de Krudener found herself
in constant requisition at the grand-ducal palace for
the sake of her brilliant and witty conversation.   In
the month of May 1808, having rejoined her nephew
Baron Louis Krudener at the baths of Baden, she
further made the acquaintance of the Queen of
Holland, Hortense Beauharnais.   The latter was so
charmed by the religious enthusiasm and elevation
of sentiment displayed by Mme. de Krudener, that
she not only received her in an unceremonious
manner at all hours of the day, but was anxious to
attach her permanently to her Court—an offer which
was respectfully declined.   At the same time the
foundations were laid of an intimacy that extended
over many years between our heroine and Mdlle.
Cochelet, reader and *confidante* to the unhappy
Queen.[1]   In her valuable Memoirs, Mdlle. Cochelet,
who was possessed of a warm, sympathetic heart
and considerable intellectual ability, writes enthusiastically of this period as " the happy time when she
(Mme. de Krudener) won my admiration and my
friendship, when we talked for hours together, and
when her exquisite soul revealed itself to me in all

---

[1] Louise Cochelet, afterwards Mme. Parquin, for twenty-five years companion to Queen Hortense, and authoress of *Mémoires sur la Reine Hortense
et la Famille impériale.*

simplicity without any trace of exaggeration."[1] It is pleasant to observe the undisguised admiration which Mme. de Krudener was able to evoke in members of her own sex; and this friendship with Mdlle. Cochelet is specially noteworthy as having called forth some of the most important letters on public matters, that have come down to us from the future prophetess.

[1] See *Mémoires* by Mdlle. Cochelet, vol. ii. chap. vi.

CHAPTER VII

1808-1810

THE residence of Mme. de Krudener in the family circle of Jung-Stilling was destined to have a marked influence not only on her immediate spiritual development, but on her whole future course of action. She arrived at Carlsruhe imbued with much religious fervour, deeply stirred by the fact of her own conversion, and with her receptive enthusiastic nature more than ever open to new religious impressions and modes of thought. She had acquired from the Moravian Brothers a firm belief in the redemption of mankind through Jesus Christ, and in the possibility of an instantaneous conversion to God through His grace, as well as a strong faith in the efficacy of prayer. Further than that her dogmatic teaching did not go, and her piety was of a simple, active kind, entirely free from any hysterical tendency. But from the instant of her becoming a member of the Stilling household she was launched on the deep waters of mystical pietism, in which all the remaining years of her life were destined to be spent.

Side by side with the growth of religious free thought in the more educated classes of Germany, as of France, during the course of the 18th century, there had been amongst the humbler classes a far more widespread growth of a mystical and pietistic form of religious faith, which had become engrafted on many of the Protestant Churches in all parts of the empire. Jung-Stilling, sprung from peasant stock, had been brought up in the midst of it from his very cradle, and at the time of his first acquaintance with Mme. de Krudener, when he was already in his 69th year, he was perhaps the most important representative of the religious national movement in Germany. From his earliest youth he had looked forward to a high career. Converted to God under special circumstances in his boyhood, he maintained that every step of his life had been taken under the marvellous indications of Providence, and that the power of prayer had unfailingly assisted him in every necessity. The doctrines of the French Revolution filled him with horror, and he preached against them with all his might. Like Swedenborg, of whose writings he had made a special study, Jung-Stilling believed that certain persons possessed the faculty of communicating directly with the spiritual world, and, as a natural corollary, that he himself possessed such a power. Like all mystics, he indulged in much literal interpretation of the prophetic books of the Bible, and announced a second advent of Jesus Christ, and the speedy commencement of the Millennium. Such, in brief outline, were the doctrines into which the venerable old man initiated his visitor, who on her side was only too willing to accept without questioning his religious experiences. Many of Stilling's views were shared by one whose name is revered by posterity far more for the sake of his great love for humanity and his practical philanthropy, than for his mystical teachings. The Pasteur Oberlin,[1] who is best known to English readers as one of the first and most enthusiastic continental adherents of the then recently started British Bible Society, was also the recipient of a visit from Mme. de Krudener, who arrived from Carlsruhe armed with a letter of introduction from Jung-Stilling, and who was filled with amazement and admiration for all that had been accomplished in the Ban de la Roche by the self-sacrificing labour of a single man. It is impossible not to feel a moment's regret that this practical side of the ministry of Christ did not tempt Mme. de Krudener away from the visionary dreams of world-wide evangelisation, which were already beginning to take shape in her eager heart and brain. Had all the leaders of the pietistic school in Germany been men of the scientific attainments and broad sympathies of Jung-Stilling, or of the splendid humanitarian zeal of the Pasteur Oberlin, the future developments of the movement might have been

---

[1] John Frederic Oberlin (1740-1826), Pastor of the Ban de la Roche, in Alsace, for over fifty years, during which time he transformed the district from a barren tract of mountain land, inhabited by a miserable peasantry, into a flourishing agricultural community, with schools, public library, spinning factories, and every known means for promoting physical and spiritual welfare.

very different from what they ultimately became, and Mme. de Krudener herself would have been saved from many of the errors of her religious teaching. Unfortunately the belief in the speedy establishment of the Millennium and in spiritual manifestations in daily life, the prevalence of distorted interpretations of the Scriptures, and more especially of the Book of Revelation, together with the encouragement afforded to every form of prophecy and so-called divine inspiration, inevitably opened the door to superstition and charlatanism of the grossest kind, to which the credulous and the ignorant fell easy victims, and of which the clever and unscrupulous were only too quick to take advantage for their personal benefit and aggrandisement.

Such a man was Frederick Fontaine, who, as pastor of the little village of Ste. Marie-aux-Mines, in Alsace, had gained much credit in the surrounding country by a constant display of unctuous piety and mystical pretensions, and whom Oberlin himself, in the goodness of his heart, trusted as a friend and exalted as a teacher. In reality Fontaine was nothing more than a religious impostor of the most vulgar description, with a natural capacity for eloquence of the evangelistic order, and whose spiritual successes served not only to feed his personal vanity, but opened up the way to advantages of a more substantial kind. It was an evil day in the life of Mme. de Krudener when, in the summer of 1808, she first alighted at the door of the minister of Ste. Marie-aux-Mines. A short time previously, Fontaine had strengthened his position by securing the services of a certain middle-aged peasant woman, Maria Kummrin by name, of no education, but possessed apparently of some thought-reading faculty, which gained her much credit amongst her neighbours. She frequently related events that took place at some distance from her home, and many of her prophecies were currently reported to have come true. In her states of ecstatic contemplation, in which she would remain for hours, she would offer up prayer in unctuous and flowing language, and on returning to her natural self, would maintain that she had been in direct communication with the angels of God. It is easy to see the advantages which accrued to Fontaine, by the presence in his parish of this misguided but apparently well-meaning woman. Encouraged by the minister in all her spiritual extravagances, and flattered by the consideration with which she was treated, her prophecies and visions increased apace, and she was ready to announce in her ecstasies any-thing suggested to her by the crafty minister. Whether Fontaine and Maria Kummrin were part-ners in the deception practised, or whether the peasant woman was merely the dupe of her more accomplished companion, it is difficult to ascertain ; certain it is that, for a time at least, Mme. de Kru-dener was the dupe of both, and was urged on by them to a credulous belief in the most barefaced deceptions, practised under the pretence of divine inspiration. It would appear that Maria Kummrin had publicly predicted the arrival in the village of some important stranger, who was to achieve great things for the kingdom of God, and that when Mme. de Krudener drove up to the door of the pastor's house, Fontaine welcomed her solemnly in words similar to those addressed by the disciples of John to Jesus Christ : " Art thou she that should come, or look we for another ?"   Such a *début* was quite sufficient to excite the restless aspirations of our heroine, and she lent herself only too readily to the assurances of her host, that they had both been specially elected by God to labour together for the conversion of sinners.   All the scruples which a knowledge of the world might naturally have in-stilled into her mind were regarded as the unworthy promptings of self-interest ; and before many days were passed she was ready to make the sacrifice of time, strength, and money on behalf of a course which she regarded as directly inspired by Heaven. Of the complete good faith of Mme. de Krudener herself throughout this regrettable phase of her life, there exists no shadow of a doubt ; her most bitter opponents are agreed in recognising the absolute honesty of her intentions.   Her innate refinement of mind, combined with the purity of her motives, enabled her to pass untainted through this unwhole-some atmosphere of combined charlatanism and hysteria.   Yet one cannot but feel that she too was flattered by the predictions of the village prophetess on her behalf, and that but for her unconquerable vanity, which was to crop up in the course of her life in so many strange disguises, she could hardly have been so blind to the self-interested manœuvres of Fontaine. Nevertheless, her own peace of mind and simplicity of purpose remained singularly unaffected by her surroundings. The following letter, written to Mme. Armand shortly after her arrival at Ste. Marie-aux-Mines, will best explain how far she had travelled, since the time of her first arrival in Carlsruhe but a few months previously.

STE. MARIE-AUX-MINES, 21st June 1808.

DEAREST FRIEND—The most fortunate of experiences makes me say of myself that I am the happiest of women. I can only explain to you in person all I have undergone; but, in the meanwhile, I pray for you, and I believe that you too will become blessed in this life. Dear friend, think that I have experienced miracles in the true sense of the word; that I have been initiated into the most profound mysteries of eternity, and that I could reveal to you many things about the future life. No, you have no conception of the happiness which awaits all those who give themselves entirely to Jesus Christ. Persevere; go to Him day by day. I have received the most positive promise through His goodness and mercy that He will deign to grant my prayers for my friends and relations. I ask of His mercy the gift of eternity on their behalf. Oh, if you only knew how He loves us! The time is coming when the most frightful calamities will overtake the earth. Do not fear; remain faithful to Him. He will gather together all the faithful, and afterwards His kingdom will come. He Himself will come and reign a thousand years on the earth. Give yourself to Him, and ask of Him only Faith and Love for Himself and for His divine Father. Adore the Father and ask of Him His Holy Spirit.

We do not propose following Mme. de Krudener in detail through the wanderings of the next few months. During a short visit to Geneva in the autumn of 1808, undertaken with the express sanction of Maria Kummrin, she had the inexpressible joy of completely converting her friend Mme. Armand to her religious views. Back at Ste. Marie-aux-Mines, she writes (23rd October): "Our little household breathes peace. We read, we work ; in the evening after tea we read aloud the letters of Mme. de Sévigné." The influence of Maria Kummrin was still all-pervading, and was enhanced by the following incident. Some time previously, Mdlle. Sophie de Krudener had given her hand in marriage to a Spanish officer, the Chevalier d'Ochando, who was taken prisoner by the French during one of the Peninsular campaigns. He was detained for some months in Denmark, in spite of the urgent petitions for his release forwarded by his anxious relatives. The village prophetess had frequently predicted his return, and one day, during a temporary absence of Mme. de Krudener and her daughters from Ste. Marie, it was revealed to her in an ecstasy that important letters on the subject were on their way. The very next day Mme. de Krudener received an official dispatch from the French Minister of War, announcing to her, by the special favour of the Emperor, the immediate release of her son-in-law, who in point of fact shortly afterwards rejoined his wife. After this fortunate occurrence Fontaine no doubt felt that the time had come to act on the old proverb of making hay while the sun shines. Maria Kummrin accordingly announced that it was the will of God that a Christian community should be founded in Würtemberg, and, descending to particulars, that an estate

near Bonigheim was marked out for the purpose.
Yielding to the persuasions of the minister, Mme.
de Krudener not only purchased the house and
land, but bore all the expenses of installation.
Maria Kummrin, Fontaine, his wife and children,
and one or two other recipients of charity, were all
to form part of the new community, the whole
expense of their maintenance falling on Mme. de
Krudener. The winter was spent in the necessary
preparations, and on 31st March 1809 the lady
writes from her new home in the spirit of serene
content which has become habitual to her :—

> The house is in the midst of woods and vineyards at the
> foot of a mountain. . . . My bedroom has a green paper covered
> with hydrangeas, and gets a great deal of sun. It is delicious.
> . . . It is at the bidding of our Lord that we have taken this
> house, otherwise I should never have dared to incur such an
> expense. It was in such bad condition that it has cost over 100
> louis to repair. But now it is quite charming.

The new community were not destined to be
left long in peace. The growing fame of Maria
Kummrin attracted numerous pilgrims to Bonigheim,
and King Frederick I. of Würtemberg, who had his
own reasons for regarding the village prophetess
with disfavour, determined to put an end to these
manifestations of her power. The police accordingly
made a raid on the establishment, and carried off the
peasant woman to prison, whilst Mme. de Krudener,
who appealed loudly and eloquently on her behalf,
received shortly afterwards an intimation to leave
the kingdom within twenty-four hours. In this pre-

dicament she applied to an old friend, M. Bignon,[1] then acting as Napoleon's representative at the Court of Baden, to arrange for her friendly reception in the Grand-Duchy. This task appears to have been accomplished without difficulty, and the refugee found the warmest of welcomes awaiting her not only from the Hereditary Grand-Duchess Stéphanie,[2] but also from Hortense Beauharnais and her lady-in-waiting, Mdlle. Cochelet.

The arrival of Mme. de Krudener (writes M. Bignon) added largely to the enjoyment of our little society. She had not yet taken to composing prayers and sermons, but only stories full of visions, spectres, apparitions, and ghosts, which made an immense impression upon us, especially when she told them in the evening seated amongst the ruins of the old castle of Baden. Her stories were all delightful, or at least appeared so to our little circle, which included M. de Norvins. I must add, and the detail is not without importance, that Mme. de Krudener had not arrived alone; she was accompanied by her daughter Mdlle. Juliette, a pretty girl of seventeen, a companion who spoilt nothing of the charm that is diffused around her by a *femme d'esprit*.

The above allusion to M. de Norvins[3] brings us to one of the most interesting friendships of Mme.

---

[1] L. P. E. Bignon (1771-1841), a celebrated statesman and diplomatist, one of the ablest and most faithful servants of Napoleon I. In the will of the latter there occur these words: "I bequeath to Baron Bignon frs. 100,000, and request him to write the history of French diplomacy from 1792 to 1815." For note on Mme. de Krudener's expulsion from Würtemberg, see Preface to the 10th vol. of Bignon's *Histoire de France sous Napoleon*.

[2] Stéphanie de Beauharnais, niece of the Empress Josephine, and consequently cousin to the Queen of Holland, had married the Hereditary Prince of Baden in 1805.

[3] Jacques Marquet, Baron de Norvins (1769-1854), filled many important administrative posts under the Empire, and devoted his declining years to the composition of several able works on French history. He also left Memoirs, which have never been published.

de Krudener's later years.   An enthusiastic supporter of the Napoleonic policy, and the right hand of Jerome Bonaparte in the organisation of the new kingdom of Westphalia, M. de Norvins was not only a man of marked administrative ability, but also of elevated character, whose warmest sympathies were aroused by the religious zeal of Mme. de Krudener.   They had many opportunities of meeting about this period, and the friendship that sprang up between them is at once a testimony to the faculty of being "all things to all men" which was one of the distinguishing traits of our heroine, and also to the impression of sincerity, which, in spite of the compromising extravagances of Fontaine and Maria Kummrin, her religious conversion made upon men of the world.   There exists a charming description, from the pen of the statesman, of the Krudener household as it appeared to him on the occasion of a visit, shortly before their expulsion from Würtemberg :—

Mme. and Mdlle. de Krudener carried their passionate love of good into all they did, without pretension, without intolerance, without display, without vanity.   They were primitive Christians who had taken the Bible literally.   Charity, resignation, forgiveness of injuries, and humility, were their practical virtues.   I often found them dining very merrily off black bread, after having given their own dinner to some poor persons, whom they waited upon quite naturally: one only discovered it by seeing it.   Regarding her private fortune in the light of a legacy for all who had need of it, Mme. de Krudener gave alms to the extent of causing herself positive embarrassment.   But her charity was not limited to material help ; it was the task of comforting broken hearts which displayed her in her most pleasing light.   Humble with the poor,

Mme. de Krudener was quite at her ease with the rich, and spoke to them of the Gospel with complete freedom. Remarkable intelligence, acute sensitiveness, a very extensive education, a knowledge of the French, German, English, Russian, and Italian languages, all of which she spoke with exceptional facility, joined to her delicate tact and the exquisite grace of her manners, all gave her access to the most cultivated minds. Her daughter was still so shy, that the glance of a child was enough to make her blush. Sometimes however the recital of a heroic deed, the accent of eloquence or of some sublime poetry, freed her from her self-distrust, and nothing could be more charming than the expression of her enthusiasm. Frequently I caught myself regretting, that our meetings had no other witness than myself, capable of admiring the elevation of thought and nobility of feeling of these two remarkable women.

M. de Norvins, as we have seen, was one of those who welcomed Mme. de Krudener on her arrival at Baden, and the following extracts from a lengthy letter written to him shortly afterwards, make it evident that much religious discussion had taken place between them. Free from any hysterical exaggeration, and penned with a charming candour, the letter gives perhaps the truest picture we have of Mme. de Krudener at this period, and goes far to explain the fascination which she continued to exercise over rich and poor alike :—

BADEN, *26th November* 1809.

Yes, my dear Norvins, sooner or later you will be persuaded that God is better, more tender, more sublime, more truly great, and more logical than all the conceptions of philosophy ; you will understand those touching and simple words suggested by love and truth: Become as little children. You will forget the falsehoods of men who agitate themselves, die, and pass away, without having known real happiness. You will say to yourself: God having nothing above Himself, nothing on a level with Himself, naturally turns His eyes towards those beneath Him.   He is too great to be like what we imagine in our miserable conceptions of greatness.   Nothing can escape Him.   All the voices of Heaven and of Earth are filled with love when once we can understand them.   If He did not know how to love He would not have created anything; and since we ourselves know, though very imperfectly, how to love, since we know how to be gently and strongly moved by the desire of being of use to that which we love, believe that we can only have learnt from Him the most sublime secrets of nature and eternity.   Thus, so long as we feel no longing for a loving God, a true friend, a father, why should He reveal Himself to us?   Do we not see the same language throughout all nature?   Everywhere prayer meets with its answer.

Oh ! if only we were not so blind, so miserable; if only we did not run after shadows, we should have the boldness to ask much.   Nothing then would satisfy us but He who holds everything within Himself: we should believe in His word; we should go to Him; our thirst would be quenched; and happiness would be our portion even on earth.

Dear Norvins, if, indifferent to everything, neglected by the world, crushed by overwhelming memories, I were to speak to you about the emptiness of all things, you might imagine that I was reduced to abandoning everything; but my heart is still very young.   I possess a lively imagination which is so easily inspired both by art and by nature !   I was born in the midst of the world, of its illusions, of its privileges; everywhere I have been spoilt.   I am credited with talents which obtain for me a welcome in society.   I had only to say " Yes," and a short time ago I might have married an immensely rich man : he bore a title, he was a prince, he offered me a splendid position.   I might have had a grand house in Paris; or have wandered about that marvellous Italy that I love.   I have always had much love given me, and I still have it.   Thus, everything that is most charming in life, and most dangerous to one's vanity, lies always within my reach.   I was born with that vanity of birth and of success.   Do you believe that mere excitement, or some disease of the imagination, could make me so reasonable in the eyes even of philosophers?   Do you believe that one can inspire

oneself with the peace, the simplicity of life, and the extreme
innocence of an existence that nothing disturbs, nothing
brightens in the eyes of the world, and nothing agitates?
When one's whole life has been spent in society, do you believe
one can be perfectly happy in absolute solitude, in the midst
of the mountains, and breathe repose as one breathes the pure
air, and only ask of the Almighty the happiness of others, one's
own being assured? Seriously, that would indeed be a profound
art of which we have completely lost the knowledge, and which it
would be worth while to study. But, my dear Norvins, I must
be credited with nothing in all this. I was no better than the
rest of mankind; left to myself I was, and I am still, as weak as
others. I was a wretched instrument; God has been pleased to
tune it, and if it gives forth occasional harmonious sounds, which
bring back harmony to the mind, it is to the Author of that
harmony that I wish to lead mankind. I have become a child
again. I believed; and the truth, simplicity, calm, and all the
hopes of an unknown happiness have filled my whole life. I
have visited Heaven, and Earth has fled from beneath my feet.
Dear Norvins, this is the whole secret of my life, which many
people regard as foolish, ridiculous, and absurd, and of which
each day flies past in the sweetest peace.

Thus love, simplicity, complete renunciation of
will, and detachment from the world, had become
the dominant notes of her religious faith. " I cannot regard suffering otherwise than as a gain," she
writes to another friend.[1] " Physical pain, hours of
darkness and depression, are painful to bear, but
love consoles us by its tenderness." Some months
previously the works of Mme. Guyon had been put
into her hands by a Geneva friend, the Marquis de
Langallerie, and it is easy to trace the influence of
that long-suffering and much-maligned woman in
the later writings of one who, under very different

<hr>

[1] M. Weguelin, 23rd January 1810.

circumstances, had much in common with the mystical authoress of the *Moyen Court*. Mme. de Krudener, too, aspired with all the strength of her ardent nature after pure love; and her study of Fénelon and Mme. Guyon, of Saint Theresa and other contemplative Saints of the Catholic calendar, was destined, before her death, to lead her almost to the threshold of the Church of Rome. The following passage, written about this period, might almost be a page out of the mystical writings of Mme. Guyon, and reveals how deeply Mme. de Krudener was already imbued with the doctrines of Quietism.

This love ought to reduce to ashes everything that is impure, personal, or selfish in our hearts. It is opposed to all idea of property, which it regards as a theft from God. It desires to receive everything from Him, that it may give Him everything. It makes us capable of the most heroic sacrifices, and produces in us a devotion to our fellow-creatures similar to that of Jesus Christ. It will constitute the glory of the redeemed Church, which will be called to reign with Christ on earth for a thousand years. At present our Judge is still crucified in all His members; those whom He wishes to employ are persecuted and despised. They have to pass through much suffering, bear heavy crosses, and walk in mysterious ways; they are the laughing-stock of all, and are not even recognised by many true Christians. They form a little flock which desires to have nothing for itself; but how precious they are in the sight of the Divine Shepherd! They will be like the disciples of old, of whom Christ asked: "What seek ye?" They will even be a cause of scandal to many eminent Christians, who are not acquainted with the mysterious and special ways of God.

Let not that restrain them! The pledges of their divine vocation are precisely that despicableness, that disgust, with which they inspire the learned. That divine love which causes them to be accused of exaggeration and fanaticism, but which burns within them, is the best proof of their noble origin.

But if, as a rule, Mme. de Krudener felt all the ecstasies of a close and conscious union with God, she did not escape from those occasional periods of darkness and that sense of desolation to which even the greatest of saints have been liable. Thus we find her writing to Mme. Armand :—

Alas! those happy days are past in which I followed my Beloved through the valleys, His voice calling me, His sweet odour preceding me, and when I was in the joys of Paradise. Oh! who can depict the celestial mysteries of His Beatitudes! My heart, which formerly He had summoned to these felicities, is often cold, dead, dry, barren ; but now my will is unceasingly united to His, and I follow Him past precipices at which nature shudders.

In point of fact, the lady had reason enough for anxiety on more subjects than one. Her connection with Fontaine and Maria Kummrin—the latter of whom had been released from prison—was a fertile source of trouble and misrepresentation. The pride, arrogance, and utter want of refinement of feeling displayed by the minister, constantly compromised his patroness, who, with a faith and charity which would have been touching, had they not been so unfortunately misplaced, continued to leave her house and purse at his disposal. As a result, she was constantly exposed to positive pecuniary destitution ; and more than once she relates with joy how, when she and her daughter were literally reduced to their last halfpenny, help from some unexpected quarter would be vouchsafed to them in answer to their prayers.

Moreover, the very excess of her religious zeal

was sufficient to raise up enemies in the fashionable society, in which circumstances still compelled her in part to live. Every woman who forsakes the well-worn tracks of conventional conduct, even from the purest of motives, runs the risk of vulgar misrepresentation and abuse; and Mme. de Krudener was to prove no exception to the rule. To be sure, she was never deserted by a little band of devoted and admiring friends; but it was inevitable that the somewhat exaggerated language in which she was accustomed to clothe her mystical thoughts, should have excited the cynical contempt and laughter of all those to whom the joys of the spiritual life are as a closed book. Her friendship with Fontaine, and the unhappy circumstances connected with her own married life, gave a handle to her detractors of which they did not fail to take advantage, and the most calumnious accusations began to be rumoured about her. The opinion of the world was by this time a matter of very small concern to Mme. de Krudener. But she was struck in the tenderest part of her nature by the disapproval which Mme. de Wietinghoff expressed regarding her conduct, and which threatened to destroy the confidence that had existed for so many years between mother and daughter. Partly in the hope of removing the misunderstanding, and partly from a sense of duty to a parent both aged and infirm, Mme. de Krudener resolved on undertaking the long journey to Russia in the summer of 1810.

How little at this period Mme. de Krudener

valued the good opinion even of her friends, may be seen from the following letter, written to Mme. Armand, in answer to one in which her correspondent gives expression to the respectful admiration, which a perusal of Mme. de Krudener's letters had excited in a little circle of Geneva well-wishers :—

MME. DE KRUDENER TO MME. ARMAND.

9th March 1810.

MY SWEET FRIEND—Pray forget the mere creature, and do not love me, I entreat you, as though there were anything the least lovable in me. Remind yourself that my life has been nothing but a tissue of horrible sins; that no one has been more favoured, and no one more unworthy. I request you particularly, if you communicate my letter to your friends, to read them this passage. Do not listen to a vain friendship, but give glory and honour to Him to whom glory is due. The point is not that a miserable creature, who has deserved to be rejected, should be admired, petted, and shown off to advantage. No, my dear friend, the point is to glorify Him who creates out of nothing, and who summons the most unworthy; to adore His ways, to show the depths of His mercy, and to console those who are afflicted by their misfortunes. The point is to love, and to cause to be loved, the most loving, the best, the most tender of Fathers, who is for ever speaking and calling to us. The point is to allow ourselves to be so penetrated with love and gratitude that we spend all our time thinking how we may glorify Jesus Christ, and how we may prepare the way towards that reign of peace and glory which is to come.

CHAPTER VIII

1810-1814

On arriving at Riga, Mme. de Krudener had the pleasure of finding her mother convalescent, and overjoyed at the prospect of seeing her daughter and grand-daughter once more at her side. The next few months seem to have been spent in quiet domestic life, and in trying to wean Mme. de Wietinghoff from those social pleasures, which still exercised a certain fascination over the imperious old lady. The following letter to Mdlle. Cochelet throws a pleasant light on the relations of the writer with all that was highest in the society of the day, and is noteworthy as giving a first indication of that interest in the *haute politique* of Europe, which was soon to become of such absorbing importance to her.

Mme. de Krudener to Mdlle. Cochelet.

Riga, 10th December 1810.

I have but a single moment, dear and kind friend. You will permit me to call you by that name, for you have been good enough to give me all the proofs of affection which justify me in using it. I received your most kind letter a few weeks ago, and you may judge of the joy it caused me to find you the same as when I left you, and to discover that in spite of all the apparent wrongs of which I must be guilty in your eyes, you have not changed towards me! Oh, how well you have read my heart! I cannot express to you how full my heart is of grateful remembrance and good wishes towards you. I am afraid I explain myself very stupidly; I do not even know how to collect my ideas, for I should like to write you a volume, and I must choose from amongst the most necessary, the most indispensable.

Just imagine to yourself a Russian courier aspiring to travel as fast as the north wind, who yet was ready to stop for a moment, and who, luckily for me, had a carriage that wished to be left behind, and which is for the moment out of repair. The courier is M. Divoff, who has the happiness of knowing you. How I wish I could see you too, if only for a few seconds! You tell me you have been good enough to write me two other letters; I have never received them, which I regret extremely. I also have written to you, but I know that my letters have never been delivered, for reasons which I will explain at the first opportunity.

How often I have thought of Baden and of the happy days there, of the majestic mountains, and of the ruins teeming with memories! In this glorious setting how often have I not retraced the portrait of an ideal woman,[1] of a queen whom I know how to love and respect with the enthusiasm that she deserves. What misfortunes she has undergone! But the dawn would not be so beautiful if it did not rise up in all its splendour from the darkness, and her virtue is like the ocean which owes its most beautiful effects to its storms.

I remember making the remark more than once to that angelic woman[2] who is now dead, and who shed so many tears beneath her crown. You say you have felt something of what I must have undergone; well, I must tell you that I am quite consoled. I loved her very dearly, with her superior nature. I knew intimately her soul, which was so little fashioned for the world; and it is just that love which was too pure to contain any alloy of selfishness which has consoled me. She has disappeared; she is not taken away from me. Frequently, alone, on my knees, on these cold Baltic shores, I still pray for her, and ask of God what

---

[1] Queen Hortense.
[2] Queen Louise of Prussia, who died in the previous July.

she longed for so ardently: that she may grow yet more pure, and, as she becomes more perfect, that she may be more susceptible to celestial joys. In my fancy I see her radiant, calm, and smiling at her past griefs. I think how, on her deathbed, when everything disappears, when illusions vanish and pleasures are wrapt in mourning, I think how she must have welcomed her troubles, and how all the sacrifices and bitternesses of her life must have appeared radiant before her and have said: "We used to seem terrible to you, but in reality we were blessings in disguise, sent from Heaven to purify you, to detach you from everything that is fragile and perishable, and to teach you the virtues which it is necessary to cultivate on Earth, so as not to be disinherited in Heaven." Faith, confidence in God, resignation, that profound love for a glorious God who only wishes to love and to overwhelm with gifts, the craving for a Saviour full of pity who adopts us and discharges our immense debts—all these treasures, beside which the splendours of a throne and of days strewn with flowers are but miserable nothings, all these awe-inspiring secrets can only be learnt in days of adversity.

Dear friend, such language must seem to you austere, and my letter is indeed a serious one. Life has no more secrets from me, and I have done with illusions. Truth is to me a primary necessity, and the joy of Heaven has long dwelt in my soul. Thus I should have to cease to be myself in order not to describe that which rules me.

I imagine myself in the presence of that Queen whom you have the happiness of approaching; I call to mind all her touching kindnesses, and I say to myself: "If I could ask Heaven for thrones for her, should I see her happy?" No. She requires far more than that. Intense suffering, that Daughter of Heaven, has purified her angelic soul; she was almost crushed beneath the load of her sorrows. I have seen her, in imagination, separated from her children, and I know her well! I have felt so much! But I have also seen vast regions of unalterable happiness opening out before her.

I have seen the same God who called to Himself her who is no longer on earth, say to the Queen: "Nothing on earth can satisfy a heart created for immense favours. I will send the peace of Heaven to that heart torn by men." Oh how frequently my thoughts have offered up the purest homage to your Queen! Pray tell her all this, and pray describe me to her as possessing a heart which has felt and suffered much and yet is not embittered, and which, after all the joys and ills of this life, has been purified in that consoling and vivifying faith which I desire for her.

Time is short, and I have yet so much to say to you. Let me first acquit myself of a sacred duty.

Shortly before the death of the Queen of Prussia, I received from her a letter. I had talked to her with enthusiasm of the Queen of Holland. I had told her that she had in her one who could appreciate her. Here is what she wrote to me: " What you tell me about the Queen of Holland has interested me extremely; all those who know her, love her and do justice to her; the friendship which she· has been pleased to bestow upon me came as a very agreeable surprise, and I should like her to know how much I appreciate being distinguished by her."

I acquit myself of this order, with extreme joy, dear Mdlle. Cochelet. I have been long waiting for a favourable opportunity of writing to you, and I hope that many more will occur. If time permits, I will explain to you a few of the most striking passages in the letter the Queen wrote me.

Now I must beg of you most earnestly always to love me a little, to write to me either through the post or by couriers, to tell me about the Queen—her health, the little Prince [1]—about yourself and your pleasures; I implore you to let me hope for this favour. My address is at Riga, where I have been for several months. I am nursing an aged mother, and between her and my daughter my days slip peacefully by. I write little, having but little time. Here there are no solitary valleys, there is no laughing nature; there is nothing enchanting in gloomy Russia; but everywhere, within the soul of man, there exists a universe, and the whole world would be but a prison-house without the faculty which allows us to dream of a world beyond. . . .

Here are twelve pages, and I am still writing. Some time ago I entrusted M. de Norvins with all sorts of messages for you. Did he deliver them? What is he doing? Where are you going to spend the summer? Is the Queen's health any better?

---

[1] Charles Louis Napoleon, third son of King Louis and Queen Hortense, born 2nd April 1808.

Whilst here, I have seen the young Empress of Russia—good, beautiful, and unhappy. I described the Queen [1] to her as being like one of those wonderful pictures by Raphael which attract the eyes of everybody. . . . What is the Empress Josephine doing? I feel for her an electric sympathy and devotion; her happiness is a necessity to me. Tell me about Navarre. Is Mdlle. de Mackau still with her? I saw that charming Princess Stéphanie [2] for a moment, and we talked about the Queen.

I am awaiting news from you, and implore you to write to me. Live happily, my dearest friend; few people love you as I do. Pray continue your kindness to Paul,[3] and cherish friendly sentiments towards him, his mother and Juliette. I would I could see you once more, and that I could renew to the Queen the homage of a profound respect, the chivalrous devotion of the Middle Ages, which I have sketched in my *Othilde*. Oh how much you would enjoy the book! It was written with the help of Heaven, and that is why I dare to say that it contains beautiful passages.

Good-bye, good-bye! Mary Queen of Scots used to say, in speaking of her native land, "Tant doux pays de France." My heart says to you, in spite of all intervening space: "Live happily under this beautiful sky, and live for immortality; begin here, on earth, those peaceful days wrested from human fragility: give to God everything of this earth, and let us live on our happy emotions; may they endure for ever!" Press respectfully against your heart those royal hands, which I should like to bathe with my grateful tears. I embrace you a thousand times, dear friend: always your most devoted! . . . B. KRUDENER.

The improvement in Mme. de Wietinghoff's health was not destined to be of long duration, and early in the year 1811 a paralytic stroke brought her life to a sudden close. Though released from her filial duties, Mme. de Krudener was detained at Riga for almost a year longer, settling legal business

---

[1] Queen Hortense.   [2] The Hereditary Grand-Duchess of Baden.
[3] Her son, Paul de Krudener, who had entered the Russian diplomatic service.

in connection with the property of the deceased, and in the well-nigh hopeless task of reducing her own much embroiled pecuniary matters into some sort of order. Needless to say that much time was devoted to Mme. Blau and her other Moravian friends, whom she initiated into the mysteries of Quietism. Many persons were converted to God by her means, and amongst them her own brother, the Councillor Wietinghoff, now head of the family.

After preaching the doctrines of pure love at Königsberg, at Breslau, and at Dresden, Mme. de Krudener arrived once more at Carlsruhe, in the neighbourhood of which town Fontaine had been appointed to the charge of a parish, where he preached the gospel with much unctuous zeal. Unfortunately her two years of absence appear to have been of no effect in freeing Mme. de Krudener from the domination of the minister and his satellite. "God Almighty is with him, and the most astounding conversions and benedictions are effected by his means," she writes. Indeed, there appears to have been some mysterious project at this time, promulgated by Maria Kummrin in her moments of ecstasy, of a mystical union between Mme. de Krudener and a brother of Fontaine, who was both infirm in health and devoid of any attractions, either mental or moral. That the lady should ever have lent herself to such a scheme for a single moment, shows the extraordinary lengths to which human credulity can go, under the influence of misdirected religious fervour. As far as can be ascertained, the

only practical result of the arrangement, and one
that Fontaine no doubt had mainly in view in promoting the scheme, was that Mme. de Krudener
was for years burdened with the support of this
individual, who was sent to live at Geneva under
the care of Dr. Butini, and whom she can only have
seen at very rare intervals.

In October (1812) we find Mme. de Krudener
temporarily established at Strasburg, her peace of
mind quite undisturbed by the fact that events in
Russia were threatening to leave her, without any
regular means of subsistence.   Her days were
wholly spent in prayer and religious intercourse :
the mornings being devoted to persons who could
only speak French, whilst in the evening prayer-
meetings were held in German.   On her first arrival
at Strasburg Mme. de Krudener had not only
enjoyed the pleasure of a meeting with her son
Paul, but had also renewed acquaintance with her
old friend the Comte de Lezay-Marnésia, whom she
had not met since her frivolous and pleasure-loving
days at Barèges and Montpellier, more than twenty
years previously.   A man of considerable ability and
upright character, M. de Lezay, after filling various administrative posts, had been appointed prefect
of the department of the Bas-Rhin, and together
with his wife, "an admirable woman, noble, generous, and worthy of the early days of the Church,"
accorded the warmest of welcomes to Mme. de
Krudener.   Indeed her piety and her gentle refinement appear to have exercised as powerful a fascina-

tion over him as did the coquettish beauty of her younger days; and though up to this time he had kept aloof from all evangelistic meetings, Mme. de Krudener was soon able to write in pious triumph to a friend :—

We have had the happiness of seeing the Préfet in our midst, praying to and adoring on his knees the Saviour of the world. You can imagine the impression it has made. He is the first in rank, the first in public estimation, both from his uprightness and his virtues; he is naturally the most independent and proud of men; and yet he is now submissive as a docile child, great with true greatness, a Christian adoring the true God and Christ crucified."

In the following summer Mme. de Krudener felt spiritually impelled to visit Geneva, a journey which might well have been naturally inspired by a desire to see her much-loved friend Mme. Armand, from whom she had been separated for four years. The two months which she spent on the shores of Lake Leman are noteworthy as marking the commencement of her friendship with Henri Empaytaz, the young theological student who was to become her spiritual guide and companion throughout the later years of her evangelistic labours. At this period, however, the guidance and encouragement all proceeded from the lady herself. Empaytaz does not appear to have been a man of any general culture, or gifted with much intellectual power, but as a spiritual *confidant* he was a vast improvement on Frederick Fontaine, being a man of gentle and refined nature, deeply imbued with real devotional feeling. If, in later days, his judgment may often have been at fault, his sincerity seems to have been always above suspicion. About this time the independent evangelical movement in Geneva was at its lowest ebb, and Empaytaz who, with a few friends, had attempted to carry on both a Sunday School and Bible Classes, had brought himself into serious theological dispute with his spiritual superiors. Needless to say that Mme. de Krudener's warmest sympathies were immediately enlisted on his behalf by the trying circumstances in which he found himself, and all through the autumn and winter of 1813 eloquent letters of spiritual advice and pious exhortation found their way from Carlsruhe and Basle to Geneva. At length, in the month of June 1814, when the dispute was brought to a close by the definite refusal of the ecclesiastical authorities of Geneva to admit the young candidate to the ministry, accompanied by an injunction to refrain from public preaching, Mme. de Krudener wrote to her protégé in one of her most exalted moods, congratulating him on his defeat, and imploring him to rejoin her in the Grand-Duchy of Baden, where the work of the Lord was making marvellous progress, and where she found herself sadly in need of spiritual assistance. The lady appointed a rendezvous at the house of the Pasteur Oberlin at the Ban de la Roche, whither the young man accordingly repaired, but it was 12th September before Mme. de Krudener was able to tear herself away from her manifold engagements at Baden.

The year 1814 was in truth a time of the most

intense popular excitement, and the enemies of France were everywhere in a mood of triumphant jubilation. The retreat of the French army after the disaster of Leipsic and the dissolution of the Confederation of the Rhine, followed by the immediate invasion of France by the allied armies and the abdication of Napoleon at Fontainebleau, seemed to announce the close of the great struggle which had torn Europe in pieces since the opening years of the century. In public estimation the Emperor Alexander I. of Russia stood head and shoulders above his royal allies, and it was to him that all eyes were turned as the restorer of peace to Western Europe. At the little Court of Carlsruhe, antagonistic interests added an element of personal bitterness to the tension of the moment. The Grand-Duchess Stéphanie, niece of the Empress Josephine, filled with grateful devotion to Napoleon, could not conceal her sorrow at the calamities which were daily befalling the Imperial family. On the other hand, the presence at Court of her sister-in-law the Empress Elizabeth of Russia, together with the sisters of the latter, the Queens of Bavaria and Sweden, made it impossible to restrain the open expressions of delight over the successive triumphs of the Allied Sovereigns.

Whether the Court was in residence at Carlsruhe or at Baden, Mme. de Krudener, both by her personal attractions and by her position as the widow of an imperial ambassador, was enabled to take her place within the royal circle. Indeed, the

charm of her conversation was so universally recognised, that her society was much sought after, and it
became impossible for her to adhere to her original
resolution of devoting herself solely to her poorer
neighbours.   In this way she frequently found
herself in the presence of the Empress of Russia.
"The Lord has been pleased to unite the soul
of the Empress to mine, in ardent prayer," she
writes to Empaytaz (20th August).   "I have had
more than one conversation with that angelic
woman."   Beautiful, talented, and virtuous, though
of a somewhat cold temperament, the Empress
Elizabeth suffered keenly from the estrangement
which existed between her and her husband.   She
had followed him to Western Europe in 1813, but
partly owing to the exigencies of the campaign,
though still more largely owing to the indifference
of the Emperor, they had been separated during the
whole period, the Empress staying in turn at Berlin,
at Weimar (of which the Grand-Duchess Mary
was a sister of Alexander), and at Carlsruhe, but
principally with her mother, the old Margravine
of Baden.

In close attendance upon her was Mdlle.
Stourdza, her favourite lady-in-waiting, a person of
singular sweetness and elevation of character, who
was united to her Imperial mistress by the warmest
ties of affection and confidence.[1]   Mdlle. Stourdza

---

[1] Roxandra Stourdza, born 1786, sister to Count Alexander Stourdza, came
of a well-known Greek family, which took refuge in Russia from Turkish persecution; she was appointed maid-of-honour to the Empress in her sixteenth
year.   In 1816 she married Count Edling, who occupied a post at the Court of

also enjoyed at this time the ardent friendship both of Mme. Swetchine (then on the eve of her reception into the Catholic Church) and the Comte Joseph de Maistre; and it was not long before Mme. de Krudener, with her quick insight into character, discerned in the lady-in-waiting a refined spirituality and seriousness of purpose rarely to be met with in Court circles. Mdlle. Stourdza responded gratefully and enthusiastically to the advances of the elder woman, and there sprang up between them an intimacy which was destined to pave the way towards events of the very highest importance. Up to this time, in spite of numerous assertions to the contrary, Mme. de Krudener had had no possible opportunity of bringing her religious views to bear in any way on the Emperor Alexander. Indeed, the acquaintance between them had not passed the stage of the merest official recognition. "Nothing surprised me more," writes Mdlle. Cochelet in the autumn of 1814, "than that Mme. de Krudener at that time should be barely acquainted with the Emperor. She only saw him at a later date." But the correspondence which was carried on between Mdlle. Stourdza and Mme. de Krudener was to establish a hidden means of communication between the lady and her sovereign, and contributed directly towards that first momentous interview which took place in the ensuing year.

Saxe-Weimar, but ultimately she and her husband founded an agricultural colony called Mansir, in Bessarabia, and devoted themselves to the welfare of their peasantry. Many of Mme. Swetchine's most delightful letters are addressed to Countess Edling.

Read in the light of coming events, the following letters, written during the occasional separation of the two friends during the summer of 1814, are full of the deepest interest.

To Mdlle. Stourdza.

RASTADT, *2nd April* 1814.

You possess one of those souls which make a mark, which leave an impression, and which it is impossible to watch without longing to see it arrive at its real destination. I aspire after true happiness, and that happiness is partly composed of that of others. After having sought the peace of God, after having found at the foot of the Cross, and of my adorable Saviour, peace, the forgiveness of my sins and boundless hope ; illuminated by a spark of that divine love which alone can give to man an idea of true felicity, my most ardent desire is to see that glorious God loved and adored, who for our sakes went down into hell, and who, taking on Himself our sins and the curse which condemned us to eternal destruction, suffered death in order that we might have life. . . .

It was in the school of vexations and of human passions, it was in the midst of false joys and the unfathomable sadness of a life, which I had wasted by not consecrating it to God and to my Saviour, to whom alone it belonged, that I learnt to speak to all those whom the world still afflicts and fascinates. It is because I have been my own idol, because I have wished to shine and to win approbation, that I have learnt to despise myself sufficiently to feel only indulgence for others. It was in receiving an un-merited pardon from a merciful God, that I entered into a solemn obligation to forsake all things, according to the Gospel, in order to follow Christ ; and that the scorn and persecutions of men, should I ever have to submit to them, and even death itself, would seem easy to me through the grace of Him who said that those who wished to be His disciples would be rejected by the world and persecuted for His sake. Forgive me this long letter, too long perhaps, but God, in making it helpful to your soul, can bless it. You are reading Madame Guyon : that admirable woman who was endowed with every gift, and who became so powerful an instrument of grace, will teach you much ; so also will Fénelon. Pray on your knees, Madame, that you may be enlightened by that grace with which the Saints and the Blessed are endowed. Pray frequently, even when your prayers are but short ; pray from your heart, and offer that heart to Him who alone is worthy of it, and who died for our sake. Follow the holy inspirations with which Christ will endow you by the Holy Ghost. Become as a child, and pray that you may love : that is the great secret of eternity, the reward of Saints, the joy of Angels ; and I venture to predict for you even on this earth an inconceivable happiness, of which those who have not tasted it can have no idea. But add to your prayers the renunciation of self. Each day try and do something to the honour of our Saviour who desires to make you His temple. Break your idols valiantly. . . .

Go to the fountain of love, pray constantly, weep over your sins and your incapacity to love, and God will hear your prayers. May the God of peace grant you His peace !

2nd May 1814.

Cultivate the generous faith of childhood—an age so much closer to Heaven. In the midst of the world and its miserable falsehoods, we lose all trace of happiness and truth, for we lose the living God. He unceasingly desires to reveal Himself to us, and we unceasingly reject Him by trying to intoxicate ourselves with wretched pleasures, and with sad and disgraceful passions. Happy indeed, a thousand times happy, are those who are considered worthy to suffer ! They have the promise of a radiant dawn, after passing through the terrible night. You must be regenerated in the stream of life. Christ alone is the way, the truth, and the life. Religion is gentle, sweet, simple and easy, when we receive it from the hand of God. His yoke is light, and what He gives is far beyond all the conceptions of human weakness, for He gives Himself. Try and forget little by little what you have learnt from man. Everything is distorted and perverted, and all the traces have been lost which should have served to guide those who wish to live for eternity. Thus we must have recourse to the Gospels ; and, as I have already said, you must become simple and calm and as a child, you must relinquish your will and your heart to the great and loving Power that created the world, but to whom tears of sorrow and of suffering are of greater value than all the adoration offered up to His great and omnipotent Majesty.

Yes, God is love, *mon amie ;* allow me to make use of that expression of affection ; allow me, whilst traversing the regions of faith and of love, to put aside all worldly forms and conventionalities, for my heart loves and cherishes you, and your happiness has become very dear to my soul. You have received much homage, but you have never inspired a more pure and tender passion than that which I entertain towards you. I have discovered you, and I foresee your splendid career. Be faithful to the call, have the courage to be happy, and to give yourself to the God who died for you, and whose only desire is to overwhelm you with blessings. Your intelligence is sufficiently wide that you need not dread the idiotcy of worldly people and of their usual arguments, and you are too enlightened to believe that one can exalt oneself by becoming simple. Alas! if man cannot create for himself a single day of happiness, is it likely he can procure for himself the most beautiful of all gifts, that of faith? No, it is God Himself who alone can teach us to believe and to love. When we are resolved to live for that which is alone worthy of mankind ; when we are determined to waste no more precious days, nor to drown them in miserable pleasures ; when a new universe spreads out before our eyes immense faculties, sublime duties, ever new joys, admirable results, a peace which the angels contemplate with pleasure, and the Almighty alone can bestow : what need we care for the judgment of men, whose only happiness lies in scoffing, and who drag themselves wearily through a disinherited life?

Do not feel alarmed. I do not ask of you any violent shock, any painful or unhappy sacrifice. The God of the Gospels is loving and generous. He will lay on you commands which will strengthen you when the time comes ; He knows how to give what we do not even dream of. . . .

CARLSRUHE, *7th July* 1814.

DEAR CHILD—You wish me to call you by that name. I beg you always to have the courage of devotion, and to pray on your knees to Him who loves to give. He is the sun in whose rays you can always warm yourself, and who will bless your undertakings. Do not fear suffering ; it is the seal of a high destiny.

. . . It was on the Cross, covered with shame, that He perished who had made Himself man, and who relinquished the glories of Heaven in order to save a perverse and ungrateful race. It was there that He laid the foundations of His Church against which the gates of hell shall not prevail. The Blessed Mary, John the apostle of love, and a sinful woman steeped in sacred sorrow, were the first depositories of the great mysteries of the Church. You are called to belong to Christ, not only for your salvation, but in order to glorify Him, and to be a help to your brothers. Do not hesitate, dear child; a very strong duty directs me to write to you in this tone. I know more than you can know. Oh do not allow yourself to be held back in the midst of a life, where mere nothings dare to dispute with God the possession of the soul of man.

. . . Let these words, "My son, give me thine heart," resound frequently in your ears. "Watch and pray."

Mdlle. Stourdza's replies have not been preserved; but we can judge of the deep impression made by Mme. de Krudener's eloquent and prophetic words on the soul of the recipient, by the frequent references to the subject which occur in the letters of another correspondent.[1] It is evident that Mme. Swetchine was deeply concerned at seeing her young friend fall under the influence of one whose religious teaching she honestly regarded as pernicious, and her letters are full of solemn warnings against the dangers of Protestant mysticism and unregulated religious fervour. " If only I could preach like Julie," she writes regretfully, feeling herself helpless to stem the current of Mme. de Krudener's rising popularity.

In the month of August the royal circle at Baden was further increased by the arrival of the ex-Queen

---

[1] See *Mme. Swetchine, sa Vie et ses Œuvres*, par le Comte de Falloux.

of Holland, upon whom had been conferred the title of Duchesse de Saint-Leu. During his residence in Paris the Emperor Alexander had been a frequent guest at La Malmaison, and had been all kindness and consideration for the children of the Empress Josephine; and when the death of her mother (29th May 1814) inflicted a final blow on the unfortunate Hortense, he promised to befriend her in every way in his power. Thus at Baden the Queen not only met with the kindest reception from the Grand-Duchess Stéphanie, and from her brother Eugène and his wife,[1] with whom she took up her residence, but also from the Empress and her sisters. It is from the lively pen of her lady-in-waiting, Mdlle. Cochelet,[2] that we have all the details of her stay at Baden, together with a vivid account of the visits paid to her by Mme. de Krudener, of which we give an abridged version.

I was alone in my room when Mme. de Krudener entered. I sprang up with an exclamation of joyful surprise, and was about to throw myself into her arms, when she arrested me with a solemn gesture. Her inspired mien, her prophetic accent, and her impressive pose filled me with surprise.

"I have come to see your Queen," she said. "I must save her from a danger that threatens her. . . . I have come to declare to her what God wishes her to know. You know how deeply I love her. I have not seen her since 1809, but I pray for her frequently. She must submit to her fate. She is beloved of God. . . . She must be resigned; she is not yet at the end of her troubles."

---

[1] Princess Augusta of Bavaria.

[2] See her *Mémoires sur la Reine Hortense et la Famille impériale.*

In answer to Mdlle. Cochelet's eager questioning, Mme. de Krudener at length became more explicit.

"Above all do not let her return to France, let her go to Russia; the Emperor Alexander is the refuge of the destitute. . . . Ah! you do not know what a terrible year 1815 will be! You imagine the Congress will finish its labours. Undeceive yourself. The Emperor Napoleon will leave his island. He will be more powerful than ever, but those who support him will be pursued, persecuted, punished. They will not know where to lay their heads!"

She had remained standing (continues Mdlle. Cochelet), gesticulating as she talked. Her slim figure, her extreme emaciation, her fair hair all in disorder, her eager eyes, all combined to give her a supernatural air which filled me with an unaccountable sense of alarm.

The Queen of Holland was away from home on this occasion, and it was only on a second visit that the interview took place. On rejoining her royal mistress after Mme. de Krudener's departure, Mdlle. Cochelet found her with red eyes. Queen Hortense admitted that she had been much touched by her visitor's sympathy, but it is evident she placed far less faith in her prophetic utterances than did her more enthusiastic lady-in-waiting.

A second visit appears to have been somewhat disastrous in its effects, and, in spite of her very real devotion to Mme. de Krudener, the lively lady-in-waiting allows a spice of malice to flavour her description of the scene. Interested in his sister's account of the prophetess, Eugène Beauharnais expressed a desire to make the lady's acquaintance, and it was arranged that she should pay her respects both to him and to his wife, the Princess Augusta.

I remained in the salon awaiting the end of the visit, and the Queen conducted Mme. de Krudener to her sister-in-law's apartment.   The next moment she reappeared in such fits of laughter, that it set me laughing without waiting to hear the cause of her merriment.

When Hortense had sufficiently recovered her gravity, she gave the following account of the introduction.

Prince Eugène had failed to warn his wife, and was possibly himself ignorant, of the religious enthusiasm of Mme. de Krudener, which prompted her to hold forth without preamble on the will of God. The Princess Augusta accordingly expected an ordinary presentation, and when the prophetess advanced gravely towards her, she bowed with her usual grace, and invited her to sit beside her.   Not at all; Mme. de Krudener stops, raises her head, lifts her eyes and her arms towards heaven, whilst speaking with emphasis of resignation and of future misfortunes greater than any they had yet suffered.   Instead of groaning under them, they were to thank God who sent them out of love. . . . The Princess Augusta, quite mystified by her visitor, remained in open-mouthed astonishment; Prince Eugène, equally puzzled, looked as though he thought she were mad, and the Queen, seeing their dismay, felt the situation to be so comic, that she fled from the room to save herself from exploding with laughter in their presence. When she was once more sufficiently mistress of herself, the Queen re-entered the salon in order to deliver her sister from the tragic prophetess, and poor Mme. de Krudener was dismissed with all speed, that she might not perceive the impression she had made.

Fortunately this prophetic mood was not habitual, and Mdlle. Cochelet gives a charming description of a long day which she spent with mother and daughter, "those two angelic creatures," in their little house near the Lichtenthal valley, where they devoted their days to nursing the sick and feeding the hungry. Of Juliette de Krudener, that gentle shadowy figure that flits through the pages of her mother's life, correcting by its tender grace whatever may be at times harsh or repellent in the later career of the prophetess, their visitor writes :—

Her slim figure, the delicacy of her whole being, seemed to indicate that but a slender thread bound her to this life, and the purity and sweetness of her expression was the exact reflection of the unspotted and naïve soul which only existed for the sake of doing good. . . . Their room, most simply furnished, possessed no other ornament than an enormous wooden crucifix, before which Mme. de Krudener knelt with those whom she wished to fortify in that vivid faith which burned in her heart, and which her inspiring words communicated to her hearers. I felt myself better for being with her, and I joined fervently in the simple and touching prayer which she offered up before our meal, the most frugal of which I had ever partaken. And yet hospitality had not been forgotten : a dish of meat, an unaccustomed luxury, testified to their desire to make me welcome.

In the meanwhile Mme. de Krudener's friends at the Ban de la Roche were eagerly awaiting her arrival in their midst. She excuses herself more

than once for the unavoidable delay in her departure,
and writes 7th September to M. Empaytaz :—

I have been repeatedly detained by important business, and I
have felt strongly that my work was not finished. The Lord has been
pleased to conform the soul of the Empress to my ardent wishes.
I have had more than one interview with that angelic woman,
and lately, on seeing her depart, I thought myself free, and I
burned to rejoin you in my beloved valley, but a voice within me
said, It is not yet finished. . . . I have lived through a momentous
and blessed time, having been ceaselessly occupied with souls,
having been enabled to preach Christ to the Queens and the
Empress, and having lately spoken of our Saviour to the Queen
of Holland and the Viceroy, whilst announcing to them the great
events that are approaching.

A few days later Mme. de Krudener appears to
have left Baden with her daughter in order to
indulge herself in the rare luxury of a few weeks'
much-needed rest in the peaceful valley, over which
the Pasteur Oberlin held spiritual sway.

M. de Capefigue, in his volume entitled *La Baronne de
Krüdener*, describes the lady as having been present in Paris at
the time of the first Restoration. He even invents her receiving
the Emperor "in her retreat, surrounded with images and
amethyst crosses, illuminated by a thousand candles, and per-
fumed with incense." A similar statement is to be found in the
palpably prejudiced and inaccurate article by "Parisot," which
was unfortunately contributed to the supplement of the *Biographie
Universelle.* It is hardly necessary to state that both assertions
are entirely devoid of foundation. Mme. de Krudener's own
letters sufficiently testify to her presence in Germany during the
spring and summer of 1814, and, as we shall see, there is ample
evidence to prove that her personal relations with the Emperor
Alexander only date from the month of June 1815.

ALEXANDER I, TZAR OF RUSSIA.

From a Print in the British Museum.

CHAPTER IX

THE eyes of all Europe were turned towards Vienna, when, in the month of September 1814, the Congress commenced its sittings, with the duty before it of determining the boundaries of the new map of Europe, and of ratifying the position of France under her restored régime. The momentous nature of the questions to be discussed, attracted an unparalleled number of crowned heads to the Austrian capital, as well as the accumulated talent of the diplomatic world of the day. The Emperors of Russia and Austria, the Kings of Prussia, Würtemberg, Bavaria, and Denmark, Nesselrode and Capo d'Istria on behalf of Russia, Hardenburg and Humboldt for Prussia, Castlereagh for England, Talleyrand for France, and the great Metternich for the Emperor Francis, with Gentz as official Secretary, besides Blücher, Eugène Beauharnais, Pozzo di Borgo, Prince Adam Czartoryski, and many more, were all gathered together to take part in the proceedings, animated by the hope of receiving some portion of the spoils for themselves or their masters.   Nor were the ladies absent from the scene.   Most of the sovereigns of Europe had arrived accompanied by their consorts, and hence a series of the most sumptuous fêtes and festivities which flung a veil of brightness over the grave and protracted labours of the Congress, and prompted the old Prince de Ligne to the witty remark, " Le Congrès danse, et ne màrche pas."

Foremost in the brilliant throng towered the majestic figure of the Emperor Alexander I., on whose will, more than on that of any one present, depended the fate of Europe.   Strikingly handsome, with a tall well-built figure, imposing carriage, and singular charm of manner, it is little wonder that Alexander was idolised by his own people, and won the hearts of all, men and women alike, on their first coming in contact with him.   The whole personality of the Emperor, with his brilliant qualities and lamentable faults, offers a study of the greatest psychological interest.   Endowed in his youth with the highest and most generous aspirations, he was destined in later life to be identified with a policy of the most reactionary despotism. Of loose private morals and philosophic views on the subject of religion, he was to pass, in middle life, through a phase of the most intense religious fervour, which, for the time at least, completely metamorphosed his life, both public and private. But in order to appreciate in all its significance the very curious relation that was shortly to spring up between him and Mme. de Krudener, it is necessary to turn for a moment to the moulding influences of his early surroundings.

From his first boyhood the Emperor Alexander had been brought up under the immediate supervision of his illustrious grandmother, the Empress Catherine II., whose long reign of thirty years had been so glorious to Russia, in spite of the extreme immorality of the Empress's private life. Possessed of striking political genius, Catherine would brook no interference with her authority. Her son Paul (afterwards Paul I.), of violent and suspicious temper, though not wanting in intellect, was forced to lead a life of indolent seclusion, deprived even of the companionship of his numerous children, until the death of his mother in 1796. It was Catherine who placed her two eldest grandsons, Alexander and Constantine, under the charge of the Swiss Republican, César Laharpe, from whom they imbibed both philosophic ideas on religion and enlightened views on political government. Laharpe only quitted his royal pupil after the marriage of the latter, and for years Alexander kept up an intimate correspondence with his old tutor, and retained the highest respect both for his moral character and his political principles. Married at sixteen to the Princess Louisa Augusta of Baden[1]—who, on her baptism into the Orthodox Church, took the name of Elizabeth Alexievna,—Alexander, in the first flush of

---

[1] Second daughter of the Hereditary Prince Charles Louis of Baden, and grand-daughter of the Grand Duke Charles Frederick, who reigned seventy-three years. Her two sisters became respectively Queens of Sweden and Bavaria.

early manhood and youthful enthusiasm, was expected by Catherine to settle down to the dull routine of Court ceremonies, unrelieved by any political responsibility. His friend and confidant, Prince Adam Czartoryski,[1] has related in his Memoirs how the young heir to the throne was inspired at this time with the most exalted sentiments of liberty, and an ardent love of humanity. He regarded his grandmother's policy with the greatest aversion, deplored the fate of the unhappy Polish nation—then in the last throes of her existence,—announced himself as an uncompromising opponent of absolute power, and looked forward eagerly to inaugurating a new epoch of freedom and justice in Russia.

Nor did the early acts of his reign belie the sentiments of his youth. After the midnight murder of Paul I., a murder which his son was practically powerless to prevent, and which he never ceased bitterly to lament, Alexander ascended the throne amid the high hopes of a nation groaning under the weight of five years of reactionary tyranny and military despotism. Freeing himself from the dominion of Count Pahlen and his associates in the midnight tragedy of the St. Michael's Palace, the young Emperor surrounded himself with a set of young men representative of all that was most

[1] A member of the celebrated Polish family of that name, and the ardent advocate of his country's claims on the protection of Russia. Prince Czartoryski was for a time Minister of Foreign Affairs to the Emperor Alexander. He was well known in England, and was a personal friend both of Earl Grey and Lord Brougham. His interesting Memoirs have been recently published in French and English.

liberal in Russian contemporary thought : Prince Adam Czartoryski, Counts Paul Strogonof and Victor Kotchoubey, Prince Alexander Galitzin and Michael Novosiltsof. With their help he instituted a period of emancipation and reform. The censorship of the press was practically abolished, corporal punishment partially suppressed, the condition of the serfs ameliorated, religious persecution prohibited, and the frontier thrown freely open to foreigners. Large schemes of reform in the administration of law and justice, and a whole system of popular education were planned and partially carried out.

Unfortunately this happy state of affairs was not destined to last long. Foreign complications, Napoleonic wars, and the ambition to make a figure in European politics, distracted the Emperor from his internal reforms. Though filled with sympathy and enthusiasm, and endowed with great intellectual gifts, there was a strain of weakness in Alexander's character. He was emotional, changeable, and wanting in firmness and patience. His enemies have accused him, moreover, of a certain cunning and power of deception, a view which finds its most exaggerated expression in Napoleon's well-known and scathing epithet, *Un Grec du Bas Empire.* After a time the magnitude of the task before him seems to have oppressed and discouraged him. Moreover, his domestic life was full of disappointment. Married whilst a mere boy, it could hardly be expected that in the corrupt court of St. Peters-

burg his heart would remain irrevocably faithful to
the Princess, whom he accepted at the bidding of
Catherine.   And   Elizabeth,   beautiful,   virtuous,
gentle, and serious-minded, did not possess those
more brilliant qualities which might have served to
retain her husband's wandering affections.   Deeply
hurt by his repeated infidelities—he was for eleven
years the acknowledged lover of the beautiful
Countess Narishkine,—the Empress treated him
with coldness and reserve, the absence of any heir
to the throne still further estranging the Imperial
couple.   The Congress of Vienna was indeed the
occasion of a partial *rapprochement* after years of
separation and indifference.

Alexander's impressionable nature had been profoundly stirred by the sight of the terrible suffering
inflicted on his subjects, by the French invasion of
Russia and the burning of Moscow.   His mind became filled with the most gloomy forebodings, and his
thoughts began to turn towards those deep problems
of existence, which until then had caused him but
little uneasiness.   Prince Galitzin,[1] who had himself
recently passed through the religious crisis of his
life, advised him to have recourse to the Scriptures,
and it is related how one day he surprised the
Empress Elizabeth by entering her apartment and
begging the loan of a Bible.   It was under the
influence of the religious emotions excited by this
new study, that the Emperor resolved on placing

---

[1] Alexander Galitzin, one of the early companions of the Tsar, and later
Procurator of the Holy Synod and Minister of Education and of Public
Worship.

the sacred volume in the hands of even the poorest of his subjects. With this object in view, aided by the metropolitan Seraphin, Alexander, in the midst of the overwhelming difficulties of his campaign against Napoleon, founded the Bible Society of Russia,[1] with Prince Galitzin as President and Alexander Tourguenief and M. de Wietinghoff, the brother of Mme. de Krudener, amongst its most energetic members.

In the following year, still animated by the same suddenly-awakened interest in religious manifestations, Alexander entered into friendly relations with some communities of Moravian Brothers in Germany, and held several long conversations with Jung-Stilling at Carlsruhe; whilst in 1814, during his brief visit to England, he not only received a deputation from the British Bible Society, but also granted an interview to a deputation of Quakers, with William Allen at their head, of whom he made special inquiries as to the position held by women in their religious organisation.

During the arduous months that preceded the abdication of Napoleon at Fontainebleau, the vastness of the issues at stake roused the Emperor to a noble sense of his responsibilities; but when, crowned with victory, he found himself in Paris the object of universal adulation, the pleasure-loving

---

[1] This Society enjoyed a few years of extreme activity; the Bible was translated and published in forty-one different dialects, and half a million copies were distributed throughout the Empire. In 1826, however, in consequence of the opposition of a reactionary section of the Orthodox Church, the Society was suppressed, and its work abandoned.

side of his nature became once more in the ascendant. At Vienna he felt himself torn in two between
the brilliant fêtes at which he was bound to appear,
and the serious work of the Congress, together with
the unexpected opposition he encountered, chiefly
from Lord Castlereagh, to his schemes in reference
to Poland. Then it was that the Empress Elizabeth,
ever anxious to draw her husband's mind under
religious influences, laid before him the letters which
Mdlle. Stourdza continued to receive from Mme. de
Krudener. The effect was to excite in the Emperor's
mind the most lively curiosity in regard to the
unknown correspondent, and a keen desire to be
brought in contact with one whose letters breathed
so courageous a spirit of mystical devotion and self-
abnegation.

Mme. de Krudener, as we have seen, retired to
the Ban de la Roche at about the date of the opening of the Congress of Vienna. After a few weeks
of spiritual refreshment in the company of Pastor
Oberlin, she returned to Strasburg with her daughter
and M. Empaytaz, summoned hastily to the death-
bed of her old friend the Comte de Lezay-Marnésia.
From the house of the bereaved widow the following letters are dated :—

To M. Bauzet, Theological Student, Strasburg.

My Son—The Cross, and humble submission at the feet of
Christ—there is a vast library where you may learn much. It
is in times of sorrow that we cling to the hand of our Divine
Jesus, the friend of our souls, that we allow ourselves to be purified, that we realise our wretchedness, that we see what man is
in the flesh, and whether he knows how to love, suffer, or sacrifice

himself. It is then we discover that it is the eagle above who builds his nest on the summit of the rocks, that Faith is a splendid gift, a daughter of heaven, and that the incredulity and pride of which the whole world boasts, are really sunk in the mud and produce discordant cries, in salons as well as in the streets. How easy it is to be revengeful, to agitate, to clamour, to reject what one does not understand, to scoff at wise men, and to blush at the idea of confessing Him, who forsook the glories of heaven and the adoration of the angels, that He might be insulted, despised, crucified, in the midst of a perverse and ungrateful race, who up to the present day still revile the God of mercy, whilst He never grows weary of loving them and inviting them to the marriage supper of the Lamb . . . Every Christian ought to be a missionary; but you need not go to the North Pole for that; you will find plenty of Samoyedes in your own country, and hearts colder than those of the Lapps : call down upon them the rays of life and of grace. Do not be discouraged. Love and charity will teach you many things, for they are born of God.

MME. DE KRUDENER TO MDLLE. COCHELET.

STRASBURG, 19*th October* 1814.

I have been meaning to write to you, dear friend, for a long time. I have been busy with many things, and it is a very real feeling which binds me to you. I spent four *months*[1] at the Ban de la Roche. It is the valley that I mentioned to you. I have inscribed your name there, and have entrusted some holy women with the task of praying for you. In the midst of these mountains, surrounded by the most sublime lessons and the purest joy, I have spent some most helpful moments of which the world can know nothing.

Oh, my dearest friend, what a comfort it is to be freed from all vanities, to realise the emptiness of everything, and to draw the purest happiness from the bosom of God Himself! If you could only feel it as I do, if you could turn towards Christ, the Saviour of souls, and be thoroughly persuaded that you forfeit nothing by loving Him, that indeed life only begins then, and

---

[1] *Months* is presumably a misprint for *weeks*, as Mme. de Krudener did not arrive at the Ban de la Roche before the middle of September. The letter is taken from Mdlle. Cochelet's Memoirs.

that there still remains an inexhaustible treasure which one has never touched, even though one possessed everything on this earth !

What remains to man, wearied by all the disappointments of life, crushed by the injustice of his fellows and by the transitory and unsatisfying nature of all pleasures ? What remains to him, I ask ? Everything remains for him still in that elevated region of which he did not suspect the existence whilst in the world. There are raptures which the earth cannot give, there are thoughts which men in the full current of life have never had, a glorious revelation which manifests itself day by day, and discloses to us the unbounded love of God; finally, there are treasures before which we stand as disinherited beggars, even if we have been the possessors of crowns.

Yes, life has revealed everything to me ; I have possessed everything, and weariness and indifference have swallowed up longed-for days. I have been present in turn at all the feasts of life, and I have seen them all struck by an eternal mourning. And I myself, proscribed and with a withered heart,—I had no pleasures beyond a few vanities !

Oh ! how completely everything is changed ! I can no longer endure the pomps of life. Brilliant men have the same effect on me as a foolish, dull book, which I know by heart the moment I have read the first page. Art reveals nothing to me which attains to the ideal of the celestial thoughts which I find in my own soul. The pleasures that men pursue appear to me as a foolish and vulgar squandering of time, which might have produced the most heavenly joys that unceasingly exalt and ennoble our existence.

In a word, Truth alone, simple and fascinating, forms the sole attraction of my life. I realise that it was that noble thirst which tormented me through all the enchantments of the world. God Himself first offered me the cup; and later, when I learnt at the foot of the Cross to love Him who did not disdain to die for an ungrateful race, I felt that He alone was worthy to fill this heart which was larger than the earth ; His will became the aim and object of my life.

To love that which alone is lovable, to wish to love it, at all events, became henceforth the aim of my whole being. . . . What things I learn, what veils are lifted for me and for all who have cast themselves free, both from the world and from its illusions !   But also what a summons to appeal to the unhappy creatures, who go through life without realising the obligation under which they will be to render an account of every moment ! What a summons to exhort them to profit by this period of grace, and to seek for the mercy of our Saviour and for a new heart !

Oh ! my dear friend, fling yourself boldly on that heart which contains an ocean of charity, and pray every day that you may love Christ, the living God.   He will overwhelm you with graces ; your prayers, which at first will be short, will grow every day more sweet to you.   Every day you will offer up to Him the sacrifice of some habit.   His hand is gentle, and will not hurt you ; little by little He will deprive you of that which you are to relinquish, and will give you, by His grace, that which you are to acquire.

Walk in the royal road of the soul, and learn to confess Him who has said that those who confess Him before men, He also will confess before our Father who is in heaven.

Is He not our sovereign ?   Patience, humility, silence, when we wish to speak about useless things ; purity in every thought, charity in all things, in opinions as well as in actions ; finally, the desire of glorifying Him in all that we do : such are the tokens of this new heart, of this Christian life, to which you also, dear friend, are called.   Prayer teaches you to ask for all things ; faith, to obtain all things.

The most horrible disasters will overtake our guilty France, but an abundant grace calls to repentance all those who may and can be saved.   For the sake of so many who are dear to you, I entreat you to become a means of obtaining favours for them by your prayers and by the gift of your whole heart.   Tell them that man without faith falls under the most terrible scourge.

I have just been present at one of those scenes in which the world can offer nothing beyond the bitterness of its regrets, or the barren comfort of philosophic reasoning, but in which the Christian, surrounded by the glory of his faith, flings himself into eternity.

Death has just overtaken a man who was beloved throughout the province.   M. de Lezay, Prefect of Strasburg,[1] was in

---

[1] M. de Lezay was fatally injured in a carriage accident whilst driving with the Duc de Berri on a tour of inspection.

every way distinguished, both for his great talents and his great
virtues; but all that was as nothing compared to his sublime
Christianity, which made him die like a saint. Descended from
the family of St. Francis of Sales, he seemed to walk in the
footsteps of that illustrious teacher. Putting on one side all
the admiration of those who were to mourn him, he calmly
approached the moment in which everything leaves us, and
casting himself on the Divine mercy, he invoked the blood of
our Saviour, and declared that his hope lay in Him.

When his friends tried to remind him of his good works,
he realised all the futility of human virtues; he declared they
were all soiled by pride, and he would not listen to anything
except about Love which receives us as sinners. He requested
as a special favour of the authorities not to pay him funeral
honours, and in the midst of so many expressions of the deepest
devotion he shed no tears, except at the thought that he did
not love enough the God who had loved him so deeply, as to
suffer for his sake on the cross of shame.

"I am a very youthful penitent!" he declared, forgetting
the terrible pains of his tortured body; and when he feared that
patience might fail in moments of acute suffering, he would
press his dying lips to the crucifix which was offered him.
And remembering the precepts of our divine Master, his lips
and his heart breathed forth nothing but peace. He called
together his servants, and begging their pardon for not having
set them a better example, he prayed with them and exhorted
them to lead Christian lives.

Perfectly calm, and feeling the approach of death, he begged
his wife, who has been the angel of his life, to recite the prayers
for the dying. He died in order that some day he may live
again at the feet of Him who is the Resurrection and the Life.

Yes, he is prepared for the heavenly joys, carried off from
this life like a victim, testifying to the deep mercy which has
crowned a sincere repentance with a sublime death. He has
had the happiness of setting a grand example to our unhappy
century. With a genius for administration, with the very highest
courage and the gentlest of souls, he possessed the gift of
charity, a love for the poor, and all the nobility of the
old French character, and above all, the beauty of humility

and of faith that are not of the earth, but are a gift from heaven.

His wife, as noble as himself, is worthy to be his widow, and that love, so tender and so rare, by which they were united will continue, and will separate her for ever from the world.

I see that my letter has grown into a long one, but how many more things I still have to tell you! Let me beg of you to present my respects to the Queen, and keep a little friendship for me. My warmest aspirations are on behalf of that Princess whom you love so deeply, and who is so deserving of the purest happiness. Oh, may she be blessed with all the joys of Eternity! My daughter and I beg to assure you of our devotion.

B. KRUDENER.

To MDLLE. STOURDZA.

STRASBURG, 27th October 1814.

I hope, my dear friend, that you have received the letter that I sent you by young Mme. de Fries; I had the pleasure of receiving yours, which made a very pleasing impression upon me, and which showed me the state of your soul. What comfort I derive from the thought of seeing you advancing towards the only goal that should attract you! Do not let anything hold you back. Ascend the mountain whilst those who worship false idols are descending it. The living God summons you, and the altar to which He conducts you is that Cross that cannot be combined with the pleasures of a corrupt world. And such pleasures! No, the poisoned cup at which the mob quenches its thirst can never tempt you. No, you have tasted of the Fountain of Truth, and you will turn away in horror from the banquet of the enemies of your God. The boundless love that summons you will not find you ungrateful, for you have been brought up to belong to that nation of children and of heroes, which, in the horrible struggle that is approaching, will vanquish through love.

I speak solemnly, but I live at the foot of the Cross. The events of life are foreshadowed, and visions of the future, the voice of the apostles, the miracles which God has lavished on His people and on the unworthy individual who is writing to you, all urge my conscience to speak to you with energy. There is no time for hesitation. *Let the nation of follies amuse herself; she possesses nothing beyond those miserable pleasures which enslave and dishonour her;* but Christians should watch and pray. The angel who noted the preserving blood on the doors of the elect is passing, though the world sees him not; he numbers the heads; the judgment day is approaching; it is close at hand, and the world dances on a volcano! *We are about to see guilty France, which according to the decrees of the Eternal ought to have been spared by the Cross with which she had been afflicted,—we are about to see her chastised.* Christians have no right to inflict punishment, and the man whom the Almighty had chosen and blessed, the man whom we are privileged to love as our sovereign, could only bring peace. *But the storm is approaching; those lilies preserved by the Almighty, that emblem of a pure and fragile flower shattering a sceptre of iron, because such was the will of the Eternal, those lilies which should have been as a summons to purity, to the love of God, to repentance, have appeared only to disappear.* The lesson has been inflicted, and mankind, more hardened than ever, dreams only of rebellion. Oh, let us pity these men of the torrent; they are in barren deserts; they are cast by their passions on a stormy ocean where they count the shipwrecks of others without caring to avoid their own! Oh, let us pray for them; it would be our duty, even if we were not Christians. Let us shudder at the approach of these calamitous times, of which every one feels a certain presentiment, even where it does not amount to a certainty. Is it possible to dance and to adorn oneself with sumptuous garments when millions lie groaning, and when dark hatred divides the human race? What! Shall these heartless festivities, which rise up on the mourning of nations, and will replunge them in sorrow, never inspire us with horror? Should we not shudder at the thought of offending our great and loving God, who loathes to see us prostituting life instead of regarding it as a sacred trust, a service of love and of joy? As for us, let our feasts consist of the praises of God our Saviour. Let us honour Him with holy and generous offerings—the offerings of our hearts; let the cultivation of all our faculties produce marvels of thought and generous pleasures; it is then that we shall know true festivities and enjoyment, in which angels will take part instead of the demons who preside over the coarse pleasures of the people, and over those of more refined passions.

After giving an account of the death of M. de Lezay-Marnésia in terms almost similar to those we have already quoted in the letter to Mdlle. Cochelet, Mme. de Krudener continues :—

You wish to speak to me of all the deep and striking beauties in the soul of the Emperor. I believe I am already fairly familiar with his character. *I have known for a long time that the Lord will give me the pleasure of seeing him.* If I live, it will be one of the most blessed moments of my life. No earthly duty can be more pleasing than that of loving and respecting him whom we are ordered by God Himself to love and respect. *I have great things to say to him*, for I have suffered much on his account. The Lord alone can prepare his heart to hear them. I do not allow myself to be disturbed about it; my business is to be without fear and without reproach; his is to embrace truth at the feet of Christ. May the Almighty direct and bless him who is called to so high a mission ! . . . May he receive from Christ on his knees those great lessons which always did, and always will, astonish the world, and which will fill with holy joy that heart which is now filled with holy fear. As for the unworthy servant of the Lord who is speaking to you, you know that she wishes for nothing for herself; the glory of Christ alone inflames her heart, or at least she aims at dying to all that is not Christ. His blood alone is the sole interest of my life—the blood which has saved and regenerated me. All other purple has disappeared from before my eyes. My soul thirsts after the living God, and no terrors alarm me. It is for me to give my heart; it is for Christ to form it, to enlighten it, and to strengthen it. Amen.

Prince Galitzin has sent me a thousand crowns (3000 francs) for our old Jung (Stilling). I guess the hand that sent them, but I hold my peace. May the Most High bless the hand, and may the feet of Him who brings peace walk before him.

It is little wonder that this powerful and eloquent

letter, placed in the hands of the Tsar by his wife's lady-in-waiting, should have made so profound an impression on his soul. The stern denunciations of the reckless frivolity which reigned at the Austrian capital, the mysterious prophecies in regard to the Lilies of France, and the undisguised references to himself as the regenerator of the world, were all calculated to strike home to the Emperor's conscience in its most tender parts. In reading both this and subsequent letters in which Mme. de Krudener refers so ecstatically to her sovereign, some readers may be tempted to scoff at her enthusiasm, and attribute it to hidden self-interest. But they must bear in mind the very unique position filled by the Emperor of Russia in the eyes of his subjects, as visible head both of the Church and the State. This, combined with the halo of glory which surrounded Alexander as the vanquisher of Napoleon, fully explains the fact that Mme. de Krudener, filled with religious enthusiasm, should have looked to her sovereign as the restorer of peace to Europe. As a patriotic Russian—and all Russians are intensely patriotic—she could not indeed look to any one else.

In one of her letters to Mdlle. Stourdza, Mme. de Krudener inquired after an old friend who, unknown to her, was already on his death-bed.

There is an old sinner at Vienna for whom there is a soft corner in my heart—there are many such—it is the Prince de Ligne.[1] He used to call me "la sœur grise des cœurs," and we

---

[1] The Prince de Ligne (1735-1814), an Austrian general and French writer, chiefly celebrated for his wit and his cynicism. An octogenarian at the opening of the Congress of Vienna, though still in full possession of all his intellectual

were very fond of one another. Do you ever see him? No doubt you do. He has an excellent heart. I am so dead to the world, that nowadays he would be afraid of me as of a corpse. But neither his fear nor his laughter would deter me, if I could only hope to see him turn towards that life which saves us from eternal death. There were moments when his conscience troubled him, and at such times he desired to see me a Catholic, and I hoped to see him a Christian.

That Mme. de Krudener herself was never present at Vienna during the protracted sittings of the Congress, is amply demonstrated by her own letters written during the winter and spring of 1814-15. The mistaken belief in her presence is founded on a statement contained in Capefigue's *Histoire de la Restauration*, in which he quotes a supposed secret dispatch from Talleyrand to Louis XVIII., describing the Emperor of Russia as "agenouillé dans un oratoire avec Mme. *Crudner.*" The absence of any such dispatch in the recently-published Talleyrand Memoirs, which contain (vol. ii. Part VIII.) his complete public and private correspondence in reference to the Congress, may be regarded as finally disposing of M. Capefigue's statement.

In the course of her evangelistic labours at Strasburg, Mme. de Krudener had the happiness of touching the heart of one who was destined to prove himself the most faithful of friends and the most ardent of disciples. This was the Baron Franz von Berckheim, a member of an old German family, and at that time Commissary of Police at Mayence.

faculties, he was visited by all the sovereigns and diplomats ; and dying 13th December, contributed, as he himself said, to the general entertainment by providing the spectacle of a field-marshal's funeral.

Having been present at one of Mme. de Krudener's religious conferences on the occasion of a temporary visit to Strasburg, he was so penetrated with the necessity of giving up his life to the service of his divine Master, that without delay he resigned his appointment, sacrificed a brilliant administrative career, and made a humble offer of his person and his possessions to Mme. de Krudener. His marriage to Juliette de Krudener in June of the following year, added a yet closer bond to that which already united him to the little band of wandering missionaries; and from that time forward we shall find him associated in all the labours of Mme. de Krudener, and supporting her in times of trouble by the most unfailing courage and affectionate devotion.

CHAPTER X

AFTER quitting Strasburg Mme. de Krudener spent a few weeks at Carlsruhe, where she was overwhelmed by a throng of visitors, both rich and poor, eager to take part in the daily prayer-meetings, and to obtain from her spiritual advice and consolation. Frederick Fontaine also reappeared on the scene with a request for the purchase of land at Rappenhoff in Würtemberg, where he proposed to found a second Christian colony. To this, after considerable hesitation, his patroness agreed, though the transaction was not completed till some months later. In spite of all previous experience, it was apparently impossible to open the eyes of the lady to the real character of this self-styled servant of Christ, whose spiritual requirements were invariably clothed in so very material a form. The strain and the publicity of the life at Carlsruhe soon proved too exhausting for the prophetess, and at the beginning of the new year we find her established, with Juliette, Empaytaz, and De Berckheim, in the comparative calm of Baden. Here she had once more leisure to take up her pen, and indite stirring and prophetic letters to her absent friends. To Mme. Armand she writes :—

A great period is approaching. Everything will be overthrown : schools, human science, states, thrones. The children of God will be collected together. Pray, my dear and precious friend, pray for a great zeal.

But it is to the two ladies-in-waiting—the one in Paris, the other at Vienna—that she dwells most solemnly on coming events.

MME. DE KRUDENER TO MDLLE. COCHELET

BADEN, *2nd January* 1815.

MY VERY DEAR FRIEND—More than two months ago I wrote you from Strasburg a long letter containing many details respecting the death of the prefect. I wish you would let me have just two lines to say if you have received it. Tell me also, dear friend, what you are doing, how you are, and what is the condition of your soul, which displayed such great and happy emotions. I should really like to know whether my letter ever reached you, that I may discover if it fell into other hands.

We came here in order to enjoy a few days of solitude. Baden is always beautiful. Rest is indispensable to me, for often I have not a moment in which I can enjoy quiet. Nevertheless we are so busy here that I can hardly answer a fraction of the letters which I receive.

Being very hurried because of the courier, I must conclude by begging you earnestly to let me have a line from you. Pray do not stand on ceremony with me : you know that I am not at all *exigeante.*

I long for the true happiness of my dear friend : I long to see her turn to those springs of living water which alone can quench our thirst.

I tell you once more that we are approaching the most terrible crisis. Woe unto him who is not converted unto Christ, and who does not possess the living faith that assures him of the pardon of his sins. A terrible judgment awaits him.

Oh, my dear friend, how delightful it is to possess in one's heart that divine peace, that harmony between God and ourselves ! Let us begin to taste that joy which nothing else has ever given us ! Let us go daily for a few moments to the feet of Christ. Let us go with humility and confidence ; let us speak with Him, and beg Him to adopt us by the precious blood that He shed for us ; and let us give Him our whole heart, in order that He may rid it of that which displeases Him, that His Holy Spirit may renew it, and that we may each live a new life in Him.

Every day will bring fresh strength. The gift of prayer will soon come, and prayer will be your delight. What can be equal to the converse that we may hold with the best of friends, the Lord of the whole universe, the God who loved us so deeply that He sacrificed Himself for us ?

Pray forgive me for telling you all this, but I do so long to see you happy, as I am myself. You have a great soul and an intellectual mind ; a vast career lies before you, and the world is so soon exhausted. What remains to us of it but bitterness ? whilst with God there are endless new treasures.

If it be possible, write me a line. You know, and I repeat it, that I require no formality, no ceremony ; you must do just as you like. You know that my heart is entirely devoted to you, and quite removed from every worldly interest.

How is that angel, whom you love so dearly, and for whom my heart feels such respectful devotion ? We see a great number of wonders unrecognised by the world, of great conversions, of great marvels, and of streams of grace granted by God in these days in which God is not yet weary of inviting mankind to come to Him before the abyss opens up. Happy are they who shall profit by it !

The wars, the desolation, will be terrible ! *Remember the year XV, for it will be memorable.* The Viceroy,[1] if he is in Vienna, must have learnt many things. . . . Peace cannot be arranged, and it is evident that the power of making it does not rest with men. Blessed are they who give glory to Him to whom alone it is due ; who know that He chastises His people and afflicts them with plagues ; that He is a mighty God who wishes only to act by love, and whose voice is always tender ; who only punishes to

---

[1] Prince Eugène, Viceroy of Italy.

correct, and who, even when He sends storms against those who will not hear Him, is nevertheless always ready to pardon and to save those who are willing to be saved! Pray tell me whether the poet Ducis is better: I hear he was ill. I am much attached to him. Address your answer to Carlsruhe, dear friend. Juliette and I both embrace you tenderly.

To Mdlle. Stourdza.

4th February 1815.

I was afraid for a moment that my letter might have made you anxious. In it I spoke to you also of my profound and respectful admiration for the Emperor. Quite recently the greatness of his mission has been revealed to me so clearly, that I have no longer any doubts on the subject. I adore the generosity of our Lord, who has so blessed His instrument of mercy. How little the world realises all that awaits him when the divine ruling will be everywhere in the ascendant, and the sun of righteousness will be manifest to the most blind! Yes, dear friend, I am convinced that I have most important things to communicate to him, and although the Prince of Darkness will do all in his power to prevent it, and to keep at a distance all who can speak to him of the divine will, the Almighty will be the strongest. God, who is pleased to make use of those, who, in the eyes of the world, are objects for disdain and derision, has prepared my heart for that humility which does not seek the approbation of men. I am nothing; He is everything, and the kings of the earth tremble before Him, and are as dust. Not daring to accept anything, having renounced all things, neither favour nor blame can intimidate me. That is what I said to you in my letter. The one to which you have written an answer was twelve pages long. Did you receive the whole of it? It is a curious question to put; but perhaps some one did you the service that Mme. de Sévigné apparently wished for at times when she used to say: " Read my letter through, though it is so long; I have no time to make it shorter." Moreover, I put the question to you because you ask me whether I know Werner, and that in my letter I spoke to you myself about Werner. However, I shall not bear you any grudge if you had not time to read it, and that others did so. I will tell you what the Queen of Prussia once wrote to me : " Have you received my letter? The postmasters, and the masters of the postmasters, will only find in it a heart that belongs to God."

The news of Napoleon's midnight flight from the island of Elba, which reached Vienna in the early days of March, fell as a bombshell amongst the members of the Congress. A few weeks previously Mme. de Krudener, moved, as she herself declared, by some divine inspiration, had taken up her abode in an old mill near the village of Schlüchtern, in the Electorate of Hesse, there to await the momentous interview with Alexander which she felt to be approaching. Her letters to Mdlle. Stourdza, who had accompanied the Empress Elizabeth on her return to Baden, display no surprise at the sudden change in the political aspect of Europe.

To Mdlle. Stourdza.

Schlüchtern, 10*th April* 1815.

We were so faithfully warned by the mercy of our Saviour that we knew beforehand all the important periods, so accurately indeed, that 20th March, the day on which some important event occurred in Paris, had been announced to us three months previously by a member of our society; but what I wrote to you from Strassburg about the lilies that had only appeared to disappear, I wrote under an inspiration that overwhelmed me at the moment of writing. In the same way, the great influences which are at work in the soul of the Emperor, and which are preparing him for the glorious destiny which will astonish the world, are not unknown to the humble servant who is to announce these things to him; but I have known from the beginning that there will be great difficulties in the way, and many false accusations will be brought against me, and I do not dare justify myself on any point until the Lord makes all things clear. . . .

I have recently been forced into several journeys, and a refuge has been indicated to me which will be the witness of great things. All that has an appearance of caprice, and many people, seeing that I have been warned beforehand of so many events, imagine me to be mixed up in political matters. Alas! if I only knew what passes in the various cabinets, I should know but little, and should be groping in the dark.

To Mdlle. Stourdza.

Schlüchtern, 18th May 1815.

I cannot refrain, my dear friend, after receiving your last letter, from telling you how touched I was by the kindness and indulgence you have shown me, when you think me guilty of so long a silence. Oh, my dear Roxandra, how much I love you! My heart cannot be drawn from you while I am writing to you, in spite of a thousand things that summon me, to such an extent that I am quite feverish; for my heart is much agitated at the sight of so many miracles, and by the number of letters asking me for spiritual advice, and announcing the progress of the Church. Oh, my dear friend, what things I have learnt since I saw you, what things I have seen confirmed, of which the world has no idea! How I long to talk to you of our beloved Emperor, and of the great future of the world! I have no longer the slightest doubt that the Lord desired to enlighten the miserable and unworthy creature who writes this to you. Dear friend, pray, pray; the moments are very precious. Pray for the elect of the Lord; pray also for your poor friend, who is in great need of prayers, who fears every moment to be unfaithful to her great duties, and who feels so guilty at not loving sufficiently the most merciful God, who overwhelms her with favours, and grants all her prayers. We cast ourselves frequently on our knees in order to pray for those we love. Oh, how little the world anticipates the future!

Alexander left Vienna on 26th May, and travelled across Germany night and day in order to join the headquarters of his army at Heidelberg. The uncertainty of the political outlook, the possibility of a further prolonged war against Napoleon, the anxieties consequent on the discovery of the secret alliance between France, Austria, and England, and all the responsibilities which rested on his shoulders as the most powerful potentate of Europe, filled the soul of the Emperor with a more than usual sense of depression and anxiety. In this gloomy frame of mind he was obliged to submit to the enthusiastic receptions, forced upon him by the inhabitants of the towns through which he had to pass. At length, on 4th June, he entered Heilbronn, in Würtemberg, and, wearied out with his exertions, he retired at nightfall to his apartments, giving orders he was not to be disturbed. The strange sequel must be told in his own words, as contained in a letter to Mdlle. Stourdza.

At last I was able to breathe, and my first movement was to take up a book that I always carry with me, but my intellect, darkened by heavy clouds, was unable to grasp the meaning of what I read. My ideas were confused and my heart oppressed. I allowed my book to fall from my hands, while I thought what a consolation the conversation of a pious friend would have been to me at such a moment. That thought brought you to my mind. I remembered also what you had told me of Mme. de Krudener, and of the wish I had expressed to you of making her acquaintance. Where can she be at this moment, and how am I ever to meet her? The thought had barely flashed through my mind when there was a knock at my door. It was Prince Volkonski, who told me, with an impatient expression, that he troubled me at such an hour in spite of himself, but it was in order to get rid of a lady who absolutely insisted on seeing me. He mentioned the name of Mme. de Krudener. You may judge of my astonishment. I seemed to be in a dream. Mme. de Krudener! Mme. de Krudener! I exclaimed. So immediate a response to my desire could not be a mere chance. I received her on the spot, and as though she had been able to read my very soul, she addressed me in hopeful and consoling words, which calmed the agitation with which I had been overcome for so long.

Further details of this striking scene have been recorded by M. Empaytaz. Mme. de Krudener, on hearing of the approach of the Emperor, had left the village of Schlüchtern with the express intention of intercepting him at Heilbronn. From the first moment of entering his presence, she addressed her sovereign in the same tone of fearless and outspoken reproof, which she was accustomed to make use of towards all those who came to her for spiritual guidance. She pointed out to him the immorality of his past life, the state of sin in which he was still living, and the spiritual pride which had been at the bottom of all his plans of self-reform. And, carried away by religious emotion, she exclaimed: " No, sire, you have not yet approached the God-Man as a criminal begging for mercy. You have not yet received the grace of Him who alone hath power on earth to forgive sins. You are still living in the midst of your sins. You have not yet humbled yourself before Jesus. You have not yet cried like the publican from the bottom of your heart, ' Lord, be merciful to me a sinner.' And that is why you enjoy no peace of mind. Listen to the voice of a woman who also has been a great sinner, but who has found pardon for her sins at the foot of the Cross of Christ."

The interview lasted far into the night, for three whole hours, the sternness of Mme. de Krudener's words being tempered by the invariable sweetness and gentleness of her voice and manner. The Emperor was almost incapable of speech.

Stirred to the very depths of his being by the eloquent words of his visitor, he sat, with his head resting on his hands, shedding silent tears. At length Mme. de Krudener, alarmed by his emotion, and recollecting that it was to her sovereign she was speaking with so much freedom, feared she had gone too far, and said: "Sire, I must crave your forgiveness for the tone in which I have been addressing you. Pray believe that it is out of the sincerity of my heart, and as in the presence of God, that I have told you truths which hitherto have never been said in your hearing. I have merely acquitted myself of a sacred duty towards you."

Alexander, whose natural sweetness of disposition saved him from any feeling of resentment or injured pride, replied at once, " Do not be afraid; your whole speech is justified in my heart. You have made me discover in myself things which I had never seen. I give thanks for it to God ; but I feel the want of many such conversations, and I beg of you not to go far away."

Such was the dramatic scene that marked the commencement of a friendship, which for the ensuing four months was to provide scandal and gossip for the whole diplomatic world assembled in Paris. In view of the many misrepresentations to which the intimate relations between the Tsar and his mystical directress have given rise, it is perhaps as well to state at once that the friendship throughout was of a purely spiritual nature. So little indeed was there anything of self-seeking on Mme. de Krudener's side, that although at this period she was specially pressed for want of money, and although the Emperor with one stroke of the pen would gladly have made her independent for life, she never appealed to him for a single rouble.   In answer to the insinuations in which men of the world feel it necessary to indulge, whenever a warm friendship between man and woman is in question, it need only be pointed out that Mme. de Krudener was at this time over fifty years of age, and thirteen years senior to the Emperor.   Except for her still beautiful and expressive eyes and her graceful carriage, the lady retained no trace of her earlier fascinations. Pale, thin to emaciation, with drawn features, her once luxuriant hair hidden under a simple white kerchief, falling on either side of her face, and pinned together beneath her chin ; her dress of some dark woollen material, with long sleeves closed at the wrist, and quite devoid of any worldly embellishment—thus Mme. de Krudener appears in an old German print of the period still in existence, and thus, no doubt, she appeared in the presence of Alexander during the many evenings he spent in her society.   That a monarch, at whose feet it may be said without exaggeration the most beautiful women of Europe were ready to fall, should have voluntarily relinquished all social triumphs, and have been willing to incur the inevitable ridicule of friends and foes alike, in order to spend long hours of prayer and religious converse with one who at best was regarded as but a mistaken enthusiast, can only be explained on the theory that he acted under the influence of the most intense spiritual emotion. And, indeed, the marked transformation observable in the Emperor during the period of his second visit to Paris, both in his public acts and his private demeanour, renders any other explanation of his conduct quite untenable. For months and years Alexander had been, spiritually speaking, groping in the dark, searching for that immediate sense of personal union with Christ which the magnificent but lifeless services of his own Church entirely failed to supply, and which, indeed, he had never been taught to seek for in them. And now, in Mme. de Krudener, his emotional nature had found, or believed it had found, just that guidance towards the true spiritual life after which he had craved so long in vain. Full of the highest impulses, in spite of the inherent weakness of his character, it is little wonder that the most autocratic sovereign of Europe should have placed himself under the guidance of one from whom, for the first time since he mounted the throne, he heard the undisguised truth as to his own shortcomings. What to the superficial observation of his contemporaries was conduct of almost inconceivable folly and weakness, was in reality only one more testimony to a universal spiritual truth : the magnetic influence of self-sacrificing religious fervour.

The morning after his momentous interview, the Emperor Alexander continued his journey to Heidelberg, where he rejoined the headquarters of his army, and was to await the advent of his guards.

Immediately after his arrival he wrote to Mme. de Krudener begging her to follow him, on the ground that he was filled with an intense longing to discuss more in detail what had for so long filled his thoughts. "You will find me established," he wrote, "in a little house outside the town. I have selected the spot in preference to all others because I found there my banner : a cross which stands in the garden."

On receiving this letter, Mme. de Krudener hastily wrote the following note to M. Empaytaz, who had remained at Schlüchtern :—

DEAR FRIEND—I feel an intense desire that you should come with me to visit Alexander, for I feel strongly the necessity of being with you, of praying, and of going over once more the many passages of Scripture which you are in the habit of finding and reading to me. I wrote yesterday to Alexander, and by the grace of God the letter will bear fruit ; it was strong and tender.

My soul is in the expectation of great things. The war has begun ; the moment is a decisive one. . . . Pray hasten, my dear friend and brother !

On the 8th of June the little party, consisting of Mme. de Krudener, her daughter, De Berckheim, and M. Empaytaz, left Heilbronn, arriving at Heidelberg on the following day. They took up their abode in a simple peasant's cottage, situated on the banks of the Neckar, at ten minutes' distance from the Imperial headquarters. Here, in this humble abode, in a room separated only by a partition from a cattle-shed, the Tsar of all the Russias spent long hours in prayer and eager study of the Scriptures with his hostess and the young Geneva minister, arriving with great regularity every alternate evening at ten o'clock, and remaining frequently till two in the morning. Politics and questions of current interest were entirely banished from these interviews, the conversation turning exclusively on the fundamental truths of religion and the necessity of personal salvation, Alexander himself frequently selecting the portion of Scripture which he desired to have expounded and discussed.

M. Empaytaz has chronicled[1] several curious details of these nocturnal prayer-meetings, which place beyond a doubt the absolute sincerity of the Emperor's religious professions, and which are all the more remarkable as referring to a period of the most intense political excitement, when the whole fate of Europe was trembling in the balance.

He told us one evening that for a long time God had inspired him with an affection for reading the Bible and with a great attraction to prayer; that every day, whatever his occupations might be, he read three chapters, one from the prophetical books, one from the Gospels, and one from the Epistles. Even during the war, with the cannon roaring round his tent, he did not allow himself to be distracted from his devotions. He added that he made every effort to conform his life to the precepts of the Scriptures, and to renounce whatever they forbade; but that he had never succeeded in uprooting a single sin from his soul; that now he realised the power of grace and the Spirit of Christ which could alone bestow the strength to follow His commandments; finally, that he now experienced a peace of mind which accompanied him under all the circumstances of his life.

The conversation having turned on the efficacy

---

[1] See his *Notice sur l'Empereur Alexandre*, a small pamphlet published at Geneva.

of prayer, he exclaimed: "And as for me, I can assure you that having frequently found myself in dangerous (*scabreux*) situations, I have always been saved by prayer. I will tell you a thing which would certainly greatly surprise the world if it were known, and that is, that in my audiences with my ministers, who are very far from sharing my views, when they express a contrary opinion, instead of discussing the point, I pray silently, and I can see them by degrees attracted towards the principles of charity and justice."

During his stay at Heidelberg the Emperor was reading the Psalms; on Monday, 19th June, he happened to read the 35th Psalm, "Plead my cause, O Lord, with them that strive with me," and in the evening he assured Mme. de Krudener that the last trace of anxiety as to the result of the war had thereby been removed from his soul, and that he was convinced he was acting in conformity with the will of God.

Two days later arrived the news of the French successes at Quatre-Bras and Ligny, which threw the whole Russian and Austrian armies into consternation. Alexander alone retained his peace of mind; after fortifying himself by fervent prayer and by reading the 37th Psalm, "Fret not thyself because of evildoers," he rejoined the assembled generals, rallied their courage, exhorted them to an immediate advance, and assured them of victory. When at length the news of the battle of Waterloo reached the Russian headquarters, "the Emperor," writes Empaytaz, "came to me with an expression of the most cordial joy, seized me by the hand, and exclaimed: 'Oh, my dear friend, to-day we must indeed render thanks to the Lord for the great benefits he has conferred upon us.' He fell on his knees, shedding abundant tears of gratitude, and at the conclusion of the prayer exclaimed: 'Oh, how rejoiced I am, now that my Saviour is with me! I am a great sinner, but He has deigned to make use of me to procure peace for His people. Oh, if only all nations could realise the ways of Providence, if they would only obey the Gospel, how happy they might be!' A few minutes later he said: 'Oh, how I wish I could convert my brother Constantine; I love him deeply, and it is a great grief to me that he should still be living in the shadow of sin; I bear him in my heart, and shall not cease to pray to the Almighty to open his eyes to the truth.'"

On the 25th of June the Emperor Alexander started for Paris, having previously presented Mme. de Krudener and her party with the necessary passports to enable them to follow him without delay. Owing to the disturbed state of the country, however, it was not found practicable for the ladies to set out on the journey before another fortnight had passed, and during the interval Mme. de Krudener enjoyed the double pleasure, firstly, of giving her beloved daughter in marriage to the Baron de Berckheim, and secondly, of welcoming her old friend Mme.

Armand from Geneva.   She further found time in the midst of her manifold engagements to visit some condemned criminals in the prisons of Heidelberg, in order to exhort them to a final repentance.   Her eloquent words of prayer and intercession touched the hearts of most of her unhappy hearers, and she had the ineffable joy of feeling that her presence had not only softened their last hours on earth, but had also been the means of teaching them to prepare more worthily for the supreme moment of death.

The following letter to a friend, written immediately after the departure of the Tsar, gives a glimpse of Mme. de Krudener's own feelings towards her sovereign, now that she had been brought into relations of daily intimacy with him.

Oh, how truly great he is with the greatness of the sincere Christian!   How his faith, his charity, his childlike simplicity show through his whole life the influence of the God whom he loves so deeply, of Jesus Christ!   What disinterestedness he displays in this great cause. . . . Every one admits the superiority of the Emperor, his calmness, the depth of his thoughts, which are invariably inspired by prayer, his great confidence in the Almighty; everything conspires to elevate him into the only man of the day in whom we can place our hopes.   I trust, under the will of God, to be able to rejoin the Emperor at Spires to-morrow, and to remain there as long as he remains.   It will not be for long.   Pray for him.   We do so faithfully, yet not sufficiently. . . . My little cottage gave him the greatest pleasure.   " I also have my guards," I used to say to him.   They were the three cows at the entrance to the house.   My porter was a solitary Cossack, whom he presented to me, for the cottage was so tiny that it did not contain the whole of my party.

After a fatiguing and distressing journey in the
rear of the allied armies, the little party arrived in
Paris in the middle of July, and found a first resting-
place at the Hôtel de Mayence, Rue Cordière, near
the Faubourg St. Germain.

CHAPTER XI

IT was eleven years since Mme. de Krudener had last quitted the French capital. She had left Paris in 1804, flushed with triumph at the success of her *chérissime Valérie*, and in the enjoyment of a St. Martin's summer of youth and beauty. She returned in 1815, aged and haggard, dead to all sense of worldly triumph, leading a life of poverty and asceticism modelled on that of the saints of the Catholic Church, animated with the one object of preaching to all men the message of the Gospel, and exhorting them to a new life in Jesus Christ. Moreover, she returned as the inspired prophetess of the great events of 1815, and as the keeper of the conscience of the Tsar Alexander, who was believed to defer to her judgment in all matters of religion and morality. Under such exceptional circumstances it is not surprising that even during the exciting months which followed the second return of the Bourbons to the throne of France, the presence of Mme. de Krudener in Paris should have created a profound sensation in all circles of the gay capital. The world that she had renounced crowded around her, and busy politicians and women of fashion were to be met at all hours on her staircase, eager to see, if not to hear, the converted *mondaine* of earlier days.

The Elysée Bourbon having been assigned as a residence to the Emperor of Russia, the Hôtel de Mayence, on the south side of the river, where Mme. de Krudener had alighted on her first arrival, was at an inconvenient distance ; and accordingly, two days later, at the special request of Alexander, she removed herself and her party to the Hôtel Montchenu, 35 Faubourg St. Honoré, which belonged at that time to Mme. de Lezay-Marnésia. Both the Hotel and the Elysée Bourbon communicating through their garden doors with the Champs Elysées, a means of communication was established between them, which permitted the Emperor to go backwards and forwards at all hours without exciting observation.

Alexander appears to have taken full advantage of his right of private *entrée*. Every alternate evening, when his official duties were over, he walked across, attended by a single valet, to the Hôtel Montchenu, and joined Mme. de Krudener in her little salon, often remaining until a very late hour. On these occasions either Mme. de Berckheim or M. Empaytaz was usually present. As at Heidelberg, the avowed objects of the visits were prayer and the study of the Bible, to which the lady added eloquent and outspoken exhortations on the practical duties of a truly Christian life. Sometimes

she would fear that her enthusiasm had carried her
too far, but Alexander would be the first to reassure
her on that point. "Do not fear, Madame," he
would exclaim. "Scold me well; by the grace of
God I will carry out all your instructions." Mme.
de Krudener always protested, and no doubt sin-
cerely, against the accusation that she attempted to
regulate the politics of Europe during these evening
séances; but the moral and political duties of a
sovereign are too closely intermingled for it to be
possible to maintain the distinction for any length of
time, and there is no doubt that by degrees the
political questions of the day occupied a larger and
larger space in the minds of both the Tsar and his
Egeria, with results of the first importance to
Europe.

The Parisian world was not long in discovering
that the gay and amiable monarch of the preceding
year had undergone a considerable moral transformation. Alexander appeared neither at balls
nor at the theatre, and as far as possible abstained
rigidly from every sort of social and official festivity.
During the absence of the Empress in England, he
shut himself up in his apartments at the Elysée,
devoted himself to State business and the study of
the Bible, and denied himself to all visitors whom it
was possible to exclude. His conduct appears to
have been based on a sense of his own weakness.
"Pray for me," he said one evening to Mme. de
Krudener; "pray to the Almighty to strengthen
me against the bad influences of this city. Until

now I have resisted its seductions, but man is so weak, that if he is not sustained by grace he succumbs to the temptations which besiege him on every side. I feel the necessity of avoiding society ; that is why I asked for a retired residence. In the rooms which I occupy I enjoy a great deal of peace ; I neither see nor hear anything which distracts me from my duties ; I work, I read the Scriptures, I commune with God in prayer, and I trace His merciful and tender protection in all that He helps me to avoid." For the same reason, no doubt, he cultivated in society a dignified courtesy and restrained gravity of manner very far removed from the easy *sans-gêne* of his earlier days.

" People have noticed," said Mme. de Krudener to him one day, " that you are more virtuous this year than you were before."

" How is that ? "

" They say that you put on a severe expression whenever you are praised."

" That is true," returned the Emperor; " but it is because I attribute to God what men attribute to me."

It must not be imagined that the very evangelistic development of the Emperor's religious ardour, under the direction of Mme. de Krudener, in any way affected his allegiance to the Orthodox faith of the Empire. At no period of his life was he more strict in fulfilling all the fasts and ceremonies imposed on its members by that Church. Feeling the necessity of being at all times united in prayer with the sympathetic soul of his spiritual directress, he invited her to be present in his private chapel at the Elysée Bourbon at the celebration of Mass on Sunday mornings. Accordingly every Sunday Mme. de Krudener, her head covered with a white veil, took her place in a seat reserved for her use in a room overlooking the Imperial chapel.

It may readily be supposed that these private relations between the Emperor of Russia and Mme. de Krudener quickly gave rise to every sort of spiteful report and exaggerated rumour. The diplomatic world assembled in Paris were much mystified by this unexpected development, and made use of all the private sources of information at their disposal in order to discover the key to the situation. When, at length, the fact appeared to be established beyond any reasonable possibility of a doubt, that the connection was of a purely religious nature, the scorn and amusement of the unbelieving world of the day knew no bounds. The Liberal party, who had always regarded the former pupil of César Laharpe as a member of the philosophic school of thought in which he had been reared, were especially indignant at his defection. The position threatened to throw all the calculations of state-craft out of gear; no one could foretell what new developments might not arise from so unprece-dented a situation, and various methods were employed to seduce the Emperor from his allegi-ance to his middle-aged enchantress. Talleyrand cynically proposed to inveigle him into a rival salon,

in which he should be captivated by all that was
. most *recherché* amongst the wit and beauty of the
Parisian world.   The bait failed to draw the victim,
but Metternich, undeterred by the non-success of
his rival in diplomacy, undertook the formation of
an Austrian coterie, which should be irresistible in
fascination, and for that purpose secured the services from Vienna of some of the most renowned
beauties of the Austrian Court.   Alexander proved
himself superior to such intrigues.   " The three
ladies have been presented at Court," he announced
laughingly to his friend.   " They were attired in
Vienna toilettes *qui n'étaient pas fameuses;* the
whole thing was a failure, and no doubt it will put
an end to the gossip."

Amongst the many inaccurate rumours current
in Paris regarding Mme. de Krudener, and which
have been chronicled by certain of her critics, we
find glowing descriptions of reception rooms artfully
arranged with a dim religious light, in order to
enhance the mystical appearance of the prophetess,
clothed in majestic costume.   In reality, the very
reverse was the case, and the rigid simplicity of all
that appertained to the inmates of the Hôtel
Montchenu contributed more than anything else
to impress the luxury-loving Parisians with a belief
in the sincerity and genuineness of the doctrine
that was preached.   " Notre très bonne mais très
extravagante cousine de Krudener," writes the
Comte d'Allonville [1] in a short biographical notice,

---

[1] See the *Mémoires Secrets du Comte d'Allonville*, vol. vi. chap. xxxvi.

composed throughout in a tone of affectionate indulgence towards the fantasies of a charming
woman, "resided in 1815 in the very dilapidated
hôtel of the Comte de Montchenu. I have seen
her there almost entirely destitute of furniture."
The lady herself explains the matter in a letter
written a few months later from Switzerland.

It is a curious fact that I never dared to have my Paris
apartment furnished.   At first I intended doing so; I said to
myself: a simple apartment decently furnished—that is what I
require.   But many things seemed to indicate clearly that I was
to keep my salon as it was—without mirrors, with a few rush-
bottomed chairs, and nothing beyond the very barest necessaries.
At a later date I realised what an impression was made upon
people by the great contrast between the luxury in which I had
always lived, and this complete renunciation of all things; how
struck they were by seeing me, before the eyes of all Paris,
braving the conventionalities of which we are all the slaves, and
showing, by the liberty of those who are detached from all
worldly possessions, how happy one may be.   They realised that
I was indifferent to all things; and possibly it occurred to some,
who had never previously reflected on the subject, that there must
be a positive joy in this religion of the Gospels, which the divine
Master lived in its full perfection, when He had relinquished the
glories of heaven in order to clothe Himself in human form and
suffer every degradation.

Mme. de Krudener, in the rigid simplicity of a
dark woollen gown, offering a rush-seated chair to
the *grandes dames* of Parisian society, brings to our
mind distant reminiscences of the tender figure of
St. Elizabeth of Hungary, in the gray serge habit
of a tertiary of St. Francis, leading a life of prayer
and poverty, surrounded by all the ducal splendours
of the Castle of Wartburg.

BARONIN KRÜDENER

Zwickau b. Geb. Schumann

Of all the novelties that could possibly have been offered to the inhabitants of the French capital in 1815, a religious salon was undoubtedly the most striking.   At no period have the prospects of religious faith and sentiment seemed at a lower ebb throughout the nation at large than at the moment of the Restoration—prospects which were soon to be brightened by the appearance on the scene of a De Bonald, a Lacordaire, a Montalembert, and many other talented champions of the Church.   In the bitter struggle between Catholicism and scepticism, which was to be one of the distinctive notes of the next fifteen years in France, salons in which the religious element was predominant were formed by degrees from amongst all that was noblest in the Legitimist circles of Paris.   Of such salons, though belonging to a slightly later date, none have left more graceful souvenirs than that of the Russian convert, Madame Swetchine.   But when in July 1815 Mme. de Krudener threw open the doors of the Hôtel Montchenu to all her friends, rich and poor, young and old alike, who cared to take part in evangelistic services, it is not surprising that in the first instance curiosity and love of novelty supplied the main motives of many who presented themselves for admission.

The service took place at seven in the evening, and consisted mainly of an extempore prayer and an exposition of a portion of Scripture.   Empaytaz alone, dressed in a black Geneva gown, held forth on these occasions, speaking with much fluency and simplicity, rendered impressive by the evident strength of his own convictions. Mme. de Krudener usually knelt amongst the congregation, which assembled in a large drawing-room overlooking the garden on the one side, and on the other opening into a broad corridor. On the farther side of this corridor were situated the family dining-room, and a little private sitting-room in which Mme. de Krudener received the Emperor at night, and during the day any of her friends or disciples who wished to talk to her in private. As the fame of her piety and wonderful sweetness of manner spread through the capital, these daily visits became overpoweringly numerous, occupying the whole of the hostess' time, so that she complains in her correspondence of having leisure neither for food nor for rest.

Amongst this crowd of visitors might be discerned not only many of Mme. de Krudener's old friends and admirers, but also many of the most celebrated men and women of the day,—Chateaubriand, Benjamin Constant, the mystical Bergasse, who also enjoyed the confidence of the Emperor Alexander, the Baron de Gérando, councillor of state and philanthropist, the Duchesses de Bourbon and d'Escars, the Duchesse de Duras, who was soon to be distinguished as the holder of the most refined and intellectual salon of the Restoration, Mme. de Récamier, still in the full possession of her marvellous beauty, the Princess Sophie Volkonski,[1] and many others.

---

[1] Wife of Field-Marshal Prince Peter Volkonski.

Chateaubriand, it would seem, was attracted to the Hôtel Montchenu more by the pleasant remembrance of his old friendship with the authoress of *Valérie*, and possibly also by the hope of entering into personal relations with the Emperor Alexander, than by any sympathy with the evangelistic methods adopted by his hostess. A reference to his visits to Mme. de Krudener at this period, which occurs in the *Mémoires d'Outre Tombe*, is couched in a tone of supercilious cynicism.

Mme. de Krudener had invited me to one of these celestial performances. I, a man of many chimeras, hold all folly in detestation, all nebulosity in abomination, and all jugglery in disdain ; we cannot all be perfect. The scene bored me ; the more I wished to pray, the more I felt the aridity of my soul. I could find nothing to say to God, and all the while the devil was tempting me to laugh. I much preferred Mme. de Krudéner, when, surrounded with flowers and an inhabitant of this miserable earth, she composed *Valérie*.

Fortunately other eye-witnesses carried away a more pleasing impression. "Curiosity," writes Grégoire, former Bishop of Blois and a constant visitor, " was powerfully stimulated by the appearance of a woman, who, born in luxury, had deserted palaces in order to tend the unfortunate under thatched roofs, of a woman whose natural graces were embellished by the brilliancy of her talents, who expressed herself with elegance and fluency, with the accent and intonation of a prophetess, and with the appropriate gesture which prepares the mind for conviction and pours unction into the soul."

Mme. de Genlis, then living in retirement at

the Carmelite Convent in the Rue de Vaugirard, writes in her Memoirs in a strain of grateful appreciation of the visits paid to her by our heroine.

. . . She wrote to me asking if she might call, and I consented with pleasure. I had read a most charming little novel of hers called *Valérie*, which contained no indication of the exalted sentiments that I heard attributed to the authoress. I was curious to meet a person who apparently united an exaggerated imagination with much simplicity and naturalness; and such were precisely the qualities I discerned in her. She would say the most extraordinary things with a calmness that carried conviction; she was certainly most absolutely sincere; she appeared to me most amiable, witty, and possessed of a quite *piquante* originality; she came to see me several times, showed me the greatest kindness, and inspired me with a deep interest. She was gifted with a sensitive soul, much tenderness, and most excellent intentions; she was still comparatively young, and her death has caused me much sorrow.

Very interesting too are her relations with Benjamin Constant, the brilliant orator and journalist, the friend and fellow-exile of Mme. de Staël, whose many-sided character was founded on a strong basis of religious sentiment, and an intense love of justice and liberty, but who was subject to constant fits of bitter irony and morbid discouragement. It was in these moments of depression that he would turn to Mme. de Krudener for the sympathy and consolation which she knew so well how to bestow—"an unchanged Adolphe in the presence of a regenerated Valérie." To Mme. Récamier, the recipient of all his confidences at this period of his life, Constant writes on the morrow of one of his visits :—

Yesterday I saw Mme. de Krudener, first in general company,

and afterwards alone for several hours. She affected me in a way that I had never felt before, and this morning the impression was heightened by the following circumstance. She sent me some manuscript writing, with a request to forward it to you and to no one else. I should much like to read it with you; it has done me good; there is nothing very new in it; that which all hearts undergo, whether joy or pain, cannot be very novel; but it has appealed to my soul in more places than one. . . . It contains truths that are trivial, and which yet tore my heart. When I read the following words in no way striking: "How often I have envied those who laboured with the sweat of their brow, added one burden to another, and lay down to rest at the end of each day without knowing that man bears within himself a mine which he ought to work! A thousand times I have said to myself, Be like other men,"—I burst into tears. The remembrance of a life, so stormy, so wasted, which I myself have flung against the rocks in a sort of fury, impressed me in a way that I cannot describe.

And again:

I had spent the whole day alone, and I only went out in order to call on Mme. de Krudener, The good excellent woman! She does not know all, but she sees that I am devoured by some frightful grief; she kept me three hours in order to console me; she told me to pray for those who caused me to suffer, to offer up my sufferings in expiation for them if they were in need of the sacrifice.

Naturally Mme. Récamier found herself in time drawn by this curious fascination to the salon of the Hôtel Montchenu, and there exists a gracefully worded little note, preserved by Chateaubriand —himself the intimate friend of all concerned—in his Memoirs, which gives a charming glimpse of the relations between the two women, each so supreme in her own particular sphere. B. Constant writes to Mme. Récamier :—

I acquit myself with no little embarrassment of a commission that Mme. de Krudener has just laid upon me. She entreats you to come to her house as little beautiful as possible. She says you dazzle every one present, and in that way souls are troubled and all real attention becomes impossible. You cannot, I know, deprive yourself of your beauty, but pray do not add to its power. I might add many things about your looks on the present occasion, but I do not possess sufficient courage. It is easy to be ingenious about the charms that please, but not about those that kill. I shall see you shortly; you told me five o'clock, but you do not return home till six, and I shall not be able to say a word to you. However, I will do my best to be amiable once more.

But it is time to let Mme. de Krudener herself speak on the exciting events through which she was living. Surrounded as she was by her friends, with every moment of her time occupied, few letters of this period have come down to us. But there was . one friend, Mdlle. Stourdza, then absent with the Empress Elizabeth in England, who had a primary claim on her time and attention. To her she writes as follows :—

Paris, 17th August 1815.

My very dear Friend—You will have been surprised to see the couriers arriving, and especially the last, without receiving a letter from one who is devoted to you for life, and who will never cease loving you. But my position has been an embarrassing one, and I spoke of it to your brother. It was quite impossible for me to write openly, and I can write in no other way. The roads are very unsafe, and letters are exposed in every sort of way to being read; although I never meddle in politics, it was impossible for me to write to you on any but insignificant topics, and they no longer appeal to you. I wrote to you on the journey from Bar-sur-Aube, and the courier who took charge of my letter promised faithfully to deliver it. We arrived here as by a miracle, under the protection of that powerful mercy that watches over us, and without arms, as the idea of making use of them was already forbidden me. The Cossack who had escorted us had broken his lance, and I did not dare have it repaired. We were always arriving on the morrow of some pillage or revolt, and we passed like a band of children through a country distracted by crime and passion. Almost everywhere in the villages crowds collected round our carriages. Both Empaytaz and I preached the Gospel and just retribution, but also the mercy of the Saviour, who in His boundless love wishes only to save us. Tears flowed abundantly, and it was a sad picture which was formed by those deserted villages with the houses destroyed by the last campaign, and the people dazed and awe - struck. Our dear Emperor had had money distributed all along the route in order to alleviate the suffering; everywhere he is regarded as an angel. His attitude has been that of the Christian hero, such as, with the help of the Almighty, I had dared to predict and hope for last year. His greatness is apparent even to the blind. He announces even by his silence the God who has chosen him. His quiet simple life, devoid of all the frivolous pleasures that go to make up worldly happiness, is a splendid spectacle, which is as a sermon to men on the forgotten Gospels. He works very hard. In the evening he comes frequently to visit a person who is very devoted to you, and who lives in his immediate neighbourhood; she rejoices at seeing him always advancing on the great path of worldly renunciation, given and offered to us by Christ. He is very popular here, and the people call him by all sorts of affection- ate names. Evil alone flees from before him. He enjoys those pleasures that come from God and from the Saviour to whom he testifies by his life.

Paris is still agitated, and France as well as the capital. People are being murdered in the south; let us weep and pray. Pray for me, for I feel my incapacity to fulfil my duties, which for many years have made my life a remarkable one, causing me sometimes to live in the country and to lodge with peasants in a mill, as during the spring; and sometimes transporting me into the midst of the splendours of society, and the very highest ranks.

As far as possible, I keep my presence in Paris a secret from certain people, but I see duchesses and servant-maids, and men of every political party, without allowing them ever to talk politics to me. I say to them: "I have arrived at a point at which I only care about charity: if you wish me to point out to you the only remedy both on earth and in heaven for your troubles, your sins, your deceptions, your torments, I will preach to you the mercy of Christ ; but if not, my time is too precious."

To the Same

Paris, 30th August 1815.

. . . Alexander is the elect of God ; he walks in the path of renunciation.   I am acquainted with every detail, I might almost say every thought of his life ; he comes here with great regularity, and the spiritual bond originated by God grows ever closer. When occasionally he is obliged to go into society, it is neither to the theatre nor to a ball, and he told me it always affected him like a funeral, and he could no longer conceive how men of the world should propose such amusements. . . .

Yesterday the Duchesse de Duras and Chateaubriand were chatting with me.   We were speaking of the chastisement that weighs upon France, and I replied, when they spoke to me of the enormous influence I possess over a certain personage, "That personage is nothing but dust and an instrument of flesh.   God permits me to speak the truth to him.   God inspires him with a love of truth, but he can do nothing for France.   The only way open for your country is to make *amende honorable*, to humble herself and cry for mercy at the foot of the Cross she has deserted for so long, and to openly confess Jesus Christ.   Then, clad in sackcloth and ashes, and, if you like, with a rope round my neck, I will be the first.   I too have sinned in the midst of this great Babylon.   Let the King and the nobles and the people do penance also, and strike their breasts.   And you, Mme. la Duchesse, who are a woman of great courage, you will be among them ? "

"Oh yes ! " she said, "certainly ! "

A few days previously an old friend of mine, the Duchesse d'Escars, told me she was ready to do penance in public. Chateaubriand quite agrees with me ; he has just published a remarkable speech.   Indeed, the Almighty is turning all hearts. . . . My health and my life are a positive miracle.   People are coming and going all day. . . . I hardly know whether I eat or not, and I talk the whole time.   In the evening I rest while talking gently to the Emperor and hearing him talk, but he comes late and goes late.

P.S.—Can you read my letter and understand it? Your heart will help you. I have no time to collect my ideas and to write them down. Since I finished my letter, I have seen a whole crowd of people, and have not even had time to change my dress. The Duchesse d'Escars has just left; an Englishman named Bruce, who has been round the world; young de Staël, the son of Mme. de Staël; Mme. de Gérando; and your Princess Bagration, all spent an hour with me.

The natural common sense of the Emperor Alexander enabled him about this time to confer a lasting benefit on his spiritual directress, by ridding her for ever of the grasping demands of Frederick Fontaine and of his dupe Maria Kummrin, who had naturally hastened to follow their benefactress to Paris, in the hope of sharing in the pecuniary advantages which might be expected to accrue from her friendship with the Tsar. We relate the incident as it is given by M. Eynard.

The visionary had already indulged in a first ecstasy, and had announced that she would have a second on the following evening in the ante-chamber. Mme. de Krudener spent many hours in prayer, imploring God to manifest His will. When the hour came at which the Emperor was in the habit of passing through the ante-room, he found Maria Kummrin reclining on the sofa. He asked for explanations; Mme. de Krudener not vouchsafing any reply, Fontaine took upon himself to explain to the Emperor that she was a prophetess of the Almighty, who had a message to deliver to him from God. Alexander sat down to listen, and Maria Kummrin commenced a sententious discourse which wound up with a demand for money with which to found a Christian community in the neighbourhood of Weinsburg. Mme. de Krudener had risen from her knees whilst the woman was still speaking, and had left the room with her daughter. A few moments later she returned, and begged the Emperor to accompany her into the salon. Alexander followed her, and interrupted her apologies by assuring her that he was sufficiently acquainted with human nature not to allow himself to be duped by the piety of people so very prompt in asking for money, and advising her to get rid of them as quickly as possible. Two days later Fontaine and Maria Kummrin took their departure for Rappenhoff.

Two anecdotes, both characteristic of the Emperor at the time of his most complete submission to the doctrines of practical Christianity as preached by Mme. de Krudener, and indicative also of that Russian simplicity of character which his western critics have so frequently mistaken for conscious duplicity, find an appropriate place at the close of this chapter. On his nocturnal expeditions to the Hôtel Montchenu, Alexander was accustomed to be followed on foot by a valet of Prince Volkonski, named Joseph. On one occasion the key of the garden door opening on to the Champs Elysées declining to turn in the lock, Joseph jumped over the low railing into the hôtel garden, in order to open the door from the inner side, after which he preceded the Emperor down the path. Suddenly the figure of a man emerged from the shrubbery, and flinging himself upon Joseph, struck him a blow with a knife which grazed his ear. The next instant the Emperor, on coming up, received from the same unexpected quarter a great armful of onions and other vegetables full in the chest. The shouts of the valet attracted the attention of Mme. de Krudener's servants, who rushed to the rescue, and after a short scrimmage the assailant, having been captured and dragged to the light, it was discovered that he was an English soldier disturbed in the act of robbing the garden of the Hôtel Montchenu. He was brought up into the salon. At the sight of the Emperor he was so overwhelmed that he could barely speak, but Alexander addressed him encouragingly, poured him out some coffee, and having heard his story, sent him away with a gift of money, so that he should not be tempted by want into such evil courses again. The lucky soldier, relieved from his terrors, preserved sufficient presence of mind to request the Emperor before leaving not to mention the matter to his superior officers, a request which was smilingly granted.

The same Joseph is the hero of the second incident, as related by Empaytaz. In spite of the rigid watch which the Emperor kept over his daily conduct, expressions of anger and impatience still escaped him from time to time in moments of irritation. One evening, as he was crossing the ante-room of the Hôtel Montchenu, he turned to the attendant valet and asked whether he had executed a commission previously given. "Sire, I had forgotten it," replied the confused Joseph. "When I give an order," retorted the Emperor in an angry tone, "I expect it to be carried out without fail." Saying these words, he passed into the salon, but Mme. de Krudener, advancing to greet him with words of welcome, noticed at once that his manner was constrained and confused.

"Sir, what is the matter? you seem troubled," she inquired.

"Nothing, madam," was the answer; "it is nothing. . . . Pardon, madam, I will return immediately." Alexander left the room, and went up to the valet.

"Joseph, I must apologise; I was too severe in my manner just now."

"But, Sire!"——

"I must beg you to forgive me," continued the Emperor; and finding his servant still too overwhelmed to reply, he seized him by the hand and repeated, "Say that you forgive me."

"Yes, Sire," stammered the mystified valet; and his Imperial master, after warmly thanking him, returned in a more peaceful frame of mind to the presence of his spiritual directress.

Many people, doubtless, will scoff at the incident as merely quixotic; but when we recollect the almost universal barrier of reserve and pride which separates a master from his servant, it must be admitted that a little act of social reparation like the above, from the most autocratic sovereign of Europe to an ordinary domestic attendant, implies a degree of Christian humility which the majority of us find quite beyond our reach.

CHAPTER XII

IN spite of Mme. de Krudener's repeated assertions concerning the non-political nature of her regenerating mission, it was not long before her name became intimately connected with the political events of the day. The trial and death of General de Labédoyère first brought her supposed political influence prominently before the public, and she has been much censured by her critics, not, curiously enough, for having attempted to intercede on behalf of the brilliant and unfortunate young officer, but for having interfered with so little practical result.

Charles de Labédoyère was one of the most talented and patriotic of all Napoleon's younger officers. As a boy of twenty he had fought valiantly at Jena; as colonel of the 112th regiment he had distinguished himself at Lutzen and at Bautzen, and had shared in all the defeats of the campaign of 1814. Thanks to the intercession of his royalist connections, after the abdication at Fontainebleau he was given the colonelcy of the 7th line regiment, and stationed at Grenoble. Of an ardent and enthusi-

astic temperament, Labédoyère's soul had been fired
by the magic touch of Napoleon's genius ; and when
his former chief landed in Provence, the impetuous
young officer hastened to rejoin the imperial standard
at the head of his whole regiment. "Sire," he
addressed the Emperor, with characteristic frankness,
"the French nation will do everything for your
Majesty, but it is essential that you should do everything for them. No more ambition, no more
despotism ; we mean to be free and happy. Your
Majesty must abandon the system of conquest and
absolute power which has proved a misfortune both
to you and to France." Napoleon smiled at this
harangue, but he knew the value of the young officer
too well to take offence at his outspokenness, and
during the Hundred Days Labédoyère saw himself
loaded with favours. Hence it is hardly surprising
that after the second Restoration his name was
placed in the list of nineteen persons who, by the
proclamation of 21st July, were ordered to be tried
by court-martial, and that the ultra-royalist party
clamoured for his execution. Nevertheless Fouché,
anxious if possible to save his life, provided him
secretly with blank passports, and allowed every
facility for his escape from the neighbourhood of
Clermont-Ferrand, where he had taken refuge, to the
Swiss frontier. Labédoyère's conduct at this juncture has always remained an inexplicable mystery ;
whether, as his friends assert, he was filled with an
uncontrollable desire to embrace once more his young
wife and child, then resident in the capital, or

whether, as his enemies insinuate, he harboured further treasonable schemes against the Government, certain it is that he returned to Paris in the ordinary diligence, was recognised at the barrier, and within a few hours was lodged in the military prison of the Abbaye. Arrested on 2nd August, he was summoned to appear before a court-martial on the 9th, when he defended himself with calmness and dignity, and on the 15th was condemned to be shot as a traitor, with three days' grace to prepare for death. The trial produced the most intense excitement throughout France : on the one hand the supporters of Louis XVIII. clamoured for justice, whilst on the other the youth, the courage, the high birth, and the melancholy beauty of the prisoner, not yet thirty years of age, raised up a chorus of sympathy on his behalf. Mme. de Labédoyère and her friends moved heaven and earth to obtain a favourable verdict, the young wife even penetrating to the presence of Louis XVIII. himself, and flinging herself at his feet to implore his pardon for her guilty husband. The heart of the sovereign remained unmoved. It was known that the kindly sympathies of the Emperor Alexander had been touched on behalf of the young officer, and that he earnestly desired his acquittal, without, however, feeling justified in making an official protest on the subject. Talking one day to the king's niece, the Duchesse d'Angoulême, Alexander openly advocated a policy of clemency.

"Sire," replied the Duchess, embittered by her

many years of exile, "justice demands firmness and measures that strike terror."

"Madame, if justice has its rights, so also has charity."

"Charity," exclaimed the Duchess, "cannot be distinguished from weakness."

"You are mistaken, madame," was the answer; "charity wins and softens all hearts."

The last hope of the distracted wife lay in Mme. de Krudener, and day after day Mme. de Labédoyère hurried to the Hôtel Montchenu to implore her friend to use her great influence with the Emperor to procure her husband's pardon.

Rightly or wrongly, Mme. de Krudener does not seem to have felt herself called upon to interfere actively on behalf of the General. She was far more absorbed in the salvation of his soul than in that of his body, and whilst Mme. de Labédoyère appealed piteously for the life of her husband, Mme. de Krudener talked in prophetic tones of repentance, of the love of Christ, of the day of judgment, and other cognate subjects. It is almost impossible to believe that at the moment of her greatest influence with the Emperor of Russia, a powerful appeal to his sense of justice and mercy would have proved of no avail. It seems certain that, though the subject was discussed between them, no such appeal was ever made; and one cannot but regret that Mme. de Krudener failed at this juncture to put out her hand to save the life of one who by nature was well worthy of the effort.

The following letter to Mme. de Labédoyère, written, as the date shows, when the fate of the General was still trembling in the balance, has frequently been quoted as a favourable example of the writer's style of *exaltée* eloquence. But when it is recollected that the broken - hearted young wife was imploring for deeds, not words, one cannot but feel that these irreproachable sentiments of repentance and renunciation must have sounded as a death-knell to her hopes.

MME. DE KRUDENER TO MME. DE LABÉDOYÈRE.

PARIS, 11th August 1815.

How I wish I were able to console you, dear and unhappy friend! But that is a task beyond the powers of man. I have pointed out to you the only way by which you can escape from this terrible misfortune, which may prove so salutary,—through God, and God alone. It is at His feet, it is by embracing that Cross which is the refuge of sinners and the rallying-point of all that was ruined by the Fall, that we find peace, rest, and salvation. It is for having deserted that Cross, through the most cowardly ingratitude, that thrones are trembling, and that the people are being swept from the earth.

O madame, you who were brought up in the midst of the antiquated remains of a monarchy which in former times prided itself on furnishing the first Christian kings, and that can claim those names to which was directed the only homage that does not fade, be also a Christian! Implore the mercy of the living God. Cast yourself on His bosom, not seeking for those human supports forbidden by the divine law when it says : " Cursed be the man that trusteth in man and maketh flesh his arm ! " but seeking Christ Himself. He is more loving than the mother who tends with tears the child that appeals to her. He is better than all the kings of the earth. But, madame, He is the Eternal, and consequently His ways are not our ways. Boundless eternity is the heritage of man, who is so fallen that he cannot even pass through life and exist for a few years without degrading it by his sins.

If God strikes us, let us adore Him! It is only to correct us! Let us resign ourselves, let us weep and pray, but remember that it is not for us to restrain His arm; that He alone in His fathomless mercy can hold the reins that guide His rebellious creatures, who would fall into the abyss if a loving God did not stoop to guide and to hold back those whom He constantly desires to save.

Ah, madame, you have been witness of my tears, and you know if my heart is cold! Before your name was brought in to me I was at the foot of the Cross praying for the unhappy Labédoyère. When I saw you my heart was torn in two. But religion, which sheds tears of pity, has also great lessons to teach, and, even whilst living, its most sublime ministry consists in warning, with that strength that can only be imbibed at the feet of Him whose immutable decrees we adore.

I have shown you your great duties. The ordinary woman has only tears; she who is truly a wife has eternity, where her bonds become sublime. Such is the marriage offered us by the Church; all other is but adultery. That which is not founded on God is but one of the incidents of life on which rest the actions of mankind, either passion, or cupidity, or ambition, to which we give polite names, or finally, all those follies which men try in vain to ennoble, but which belong in reality to the dominion of sin, and are stamped with the disapproval of the Almighty.

I implore you to be truly Christian, and to have the courage to point out to your husband his terrible sins. But show him also God our Saviour, who became man that He might wash away our sins with His blood. Do not excuse him, do not rejoice to see him calm. Impress on him that he must be prepared for a terrible judgment if he does not turn to Christ. Do not excite vain hopes in him! Where is the sovereign that dares to correct the hand of God? Pray, pray both for him and with him!

Such are your duties, my dear young friend, and I promise you, in the name of our Saviour, who has deigned to show me also His mercy, and to rescue me from a world where I was not happy in the midst of everything that people envy—I promise you, I repeat, the peace that comes from Him alone, and a joy which men cannot conceive. You can easily be great in their eyes by possessing the virtues which they admire, by weeping, by sacrificing yourself, possibly by dying of grief. Any dramatic scene strikes their imagination. But try to be truly great, by weeping at the foot of the Cross, by giving all your heart to God, and by saying to yourself: My duty is to enlighten my husband, and not to deceive him, to show him the sad fruits of a life given to the world where, not being a Christian, he fell into the abyss, from which the inexhaustible love of God can alone rescue him, and will rescue him, when all men have abandoned him. Oh, may he weep at having offended the great and glorious God, who, by becoming man, bore our crosses and died on a cross of shame! May he beat his breast. He will be once again great when he raises himself; for God alone, His grace alone, can raise him, and man dare not judge him when God has pardoned him. He will weep at having been faithless to his king. Such tears are those of men who have returned to their natural dignity. No great man exists who has not shed tears over himself, and there is no man living who is not guilty in the eyes of God. He will then see the worthlessness of false glory. He will then groan over his errors. If he makes excuses for himself he is lost.

I have spoken to you with truth; it is the only language I know. Charity is my duty. She is in turn gentle and stern. I am a Christian, and in humiliating myself in my worthlessness at the feet of Christ I have the courage of the highest hopes, for I know the depths of His mercy, and I hope for the salvation of your husband if he casts himself on the bosom of our Saviour, who rejects no one.

The prisoner himself, calm and courageous to the end, evidently did not place much faith in the efforts which were being made on his behalf, nor in the effect of the letter of submission which he himself addressed to Louis XVIII. after the death-sentence had been pronounced. Having received from his wife both Mme. de Krudener's letter, and an accom-

panying volume of spiritual exhortation, he replied
in the following dignified terms :—

THE COMTE DE LABÉDOYÈRE TO MME. DE KRUDENER.

I cannot deny myself the pleasure of thanking you for the
interest you have been kind enough to display towards my most
unhappy wife. You have appreciated her many and excellent
virtues, and you have been good enough to offer her spiritual
consolation. Do not blame me, madame, for venturing to thank
you. I am very grateful for the book you sent me. There are
times when it is a special joy to turn one's thoughts to the great
and sublime truths of religion. I trust I shall be enabled to
make a good use of the few short moments which remain to
me. I cannot believe, madame, that you can have retained even
a confused recollection of me. On the occasion when I had the
pleasure of seeing you, I had not yet attained to an unhappy
celebrity. Mme. de Labédoyère tells me that you have had the
kindness to call at the door of my unlucky mansion ; how touched
I am by this proof of your sympathy ! I beg to express to you
my most ardent gratitude. Forgive the liberty I take in writing,
and believe me, madame, with all respect, your very humble and
obedient servant,   DE LA B.

To this Mme. de Krudener hastened to reply in
the following letter :—

TO THE COMTE DE LABÉDOYÈRE.

PARIS, 17*th August* (?).

I thank you, monsieur, for the touching letter which has
caused me to shed many tears both bitter and sweet. Alas,
monsieur, who would not shed tears over so heartrending a
situation ! But my tears have been sweet also, for the disposi-
tions of your soul lead me to hope that you will fling yourself
into the arms of our Saviour, who is longing to receive you, whose
love for us is greater even than the love of a mother for her son,
who propitiated on our behalf the justice of the paternal Father,
and who desires to belong to us by virtue of that supreme sacrifice. Oh, my dear and unhappy M. de Labédoyère, cast your-

self entirely on His mercy! Think of the love of a God who became Man for our sakes, and think how little we have loved Him in return.

Oh! I entreat you by the sorrow which I have felt for you, and by the tears my eyes have shed for you, I entreat you to forget all that men say who know nothing of the truth, and therefore reject it, and let your thoughts rest on the great love of our Saviour, on Jesus Christ, who will judge us if He does not save us! When all is ended He will remain, for He is the Eternal!

One spark, monsieur, of that charity which is in His breast inspires me to pray for you, to cast myself at the feet of our adorable Saviour! Do not reject my prayers. I have been raised up, not by men, but by miracles of mercy; how should I, who have to accuse myself, dare to remind you of your sins? But we are all sinners together, and Christ wishes to save us. Is this world of falsehood, and are these sinful men, always to envelop us in their illusions? The world passes, men disappear, eternity remains. There you will find a God full of pity, if you only come to Him repentant.

Oh! when I watched your first youth, I did not know that so tragic a future . . . But all eternity remains for the true Christian. Do not blush to acknowledge the power and love of Him whom cowards desert; turn to the Saviour, call Him by His Holy Name. He does not want long prayers, He wants your heart. Your will is sufficient, and there where men only wish to see evil, He is anxious to find excuses. He wishes your repentance, and we unite ourselves with you. We pray, we prostrate ourselves. How great is the death of a Christian who turns to Christ! It unites him with all the great men of all ages, with Augustine, Jerome, Tertullian, Fénelon, St. Francis; all the holders of the most precious titles of humanity are united to Him.

And what of Bayard and Gustavus Adolphus, and all the great captains of their century? Your angelic wife will have great consolations if she may share the future with you. Nothing passes away, nothing comes to an end, and in God everything is beautiful, everything is sublime felicity. Call repeatedly on the name of our Saviour; the Scripture tells us that it is as sweet incense.

Pray forgive me whatever may have been too harsh, whatever may have wounded you in my letter to your wife. See in it only a heart convinced of its own sinfulness, but filled at this moment with an ardent desire for your salvation.

Forgive all judgments. Christians should not judge one another. How I long to see you, that my words might preach to you the mercy which I found at the foot of the Cross! I do not say good-bye to you; my hopes are immortal, and the Christian commences life there where the unbeliever enters on an existence of horrible torments.

May the Saviour in whom is all my hope, may Christ the living God, bless you !

I have heard that you entertain no bitterness against those who have been foremost in ruining you, and that you forgive your enemies. I do not know if you have any. I do not judge; but I am happy to see you in the possession of such sentiments. But, dear M. de Labédoyère, do not try to excuse yourself in the eyes of Christ; confess to Him, and confess openly, that you have sinned, and turn to that fount of mercy which caused the blood of the redemption to be shed, one drop of which will redeem the universe.

The execution took place on the Plaine de Grenelle at half-past six on the evening of 19th August. The following extract from a letter of Mme. de Krudener to the Emperor Alexander gives full details of the heroic bearing of the brilliant young officer during the last moments of his life :—

EXTRACT FROM A LETTER TO THE EMPEROR ALEXANDER.

20th August 1815.

After the sorrows which I went through yesterday on behalf of the unhappy Labédoyère, and the hours of the night spent in sadness of heart, what joy I felt on hearing in the Mass the sacred chant and the words, "Lord have mercy!"

I shed tears, and I recovered a little of the strength of which I had need in order to visit once more that poor, poor Mme. Labédoyère, who is to start to-day. I went to see her, and found her in bed. At first my presence only added to her anguish, but afterwards God helped me to show her the happiness she ought to feel at her husband's salvation.

I found the confessor who accompanied him; he is a most holy man, and I received from him the most comforting details. Labédoyère made so beautiful a death that the venerable priest said that his only desire was to make one equally good himself. He first read to him the psalms in the carriage during the entire distance. His whole soul was prepared; he was lifted up from the earth. He composed himself before death, requested absolution and benediction, confessed openly our Saviour Jesus Christ, allowed himself to be restrained by no cowardly human respect, repeatedly kissed the crucifix, adored the sacred wounds of our Lord, made an act of renunciation of his life, forgave all his enemies, and lastly, pointing to his heart, gave the order to fire, and lifting his eyes towards heaven and spreading out his arms in the form of a cross, he fell to the earth, and the smile remained for a long time on his lips.

O my God! how comforting it is to relate such details to the glory of our divine and adorable Saviour. In the midst of our unhappy century I have made acquaintance on this occasion with several pious women who prayed daily for him, also with the intimate friend of Mme. de Labédoyère, who had been a witness of the happiness of their marriage, and who, together with his relations, was present at his death. He had written to each one expressing his repentance and resignation. All were devotedly attached to him.

Let us worship the Saviour, who has drawn his repentance from his very sins, and has led him by grace to his salvation. His confessor told me that up to the age of sixteen he was very religious. He was won over by the world, but by nature he was gentle and generous, an admirable son, and a loving husband and father. . . .

Without making Mme. de Krudener in any way directly responsible for the carrying out of the sentence pronounced on Labédoyère, her undoubted failure to adopt a decided course of action in so important a crisis, leads one naturally to inquire into

the permanent result of her evangelistic labours in
Paris.　What real tangible good was effected by
her eloquent exhortations to repentance?　How
many sinners were converted to a holier life by the
prayer-meetings of the Hôtel Montchenu?　These
are questions which most missionary enterprises
show a tendency to avoid; but though it is undeni-
ably true ·that nothing is more misleading than
statistics when taken by themselves, it is equally
true that they are an indispensable factor in the
formation of any impartial judgment.　In the case
of Mme. de Krudener's Parisian labours, it must
frankly be admitted that stern fact is not at one
with the representations of some of the lady's
friends.　It is undoubtedly true that the impression
created by her preaching was intense, magnetic,
saisissante.　All who came in contact with her felt
their religious aspirations stirred by her sweetness,
her eloquence, the refined simplicity of her style,
the undoubted sincerity of her purpose.　" Many a
Parisian scoffer," writes Sainte-Beuve, "who went
to hear her in the great salon of the Faubourg St.
Honoré, which was open to all, returned, if not convinced, yet charmed and penetrated by her personality.　Even those of her intimate acquaintance
who felt called upon to oppose her in her presence,
frequently preached in a similar strain themselves
when she was no longer there."　In a word, her
personal influence was magnetically powerful, but at
the same time it was singularly transient.　Her
spiritual relations with well-known people of her

day—the Emperor of Russia, Benjamin Constant, Hortense Beauharnais, Mdlle. Stourdza, the Duchesse de Duras, and many others, all bear out, as we have seen, this view of her character. The truth is, her teaching was purely emotional; she touched the heart and the sensibilities, she inflamed the imagination, but she rarely convinced the head. Her own nature was too impressionable, too unrestrained, too undisciplined even in her spirit of self-sacrifice, to carry real fundamental conviction home to the soul of her hearers. The spirit of restlessness which distinguished her all her life, and which led her on unceasing wanderings from Paris to Riga, and back again to Germany and Switzerland, is an outgrowth of the same weakness. She habitually acted on impulse, and though towards the end of her life her impulses for the most part were dictated by the highest spirit of charity, yet they lacked the durability and stability of more measured action. As an example of the limitations of her influence, with all its magnetic effectiveness, we quote the following description of a visit to St. Lazare, as related by M. de Sainte-Beuve :—

Once, at the earnest invitation of a good man, M. de Gérando, and with the permission of the prefect of police, she penetrated into the prison of St. Lazare, and there found herself in the midst of the very dregs of society. She began to speak to these astonished and soon deeply-affected women; the corruptions of the great were laid bare; she smote her breast; she confessed herself as great a sinner as any present; she spoke to them of that God who, as she so often said, "had snatched her from the midst of the world's enchantments." The scene lasted several hours.   The effect was instantaneous, ever-deepening; there were sobs and outbursts of gratitude.   When she left, the doors were besieged, the corridors thronged.   The prisoners made her promise to return; to send them good books.   But other emotions intervened; she did not come back; and it is in this lack of discipline, of fixed order, and even of definite doctrine, that we become sensible of Mme. de Krudener's want of perseverance.

If in its main features the evangelical preaching of Empaytaz and Mme. de Krudener, as carried out both in Paris and Switzerland, differs little from that of the many revivalist movements with which England and America have been familiar since the days of John Wesley, the lady at least was saved by her innate refinement and feminine sense of fitness, from any danger of falling into the extravagances and vulgarity with which such enterprises are usually marred.   To the very end she is the same graceful tender figure whom we first learnt to love in the pages of *Valérie*.   For ourselves, it is neither on the platform, nor even at the side of the Emperor Alexander, that she excites to the full our reverent affection.   It is in the midst of her family circle. Here she reigned supreme in the hearts of all who knew her best.   All the members of her faithful bodyguard — Juliette, de Berckheim, Empaytaz, Mme. Armand—who shared so willingly in her wanderings and privations, vied with one another in enthusiastic love and devotion to the mother who was always eager to take on herself the largest share of trouble and discomfort.   Neither persecution nor ill-health, nor even absolute pecuniary destitution, was able to quench the playful cheerfulness with which Mme. de Krudener faced every misfortune of her later years. With such a picture of home-life before one, it is easy to feel indulgent towards the shortcomings of her public career.

CHAPTER XIII

THE months of Mme. de Krudener's evangelistic labours in Paris were spent by the sovereigns and diplomats of Europe in animated discussion over the conditions of peace. To what extent were the Allied Powers to be remunerated for the trouble and expense of a second time dethroning Bonaparte? The terms proposed were onerous to the French nation, and savoured far more of conditions imposed by a triumphant foe than of a friendly understanding between allies. The Prussians, smarting under the recollection of years of enforced subjection to Napoleon, were specially insolent in their attitude, even threatening to blow up the Bridge of Jena over the Seine as a salve to their outraged feelings. Wellington and Castlereagh were scarcely more gracious. Not only was Louis XVIII. to lose much territory and many fortresses on his northern and eastern frontiers, but an enormous indemnity was to be paid to each of the Allied Powers, and all the treasures of art with which Napoleon had enriched his capital at the expense of his enemies were to be returned to their original owners. Alexander had always maintained an attitude of friendly sympathy towards the French nation, with whom he was extremely popular; but his personal dislike to Talleyrand, who, contrary to his wishes, had been appointed President of the Council and Minister for Foreign Affairs on the return of Louis to power, restrained him from openly espousing the cause of France. Talleyrand in vain brought all his diplomatic skill to bear on the negotiations in order to save the future honour and glory of his country; and when he discovered that Louis was resolved on acceding to the demands of the Allies, he placed his resignation in the hands of his sovereign (24th September).[1] His successor in office, the Duc de Richelieu, was a great favourite with the Tsar, having been for twenty-four years in the service of Russia, and having acted for a considerable portion of the time as Governor of Odessa. On his advice Louis, in his dilemma, flung himself openly on the mercy of Russia. Alexander, faithful to the *rôle* of peacemaker of Europe, in which he had been sedulously instructed by Mme. de Krudener, responded to the appeal, and ultimately induced the Allies to forgo a portion of their claims.

The Russian troops had been quartered throughout the summer in Champagne, and on 10th September, the birthday of the Emperor, he proposed holding a grand review of his whole army on the Plaines de Vertus, to be followed on the ensuing

---

[1] See the *Talleyrand Memoirs*, vol. iii. Part IX.

morning by a solemn Mass of Thanksgiving. Alexander was particularly anxious that his spiritual directress should be present at the religious celebration, and accordingly, two days previously, the Duc de Doudeauville having placed his château at Montmirail at the disposal of the party for the first night of their journey, the whole Krudener household, including both Mme. Armand and Mme. De Lezay, started for the Russian headquarters. Montmirail was reached late in the evening, and the early part of the following day was devoted to prayer and meditation and the singing of hymns under the great trees of the park. Alexander had ordered rooms to be prepared for Mme. de Krudener in the house of a M. de Pinteville, in the immediate neighbourhood of the camp; and it was from here that his carriages conveyed the ladies on the morning of the 11th to an elevated spot specially reserved for them in the immediate vicinity of the Imperial tent. Before them stretched the vast plain, on which were assembled 150,000 men, whilst seven altars had been erected for the simultaneous celebration of the Mass, with all the gorgeous accessories of the Greek ritual. It was a scene well calculated to stir the hearts of all who were present; and it can easily be supposed that both Alexander and Mme. de Krudener were strung up to the highest pitch of religious enthusiasm, as they prostrated themselves in prayer in the sight of the whole vast multitude, and offered up thanks to the Almighty for the special protection accorded to the Russian troops in the recent campaign.

"This day," the Emperor declared subsequently to
the ardent participator in all his spiritual joys, "has
been the most beautiful of my life, and one that I
can never forget.   My heart was filled with love for
my enemies; I was enabled to pray fervently for
them all; and it was whilst weeping at the foot of
the Cross of Christ that I interceded on behalf of
France."   M. de Sainte-Beuve, on the authority, he
affirms, of an eye-witness, gives us a vivid and
picturesque, if somewhat romantic, description of the
memorable scene, which will well bear quoting.

The honours paid by Louis XIV. to Mme. de Maintenon
at the camp of Compiègne did not surpass the veneration with
which Mme. de Krudener was treated by the conqueror.   It was
not as the grand-daughter of Marshal Münnich, it was not even
as his favourite subject; it was as an ambassadress from Heaven
that he received her, and conducted her into the presence of his
armies.   Bareheaded—or at most wearing a straw hat, which
she flung aside at pleasure,—with her still golden hair falling on
to her shoulders, and a few curls gathered together and fastened
over her forehead; clad in a long dark gown, confined at the
waist by a simple girdle, and rendered elegant by her manner of
wearing it—thus she appeared at this period, thus she arrived
upon the plain at dawn, and thus, erect, at the moment of prayer,
she seemed as a new Peter the Hermit, in the presence of the
prostrate troops.

There is no doubt that this religious solemnity
on the Plains of Vertus must be regarded as indicating the high-water mark of Mme. de Krudener's
career in the eyes of the world.   It made patent to
all Europe what until then had only been realised
in its entirety by the initiated few, namely, the
overwhelming influence of her religious teachings

upon the mind of the Tsar. It was the signal for all the arts of diplomacy to be put in motion, in order to rescue Alexander from what, in the eyes of his contemporaries, was nothing less than a lamentable infatuation. Mme. de Krudener herself, whilst the flush of enthusiasm was still upon her, committed to paper the thoughts that had crowded her brain as she took part in the great Act of Thanksgiving, and which were given to the world in a little pamphlet—now exceedingly rare—entitled *Le Camp des Vertus.* We reproduce it at length in its translated form, for it not only demonstrates the curious belief into which the writer had worked herself concerning the divine mission both of Alexander and of the whole Russian people towards the nations of Europe, but it also contains the clue to what is perhaps the greatest, and certainly the most far-reaching in its effects, of all the events of his reign—the proclamation of the Holy Alliance.

Le Camp des Vertus.

We have recently been witnesses of one of those great scenes which connect the Heavens with the Earth, and which posterity will regard as one of those grand and sublime pages of history, which serve as a revelation for all ages.

Who would dare to write the history of our times? Where is there a Tacitus with sufficient boldness to touch on these events, which, like the Sphinx in the Fable, devour all those who do not possess the key to the riddle?

All these events are beyond the comprehension of those who do not possess the living God to explain them, and who will always remain isolated and wrapt in confusion as long as they

do not form a part of that chain of which the Almighty Himself
holds the first link, and which connects light with wisdom and
mankind of all ages with mankind of to-day, by the same current,
by a single truth.

Yes, in the midst of the universal deluge, in which every one
takes note of the shipwreck of others without perceiving his
own, when sin and passion have enveloped nations in terror
and disaster, it is all due to a single crime: that of having
attempted to ignore the living God. Such was the cause of that
first ancient philosophy of the angels of the Fall; such was the
crime of the first man. Pride stepped in between the world and
infinite Love, and hence the origin of all the infirmities of man.

But in the midst of all these proscribed nations, and in this
land of exile, there has always existed a sacred race; there has
always been one people dear in the sight of the Almighty, one
great thought which had sprung from His heart, and which,
through all ages, had sustained the universe, and united it to
God.

And it is these men of all ages who alone recognise this
great drama, this vast conflict, in which darkness continues
unceasingly to produce evil, and in which the angels, uniting
themselves with the chosen people, with the children of promise
under the eye of the Almighty, cause good to spring from the
very source of wickedness and evil passions. The conflict just
now is more fierce than ever, for it is soon to come to an
end.

Who has not said to himself: Everything must be changed,
if everything is not to crumble away? Who, in the convulsions
which have agitated the earth during the last five-and-twenty
years, has not seen something beyond an ordinary war? Who,
whilst present on those plains of Champagne which witnessed
the defeat of Attila, did not say to himself: Another rod has
been broken, and it is in the deserts of Asia that the crash of a
great fall has resounded, and it is from the midst of the most
vast empire, which seemed to be prostrate at the feet of the
conqueror,[1] that the Almighty has struck him down; that He
has scattered the colossal power as a mist from before His face,
causing the flight, as of a spectre startled by the morning light,

---

[1] *i.e.* Russia prostrate at the feet of Napoleon.

of him who advanced with all the forces of Europe, and who
left behind him only the dead to bury the dead?

And from that distant land, which was only known as in a
legend, came a simple people, who had not yet drunk of the
cup of all iniquity; who had not yet deserted the God who had
redeemed them. A long time previously they had been selected
for the purpose of repeating once more that great lesson of all
ages: that wise men know nothing, and that all things are
revealed to babes.

At their head was the man with a great destiny, designed
before all ages, and created in order to be placed in opposition to him, who, thirsting for glory, was to be crushed by his
own power.

He was humble, this disciple of the greatest of masters; he
was a child. At all times his advance was that of one who, by
a mere breath, can overthrow worlds.

The Almighty summoned Alexander, and he was obedient to
His voice. The Almighty supported him; and, full of confidence
in the future, with that infinite courage which, in the midst of
national disasters made him reject a shameful peace, he was
already the recipient of every promise; the fields of victory
were already spread out before him, and already every heart
that realised how all strength comes of God was opened to
him.

After that who would dare to praise him? No indeed! It
would imply a forgetfulness of the fact that he is great with the
only true greatness: the desire to glorify the Lord.

Happy Alexander! The boundless longings of your heart
must indeed have been satisfied when, on that blessed day, on
those same plains where, six centuries before, a hundred thousand
Frenchmen, in the presence of a king of Navarre,[1] watched the
burning of one hundred and eighty heretics by the light of the
funeral torches, when, I repeat, you saw a hundred and fifty
thousand Russians doing homage to the religion of love, and
the most intrepid of warriors bending knees which had never
been bent in the sight of danger!

---

[1] Probably Thibaut de Champagne, guilty of great severity towards the
heretical sects of his time. There exists a tradition of twenty-four heretics
who perished on Mont Aimé, overlooking the plain.

Oh, what must have been your feelings when you watched them worshipping your Christ, the God of your heart, and when you said to yourself, "They dare to pray to Him, for the Gospel, which ordains both love and peace, stands between Moscow and France"!

Yes! Glory be to the God of our armies! At last a man lives who is sufficiently great to be able to acknowledge openly, at the head of his army, which is already so splendid and so strong, according to all human standards, to acknowledge, I repeat, the Saviour who has blessed him, and the God who has given him as an example to the world!

Ah! who, in seeing that blessed day, did not entertain with us every hope; who, in watching Alexander standing beneath the great banners, was not reminded of all the victories of faith, of all the lessons of charity? Who dared to doubt the presence of divine inspiration? and who did not repeat with the Apostle: "Old things are passed away; behold, all things are become new" (2 Corinthians v. 17)?

And who but felt the need of something new in the midst of all these ruins? Men placed by their sagacity at the head of affairs have foretold this epoch by the light thrown upon it in the majesty of the Scriptures, by which it has been revealed to them. Nature confided it to her students; science suspected it; politicians, covered with shame, foresaw it in their own disasters; finally, the most mediocre of men learnt from their own misfortunes what true Christians have always said when they saw Right, not only as beauty, but as the highest conciliation of all interests.

Yes, all, whether rejoicing over the great secret, still hidden like Isis, or else trembling lest the veil of time should be rent in two, all have experienced either the hope or the terror of this epoch. And this memorable scene, in which so many mighty sovereigns adored the King of kings, appeared as an introduction of the universe to a new epoch, and as a living preface to that sacred history which is to regenerate the world.

What heart, being witness of all this, has not also throbbed for you, O France! You, who in former times were so great, and who will emerge greater than ever from your misfortunes! You, who attempted to banish the Almighty from your councils, and

who have seen the army of flesh, though supported by empires,
fall down terrified and impotent!

Say to the astounded nations that the French have been
chastised by their very glory; say to the men without a future
that the dust which exalts itself returns to its former state in the
grave.

And you, France, the first and earliest heritage of the Gauls,
the daughter of St. Louis, and of so many saints who have drawn
down upon you eternal benedictions, the inspirer of that chivalry
whose dreams have fascinated the universe, arise intact, for you
are palpitating with immortality! You are not really a captive
in the bonds of death, like those who have always ruled or served
in the domain of evil.

Already you have all been present on this day; you have all
prostrated yourselves in order to worship Jesus Christ, the glory
of the Father, and the Supreme Judge of the world!

You implored of Him to save France, when on each of the
seven altars the sacrifice of the God who became Man was offered
for all living creatures. Ah, pray that she may turn again to
God, and she will be redeemed! Yes, her virtues, her love for
her kings, her fidelity, her claims for happiness, will be given back
to her, together with that sunshine of life which has been pro-
claimed by a nation that lives according to the gospel, and that
displays to the whole universe the Cross of Victory, which, on
their departure, they will leave behind as a magnificent altar round
which all will rally, which will announce to future generations:
"Here Jesus Christ was adored by the hero, and by his beloved
army; here the nations of the north prayed for the happiness of
France."

Alexander returned direct to Paris on the
conclusion of the religious celebration at Vertus,
and was followed by Mme. de Krudener after a
day's rest at the château of Montmirail. But even
this short separation was a trial to the impetuous
monarch, who sent several times to the Hôtel Montchenu to inquire for news, and finally despatched a
courier to meet the lady on the road, and ascertain

that she had not been detained by any accident. The evening visits were at once resumed, and continued on the same footing of cordial intimacy up to the very day of the Emperor's final departure from Paris, which was to take place very shortly.

Before returning to his own dominions, where his presence was urgently required, Alexander felt strongly the necessity of openly testifying before all nations to the faith that was in him, and of setting an example to Europe of the practical application of the doctrines of Christianity to the problems of international policy. The very fact of his having been connected in his youth with the philosophic school of thought of the 18th century, made him doubly anxious to emphasise his new standpoint before the world. Moreover, the really wonderful course of events by which—mainly through the valour and energy of Russia—the power of Napoleon had been crushed, and Alexander himself raised in his stead to the position of arbiter of the fate of Europe, appeared to him as the unmistakable proof of the hand of Providence intervening directly in his behalf. The haunting recollection of the midnight murder of Paul I., in which he had been unwittingly implicated, and the memory of the manifold errors of his private life, filled the Tsar with a morbid sense of remorse which further impelled him to some step, that would definitely mark the advent of a new era in his life. Add to all this the almost daily intercourse with the *exaltée* soul of Mme. de Krudener, who constantly incited him to confess Christ before all men, and to rise superior to any considerations of merely worldly advantage, and the veil of mystery which for so many years obscured the origin of the Holy Alliance seems to roll away.

The fundamental thought of the Emperor Alexander was the formation of an international law, founded on Christianity, which should unite on a single broad basis all the Churches of Europe, Catholic and Orthodox, Protestant and Anglican. This, the Tsar believed, would lay the foundation-stone of that era of universal peace which it had been his lifelong dream to establish throughout Europe. If, he argued, the Allied Sovereigns are resolved on peace, peace will be secured—forgetful that outside of Russia the voice and will of the people is of infinitely greater moment than that of the sovereign.   There is something very naïve and curiously characteristic of the Russian temperament, in the Emperor's belief that this solemn enunciation of unimpeachable sentiments would have the power to work a miracle in the hearts of men.   That the act should have been totally misinterpreted by the majority of contemporary statesmen and historians, that it should have been regarded by Castlereagh as the senseless act of a madman, and by Metternich as the insidious plot of a Machiavelli, is, on the whole, not surprising, considering the extremely small part habitually allotted to Christian principles in the regulation of international relations.   Nor is it altogether incomprehensible that a proclamation which had its birth in an outburst of religious fervour and humanitarian zeal, should, at a later date, mainly through the instrumentality of diplomatic machinery, have been transformed into a weapon of oppression and despotism. But it is in no way our intention to venture into the broad realms of European history during the first half of the present century, in which the Holy Alliance was one of the determining factors in the fate of nations ; our immediate object is to clear up as far as may be the much-debated question of Mme. de Krudener's personal share in the composition of the famous document.

It has been asserted on all sides that the Holy Alliance in its completed form was the work of the pen of Mme. de Krudener, or, at the very least; that it was directly inspired by her. Although undoubtedly the Proclamation was the outcome of a whole train of religious influences, amongst which Mme. de Krudener was the most potent factor, it has now been made clear, from the testimony of contemporary witnesses, that the lady only played a secondary part in the drawing up of the document, the main responsibility for which rests on the shoulders of the Emperor Alexander alone.

A few days before his departure from France (writes Empaytaz) the Emperor said to us : " I am going to leave France, but previous to my departure I wish to render public homage to God the Father, the Son, and the Holy Ghost in return for the protection He has vouchsafed to us, and to invite the nations to enrol themselves under the banner of obedience to the Gospel. Here is the draft of the act, which I beg you to go through carefully, and if it contains any expression of which you do not approve, I trust you will inform me of the fact. I wish the Emperor of Austria and the King of Prussia to unite themselves with me in this act of adoration, so that, like the wise men of the East, we may be seen openly acknowledging the supreme authority of our divine Saviour. You will unite yourselves with me in prayer that my allies may be disposed to sign." . . . The following day he returned for the draft. We were profoundly touched by the humility with which he was pleased to listen to the suggestions we made to him. The next day he took the document to the Allied Sovereigns to sign, and he had the satisfaction of seeing them enter at once into his views. That same evening he came to inform us of the steps he had taken, and to render thanks to God for the success with which they had been attended.

We subjoin a literal translation of the Proclamation, the original of which is drawn up in the French language—a very short document when one recollects the immense issues with which it was fraught:—

IN THE NAME OF THE HOLY AND UNDIVIDED TRINITY.

Their Majesties the Emperor of Austria, the King of Prussia, and the Emperor of Russia, in consequence of the great events which have occurred in Europe in the course of the last three years, and especially in consequence of the benefits which a divine Providence has been pleased to confer on those states whose governments have placed their confidence and hope solely in it, having become profoundly convinced that it is necessary to base the principles of conduct to be adopted by the Powers in their mutual relations on the sublime truths contained in the eternal religion of Christ our Saviour ; declare solemnly that the present act has for its sole object to manifest, in the face of the universe, their unalterable determination to adopt as their rule of conduct, whether in the administration of their respective states or in their political relations with all other governments, no other principles than those of their holy religion, precepts of justice, of charity, and of peace, which, far from being exclusively applicable to private life, ought, on the contrary, directly to influence the resolutions of princes and guide all their decisions, as offering the only means of consolidating human institutions and remedying their imperfections.

In consequence their Majesties have adopted the following articles—

Art. I. In accordance with the words of Holy Scripture, which command all men to regard one another as brothers, the three contracting monarchs will remain united by the bonds of a true and indissoluble brotherhood, and, regarding each other as compatriots, they will lend one another aid and succour in all places, and under all circumstances; believing themselves to be placed towards their subjects and their armies in the position of a father towards his children, they will direct them in a similar spirit of brotherhood, for the protection of religion, peace, and justice.

Art. II. As a result, the only principle in operation, either between the said governments or between their subjects, will be that of rendering reciprocal service; to display to one another, by an unalterable good-will, the mutual affection with which each should be animated; to regard one another without exception as members of one and the same Christian nationality; the three allied princes themselves only considering themselves as delegated by Providence to govern three branches of one and the same family, to wit :—

Austria,
Prussia,
Russia ;

thus confessing that the Christian nation of which they and their people form a part has really no other sovereign than Him to whom alone supreme power belongs, because in Him alone are contained all the treasures of love, of knowledge, and of infinite wisdom, that is to say in God, our divine Saviour Jesus Christ, the incarnate Word.

Their Majesties consequently recommend to their people with the most earnest solicitude, as being the only means of enjoying that peace that is born of a good conscience, and which alone is lasting, daily to fortify themselves more and more in the principles and practice of those duties which our divine Saviour imposed on mankind.

Art. III. All the Powers that may wish solemnly to avow the sacred principles by which this act is inspired, and that recognise how important it is to the happiness of nations so long distracted that in future these truths should exercise their due influence over the destinies of man, will be received with much ardour and affection into this Holy Alliance.

Signed in Paris in the year of grace 1815 the 14 (26) September.

(Signed) François.
Frédéric-Guillaume.
Alexandre.

The above account, furnished by Empaytaz, receives confirmation from a statement made by M. Capefigue in his *Histoire de la Restauration*, to the effect that he had personally inspected the original of the treaty, written throughout in the hand of the Emperor Alexander, with corrections by Mme. de Krudener, by whom the word *Sainte-Alliance* was interpolated. It appears, however, at first sight to be partially contradicted by the version supplied by M. Alexandre Stourdza, the distinguished brother of Mme. de Krudener's correspondent, then acting as secretary to Alexander. He writes: "I was the first to copy and retouch the Act of the Holy Alliance, written throughout in pencil by the hand of the Emperor. I am ignorant as to whether Mme. de Krudener had any part either in the inspiration or the form of this memorable document; what I do know for certain is that it was in complete harmony with the thought and religious sentiment of Alexander. Outside these Christian principles every form of international fraternity will be but a phantom, and a sanguinary phantom." The apparent discrepancy between these two versions disappears if we assume that Alexander re-copied the work of his secretary, so as to possess a complete copy of the Proclamation written out in his own hand.

It is more difficult to reconcile the Russian Emperor's own account of the proceedings, as given three years later in a lengthy conversation which he held with the Prussian bishop Eylert during his visit to Potsdam in 1818. In this conversation, committed to paper by Eylert the moment he had left the Imperial presence, no mention whatever is made of Mme. de Krudener, and the whole original credit of the scheme is attributed to that most unimaginative and undemonstrative of monarchs, King Frederick William III. !

Few people (Alexander is reported to have said) have a true and correct idea of the Alliance; many have a quite inaccurate impression of it; whilst some even regard it with aversion, and do not hesitate to insinuate that it is inspired by some hidden selfish motive. This is what really happened. During the campaign of Lutzen, Dresden, and Bautzen, when the greatest heroism on the part of our troops did not save us from defeat, your king and I were forced into the conviction that mere human strength was of no avail, and that Germany was irretrievably lost, unless we were blessed by the special protection of Providence. In serious and thoughtful mood your king and I were riding silently side by side without even an escort. At length my truest of friends broke the silence by saying: "Things cannot go on like this. We are turning our faces eastwards, and we must and ought to be advancing westwards. With God's help we may yet succeed. If, however, as I trust, He blesses our combined efforts, let us acknowledge before the whole world that to Him alone is the honour due." We promised this solemnly to one another, and shook hands over it. Then followed the victories of Kulm, of Katzbach, of Grossbeeren, and of Leipsic; and when, in Paris, we had reached the end of our painful struggle, the King of Prussia called to

mind our holy resolve, of which he had been the originator, and
the noble Emperor of Austria, who shared in all our views, hopes,
and feelings, entered gladly into our association. The first idea
of the Holy Alliance was conceived in an hour of anxious
thought; it was realised in an hour of joy and gratitude. It
was in no way our work, but the work of God. Our divine
Redeemer Himself inspired all the thoughts that the Act contains, and all the principles that it proclaims. Whoever cannot
realise and understand this, and can see in it nothing but the
hidden designs of political ambition, should have no voice in the
matter; and it is quite superfluous to discuss the subject with
such people.[1]

In contradiction to this version comes the
positive statement made by the Grand - Duke
George of Mecklenburg-Strelitz, brother to Queen
Louise, and friend and confidant to Frederick
William, that Mme. de Krudener was alone responsible for the policy inaugurated by the Holy
Alliance. We can only account for the explanation volunteered by Alexander by the fact that
already in 1818, absence, and the cunning insinuations of courtiers, had to a large extent cured him
of his infatuation for Mme. de Krudener, to whom
consequently he was unwilling to acknowledge any
indebtedness, and, secondly, to his amiable, if somewhat misleading, characteristic of always saying
what was pleasant to the person with whom he was
in conversation.

Alexander's old tutor, César Laharpe, who
equally regretted both the evangelistic fervour and
the reactionary tendencies which marked the later

[1] See *Charakterzüge und historische Fragmente aus dem Leben des Königs
von Preussen Friedrich Wilhelm III.*, von Dr. R. Fr. Eylert, vol. ii. pp.
242-252.

years of the Emperor's reign, wrote, after the death of the latter, an apology for the Holy Alliance, which may be regarded as the unbiassed judgment of a philosophic yet sympathetic mind, equally removed from the bitter detraction of enemies and the extravagant adulation of friends.

Although intrepid in the midst of danger (he writes), Alexander held war in abhorrence. Fully realising the abuses which excited the discontent of nations, he hoped that in the course of a long peace the European governments, recognising the necessity of undertaking reforms demanded by the requirements of the century, would seriously set themselves to the task. To attain this object a profound tranquillity was necessary, and as the social revolutions of the previous thirty years seemed to have weakened the ancient ideas of order and submission, he hoped to make up the deficiency by a solemn appeal to religion. On the part of the monarch himself there is no doubt that this appeal was the outcome of a noble heart. . . . Indeed, at that moment, from north to south and from east to west, the eyes of all oppressed nations were turned towards Alexander I.; but from that moment also we must date the secret plotting which had for its object the destruction of that redoubtable moral power, which gave him as auxiliaries all the friends of learning and humanity, and the sympathies of all right-minded men. . . . Thanks to the unhappy turn which his enemies managed to give to the progress of international affairs, the confidence of the people was destroyed; and the magnanimous monarch, who had done so much to deserve it, saw his influence lost amidst the impious applause of his enemies, who dared to impute to his authority the most unpopular of the measures that they themselves had laboured to bring about.

The King of Prussia, as the natural ally of the Emperor of Russia, signed the Proclamation without hesitation. The Emperor of Austria followed suit, in spite of the objections and suspicions of

Metternich, to whose influence and secret machinations in the immediate future was primarily due the unhappy change in Alexander's political attitude. Louis XVIII. signed also at the simple request of the Tsar, not being in a position to refuse anything to the only friend France possessed amongst the sovereigns of Europe, and his example was quickly followed by most of the minor states—Denmark, Sweden, Holland, Würtemberg, Saxony, and Sardinia. The Ultramontane party, with De Maistre at its head, hailed the Alliance with delight, and Capo d'Istria, who was largely in the confidence of the Tsar, hoped to be able to turn it to the advantage of Greece, his native country. Alexander, who in his anxiety to see the matter firmly established, could not refrain from discussing the Proclamation with every one he met, received but one check in the course of his personal canvass for signatures. Castlereagh alone refused the signature of the Prince Regent to the document. It was contrary to the English constitution for a monarch to sign a treaty in the place of his plenipotentiaries, and grave complications were feared should the document be laid before Parliament for its approval. It is evident that neither Castlereagh nor Wellington regarded the Proclamation in a favourable light. The Foreign Secretary wrote to his political chief, Lord Liverpool (28th September), as follows :—

You will receive enclosed an autograph letter from the three allied sovereigns, addressed to the Prince Regent, which I have been desired to transmit. To explain the nature of this rather novel proceeding, I have obtained copies both of the letter and its enclosure. . . . I have to acquaint you that the measure entirely originated with the Emperor of Russia, whose mind has lately taken a deeply religious tinge. The first intimation I had of this extraordinary act was from the Emperor himself, who said he had communicated that morning to the Emperor of Austria his sentiments upon this subject, and he would speak to me further upon it in a few days. Prince Metternich the following day came to me with the project of the treaty, since signed. He told me in great confidence the difficulty in which the Emperor of Austria felt himself placed; that he felt great repugnance to be a party to such an act, and yet was more apprehensive of refusing himself to the Emperor's application; that it was quite clear his mind was affected. . . . In short, seeing no retreat, after making some verbal alterations, the Emperor of Austria agreed to sign it. The Emperor of Russia then carried it to the King of Prussia, who felt in the same manner, but came to the same conclusion. As soon as the instrument was executed between the sovereigns, without the intervention of their ministers, the Emperor brought it to me, and developed his whole plan of universal peace. . . . The Duke of Wellington happened to be with me when the Emperor called, and it was not without difficulty that we went through the interview with becoming gravity. . . . The fact is that the Emperor's mind is not completely sound. Last year there was but too much reason to fear its impulse would be to conquest and dominion. . . . He really appears to be in earnest. The Emperor told me that nothing had given him so much satisfaction as to affix his signature to this bond of peace in, he believed, the most irreligious capital in Europe.

Could Alexander have been enlightened as to the varying moods of reluctance, cynicism, and indifference in which the sovereigns of Europe had affixed their seals to the Proclamation of the Holy Alliance, his satisfaction would have been but short-lived. As it was, he left Paris in the early morning of 28th September 1815 on his homeward journey, buoyed up with hope and enthusiasm, and filled with generous plans for carrying out the teachings of his divine Master for the benefit of his own subjects. On the previous day he had taken an affectionate farewell of Mme. de Krudener, whose influence, destined to fade so soon under the test of absence, had remained paramount up to the very moment of parting. He warmly invited both her and her whole household to follow him without delay to St. Petersburg, there to take a share in his manifold schemes of religious and social reform, and left with her a passport, signed by his own hand, authorising her to travel to Russia by whatever route and at whatever date might best suit her convenience.

Thus came to an abrupt close the most striking and brilliant chapter in the life of our heroine. The plans of a speedy reunion at St. Petersburg were destined never to be realised. At the moment when the influence of Mme. de Krudener was deemed most irresistible, it had in reality ceased to be of any political import. Henceforth she will appear no more as the spiritual guide of queens and emperors, the confidante of duchesses and statesmen. The poor, the hungry, and the oppressed will henceforth absorb all her energies and sympathy. Persecuted, maligned, driven from place to place, often in positive need of food and shelter, she will continue her self-imposed apostolate to the peasantry of Switzerland and Germany, until sickness and disease and shattered nerves incapacitate her for further exertion. It will be impossible to follow her with accuracy through all the wanderings of these last nine years of her life; but her own letters, and the testimony of those who came in contact with her, will furnish a vivid picture of the self-sacrificing zeal with which she was inspired even to the very end.

CHAPTER XIV

THE Krudener household lingered for some weeks longer in Paris after the departure of the Emperor of Russia. The delay was principally occasioned by pecuniary embarrassments, which made it quite impossible for the moment to incur the very heavy expense of the long journey to Russia. Mme. de Krudener's boundless generosity, and her utter lack of business capacity, were continually landing herself and her family in a condition of positive penury, from which they were frequently rescued by the most unexpected means. In a letter written at a somewhat later date, the lady gives a few of her experiences at this period.

Whilst I was in Paris I required considerable sums to defray the very heavy expenses of my visit, being accompanied by so large a suite. Although I had lived very simply, you may imagine how it mounted up, with so many uninvited guests every day at my house! We learnt that the Emperor was on the point of departure. He told me so himself, and I quite expected to have to follow him immediately. We had no money; I turned at once to our beloved Saviour, telling Him there was nothing left, and the next day, or soon after, a stranger presented himself at the

door, and asked to be allowed to lodge in the house.   I had met
him once somewhere, and had been struck by him.   He heard
some one ask me to settle an account.   "Allow me," he said, "to
offer you a hundred and fifty gold louis."   They were immediately
paid down.   In the afternoon he placed four or five thousand
louis on my writing-table.   "They are entirely at your disposal,"
he said to me ; "make what use of them you please.   I thanked
him, but only accepted the hundred and fifty, which I still owe
him.   The larger sum lay for a long time on my table.   He did
not offer me anything further.   In the evening I related the
incident to the Emperor.

"Why did you not ask me ? " he replied.

Later on, after his departure, the Lord having made it clear
to us that we were to stay on in Paris, we found ourselves once
more, after a few weeks, in a critical position.

"To-morrow," declared the cook, "I shall not be able to cook
any more."

"Very well," replied Empaytaz, "then we will not eat any
more !"   But the merciful God did not allow us to be placed in
such straits.   The following day the banker from Carlsruhe arrived
with 5000 francs.   Thus it is that we are always led.

In complete indifference to matters of mere
personal comfort, and inspired by a lively faith in
the protecting hand of God, Mme. de Krudener
resolved on turning to no one but Him in moments
of want.   It must be remembered to her credit that
all through the four months of her almost daily
companionship with Alexander, she never once
petitioned him for a single tangible benefit either for
herself or her children.   More than that.   According
to Russian custom, M. de Krudener had obtained
the concession for a certain number of years of a
grant of territory as a reward for his services to the
State.   This concession passed to his widow and
children, and on the expiration of the specified term

it was customary to petition for a renewal, a request
which was never refused except for some very serious
reason. It so happened that the concession fell in
during the summer of 1815, but after making the
subject the matter of earnest prayer, Mme. de
Krudener resolved not to petition for its renewal,
but to allow the estate to pass into other hands.

It was 22nd October before Mme. de Krudener
bade a last farewell to the Paris she had loved so
long, and in which she had appeared with equal
success in so many different *rôles*, first as *mondaine*,
then as literary star, and finally as prophetess. Her
first halt was made at Binningen, in the canton of
Bâle, and here she was rejoined by a certain evangelistic worker, by name Kellner, who was to prove
one of her most active agents in her Swiss campaign.
In her present choice of a lieutenant Mme. de
Krudener was hardly more fortunate than in her
previous choice of Frederic Fontaine. Kellner, a
man of middle age, in person tall and haggard, with
strikingly black hair and a sanctimonious voice and
manner, persistently encouraged all that was most
exaggerated and sensational in the religious attitude
of his protectress, and more than once laid himself
open to charges of positive moral dishonesty. He
made a special feature in his preaching of the miracles
wrought by Mme. de Krudener, miracles related
with a marked absence of such details of time and
place as might have ensured their verification. With
her unsuspecting nature, however, the lady received
Kellner with enthusiasm into the family circle, and

the work of spreading the Gospel throughout the canton of Bâle was carried on with all dispatch. An interruption was caused by the visit of Baron Paul de Krudener, recently appointed Russian Minister to the Swiss Confederation, who persuaded his mother to allow herself to be carried off to Berne on a few days' visit to the Embassy. This natural and apparently harmless proceeding was regarded in official quarters as a confirmation of the rumours spread about as to the lady's influence at the Russian Court, all the more as her preachings were continued at her son's house, and attracted large crowds of curious hearers. The Berne police took alarm, the Austrian minister directed a protest to the Swiss authorities, and Mme. de Krudener was politely but firmly requested to curtail her stay in the canton of Berne. Thus was initiated that long course of petty persecution and police tyranny which was to turn the next three years of Mme. de Krudener's life into a ceaseless wandering from place to place, often during the severest weather, and under the most harassing circumstances.

Our heroine returned to Bâle, and took up her residence at the Hôtel du Sauvage in the town, together with the De Berckheims, Mme. Armand, Empaytaz, and Kellner. Her arrival made a great sensation in the locality, and the hotel was constantly besieged by a crowd of people, eager for a sight of the prophetess. In December, prayer-meetings, on the model of those held at the Hôtel Montchenu, were started every evening in Mme. de Krudener's salon, but the rush of visitors was so great that the meetings had to be transferred to the big drawing-room of the hotel. Even this did not suffice, and a second morning prayer-meeting had to be instituted for those who were more advanced in the religious life, whilst frequently it became necessary to throw open the windows of the salon, even in the bitterest winter weather, so that those might hear who had been unable to force their way into the room.

Indeed, the evangelistic labours of this little body of ardent workers soon began to bring forth the fruits of a religious revival throughout the town. Many young girls, who until the arrival of Mme. de Krudener had been noted for their frivolous love of dancing and dissipation, suddenly altered their mode of life, dressed in sober colours, frequented the prayer-meetings, and read their Bibles at home. It was reported that several Roman Catholics had been induced to relinquish their faith through the preaching of Empaytaz, and amongst these no less a person than the curé of Berne, M. Dolder; rumours which, if true, were sufficient to account for the hostile attitude adopted by the Catholic priests. Free-thinkers also were brought to repentance, and the conversion of M. Lachenal, professor of philosophy at the University of Bâle, who resigned his chair in order to devote himself the more completely to evangelistic work, made a profound sensation throughout the town. The religious excitement began to spread to other cantons, and from Berne, Aargau, and Schaffhausen, people poured by hundreds into Bâle in the hope of taking part in the praying and hymn-singing, which formed so large a proportion of the religious services.

But if many were attracted by the preaching of Mme. de Krudener, many more took up a position of uncompromising hostility to this new religious development in their midst. The authorities, both civil and spiritual, eyed the proceedings at the Hôtel du Sauvage with grave disapproval, though without at first seeing their way to adopting repressive measures towards one who had been so recently distinguished by the friendship of the Emperor Alexander. The passports signed by the Imperial hand made it difficult to expel the party merely on the ground of their foreign nationality. Whilst the authorities were hesitating, sermons were preached from the pulpits of Bâle condemning the doctrines disseminated by the Krudener party, and soon every sort of calumny and misrepresentation regarding them was spread about the town. Thus, Mme. de Krudener having held forth eloquently on the iniquity of worldly and loveless marriages, it was reported that she had advocated the abolition of the marriage tie. Caricatures purporting to represent the proceedings at the Hôtel du Sauvage were distributed about the town, in the hope of turning the whole movement into ridicule. In one of these, not devoid of skill, Mme. de Krudener is represented on a barrel in the midst of the Place de la Fontaine, surrounded by delighted servant-maids, to whom she is supposed to be addressing the following words :

"A time will come when your masters will go themselves to wash the vegetables and to fetch water
from the well, and when all servant-girls will walk
about in silk dresses!" More than once the meetings were invaded by angry bands of opponents, and
the public peace was in danger of being disturbed.
These occurrences, combined with the undoubted
practical inconvenience of the daily block in the
street around the hotel, and the sudden influx into
the town of large numbers of poor people, attracted
by the rumours of Mme. de Krudener's open-handed
charity, so worked on the official minds of the city
magistrates that they finally resolved to suppress
the meetings.

On 16th January Empaytaz was summoned before
the Mayor, M. Ehinger, to answer certain interroga-
tions concerning the objects of the prayer-meetings.

"M. le Bourgmestre," said Empaytaz, "I am
quite prepared to submit to the authorities; the
word of God teaches me to do so. As for the
bourgeoisie, I know nothing whatever of their relations with the government. The gospel I preach
is the gospel of peace, of love, and of holiness. . . ."

" But you occasion divisions in families."

" How so, sir? pray explain yourself."

" Yes, our young people are giving up balls and
all the pleasures of society. This really cannot
go on."

After some further argument as to the necessity
of prayer, the Mayor brought the interview to an end
by reaffirming the decision of the authorities to put

a stop to the meetings. Accordingly, that same evening, when the usual congregation began to assemble, the people were informed that no prayer-meeting would be held, and Mme. de Krudener and her friends retired quietly into their rooms. As a result an excited crowd blocked the whole street below the hotel windows until a late hour, and a serious disturbance was with difficulty prevented.

The following day Mme. de Krudener and Empaytaz sought a second interview with the Mayor, and made an eloquent appeal to his sense of justice and of religious toleration. The only reply was that they must prepare to leave the town at once. As usual, an absolute want of means weighed upon Mme. de Krudener in addition to all the other embarrassments of her situation.

I owed a hundred and twenty-five louis for our hotel bill (she writes to a friend), and I had no idea where the sum was to come from. Feeling in my heart that my creditor was impatient, I addressed our Saviour one morning, and said, " Dear Lord, Thou knowest very well that I am helpless in this matter, and that I do not know where to turn ; Thou teachest me always to let myself be led as a little child, who troubles about nothing, and surrenders himself to Thy will." The very same day some one came to me privately and said : " I have been requested by some one, whose name I am not at liberty to mention, to offer you a hundred and twenty-five louis, or a thousand florins, which he begs you to accept without interest for six months, as he knows you are in want of money." I did not accept the last clause, but I felt that we were saved by this miracle of charity. That is the sort of thing that constantly happens to me, and that is why I dare do nothing of myself.

The decision as to a place of refuge was arrived at

in almost as miraculous a manner, and is related in the same letter. Touched by the entreaties of her friends at Bâle, Mme. de Krudener was seeking for some place of retreat across the frontier of Baden.

I was praying, and I said to our Lord: "Tell me, dear Lord, if Thou wishest me to go to Grenzach-Horn." At that very instant Juliette came into the room and said: "Here is the owner of the little house." It was a pious old Christian, living close to Grenzach-Horn, who, hearing that we were obliged to leave Bâle, enjoyed no rest during the whole day because of an inward voice that kept repeating: "Go and lend your cottage to these people." So he had come to fetch us. He is a veritable angel from God, and we are very happy over it.

The house in question, known as the Hoernlein, and charmingly situated on the banks of the Rhine, consisted of but three small rooms and a kitchen. In the way of furniture it could only boast of a bedstead, a chair, and a table in each room. Such as it was, however, it was to be the headquarters of the Krudener party for over a year. Mme. de Krudener, Mme. Armand, and M. Empaytaz were the first occupants, and the two ladies had soon made the place inhabitable. Mme. de Krudener was enchanted with the simplicity of her surroundings; she insisted on doing her share of the housework, put up curtains to the room which was to serve her both as salon and sleeping apartment, dignified a plain wooden bench with the name of a sofa, and prepared to do the honours of her humble abode to the surrounding peasantry with the same gracious charm of manner which had distinguished her in the palaces of the rich. In the meanwhile the De Berckheims remained in Bâle, to watch over the interests of the party, and every morning sent their servant to the Hoernlein with provisions for the day.

Whilst Mme. de Krudener was thus enjoying to the full a short interval of much-needed rest in her village retreat, her enemies were diligently spreading the most calumnious reports concerning her all over Europe, with the express purpose of injuring her reputation in the eyes of the Emperor Alexander. Unfortunately, at this juncture, an event occurred which gave some colour to their misrepresentations. It will be remembered how Frederic Fontaine and Maria Kummrin precipitately left Paris on the refusal of Alexander to lend himself to their mercenary schemes. The minister and his satellite retired to Rappenhoff, in Würtemberg, the property purchased by Mme. de Krudener for the purpose of founding a Christian colony. Here Fontaine appears to have thrown off all pretence of leading a higher life, plunged recklessly into debt, and in various ways gave cause for serious scandal. Fortunately, the Würtemberg authorities, who had always regarded his presence with suspicion, interfered promptly in the matter ; Fontaine was arrested and ordered to leave the country without delay, whilst the property of Rappenhoff was sequestrated for the payment of his debts. It was impossible for Mme. de Krudener to entirely dissociate herself from the unfortunate results of her misplaced confidence ; moreover, it was artfully represented by her enemies to the Emperor of Russia that he too was implicated in the general scandal; and in this manner, favoured by the natural effect of separation, were sown the seeds of coldness and suspicion which were soon to replace the feelings of devotion and reverence with which Alexander had previously regarded his Egeria. The trial was a severe one for Mme. de Krudener, both in its moral and its material aspect; but she appears to have borne it with her customary sweetness and resignation. She herself refers to the subject in the following letter, written from the Hoernlein to her step-daugher, Mme. Ochando:—

. . . It is very painful to be humbled, especially on one's sensitive side.' I am perhaps more sensitive than others, and I have gone through things of which you can have no idea. I say to myself at such times: Who would not have gone through such a period of grace, when we reach eternity, where nothing is of any value but that which we suffered in order to follow our adorable Master! All is grace; it is Jesus Himself who helps us in these struggles, and makes us pass through these deaths.

We deserve nothing. He has given us all things through His blood and His sufferings. But if we wish to merit the joys of Heaven, and if we wish to work in this world, as in another world, like faithful supporters of Christ, if even we wish to be happy and to enjoy the presence of saints and of angels, ought we not to be cleansed from our infirmities, and be filled with that life of Christ which alone can render this world bearable?' Well, then, humility, the sacrifice of our will and of all that is worldly in us, demands for its accomplishment painful positions.

Worldly people have to bear it also, as the natural consequence of their faults, but they are without the boundless consolations and the actual joys which we receive from the Cross, when Christ helps us to carry it. What hidden misery, more acute than anything we can imagine, may be suffered by those very persons whom the world regards as happy!

15th March.

I began this letter a fortnight ago, dear Sophie, and have been unable to finish it; often I have not a moment to myself, people follow one another so closely. Pray for me, who have so little time to pray for myself. Juliette wrote you a long letter yesterday, and told you that we are only awaiting the moment when we shall have received Divine direction in order to rejoin you. He will also send us the means, for at the present moment we do not possess twelve kreutzers. Nevertheless, we are very happy. I borrow for the poor, and I do not even dare to pray any longer for our necessities. I lay our circumstances before the Lord, and things invariably turn out right. In the meanwhile I ask Him to prepare me for that entire destitution, without which one cannot really follow Christ, who, being Lord of heaven and earth, lived in poverty among men; but for the rest let us be what God destines us to be; it is possible to be poor even under an imperial crown.

We gather from the above extracts that Mme. de Krudener had not long been left in the quiet enjoyment of her rural retreat. Soon the little cottage of the Hoernlein became the rallying-place for all the poor and afflicted and hungry of the district. Before many weeks were passed, the whole day was occupied in tending the sick and weary, giving out soup to the hungry, and preaching the word of God to all. In the month of March the crowd was largely increased by the commencement of the yearly pilgrimages to the popular shrine of Our Lady of Hermits at Einsiedeln—the road to which lay past the door of the Hoernlein. Many of the pilgrims made a temporary halt for the purpose of listening to the eloquent exhortations to repentance and the love of God, addressed to them with such winning earnestness in their own tongue by the foreign lady, who almost invariably followed up her preaching with some more material form of help.

By this time the little party at the cottage had been reinforced by the arrival of M. and Mme. de Berckheim, their servant Fanchette, and old Mme. Empaytaz, the mother of the minister ; all of whom, undeterred by the smallness of the accommodation at her disposal, Mme. de Krudener had cordially pressed to pay her a long visit. It is surely an emphatic proof of the relations of mutual affection and confidence which reigned between the various members of the little community, that they should have joyfully consented to occupy such very inadequate quarters. De Berckheim and Empaytaz stowed themselves away in an adjacent hay-loft, thus leaving the three little bedrooms at the disposal of the ladies of the party.

In order in any way to appreciate the depth of poverty and suffering with which Mme. de Krudener came in hourly contact during the period of her evangelistic labours in Switzerland and Baden, it must be remembered that Europe was just emerging from the horrors of a most prolonged and sanguinary war. The loss by death or injury of so many thousands of bread-winners ; the taking away by conscription of all the able-bodied young men of the villages, with the consequent disruption of all ordinary conditions of labour ; the wholesale destruction of property which inevitably followed in the wake of an invading army ; the frequent absence of those whose business it was to till the ground, or to gather in the harvest when it was ripe ; the grinding oppression of forced loans and redoubled taxation, had produced an amount of abject misery amongst the peasantry of Europe of which the English nation, in spite of all sacrifices and losses, had no experience. What might otherwise appear as exaggerated or sensational in Mme. de Krudener's letters and discourses at this period, becomes, in the light of history, but the natural response of a highly-strung and sensitive organisation in continuous contact with a gigantic evil. The relief that Mme. de Krudener could afford, even with exceptional means at her disposal, was but as a drop in the ocean of surrounding destitution ; and it is little wonder that she shrank back as from a sin from the smallest act of self-indulgence, in the presence of the half-starved men and women who daily clustered round the door of the Hoernlein. Thus when Queen Hortense, as a small token of her continued affection and regard, begged Mme. de Krudener to accept of a lace veil, the gift was gratefully but firmly refused.

Beg her to forgive me (writes the prophetess to her old friend Mdlle. Cochelet) if I decline to accept it. I have renounced all the vanities of this world, and never wear any lace. If I had it, I should immediately sell it for the benefit of the poor creatures whose sufferings grieve me each day. For the last few years my daughter and I have worn nothing but the very simplest clothes ; we still possess some beautiful pearls and diamonds, whilst others of great value have already been sold. I am grieved also at the thought of quantities of fur cloaks, etc., which are getting spoilt, and which ought to bring in considerable sums, were it possible to sell them. . . . All luxury must disappear from the lives of those who preach poverty.

To another friend she writes as follows :—

HOERNLEIN, *March* 1816.

I have very few moments to myself, so that I can hardly write, much as I long to do so. The concourse of people is so great that whole villages pass by us. I preach the Gospel to them; I invite them to come to Christ, who shed His blood for them; I invite them to repentance and to hope. I, as well as those who are with me, give them books, which remind them of their salvation. Many children come to seek me; what tears! what sorrows! what misery! No one has any idea of the poverty of Baden. God in His mercy grants us the means to give an alms to every one. It is impossible to give much, but we manage a little, such as soup to the invalids and to the tired travellers. . . . The longer I live, the more I see how happy one is to be freed from all worldly bonds. The heroic courage which the living God, which Jesus Christ alone can give to His disciples, makes it possible to face and accomplish everything. How often I used to say in Paris, "I can realise nothing beyond charity; for me political parties do not exist; I preach the Gospel; I know nothing of the hatreds and interests of the world." Thank God, I have abandoned that arena, and thus it is that I have had the happiness of seeing conversions which have startled many people.

A short interruption to the work at the Hoern-lein was occasioned by two English ladies, who persuaded Mme. de Krudener to accompany them to Aarau, with the double object of procuring for her a few days of much-needed change and rest, and of introducing her to the great Pestalozzi, then quite an old man. "I have had the pleasure," writes Mme. de Krudener, "which had been previously announced to me by our Saviour, of seeing Pesta-lozzi, who was an angel of charity, but not a con-vinced Christian; he had not as yet given his heart entirely to Jesus Christ." Pestalozzi was so touched by the prayers and exhortations of Mme. de Krudener, that before resuming his journey he burst into tears, and declared that the day they had spent together was the happiest of his life.

A great reception awaited Mme. de Krudener at Aarau, whither she was accompanied by Empaytaz, Kellner, and a worthy Alsatian peasant, Jaeger by name, who for many years had devoted himself to itinerant preaching, and who had recently joined the household at the Hoernlein. Daily prayer-meetings were immediately organised, and were attended by an ever-increasing concourse of people, Catholics and Protestants arriving side by side, with the full approbation of their respective pastors. On Sundays Mme. de Krudener was obliged to preach several times, young girls and children especially crowding round to listen to the simple yet forcible words in which she entreated them to turn their hearts to God, and to walk in His ways. Her personal influence over these simple-minded people seems to have been boundless. She herself writes on this subject :—

God inspires every one with so great an attraction towards me, with so strong a desire to open their hearts, to ask my advice, to confide in me their troubles, in a word, with so great a love, that it is not surprising that the authorities, who are ignorant of the immense power the Lord confers on those who labour solely for His glory, and for the welfare of their fellows, should be mystified by it. . . . Pray for me that I may be faithful to so many graces. The Lord has granted my earnest desire to win souls to Him, which has inspired me ever since the date of my own conversion.

As at Bâle, so at Aarau ; the police began to take alarm at the vast crowds that assembled daily for the prayer-meetings, and in spite of the personal intervention of both the Catholic priests and the Protestant ministers, it was resolved to suppress the meetings. Mme. de Krudener accordingly left the house, and accepted an invitation to spend a few weeks with a Mme. de Diesbach at the castle of Liebegg. Here the same wonderful scenes were enacted. The whole countryside flocked to the castle; continuous prayer-meetings were kept up during the day in a vast barn on the property, and were attended by thousands of men, women, and children, who were restrained neither by distance nor by wet weather.

It was June before Mme. de Krudener was able to rejoin the De Berckheims at the Hoernlein. Here summer had brought no relief to the impoverished and starving peasantry. Rain had fallen continuously for nearly three months; corn lay rotting in the fields; the vineyards gave no hope of a good crop, and the price of bread had risen to fivepence the pound. Mme. de Krudener devoted herself with greater zeal than before to the task of feeding the wretched population; what remained of her diamonds and other jewellery was hastily sold, and all remittances from Russia were unhesitatingly sacrificed for the same purpose. As the autumn advanced, literally thousands were fed every day at the Hoernlein, and the concourse of beggars, idlers, invalids, helpless women and children who remained gathered together in consequence of this open-handed generosity along the Swiss-Baden frontier, was so great that the serious disapproval of both governments was once more excited, and the local papers were full of calumnious and injurious reports concerning the real objects of the mission.

It was this indiscriminate and reckless alms-giving which specially roused the indignation of Mme. de Krudener's critics ; but it must be remembered in her favour that she dealt with a period of exceptional and wide-spread distress, when any hard-and-fast rule of investigation becomes utterly impracticable. No doubt she would have held up her hands in pious horror at the principles of political economy so much in vogue in England during the present century, by which all gratuitous charity is condemned as pauperising, and the theory of the survival of the fittest is put into practice as far as the conscience of a professedly Christian nation will allow. But Mme. de Krudener would not have been alone of her opinion even at the present day, and the balance of judgment ought surely to be turned in her favour by the fact, that she at least practised the principles that she preached, and that this refined and delicate woman, reared in all the luxury of Paris and St. Petersburg, voluntarily elected to live off black bread and potatoes, to wear coarse clothing and occupy a humble peasant's cottage, in order to provide the beggars who passed her door with a daily meal of soup. She herself replied to her accusers in all simplicity as follows :—

I seek nobody; I desire to live in the most absolute seclusion. It is the people who come to me. Can I drive away the starving poor, the destitute orphan, the distraught and sin-laden soul?   I say to myself: What would our Lord have done under similar circumstances?   The answer is clear, and I act accordingly, as far as my strength will permit.   I trust I may be pardoned the only ambition of which I am yet guilty, that of wishing to imitate my Saviour.

In the curious dearth of contemporary English opinion regarding our heroine, the following extract from the diary of William Allen, who paid a visit to the Hoernlein in the summer of 1816, whilst on a tour of inspection to the Quaker centres on the continent, will be read with interest.

The Baroness has a temporary residence in a poor little house.   We found her taking tea or coffee in a small room with a bed in it.   There were present three men and three women besides our party; one an interesting looking man, a counsellor of state, with his wife;[1] another, a young man of very agreeable manners, who wore a black cross suspended from his neck;[2] and the third, an older man,[3] who, I was informed, was one of her followers; the last-named person had that morning preached to three or four thousand persons in the open air.

The Baroness was dressed in white, with a plain cap; she is an elderly person, rather tall and thin, has a good deal of vivacity of manner, spoke French fluently, and talked to us standing.   She said she felt more happiness in that poor place than she had enjoyed while surrounded with grandeur; that if we were doing the Lord's work, it mattered little where we were; that the present were no common times, but that the Lord had a great work in the earth; that there had been a great number of conversions, especially amongst the poor, but many also amongst the rich; that we had nothing to do but to come to Christ in sincerity of heart, and be anything, or nothing, as He pleases.

She said the work of religion consists in prayer and silence· On being asked whether she intended to go to Paris again, she

---

[1] M. and Mme. Laroche.   [2] Empaytaz.   [3] Jaeger.

said she knew nothing about it; that she was in the hand of the Lord, and at His disposal.

She mentioned that some had attributed to her the Holy Alliance, but that it was a great mistake, for it was the Lord only who had inspired it. She holds meetings every evening for prayer, which are crowded; she speaks with much energy, and I should have had more conversation with her if there had not been so many present. Spittler said she gave away almost all her income to the poor, but that it was done without sufficient discrimination; that their place being on the frontier of three states, many foreign poor came to it, and that the war had caused much distress." [1]

---

[1] See *Life of William Allen, with Selections from his Correspondence*, vol. i. p. 281.

CHAPTER XV

1816-1817

WITH the view of reducing to some extent the pressure of work on the occupants of the Hoernlein, and also of allowing Mme. de Berckheim to dwell once more under the same roof with her mother, Professor Lachenal generously placed his country house of Unterholtz, in the canton of Bâle, at the disposal of his friends, as a centre for evangelistic and philanthropic work. In the autumn of 1816 several members of the party took up their residence there, by which some slight measure of peace and comfort was restored to the Hoernlein. But for Mme. de Krudener herself there was no rest; her zeal, her charity, her self-sacrificing love of humanity, seemed to increase week by week. On one occasion a wretched woman entered the cottage in the last stage of destitution, and with the whole of the lower part of her face eaten away by cancer, the open wounds only half hidden by the old rags with which her head was bound up. Even her companions in poverty turned from the sight in disgust. Mme. de Krudener, not content with receiving the poor sufferer with her habitual sweetness of welcome, bent forward and kissed her. Juliette, filled with terror of infection, affectionately reproved her mother for her imprudence.

"Dearest Juliette, do not scold me," was the reply. "Only think for how many years this poor woman has been received everywhere with expressions of disgust and repulsion. Surely it was time she should know that Christians love one another."

Although it might have been supposed that the accommodation of the cottage was barely sufficient for its rightful occupants, both here and at Unterholtz a large number of destitute and sick poor were temporarily housed to be nursed and doctored into health, and to allow of greater facilities for their spiritual conversion. It was Mme. de Krudener's joy to perform the most menial services for her poor invalids. Her only happiness lay in reducing the sum of their misery, so that when the date of her birthday (21st November) came round, her friends could think of no better way of celebrating the event than by giving her presents of beans, lentils, bread, clothing, etc., which she could distribute amongst her precious charges. Mme. de Krudener was overjoyed at the thought that for a few days at least she could dole out her charity with an unstinting hand. About this time she wrote to her old friend Mdlle. Cochelet a letter describing her way of life, full of assurances of undiminished affection :—

DEAR CHILD—I am very far from having forgotten you; I think of you with an interest which you yourself do not suspect for a moment; in a word, I love you. But if you knew my life, the hundreds of suffering and wretched creatures who require my attention; the misery, the unhappiness, and the despair, which in a thousand forms, the hideous results of sin, cover the country with ruin and desolation, and are but the beginning of the just and terrible punishments by which an infinite love attempts to save that which it is yet possible to save, you would not be surprised by my silence.

You would find both me and my daughter busy in listening to the secret sorrows of the soul, in consoling, in leading despair back to the foot of the Cross, in carrying clothing and assistance and food to the unhappy creatures who besiege my door; for everywhere there is a dearth of work. We have to quiet both their hunger and their misery; the only way is to tell them to live by prayer and repentance and hope, to cleanse themselves in the blood of the Redemption and at the feet of the Saviour. . . . Oh, my dear friend! when I have a moment to myself, do you not see that I too feel the necessity of prostrating myself before the God of my soul, of imploring Him to guide and fortify me, to give me courage and patience and fidelity, and the accents of that love which the Gospel requires? Almost every one grows discouraged. People who do not know as well as I do the duties of charity, which I myself have as yet learned so imperfectly, bear me a grudge; those envious of the Cross tear me in pieces; the blind, who can see nothing beyond their own passions, accuse me of political aspirations. Those who do not love truth, fear my influence; those who are aware of the power of ridicule, and who, in the world, know only the emptiness of the conceptions of the world, try to reach me by ridicule.

Tell me, my child, in passing through all this, in steering my course through such a stormy sea, what would become of my weakness, my incapacity, and my human frailty? What would become of them in the midst of the most violent struggles, and of distractions of soul which make me suffer through the sorrows of others, and through the injustice of those who ought to know me best? What would become of me without prayer, if I did not seek for help and strength from Him who died on a cross of shame to expiate our sins, who loves us so deeply, and who summons all those who wish to love Him to follow in His foot-steps, to suffer, to love, to wrestle by prayers and tears, and to bless those that persecute them?

Therefore, my child, I try to secure a few moments for prayer, of which I stand in such great need, and I see lying round me letters from all over Europe. What am I to do? How am I to answer them? Do not condemn me; believe that I love you; I do not excuse myself, for I might be more regular, but you are willing to forgive me. . . . I leave my letter as it is; I have had to break off several times; will you be able to read it? Are you back again in Munich? Do not imagine that our angelic Emperor Alexander was vexed at seeing you at my house in Paris; it is all nonsense. I have heard nothing from him, and I am not surprised that people should attempt to injure me; but as I am resolved to love Christ my God before all things, everything else is of little import; the Lord always causes truth to prevail.

When, in the course of the winter, Mme. de Krudener went to stay with Professor Lachenal at Unterholtz, the Bâle authorities placed a gendarme at the door of the house to prevent the prophetess from addressing the crowds that assembled to hear her, whilst permitting the distribution of food and clothing. On hearing of these repressive measures the Baden police determined to follow suit at Grenzach - Horn, and accordingly stationed two gendarmes at the Hoernlein, at the expense of the occupants, with strict orders to prevent the assem-bling of any crowds. These men were changed every day, and fulfilled their duties with much rudeness and brutality. Whenever Mme. de Krudener was at the Hoernlein, relates Eynard, she invariably had a kind word for them, and often she experienced the

joy of bringing them to a better frame of mind, and
even of persuading them to second her in her charitable labours. The authorities were much annoyed
at these proceedings, reprimanded the men, and
determined to send those who would not succumb
to the lady's eloquence. Their choice fell on a
corporal well known throughout the district for his
roughness and violence of temper. The occupants
of the Hoernlein were filled with apprehensions on
receiving the news of his appointment; Mme. de
Krudener alone preserved her habitual composure,
and on hearing of the arrival of the enemy, went
straight down to confront him. She found him
swearing terribly and driving away the beggars with
blows from his sabre. She touched him on the
shoulder, and asked in her gentle voice :

"What are you doing, my friend ? Do you not
know that this is the place where all the gendarmes
get converted ? "

The man remaining dumb with surprise at this
unexpected salutation, she continued with increasing
gravity :

" I see you have many sins to reproach yourself
with, mortal sins, terrible misdeeds. Do not add
to all the other burdens on your conscience that of
driving away these poor famished people from their
mother. I implore you to leave all evil deeds to
the spirits of darkness. As for you, you have a soul
to save, and that ought to be saved. Oh, my dear
friend, listen, I implore you—listen to the voice of
a woman who has also been a great sinner ! She

has come to tell you what perhaps you have never been told before : That Jesus is the friend of sinners and of evildoers. He has come to seek and to save that which is lost. It is for you, too, that His blood flowed on Calvary. He calls you, He stretches out His arms to you, He opens His heart to you, He desires to forgive you all your sins, without any exception. Let yourself be loved by the God who has come Himself to seek you, as you would not turn to Him of yourself."

The gendarme could find no words in reply ; tears streamed down his cheeks, and he turned away to hide his emotion.

"Come, dear friend," continued Mme. de Krudener, "we will read the word of God and pray for His poor. Come with me ; you shall pray, too, and your soul will be blessed."

The man obeyed, and from that time forth the inhabitants of the Hoernlein had nothing but praise for the manner in which he discharged his duties, attending to the wants of the pilgrims with patience and gentleness, and maintaining the most perfect order.

Many more examples of remarkable conversions are recorded of this period, but the fame of them only served to confirm the disapproval and suspicions of the authorities. At the same time the German and Swiss papers were full of violent and prejudiced attacks on Mme. de Krudener and her friends, and the rough and criminal element amongst the neighbouring peasantry began to take advantage

of the openly expressed enmity of the police, to
inflict constant annoyance on the inhabitants both
of the Hoernlein and of Unterholtz. Under the
false impression that any one so generous as Mme.
de Krudener must have an unlimited supply of gold
in her possession, a gang of robbers formed the
design of looting the house of M. Lachenal. On
12th December, at the hour of the daily distribution of soup and bread, several of these men forced
their way into the house, but were fortunately over-
heard and captured by some of the occupants. On
being led into the presence of Mme. de Krudener
and Kellner, their hearts were deeply touched by
the words of gentle reproof and affectionate exhortation with which they were received. Far from
handing over the would-be robbers to the police,
Mme. de Krudener contented herself with making
an eloquent appeal to their better natures, and
before dismissing them, held out her hand to each
in turn. One of them drew back, explaining that
he was suffering from some infectious skin disease.

"Never mind that, my friend," was the answer;
"we are not afraid of anything here."

Early in the New Year (1817) the Bâle and the
Baden authorities decided in concert on the adoption
of more stringent measures. Domiciliary visits
were paid both to Unterholtz and the Hoernlein,
and all the sick and destitute who had been given
shelter were forced to quit. The indignation excited
by these despotic measures resulted in so enormous
a crowd collecting for the service on 26th January,

that the meetings had to be held in the open air, many people climbing the surrounding trees in order to have a better view of the proceedings. Both Kellner and Mme. de Krudener addressed the crowd at length, and the scene was so remarkable that sketches of it appeared in many German publications.

On 1st February, with a view to preventing a repetition of the previous demonstration, a cordon of gendarmes surrounded the Hoernlein, and once more drove out all those who had taken refuge in the cottage. No less than thirty-three patients had been admitted since the last police raid, and all these, together with the two doctors in attendance, were forced to leave without delay. A few days later a similar manœuvre was executed by the Bâle police at Unterholtz, where Mme. de Krudener was staying at the time, and Empaytaz himself received orders to quit the country forthwith. He took refuge with his mother at the Hoernlein, whilst Mme. de Krudener, the De Berckheims, Mme. Armand, and Kellner were allowed to remain under the roof of M. Lachenal. But in both places the occupants were practically under arrest, the police being stationed round the house with orders to prevent the approach of strangers or the holding of prayer-meetings.

The unexpected leisure thus imposed on Mme. de Krudener enabled her to devote her energies to the composition of a lengthy and eloquent letter to the Baron de Berckheim, brother to Juliette's husband, and Minister of the Interior at the Court of Carlsruhe, in which she defended herself against the many calumnious accusations which were current concerning her, and explained the true basis of her actions.   Space will not permit of the reproduction of the document in its entirety, but the following extracts will amply indicate the line of argument pursued, and will convince the reader that the authoress of *Valérie* had lost nothing of her old literary skill in the midst of her new interests.

GRENZACH-HORN, 14*th February* 1817.

SIR—Seeing myself publicly accused of having resisted the authorities, which would be contrary to the spirit of peace and submission that I preach to every one, and that forms the basis of my conduct, I find myself forced, for the first time, to break the silence I have always maintained in the midst of the injustice, the outrages, and the persecution of which I am the object, and which our Lord gives me the grace to endure with patience, and even with joy.   I therefore declare that I have in no way wished to oppose the authorities, in so far as the authorities by their acts have not been in contradiction to commandments which demand far greater respect than theirs, and for which I must be ready to give my life, inasmuch as they come from God.   Thus, in spite of the magistrate's order forbidding me to give hospitality to any one, either in my own house or in the rooms I had hired in the neighbourhood, and where, in the early part of my stay, I had been allowed to receive people, it would have been impossible for me on many occasions to obey such orders without being guilty of wrong-doing.

If, sir, you were aware of the calamities which afflict this country, you would easily realise my position.   Judge for yourself, and tell me whether in these times of desolation, when thousands are wandering about without food or work, when mothers, exhausted with hunger and misery, arrive at my door, and lay their poor children at my feet, telling me of the terrible temptations that beset them, and pointing to the Rhine in their dark despair—tell me, I repeat, whether I am to refuse them shelter. . . . How am I to send away people who have come expressly to see me, or who arrive so late in the day that it is impossible for them to go any farther? Moreover, sir, as you already know, it is impossible to receive any one in your country, except by official permission, without incurring a heavy fine. When I was able to do so, and it was not too late, I always asked for the permit, but very often the distance made it impossible to do so. . . .

Another complaint of the Government is that I did not send away those who revealed to me the anguish of their hearts, and begged me to pray with them, and that I did not send them to their own ministers; but frequently they came from a great distance, or from other countries; sometimes they were sent by the ministers themselves; or they were in great trouble, affected by remorse, a prey to the most terrible despair. At other times they were people who had no minister, and who did not go to church because they were not converted, or because they were too poor, and did not dare present themselves in their shabby clothes, which happens oftener than may be supposed in Protestant parishes. I have also had Jews, struck by the beauties of the Gospel, and, finally, priests and clergymen themselves, with whom I have prayed.

Being accustomed for many years to have people of every rank in life disclose to me the deepest recesses of their hearts, having repeatedly sent to Catholic priests those who for a long time had kept away from confession, how could I have dared to reject that torrent of souls whom I have seen pass by in this neighbourhood? It was not I who summoned them; it is our Saviour alone who can bestow both strength and grace. He alone can perform the miracle of conversion, and to effect it He makes use of what instrument He pleases. . . .

It is at the foot of that Cross, monsieur, that I learnt to smite my breast, and to love Christ. I listened to that voice which can make suns grow dim, and yet does not refuse to descend into the heart of man. How could I have resisted it? I shed tears over the sin of my ingratitude, for I had not yet loved our Lord God, who only created the earth and mankind that they might be manifestations of His love. From that time I had no other thought than His glory, no other need than His love. . . . After that, whether people be scandalised or not that the Lord should do great things by means of a woman, whether she be immoderately hated, or accused of being loved too much, it is of no consequence whatever. That woman prays for those of whom it is said that, "Whosoever shall cause one of these little ones that believe on me to stumble, it were better for him if a great millstone were hanged about his neck, and he were cast into the sea." She says that to love is the great magic which nothing in the long run can resist, and that the very highest power consists in believing in these words: "Whatsoever ye shall ask in my name, that ye shall receive." Yes, I possess all things, for I possess the heart of my God. When, six months ago, wishing to obey the orders of the Baden authorities, who forbade the meetings which various disciples of Christ used to hold at my house, I made every effort to hide myself on those particular days in various country cottages, crowds of people found me out, in spite of my extreme desire to enjoy a little rest.

It is, then, for God Almighty to command, and for the creature to obey. It is He who will explain why the weak voice of a woman has resounded before nations, has caused the knees of so many scoffers to bend at the name of Jesus Christ, has restrained the arm of ruffians, has caused bitter despair to shed tears, has prayed for and obtained at the foot of the Cross what was necessary to feed thousands upon thousands of starving people, as in the desert, and has preached to five-and-twenty thousand persons in these countries alone, on the boundless charity of a merciful God, who offers in His heart a refuge for the destitute whom governments and men reject and abandon.

He also knew, I suppose, what need there was for a mother to take charge of the orphans, and to weep with the mothers; for a woman educated in the lap of luxury to tell the poor that she was far more happy waiting on them, on a wooden bench; He knew the need of a woman, humbled by her sins and her errors, to confess that she had been the slave and the dupe of earthly vanities; one who would despise nobody; a simple-minded woman, not blinded by false science, who could confound the wise by showing them that she had learnt the most profound secrets by loving and by weeping at the foot of the Cross. He required a courageous woman, who, having possessed all things on earth, could say, even to kings, that everything is as nothing, and could thus dethrone the prestige and the idols of drawing-rooms, whilst blushing that she had herself wished to shine by the aid of a few miserable talents and a little wit.

I think I need no longer justify myself for having fed the poor, although the officials at Loerrach affirm that I should not have done so.

In another century I should not have been under the necessity of defending myself, and in the Middle Ages, which mystify the philosophers, and which they regard as .so unenlightened, Catherine of Siena, to whom certainly I have not the audacity to compare myself, but who preached to whole convents, and who also saw torrents of souls being converted around her, and craving her prayers, was not obliged to defend her actions, nor was she driven into exile.

Of what profit is our so-called enlightenment and our liberal ideas, if we no longer dare to feed the poor, nor to clothe him, nor to house him, nor to defend his rights, nor to console him with the Gospel in our hands? . . .

I also wish to remark, monsieur, that it is a disgraceful falsehood of the newspapers to talk of idle vagabonds at a time when no one has any work to do, and when thousands come and implore me to give them work ; when all the factories are closed in consequence of the punishments inflicted on cupidity and selfishness, which teach men to seek the Lord and to confide in no one but Him. Far from hearing of robberies as the papers declare, the only wonder is that the whole country is not given up to brigandage.

No, monsieur, far from encouraging idleness, I have reproached that wealthy town of Bâle that hates me, and that has woven the plot of which I have spoken to you, that it has done so little for the poor, and has reduced the opportunities of labour instead of supplying work.

In the communes the poor are left in charge of the poor, and at Bâle the rich are allowed to look after the rich. People depend on a few charitable institutions which, far from exciting the benevolence of the rich, appear to smother it. Crowds of destitute poor come to me for bread, from that very town of Bâle where they pretend to provide all that is needful. I also know very well that it is impossible for any government to provide for every one in such moments of universal distress. And if I could have been restrained by reproaches, the Rhine washing down corpses in its streams, the Black Forest re-echoing with cries of despair, and the sight of so many ravaged cantons, all would have summoned me before the tribunal of God for having feared your authority more than His !

Yes, I have wept with disconsolate mothers, I have flung myself more than once on my knees beside them ; and, more than once, prostrating myself before my God, and the God of the poor, I have exclaimed in tears, "Waken, O my God, the dead ! For the living no longer obey Thee by practising Thy special virtues of charity and mercy ! Where are the St. Vincents of Paul, the St. Bernards, the St. Francis of Sales, the St. Theresas, and all the great souls who founded such vast institutions ? They would help me. But no, my God ! Thou who canst do all things, Thou wilt help me." And He did help me. He alone could give me the courage necessary for my task. The outrages and insults, the dangers to which my life was exposed, they cost me nothing, for I was sustained by faith ; but I had to struggle against discouragement. He alone could give me the strength to resist, and the grace not to succumb to so much spiritual and physical fatigue. It is a miracle that I have any voice left, and that I am still alive, and that so many troubles have not crushed me. But He who calls us knows well how to strengthen us with celestial joys !

I have finished, monsieur. It only remains for me to depart, and to shake the dust off my feet, according to the words of our Lord. . . .

I offer you, sir, the hand of friendship, and at the same time I crave your pardon if I have offended you even in the smallest detail. I should be extremely sorry to be wanting in respect to the government of Baden, which I must thank for having received me during the long stay which I have made in various parts of the country. What I have just announced affects every government. It is the old combat of darkness against light. Princes and people alike are only the slaves of power, as long as they have not Jesus Christ, the living God, for their King and their Redeemer, His Gospel for their law, and His life for their example. He alone opens the gates of heaven, and closes the gates of hell. Woe unto those States of which He is not the life! The crash of their fall will soon resound.

This letter, which was made public without delay, created a considerable sensation throughout Europe, but far from putting an end to the scandalous reports that were current, it only served as a new peg on which the newspapers of the day were enabled to hang their denunciations of the writer. Both in the French and the German press the discussion was continued with increasing acrimony. Mme. de Krudener and her friends were in much the same position as were the Methodists at the close of the last century, or the Salvationists of our own time. Whilst those who came in personal contact with them were forced to testify to their piety, their self-sacrifice, their unfailing zeal for humanity, even whilst admitting the possible indiscretions and exaggerations of their conduct, for the outside world no accusation was too startling, no insinuation too base, to be levelled at men and women whose real crime in the eyes of their contemporaries was that of resolutely attempting to live up to a higher standard of Christian perfection than their neighbours. Denunciation and misrepresentation are as much the lot of the religious reformer to-day, as at any period in the world's history, and Mme. de Krudener would have been the first to protest had she not been privileged to suffer for

righteousness' sake.   Even Switzerland, which has
been so often quoted as the home *par excellence* of
civil and religious liberty, gave repeated proof of a
spirit of the most petty intolerance in its dealings
with the Russian prophetess.   Only a few days after
the publication of the De Berckheim letter, the
canton of Bâle finally made up its mind to the
definite expulsion of Mme. de Krudener and her
daughter from their territory, and this evil example
was followed in turn by every canton in which the
little band of missionaries attempted to carry on
their evangelistic labours.

CHAPTER XVI.

1817

THE weeks immediately succeeding the expulsion
of Mme. de Krudener from Unterholtz were spent
either at the Hoernlein, under the constant supervision of the Baden police, or in one or other of the
mountain villages of the neighbourhood, where the
prophetess was sure of a ready welcome from the
peasantry.   Later in the spring, accompanied by her
daughter and Kellner, and no doubt with the tacit
consent of the Bâle authorities, she appears to have
returned to Unterholtz, where M. Lachenal was
always delighted to place himself and his belongings
at the entire disposal of his spiritual benefactress.
In the meanwhile a fresh raid was made by the Baden
police on the Hoernlein ; the household was broken
up, and Mme. de Berckheim and Empaytaz decided
on retiring to Rheinfeld, where they found a promising field for their missionary labours.   Thus, for some
weeks, our heroine was left under the spiritual
direction of Kellner alone, who, of all her pious
entourage, exercised the least beneficial influence
upon her.   A professed disciple of Jacob Boehme,

Kellner persistently urged forward his protectress
along the path of exaggerated mysticism and
prophetic declamation, to which her emotional
nature already rendered her too disposed, whilst he
himself appears to have neglected no art or trick
by which to increase the prestige of the miraculous
powers which he sought to cultivate both for himself
and for her.   It was probably in the hope of creating
a sensation in his own favour that Kellner seized
this opportunity of writing and publishing a most
injudicious address " To the Poor," for which no
doubt Mme. de Krudener must be held partially
responsible, and which did more than anything else
to damage her reputation for sincerity in the eyes of
Europe, by apparently disclosing a political pro-
paganda under cover of religious exhortation.   In
this pamphlet were expressed views on the relations
between rich and poor, which, however commonplace
they may appear to us to-day, were regarded, in the
early years of the century, as nothing less than revolutionary, and which could be easily interpreted
as direct incentives to insurrection.   At the very
least, the moment was ill chosen for this new departure, and the publication was deeply regretted by
many of Mme. de Krudener's truest friends.   This
first effort was followed almost immediately by the
appearance (5th May 1817) of a *Gazette des
Pauvres*, inspired by sentiments of a similar high-
flown character.   This publication, though never
destined to reach a second number, rapidly attained
to a European notoriety.   Virulently attacked by

M. de Bonald in the pages of the *Débats*, and eloquently defended by Benjamin Constant in the *Journal de Paris*, there is no doubt that it exercised a most chilling effect on the dreams of social regeneration cultivated at the time by the Emperor Alexander, whose reforms were all dependent on the generosity of a benevolent despot, and were under no circumstances to be rudely snatched by the people themselves. In noting the chorus of abuse that Mme. de Krudener thus drew down on herself, it is interesting to remember how graciously the authorities were inclined towards her as long as she restricted her preaching to the authority of Christian dogma and to the duties of the great towards the poor. But the very instant she turned to the poor themselves, and indoctrinated them with ideas of self-help and self-amelioration, her former supporters were eager to denounce her teaching as revolutionary and socialistic in tendency.[1]

Mme. de Krudener was not long left in peace at Unterholtz. Expelled a second time from the canton of Bâle, and again from the Hoernlein, where she had taken refuge, she spent the whole of April and May, in bitter weather, wandering from place to place in North Switzerland, passing by Warmbach, Rheinfeld, Moehlin, Mumpf, Laufenburg, and Erlesbach, driven onwards by the pitiless gendarmerie, and followed everywhere by a vast crowd of starving and clamorous beggars,

[1] See on this point a very interesting study of Mme. de Krudener's teachings, contained in vol. iii. of *Die Hauptströmungen der Literatur des XIX. Jahrhunderts*, by Georg Brandes.

whose advent in her wake naturally prejudiced the minds of the local authorities against her. More than once indeed she ran grave risk of being stoned and ill-treated by the inhabitants of the villages through which she passed, made savage in their poverty by this sudden influx of idle and destitute paupers in their midst.

At length, early in June, after much discomfort and repeated separations, the little company of friends arrived safely at Lucerne, where a most enthusiastic welcome awaited them. Priests and ministers, professors and students, all united in demonstrations of joy at the advent of Mme. de Krudener in their town ; the local papers published the most laudatory articles regarding her, one of them even going so far as to compare her to John the Baptist, whilst, it is needless to add, the towns-people collected in crowds around her dwelling in hopes of an address. This gratifying period of general charity and good-will was not destined, however, to last more than a few weeks ; the increasing influx of visitors from the surrounding villages, and the indiscreet expressions indulged in by some of the lady's most ardent disciples, excited the alarm of the magistrates, who ordered Mme. de Krudener to continue her journey to Zürich. Here the concourse of people who collected to hear her was so great that within twenty-four hours the inevitable police order to " move on " was served upon her, and she was compelled to seek a temporary resting-place at Lotstetten. From Zürich, nevertheless, she found time to scribble a hasty line to her step-daughter, Mme. Ochando :—

Blessed be Jesus Christ!

DEAR AND MUCH-BELOVED SOPHIE—I have not been able to write to you, for you have no idea how engaged I have been; I have just stolen a moment at Zürich to write to Paul, and I enclose the letter open. You know they have only allowed me twenty-four hours here, being alarmed at the great crowd of beggars and sightseers. I preached according to my mission; there was an enormous crowd; you cannot imagine what a sensation I created. Priests and students, after hearing me, declared: "It is impossible to persecute that woman."

There is nothing more noteworthy in the accounts of all these preachings and peregrinations throughout Switzerland, than the sympathetic attitude towards Mme. de Krudener adopted in many places by members of both the Catholic and Protestant Churches. It is specially remarkable that, being outside the Catholic Church, her religious exhortations should have been openly approved and recognised by even a section of the Catholic priesthood. Bâle appears to have been the only town where any specific ill-feeling was aroused by the supposed conversion of certain Roman Catholics to Protestantism through the influence of the prayer-meetings at the Hôtel du Sauvage. On all other occasions the prophetess appears, on her own showing, sedulously to have refrained from any word which could close the hearts of those who came to her for enlightenment to the ministrations of their own spiritual pastors. We have seen the charity and sympathy she bestowed during many months on the Einsiedeln pilgrims. She had no wish to make converts to any particular sect or creed; her sole object was the turning of men's hearts to God. This, she maintained, might be effected with equal grace both inside and outside every Christian church that had ever existed.

The first and last word of Mme. de Krudener's gospel was Love; love for her divine Saviour, and through Him love for all His creatures on earth. "Love is life, and life is love," she wrote. In the same spirit of universal brotherhood in which the Holy Alliance was originally conceived in the mind of Alexander, she preached the union in Christian love and charity not only of man to man, and of family to family, but of nation to nation, and of church to church. There came to her the dream, which must have inspired many of the noblest souls on earth both before and since, of a universal abandonment of all minor points of difference in dogma, so that all humanity might join, as with one heart and voice, in a perpetual act of worship to Almighty God and to His divine Son our Redeemer. All narrow, conventional, loveless forms of Christianity were to her abhorrent. Thus it may easily be imagined that she had little, if any, sympathy to bestow on the so-called Reformed Churches of Switzerland and Germany, with their petty jealousies and sectarian intolerance. "How lamentable Protestantism has become!" she exclaims. And again, "Thanks be to God, I was never a Protestant!"

Nevertheless a Protestant she remained in point of fact to the end of her life, in spite of her eager protests to the contrary. Many were the rumours of her reception into the Catholic Church that floated about Europe during these years of wandering; and it is certain that she was in far truer sympathy with Catholicism—in spite of the "petrifaction" of which she was wont to accuse the Church of Rome—than with any other recognised form of faith. Nor is this in any way surprising. Her lifelong familiarity with the Greek Church, of which she was at least nominally a member, naturally prepared her mind for a belief in the dogmatic truths of Catholicism, whilst her early visit to Venice revealed to her its poetic and artistic aspects. Readers of *Valérie* will remember the vein of sadness and longing which runs through her account of Ernest praying before the altar of the Blessed Virgin in a Venetian church, and in her exquisite description of the Carthusian monastery. All through her public career as a preacher Mme. de Krudener openly advocated confession as a necessary antecedent to true repentance, and she dwelt far more on the importance of the sacraments than is usual in the Evangelical school, with which on other points she was in harmony. Casual references in her letters, to St. Bernard, St. Theresa, St. Catherine of Siena, and, above all, to Mme. Guyon, show to what extent her mind was penetrated by the teachings of the contemplative school of Catholic thought. But most especially was her sympathy shown by her habitual conformity to many of the devotional practices of Catholics, such as her habitual use of the sign of the Cross, as well as the veneration with which she regarded the crucifix, and her devotion to the Blessed Virgin. In such matters she exacted compliance from her disciples, and, above all, she dwelt on the essential importance of the posture of kneeling during prayer, herein directly differing from the recognised custom of the Reformed Churches, in which the congregation invariably stand during the offering up of prayer by the minister.

The following lengthy letter to a Roman Catholic priest, written by Mme. de Krudener whilst she was still at the Hoernlein (February 1817), reflects perhaps more clearly than any other the whole religious attitude of her mind when undisturbed by the hysterical suggestions of Kellner.

Your letter gave me great pleasure, dear friend in Christ our Saviour, and it is with a profound sentiment of humility, gratitude, and love that I kiss the hand that wrote it. Two days ago the Lord had inwardly revealed to me the great work that is beginning among the Christians of your Church. Consequently, your letter was of great importance in my eyes. It proved to me that you are one of those whom our great and only Shepherd collects in a flock, and who, as you say, are called together from the four quarters of the globe. Venerable and enlightened, you yet possess sufficient simplicity of faith to pierce the cloud which is spread by pietism over the work of our Saviour; it is a proof of your childlike honesty, and a testimony to the grace of our Lord whom you invoke. Judah persecutes and opposes Jerusalem. It is hidden from the wise, and revealed to the babes. Let us then be as children, for they alone can become heroes, for the Hero of Heroes is glorified in His little ones. . . . Let us adore, love, and die to ourselves, that we may live in Christ, who is life eternal. . . . It is under the inspiration of the Spirit of the Lord that we must bring up our children, who, at the same time, become combatants. The service of the temple ceases. The ark is there! But alas! how few Christians know anything of that time, of that harvest, of that Love that sends its followers out into the highways and hedges to save all those that can be saved.

It is by a miracle of His grace, and by a sovereign decree of His eternal wisdom, that I, a miserable sinner, have been chosen from the world by the Almighty. I did not know the outward forms, I had not met with that cold Christianity which ignores love, and misconstrues the Cross of Christ; which, whilst holding the Gospel in its hand, knows nothing of the living Christ, of the mystery of godliness of which St. Paul speaks. Consequently, it can neither know nor observe the commandments of Christ, and on the contrary, it violently persecutes the humble, who only know how to love and to bear His cross. That is why both at Bâle and elsewhere I have been the object of the greatest persecution from Christians who hated me.

But, God be praised! the persecutors have been my greatest benefactors. They have taught me to feel deeply that the Church, the bride of Christ, must have the attributes of the Lamb, and that to suffer and to love ought to be the principal objects of that flock who claim for their shepherd the Man of Sorrows, Christ the Crucified!

I have been educated by hatred and contempt; I have seen my best intentions distorted. Thus my pride was humbled; I had to carry on conflicts most trying to our human nature; I had to learn to know even more thoroughly the Incomprehensible, who dwells in light, and yet walks in the midst of obscurity, whose ways are often hidden from Christians and unfathomable by human reason. The love which supports and illuminates me leaves me no other course but to learn everything at the feet of the Saviour whom I invoke, and to forget everything that I had learnt in the school of mankind. Already for a long time He has allowed me to foresee His great schemes, and has revealed to me the secrets of the present time. He,

my mighty Friend, indefatigable in His compassion, He supports
me with a love which is beyond all words. My education has
been to learn to inhale and to exhale love all around me. It
was in the midst of sufferings such as very few Christians have
undergone, because very few have died in the deepest roots of
their former selves, that my new life arose, and that I learnt to
detest a merely earthly life, and to realise those words of the
Lord: "He that hateth his life in this world shall keep it unto
life eternal."

Thus in the midst of the great storms and the terrible
resistance of my human nature, I struggled in the dust, and I
shuddered at the thought: "Unhappy mortal, then you do not
love!" . . . Not love! That has ever appeared to me the
most terrible of all!   Not love Him! Him who has implanted in
the very depths of my soul the ardent desire that even hell
itself may love Christ, the vanquisher of hell!   Not to love Him,
my great Love, appeared to me the height of abomination.
Then I wished to make every sacrifice for Him, and to wish is
everything.   Grace alone can accomplish all things.   Profoundly
impressed by my own misery and unworthiness, I no longer
regard myself as capable of anything.   To love is my sole
occupation.   I have learnt to know the omnipotence of Faith
and of Love, not like a heroine of faith, but as a child.   The
honour and glory of my Saviour constitute my whole life.   I
have a craving to see all around me saved, so that in the end
all may unite in a joyful hymn of praise.   I know also that I
possess all things from Him who is worthy of all love.   From
thence spring the boldness of my prayers and the confidence of
my self-sacrifice.

That the blind should see, that the lame should walk, that
incurable invalids should recover, is that as great a miracle as the
spiritual resurrection of so many dead who come to life again, of so
many hardened sinners, who, filled with sacred joy and ardour,
resemble mountain torrents, carrying along others with them to
prostrate themselves at the feet of the eternal love?

Such is our life here—a constant succession of miracles; for
we follow the royal road to renunciation, the only infallible way.
To follow Christ and carry His cross through shame and persecution is above all things evangelical, and cannot lead to error.

All that is not founded on the life of Christ is dangerous; all without Him and outside of Him is dead. Love is life, and life is love.

It is of that love of which the beloved Apostle speaks when he says, "He that abideth in charity, abideth in God," and it will some day even conquer hell, for the great Prince of Life is Himself Love. He has not only overturned hell for us, but some day He will make a present of it to the Bride, for the Bride will represent to Him with tears of earnest desire that the Eternal Wisdom has said, "That at the name of Jesus every knee should bow, of things in heaven, and things in earth, and things under the earth" (Phil. ii. 5, 10).

Perhaps I am speaking too openly to a Catholic priest? Nevertheless, my dear and venerable friend, I must tell you that I have been loved and summoned not only to give up the world, but also conventional Christianity, so that I am neither Catholic nor Greek, nor, thanks be to God, have I ever been a Protestant. My divine Master has taught me to be a Christian. I did not realise, when I was seized by the omnipotent Sun of my life, that I was a sinner. I loved, and I wept with ecstasy over the transports of my love. I knew nothing of Christian societies nor of the formulas which are so easy to adopt; I had heard very little conversation on the subject, and I had learnt nothing, but I thought to myself: "Oh, if only He, the adorable One, would love me!" Penetrated by this divine flame, I thought nothing of my unworthiness, I knew nothing of my own sinfulness. Although I had suffered much, I was ignorant of my own sins, and did not hate them. I remained therefore at His feet, like another Mary Magdalen; thus the sinner who is now writing to you was called to preach the living Christ. . . . Do not be scandalised if I say to you things that your Church does not admit. It is wonderful that I dare write to you at all, for I never know beforehand, nor do I think over, what I am going to write; so I have almost given up writing, and I spend my life on my knees. For here everything is living. Hardly any one comes here who is not touched, especially if we pray with him. All is life, all is a miracle of grace.

Catholics do not ask me when they hear me whether I have been brought up in their Church; they open their hearts without questioning. In His great mercy, the Lord reveals to me many things. Some years ago I had to visit a poor sinner in a miserable hut; I preached the Gospel to her; she was converted; I heard her confession, and after that I sent her to the priest, for she was a Catholic. That is my line of conduct towards the learned and the ignorant, towards scholars, ministers of state, mathematicians, artists, and the men of every rank in life who come to me in turn. I preach to crowned heads as well as to peasants the love of Christ, not the love of those Christians who think it consists merely in singing and praying and attending meetings, but that which consists in doing the will of Jesus Christ, and of dying to ourselves so that Christ may live in us.

It is because of that, because we live for the reign of Jesus Christ, and because by His grace we rescue so many souls from Satan, that the latter is so enraged against us; it is especially at Bâle that he is most active, and that he pours forth his wrath upon us. But God having plainly warned me by the mouth of men of the intentions of the wicked, I took refuge with my friends in a house on the main road, along which thousands of people pass. The fury of our persecutors exhausted itself in horrible imprecations. One day they came to look for us in the little house that I occupied, and in the meanwhile we were all kneeling with our faces to the ground, praying for them from the bottom of our hearts. It is a fact that since then we have seen the most wonderful conversions amongst our most bitter enemies. Praise the Lord with us for His mercy! Since then, here, as formerly in Paris, the Lord has watched over me wonderfully.

The great hour of temptation which spread over the world is past. It was first announced at Bâle, as well as at Zürich and at Geneva, by a wave of Socinianism, which brought about terrible ruin in those churches. Oh, how lamentable Protestantism has become! We ought, therefore, through the mercy of God, to preach the Gospel at Bâle and in the neighbourhood, that as many as possible may be saved! Thanks be to God, this dead Christianity, like that of the Laodiceans, and of other societies who believe themselves to possess the truth, and are in reality dead, had produced no sort of vitality. They know so little of God, who is the true life, so little of the love of our blessed Saviour, and of the mighty influences of His grace, that they know very little either of the powerful action of the Lord and of the times in which we live. That is the reason why to-day, as in former times, the scribes and the Pharisees persecute Christ in His members. Pray for these unhappy people afflicted with such blindness. We have drawn their attention to their own transgressions, we have prayed for them, we have borne with their persecutions, and have forgiven their injustice.

Avarice is at the root of all evil. They will have nothing to do with the imitation of Christ, and call it fanaticism. They only know the letter of the Gospel, and are totally ignorant of the love our merciful Father bears towards sinners. That is why they judge so freely, and always condemn us. They regard me as a Catholic because of my good works, and overwhelm us with contempt and insults because we avoid no one. They are blind, and we are all the more bound to cry mercy, that through our loving mercy they too may be granted us, if it is possible; we are justified in hoping for it. Oh, they have greatly injured the work of the Lord! Several amongst them, both pietist and others, have openly confessed their sins before us, and thanks be to God, have become convinced that the *life* of a Christian is the only true life.

' Even now, when our most bitter persecutors are surprised at the way in which we have been fully justified by signs and prodigies, even now the heads of these societies persist in their blindness. It is sad, very sad, that they should persecute the work of the Lord, and lead so many into error. Thus we must pray while we work. Pray for me, my good friend, that I may have much love, and that I may have the happiness of seeing all these people converted.

At Bâle the dial points to the great hour of trial. All who are converted by us are summoned before the tribunal; many have been imprisoned, or even expelled the city, although they are Swiss subjects. When the magistrates meet them, they ask them whether they are also disciples of Jesus, or whether they belong to the horned woman! Thus people who had been stirred by us have been driven out of Huningue and other communes; it will all help towards the gathering together of the children of God, which must soon manifest itself.

Many are urged on by hatred, because we preach the Gospel

and live according to it, because we support the cause of the poor, and because by obedience and love we make men attentive to the judgments of God, judgments which were announced fifteen months ago, and which have already begun. We should never finish if we attempted to repeat all the visions and wonders which have been revealed to us, and of which many have not been published, either by oversight or through lack of time. Many of these visions bore upon my mission and the times in which we live, and as you desire to possess a full account, we shall hope, by the mercy of God, to send you one.

A great work is taking place amongst Catholics. I should have been very glad to have some conversation with Professor Seiler on his way through here, but the Lord will direct everything according to His will at the right time. I think the interview will be an important one. Our great and dear friend Booz has won my heart. Persecution has been the seal of his doctrine, which is founded on truth, and the proof of his Christianity. Soon he will be placed in a great sphere of activity. The Lord in His mercy revealed it to me some time ago. Have no anxiety on his account. . . . The Lord will soon be among us, but few know the manner of His coming. Let us watch, therefore, and pray. May the Lord bless you, worthy friend, in the name of the Holy Trinity.   Your obedient servant,

B. K.

The most striking incident of Mme. de Krudener's residence at Lucerne was undoubtedly the delivery by her of an address to the professors and students of the Catholic seminary. The hall was thronged, and the speech, which was delivered in German, was received with much enthusiasm. It seems strange that any one outside the Church should be able to throw herself so completely into the spirit of the Catholic priesthood. Mme. de Krudener's eloquent words were fortunately taken down at the time, and thus we are able to give to our readers a translation of the only complete specimen in existence of her oratorical powers.

You also are anxious to see this woman who has been so much talked about, and about whom learned and ignorant alike have exhausted themselves in conjecture; this woman, in a word, who is as much hated as loved. You are welcome, messieurs, indeed you must be so to me, as you are destined for the study of the Holy Scriptures, and some day, perhaps, you will preach Christ, my Saviour and yours. But before you can preach Christ, you must first have learned to know Him; you must first have experienced the marvellous power of His grace. It is not in the power of man to make a priest; neither does it belong to the universities to create a living church. On the contrary, was it not from their midst that so many heresies and schisms sprang up, as soon as man, abandoning himself to the pride which science inspires, allowed himself to be turned away from celestial truths to adopt worldly and carnal doctrines?

You possess, I am aware, excellent teachers; but they must have told you that the Holy Ghost alone has a right to confer episcopal ordination. It is therefore sheer audacity, when, because of worldly ambitions, of some imaginary talent, of a capacity for the study of languages, or because of any other reason you please, men destine themselves, on their own authority, for this sacred and mysterious vocation, and thoughtlessly enrol themselves under this banner, without pausing to consider that we shall have to answer not only for our own souls, but for a multitude of others who have been confided to our care.

It would therefore be very foolhardy and very rash to wish to take upon oneself a duty which the ancient Fathers of the Church, grown white with years, and the Saints of the early centuries, only accepted in fear and trembling. What man would dare to take his place before the altar without a special vocation from Him who searches our reins and hearts, and whose eyes of fire penetrate into their most hidden recesses? What lips, unsanctified by the Holy Spirit, would dare to open in intercession for sinners? Who would be so audacious as to interpose himself as a mediator between a nation of sinners and the awful majesty of the Holy of Holies? To whom could this great wrestling of man with his God be entrusted, if not to him who can say in all boldness with Jacob, "I will not let thee go unless thou bless me"?

To whom are given these holy tears, that are capable of touching the heart of the God of mercy? Most certainly only to him whom God has been pleased to select with that object, whom He has Himself educated and formed at the school of the cross of suffering. For it is only by grace, and by nothing but grace, that it is possible for man to become a priest. From whom, if not from the Almighty, can he hold his letters of credit, the omnipotence of faith and of love?

The priest without miracles is not a priest anointed of God; just as faith without miracles ceases to be the Christian faith!

How great is the importance and the dignity of the man on whom the power of binding and of loosing has been conferred; what tender strength, and what a compassionate heart must he not possess, when, seated in the chair of absolution, he receives the confessions of sinners, having himself for his great example the Friend of publicans and of sinners; how great is his privilege, who, like his divine Master, is called upon to love those who have already found in the tears of sincere repentance the absolution of all their sins at the feet that were washed with the tears of Mary Magdalen! But besides that, with what invincible courage and intrepidity must he not give battle to vice, whilst standing in the pulpit but a few feet distant from the confessional, where shortly before he had been seated as a lamb full of gentleness and humility. From that sacred tribunal, inspired by the spirit of the divine law of Christ, he dethrones the powerful of the earth, summons crowned heads before the supreme tribunal of Him in whose presence kings are but as dust; he upholds the rights of the oppressed, protects the orphan, and defends the cause of the widow. Indefatigable in all things, he may be seen during the hours of the night, at one time prostrate at the foot of the high altar, in adoration of the profound mysteries of divine love, at another, absorbed in the functions of his high vocation, which, for the true priest, has no interruption. He prays with oppressed hearts, encourages timid souls; he weeps with those that weep, and does not even disdain to beg for those who are in want; with untiring zeal and loving arms he carries his spiritual children into the very presence of our compassionate Father. At the bedside of the dying he prays for the forgiveness of sins, for the cause of all diseases and all evils is sin. Thus he appeals to the Supreme Physician, and Christ appears to him as to the apostles. But knowing well how necessary suffering is, he prays for the most part only for the saving effects of pain on the sufferer. He must be a model of sanctity in the exercise of all his sublime functions. Recognising the high importance of marriage, he unites, with the disposition of a pure and chaste heart, those whom he has taught to regard this holy bond as a solemn sacrament. The brutal desires of a wild and dissipated youth veil themselves before the purity of his gaze, and the serenity of his countenance imposes peace on the most tumultuous passions. Such is the elect of the Lord; and, such as he is, the Sovereign Priest confers upon him a power to which no worldly monarch can aspire. He learns at the feet of Christ the mysteries of the future. He hears that voice which, in speaking to the patriarch of the faithful, said, "Shall I hide from Abraham what I do?" He bears in himself the testimony of Jesus Christ, which is the spirit of prophecy. The angels are present at his celebration of the sacrifice of the Mass, and bear his supplications to the feet of Him who was, and is, and is to be.

The picture which I have just drawn for you of the venerable priest is no doubt very imperfect, and although in truth my soul realises it in all the grandeur of its various proportions, yet the meaning of it is so sublime, and at the same time so profound, that my lips refuse to utter that which my soul feels. I trust, however, I have said enough to you to give you abundant material for reflection, and to encourage you to sound yourselves on this point, feeling thoroughly convinced that it is not by means of science, but solely by the voice of the Sovereign Ruler of Souls, that you can be first called and finally directed in your holy vocation. It is only thus that the conversation we have had together can have any importance; yes, messieurs, the very highest importance for you all.

I trust that all who are here present, and whom I have had the honour of addressing to-day, and especially all those who understand the object of our mission, and who feel how needful ·

it is in this depraved century, I trust, I say, that they may turn at once to Christ, the living God! May you taste and see how sweet He is! May you all understand, you especially, the priests of the Almighty, the words that our Lord spoke to the young man in the Gospel, "Go, sell whatsoever thou hast, and give to the poor, and thou shalt have treasure in heaven: and come, follow me."

But this act, to sell all and follow Christ, includes the renunciation of all those things which still keep us bound to the earth, such as our own opinions, our own will, and all that useless *étalage* of science of which at times we are so proud, when we cultivate too high ideas of our natural capacities, which are, after all, of no avail, as long as they are not sanctified by grace. That is the cross that we are commanded to carry day by day, whilst, as we die always more and more to our natural life, we put on by degrees the divine life, until we possess it in all its plenitude. Oh, to what a height of renunciation ought we not to attain, before the Lord can take us into His service! What mystical dying are we not called upon to endure before we are capable of fully understanding the voice of the Holy Ghost in the depths of our heart!

After referring to Tauler and the inefficacy of mere intellectual attainments in the service of God, Mme. de Krudener continued—

I do not pretend to say by that that the study of languages is not necessary in order that we may read in their original tongues the sacred Scriptures, which should be of the highest importance to us. A knowledge of ecclesiastical history is above all things necessary; yet more important still is a knowledge of tradition, and most important of all is it for us to be penetrated with the spirit of the Holy Scriptures, and the Holy Ghost, who inspired them, can alone make them clear to us. It is therefore essential for us to be able, like St. Paul the great mystic, to put on the divine love, as the first and the last, and the only necessary and indispensable virtue of the Christian life. The love of Christ teaches us all things; it is the key to the divine heart of God; it alone is great above all things; it does not make conditions for the future, it offers the whole of itself as a sacrifice, because it only wishes to please, and for that very reason it hates all sin, and even the appearance of sin. To possess the heart of God is the ardent desire of love; it is its most sacred, its only ambition!

No doubt this address gave an additional impetus to the floating rumours of the lady's reception into the Church, for at Lotstetten, in the course of an interview which she granted to M. Maurer, a worthy minister from Schaffhausen, who has preserved in his Memoirs a detailed and naïve account of his visit to the prophetess, the following conversation appears to have taken place :—

"You have probably heard people say that I have become a Catholic?"

"Yes, madam."

"And you believed it?"

"Knowing you only by reputation, madam, I had no reason for either believing or disbelieving it."

"Quite so. I belong entirely to the primitive Catholic Church; it is the only true Church; it was founded by our Lord Himself, and the gates of hell shall not prevail against it. In that Church alone is the Cross elevated, and there the faithful are on their knees at the foot of the Cross. That spiritual genuflection before the crucifix is the distinctive mark of the Christian; it is this alone that saves from everlasting death, and that will save us from the approaching judgments of our own time."

She was silent for a few moments, and then began again—

"But do you suppose I am a Protestant? Oh no! I protest against Protestantism as being only a deception of Satan. If you like, I can quote a number of passages in the New Testament against Protestantism. The Catholic faith is the only true faith; you understand that I am speaking of the ancient primitive Catholic religion, not of the Roman Catholic Church."

"Then, to prevent mistakes, why not say the Evangelical Church?"

"Certainly! We are agreed, and we will say the Evangelical Church!"

From which we may gather that Mme. de Krudener attached the very smallest importance to names, and that an intermediate position of independence appeared to her the most favourable for the propagation of her religious convictions.

It is, no doubt, idle to speculate as to the secret causes which arrest the spiritual progress of a soul midway in the path that appears to be marked out for it; but, in the case of Mme. de Krudener, we may perhaps detect one reason in that common form of self-will which prompts a person to prefer the more stony path of his own choice, to the smoother road imposed by the will of another. Of such self-will, in spite of a truly heroic zeal for self-renunciation, traces may be gathered throughout the restless and stormy career of our much-suffering heroine.

CHAPTER XVII

1817-1820

DURING the last two months of Mme. de Krudener's stay in Switzerland she was under the never-ceasing surveillance of the police, being hurried by them backwards and forwards from place to place, often travelling all night, and frequently separated from her friends, whilst the crowds of poor, starving peasantry who gathered around her at every halting-place, clamouring for food and sympathy, were ruthlessly driven back and dispersed by the gendarmes.

On leaving Lotstetten (20th July) Mme. de Krudener turned her steps towards the town of Schaffhausen, where a warm reception was accorded her by M. Maurer and a little community of Moravian Brothers. Thence she passed from village to village in the canton of Thurgau, until at the end of the month she reached Constance. Here one of the town officials awaited her at the hotel with an order for her immediate departure, and that same evening, after addressing the assembled crowd from the windows of the hotel, she was forced to continue her route along the southern shores of the lake to the

little village of Hub, where permission was accorded
her for a few days' halt. The want and misery at
this time throughout the surrounding cantons of
St. Gall, Schwytz, Glarus, and Unterwalden had
reached a most acute stage, and the instant Mme.
de Krudener's advent in the neighbourhood was
made known hundreds of starving wretches poured
into the village. The sight of so much suffering
filled the hearts of Mme. de Krudener and her
companions with boundless pity, and without wasting
a moment they established a soup-kitchen, and devoted the whole day to distributing food to all who
applied for it. But once again the ruthless order
for departure was delivered by the police, and after
a final address, so eloquent and pathetic that it left
her whole audience in tears, Mme. de Krudener
continued her journey along the lake to Arbon.
Here Sunday was spent, and services were held, with
the result that by the afternoon not only were the
large salon of the hotel and all the corridors and
staircases thronged with eager listeners, but all the
streets around were packed with a silent and attentive throng. For a moment Mme. de Krudener
was overcome by emotion at the sight of this vast
multitude. A venerable priest led her to a window
of the hotel, and, throwing it open, invited her to
address the people, saying: " Madame, it is God who
has sent you to us; speak to these people; speak
to them of the salvation which Jesus Christ gives
but does not sell. Speak bravely; God will inspire
both you and them !"

The following are a few notes of the address, which was delivered in German :—

My dear Friends—We have all of us sinned ; we are all of us defiled by wrong-doing. Rich and poor alike, we have none of us loved Jesus Christ. We are now struck down by the hand of God. Let us all humble ourselves, as many as are here present. Let us beat our breasts, and I first of all, for I have sinned more than the rest of you. Let each of us repeat these words: "O God, be merciful to me, for I have sinned exceedingly ! Have pity on me ! I am as the prodigal son ! Have mercy on me, O Lord, have mercy !" Let us confess our abominations and cry unto the Lord, that His anger may be appeased. But very few really humble themselves ; it is possible that not a single one amongst you has done so. Turn yourselves unto God ; the time is short ; famine and death ravage the country. We implore you to be warned in time. Whoever does not receive the Bible will be condemned. I beseech you then to receive the divine Word—receive it with obedient hearts. Do what is commanded us. Believe in Jesus. Confess His name before men. Do not fear to confess openly the name of our Lord and Saviour. He will then confess us before the angels of the judgment, which will strike all nations. Be obedient to the Gospel ; it is the book by which we shall be judged. Let us teach our children to pray to Him alone who can deliver us ; there is no time left for hesitation.

We must humble ourselves ; as long as we do not love God we shall be condemned. That is why we entreat you in the name of our Lord Jesus, in the name of the Holy Trinity, to be converted, to have recourse to the Precious Blood. Bend your knees this very day ; begin this very day to open your hearts to the grace that summons you.

Forgive me for speaking to you so sternly, and believe that it is for your eternal welfare. May your blood not be on your own heads. Renounce the world and all the abominations of a guilty life ! Turn to Jesus and His love ; He loves you ; He loves you more than a mother loves her son ! Guard yourselves against avarice ; it is the greatest of all sins in these times of suffering. Guard yourselves against obeying those diabolic laws forbidding you to give alms, or to receive poor travellers. Guard yourselves

against obedience to such laws.   You will draw down on yourselves
more terrible chastisements than those you see carried out around
you—I mean chastisements in the life eternal.

This, my dear friends, is what we had to say to you.   This is
why the Lord sent us in the midst of you.   We implore you once
again not to despise the voice which has penetrated to your ears.
May the Lord grant you His grace to understand all we have said
to you !

The next morning (12th August) the police conducted the preacher outside the town, and for several
days she appears to have been driven backwards
and forwards across the frontiers of St. Gall and
Thurgau, without being allowed even to spend a
single night in any place.   The little party, too, were
forcibly separated, and suffered indescribable anxiety,
until at length they were allowed to rejoin one
another at Rheineck, on the Austrian frontier.   But
the Austrian authorities declining to allow them to
enter the country, it was necessary to make their
way back wearily to Arbon, through the cantons of
Thurgau and Zürich to Schaffhausen, and thence by
Neuhausen, Rafz, and Tengen, to the little village of
Daggren, in Aargau, where the exhausted travellers
arrived on 1st September, and were permitted to
make a three days' halt.   On the Sunday great
crowds collected for the services, and Mme. de
Krudener addressed them in the following words of
exhortation :—

We are sent to you by the Lord to warn you of your true
interests, and to exhort you to reflect seriously on the eternal
salvation of your souls.   Dear friends, as long as you do not
belong to Jesus Christ, you are the slaves of Satan and of the

world. I beseech you to give your whole hearts to the Lord. Address all your prayers to Him, as a child to its father. If you are hungry, ask Him for bread. If you are in anguish, appeal to Him, and He will send His angels to comfort you. We implore you to listen to this voice of warning. Seek this very day, before all things, for the forgiveness of your sins. Do you not desire to be the joy of those angels who help so much in the conversion of sinners? Give your hearts to Christ and say to Him, "My Saviour, here is my heart, which Thou desirest to possess; come and dwell in me; come and renew me utterly. I want to love Thee; I want to do Thy will. Have mercy on me; forgive me my sins; wash me in Thy Precious Blood! O Holy Ghost, come and purify me, cleanse me from the sins of the world that are in me! God the Father, reconcile me with Thyself, by the blood of Thy Son!" Pray in that manner, my dear friends, with few words, but from the depths of your hearts; a sigh, a longing of the heart, that is what God asks for. Do as I say, and you will yourselves find what joy there is in going to Jesus, what happiness is to be found at the foot of the Cross. It is that eternal happiness that we desire for you from the bottom of our hearts. Praise be to Jesus Christ. Amen.

To a little company of Tübingen students, who paid her a visit at this place, she addressed the following appropriate remarks:—

You have quitted the University, where, with great trouble no doubt, you have learnt to be sceptical. Do you know what in reality should be the first of all human studies? It is to learn to confess Jesus Christ, and to submit yourselves to His will. As long as you do not recognise the Saviour, there is nothing but emptiness and ignorance in your hearts. It is He who holds the keys of heaven, and who can open and shut the treasures of true knowledge. I have no other wish for you than this: that you may enjoy the grace of Jesus Christ, for then you will be ashamed of having spent the greater part of your lives without loving Him. . . .

Dear young people! Give Him your hearts; humble yourselves at His feet; have recourse to His grace, whilst He stretches

out His hands to you ; do this, and your visit here will not be
barren of good fruit.

These appear to have been the last public words
spoken by Mme. de Krudener on Swiss soil;
passing through Laufenburg and Seckingen, she
crossed the frontier into the Grand-Duchy of Baden
(12th September 1817), making a short halt at Wehr,
and then at Kander. Unfortunately, the Baden
police showed themselves even less accommodating
than the Swiss ; at Kander Professor Lachenal and
his wife, who, as ardent disciples, had followed
Mme. de Krudener in all her peregrinations through
Switzerland, were seized by order of the Baden
authorities, and forcibly conveyed across the frontier
to Bâle. The train of poor people who followed
Mme. de Krudener about wherever she went were
ruthlessly expelled and dispersed, and the lady herself, with a reduced suite, was hurried about, first to
Neu-Brissach, thence to Colmar, and finally to
Freiburg (in Breisgau). Here she was informed by
order of the Grand-Duke of Baden that she was to
proceed without delay on her homeward journey to
Russia, that only one or two members of her party
would be allowed to accompany her, and that the
remainder must return to their own homes.

The news of this sudden and forcible separation
fell like a thunderbolt on the little band of missionaries, who were all bound to one another by the
strongest ties of human affection and spiritual inter-
communion. After much discussion it was arranged
that Empaytaz, accompanied by his mother and

Mme. Armand, should return to Geneva, in order to take up an important work of evangelisation, to which he had been more than once urgently summoned by his colleagues.   M. de Berckheim having proceeded to St. Petersburg some weeks previously in order to convey reports to the Emperor concerning the proposed scheme for emigrating German and Swiss colonists to Southern Russia, the task of escorting Mme. de Krudener on her homeward journey was left to her daughter Juliette, and to Kellner, from whom she expressed a strong disinclination to be separated.

The whole of the winter of 1817-18 appears to have been spent in the long, dreary journey across Germany and Prussia to the Livonian frontier. Throughout the whole route the little party were escorted by police, who frequently hurried them forwards with but scant consideration for the health or comfort of the travellers, and who did their utmost to prevent the assembling of curious and enthusiastic crowds in the various towns in which a temporary halt was made. Few incidents of note occurred on the journey.   At Weimar Mme. de Krudener had the pleasure of meeting her old friend and correspondent, Mdlle. Stourdza, now Countess Edling, who, to the end of her life, retained the most affectionate veneration for one to whom she owed so much of her spiritual development.   At Neu-Dietendorff, in Saxony, a few peaceful days were spent in the society of a little Moravian community, and Leipsic was reached about the New Year.

Here a halt of some weeks was made, in order to allow Mme. de Krudener to recover somewhat from the fatigues of travelling. Police were stationed at the door of her apartment, but she was treated with all the consideration due to her rank, and a limited number of visitors were granted admission to her presence. Amongst these was Professor Krug of Leipsic, who subsequently published an account of his conversation with the lady in a pamphlet, which created a profound sensation throughout Europe at the time. Whilst her enemies affirmed that the revelations contained in the pamphlet gave the final deathblow to Mme. de Krudener's pretensions as a religious and social reformer, her friends have denounced the Professor for publishing an inaccurate version of a conversation of an exhausting and exciting nature, held with a lady who was actually at the time in bed, suffering from some feverish complaint. It must be frankly admitted at the outset that the language is exaggerated, and the statements in several instances quite inaccurate, but not more so than an intimate knowledge of the prophetess would lead one to expect, at a time when she was suffering extreme provocation from prolonged police supervision, when she was thrown mainly on Kellner for spiritual direction, and when the state of her health was such as to render her peculiarly liable to mental excitement. That Krug himself was far from regarding the conversation as placing the lady in a wholly unfavourable light may be gathered from his remark, that had he been possessed of a little

more warmth of temperament, he would have been
tempted to prostrate himself before her and venerate
her as a saint.

The Professor relates how he found the
prophetess in bed, Kellner being present in the
room, and how she gave him her hand whilst greet-
ing him with her usual salutation, " Blessed be Jesus
Christ!"   Forthwith the conversation turned on the
subject of the Holy Alliance.   "It was the immediate work of God," declared Mme. de Krudener.
"It was He who elected me to be His instrument;
it is through Him that I have carried through so
great an enterprise, of which you have not grasped
the full significance.   The mission of the Holy
Alliance is addressed to all mankind; it is to teach
them that Christ alone can save them from corruption, and preserve them from the vengeance of
God."

The Professor having suggested that the world
was no worse now than formerly, the lady retorted
eagerly : " Do you suppose it is the wicked man who
is farthest from God?   Great vices give evidence of
strength, and there is always a hope that a wicked
man may one day turn to his Saviour; but the
civilised and enlightened world of the present day is
worse than vicious : it is cowardly about all that is
good; it is weak, indifferent, without faith, without
love ; it prides itself on its much-vaunted intellect, on
its imaginary virtue.   It is the rationalism, the philosophy of the present age, which will ruin the world."

Returning to the subject of the Holy Alliance,

Mme. de Krudener explained that through her, God had caused the first conception of it to spring up in the mind of the noble and pious Emperor Alexander; that he had brought her a rough copy, which she had corrected, and that the actual Alliance had been the result. " But what bitter conflicts preceded the completion of the undertaking! It was God," she continued, " the God of love, who led me to renounce the world, that He might make of me, a miserable creature, an instrument of His grace. . . . Like a second Joan of Arc, I should have wished to seize the sword and punish every tyrant. But I was destined for another life ; it was in Italy that I had the first glimpse of it ; there, amongst the ruins of the old heathen world, in the convents, before the altars of the new world of Jesus Christ, a celestial light appeared to me, and my heart was inclined towards God. Yet insufficiently penetrated by the Creator and his divine love, I required a lesson, the most terrible lesson of all ; I saw France, with all her errors and crimes and misfortunes ; filled with horror, I renounced all the pleasures and glory of this world ; I sought my salvation in Jesus Christ ; I trusted myself to His promises ; I submitted myself to His commandments in order that I might indicate the path of salvation to my fellow-creatures. I have no need of anything ; I require nothing from the world ; I already experience celestial joys ; I am so indescribably happy that even in heaven itself I could not be more so. But I ardently long to see all mankind participating in my joy."

After an interval of rapt and silent prayer, during which Kellner carried on the thread of the conversation, Mme. de Krudener began once more: "Yes, Napoleon,—justly detested as a hardened sinner, —Napoleon has already quitted St. Helena; he will soon be amongst us; God has revealed this to me, as He revealed to me his first flight from the island of Elba; but this time Napoleon will not show himself armed with a visible power; it is by dark artifices that he will deceive mankind. France conceals within herself a sort of 'Tugendbund,' which already counts 400,000 men. They will fling themselves upon Europe, and will desolate her with fire and sword, and Europe can only be saved from ruin by a firm and faithful adhesion to the Holy Alliance. But the English, who think themselves safe, will have nothing to do with it; they abuse and calumniate it, because it threatens to interfere with their craving for gold—the sole object of their worship."

In bidding farewell to her interviewer Mme. de Krudener added a few last words. "The public press has grossly ill-treated me, but you do not believe what they say; my accusers say what they please, but I am not allowed to answer them. Good-bye; I beseech you, my dear Professor, to reflect seriously on the Holy Alliance. Turn your thoughts to faith and love; bend the knee before Jesus Christ. Alas! I would give much to see you among the faithful. God bless you!"

It were idle to deny the inaccuracy of Mme. de

Krudener's later prophecies concerning Napoleon, or indeed concerning political events in general. Thus on a later occasion she announced that Germany would be compelled to take up arms against Turkey, a prophecy which has not yet been justified by the event. Some of Mme. de Krudener's panegyrists have attempted to explain away these unfulfilled utterances, under the impression that the lady's reputation was at stake. For ourselves, we prefer to accept them as the regrettable but unavoidable outcome of an overstrained and impressionable nature under the constant influence of an unscrupulous charlatan such as Kellner. In point of fact, prophecy played a very small part in the daily life of our heroine, and her claims on our admiration and sympathy rest happily on far firmer grounds than the accuracy or otherwise of her predictions.

Although permission to await the advent of spring at Dessau was refused to Mme. de Krudener, she was treated throughout the latter part of her journey with far greater consideration than at first. Travelling in a north-easterly direction, she was allowed to make short halts and hold prayer-meetings and assemblies at all the towns through which she passed, at Lübben, Beeskow, Frankfort-on-the-Oder, Neuenburg, etc. At Beeskow the following passage occurred in her speech, which appears to have been listened to by a large number of local officials :—

The Emperor of Russia repeatedly told me himself that he had only opened his eyes to the truth, on the ruins of his

Empire, and that it was God, and God alone, who was capable of accomplishing what no human power could ever have expected from its own exertions. Do not imagine, *messieurs les militaires*, nor you, *messieurs les employés*, scholars, and philosophers, and all of you who enjoy but a paper existence, who have scattered the seeds of corruption, and have brought the world within an inch of its ruin, do not imagine that you have contributed either little or much to the restoration of Germany. Do not imagine either that that restoration should free your hearts from a reasonable solicitude, or release you from all your fears. Germany is still in a ·very tottering condition. Let us rather prostrate ourselves in the dust before Jesus Christ, and give Him thanks on our knees for our deliverance, whilst imploring Him to watch over us in the future. Oh, do not feel shame at bending the knee before God, for He is our Saviour. How often your blessed Queen, with whom I had the honour of holding frequent conversations, told me that she habitually prayed to God on her knees. And the allied sovereigns, after the great battle of nations near Leipsic, did they not prostrate themselves to render thanks to the Almighty for the victory He had given them ?

On the Russian frontier Mme. de Krudener again met with unexpected difficulties. An anecdote is related by the Comte d'Allonville, in his *Mémoires Secrets*, to the effect that the party were unable to find their passports until Mme. de Krudener, at the instigation of Kellner, had knelt down in the presence of the custom-house officers and prayed for the intervention of the Almighty, when the necessary papers were immediately forthcoming from one of the trunks. Be this as it may, it is certain that Kellner was separated from his benefactress, whilst the Governor - General of Livonia ordered Mme. de Krudener and her daughter to be kept under strict surveillance. To the credit of

Alexander, however, it must be said that the instant the news of these oppressive measures reached him he sent word that his former friend and instructress was to be treated with every consideration. "The Emperor is much grieved at what has occurred," wrote the Minister of Public Worship, Prince Alexander Galitzin, to the lady; "he does not wish Europe to imagine that he could have behaved in such a manner, when in reality he is ready to open his empire to the people of the Lord, by order of the Lord." A special courier was despatched to convey this letter to Mme. de Krudener, and to sanction the immediate return of those members of her suite who had been debarred from crossing the frontier.

Mme. de Krudener made no attempt to continue her journey as far as St. Petersburg, and there came from the Emperor no renewal of that ardent invitation which, less than three years previously, he had pressed upon his saintly friend in Paris, to come and share with him the joys and difficulties of doing the work of the Lord in his own capital. Absence, calumny, the skilful misrepresentations of enemies, the publication of the indiscreet *Gazette des Pauvres*, the unhappy *dénouement* of the Rappenhoff incident, had all combined to work on the impressionable mind of Alexander, and thus it was in but thinly-veiled disgrace, that the presiding goddess of the Thanksgiving at the "Camp de Vertus" was allowed to return to her native land. The whole of the summer of 1818 was spent by

Mme. de Krudener in quiet retirement at Jung-fernhoff, the country seat of her brother, M. de Wietinghoff, a prominent member of the short-lived Bible Society, with whom she appears to have enjoyed much spiritual sympathy. "My brother is excellent," she writes, "and his piety is sincere and active; he sends tracts for the prisoners, even as far as Siberia. . . . We prayed together the other day, with tears and much fervour."

In the autumn she took up her residence at her own property of Kosse, where the next two years were spent. Several of her Swiss friends appear to have rejoined her here, and Kellner still remained a prominent member of the household, but she suffered the grief of being separated, almost for the first time, from her daughter Juliette, who accompanied M. de Berckheim on a return journey to Switzerland, undertaken in the service of the Emperor, on behalf of the Swiss colonists for Southern Russia.

It was a great joy to Mme. de Krudener, with her enfeebled health and shattered nerves, to find herself once more, after so many years of wandering and exile, in the much-loved home of her childhood. The dreamy melancholy beauty of the Livonian landscape, which had exercised so inspiring an influence over her girlish imagination, soothed her in her old age. She spent much of her time in solitude, absorbed in prayer and meditation, or occupied with the composition of prophetic hymns and canticles, written mostly in German, and filled

with allusions to the vast pine forests and silent
level plains with which she was surrounded. When
her health permitted, she took much pleasure in
visiting the peasantry of the estate, sitting in their
wooden huts, and talking to the inmates of God, of
love, and of their duties one to another. Prayer-
meetings also were held at Kosse, and the simple-
minded religious country people, many of whom
had been influenced by the little communities of
Moravian Brothers scattered amongst them, gladly
responded to the invitation of their *châtelaine*, for
whom they had always entertained a loyal feeling of
devotion and gratitude.

Von Sternberg, the author of a short pamphlet
on Mme. de Krudener, gives the following account
of a highly characteristic little episode belonging to
this period, of which he was accidentally a spec-
tator :—

It was a fine summer's evening, when, as I was walking
along the banks of the river, an open carriage drove by, in which
an old lady, dressed in gray silk, was seated beside a young man.
Without knowing that it was Mme. de Krudener, I experienced a
singular impression at the sight of this person. A moment later
the carriage stopped, and the old lady got down, leaning on the
arm of her cavalier. Although at a short distance, I soon realised
the cause of this proceeding. There was a group of girls close
by on the banks of the river busily washing clothes, and Mme.
de Krudener, perceiving them, could not resist the temptation of
getting down and preaching them a little sermon. She accordingly made her way to the laughing country girls, who opened
their great eyes with wonder, and getting up upon a bench, she
thus obtained a commanding position, from whence she addressed
a homily to those present, of which I perfectly remember the
principal points.

"What are you doing there?" she cried out in the dialect of the country people, and with a loud voice.

The girls looked at one another laughingly, and replied that they were washing linen.

"Very good," answered Mme. de Krudener, "you are washing your body linen, but do you think of the stains that lie on your consciences, of the spots on your celestial clothing, that will drive you one day into confusion and despair, if you appear before God without having washed them? You open your great eyes, and you appear to ask me with surprise how I can know that there are any stains on your celestial vestments. Believe me that I know it most indubitably. The souls of all of us are similarly circumstanced, and the best and noblest have their stains; that is why we are ordered to incessantly keep watch over our purification, and to wash off the spots from our souls, as you do those from the linen. Neglect to do this, and God will punish you in heaven, as your master will punish you on earth if you neglect the other. But the punishments of God are as much more terrible than those of man, as heaven is higher than the earth."

And thus the discourse was prolonged, in a style that was at once familiar and yet mystical, but always borrowing its metaphors from circumstances of daily life, and that were within reach of the simplest minds. The effect was prodigious. As Mme. de Krudener spoke on, these poor girls passed from a state of stupid astonishment to gathering up fragments, and then following every sentence of the address, and as they did so their former boisterousness changed into an aspect of modest decency. Gradually they left their work, went up to the old lady, and falling on their knees they wept, whilst she, elevated above them, smiled with the smile of love, and stretched forth her hand to bless them.

The tranquil peace of the spot and cloudless sky, the inspiration of her words, which were carried away by the balmy evening breeze, all combined to produce an ineffaceable impression on my mind, and I cannot to the present day hear Mme. de Krudener's name mentioned without being reminded of that scene.

In the autumn of 1819 Mme. de Berckheim

rejoined her mother at Kosse, and in the following spring the Baron also returned from Switzerland, more than ever imbued with the doctrines of the mystical school of religious thought, and of Mme. Guyon in particular.   To his friend, the Marquis de Langallerie, to whose instrumentality this spiritual development was mainly due, he wrote several letters in the course of the year 1820, from which we make the following extracts, containing curious details as to the religious extravagances practised at this time in all good faith by Mme. de Krudener and her humble neighbours at Kosse :—

I have been to fetch Juliette from Kosse, where, by the grace of God, I spent four weeks in prayer and meditation.   Our dear mother was in very bad health during our visit.   She suffered from a bad feverish chill, but on the day of our departure for St. Petersburg, thanks be to God, her health was much improved.

I particularly appreciated the society of Kellner.   He has been introduced into the sanctuary, although as yet he can only feel the horrors of the tomb.   He and mother have received great inward graces; my mother-in-law's faith produces miracles, for the Esthonian people are so simple-hearted that they readily receive the effusion of her faith.

The separation referred to above cannot have been of long duration, for in another letter M. de Berckheim describes the. following extraordinary scenes, on which it is not easy to pass any comment :—

On Thursday, 6th May, being Ascension Day, my mother-in-law prayed on the garden terrace between eleven and twelve o'clock at night; she was enabled to offer up a marvellous prayer, of which the mere words fail to convey the full meaning.   She seemed to rise up into the celestial regions, that she might love, and be transformed into a ray of light. She flung herself into the martyrdom of love, invoked the Heavenly Jerusalem, the Blessed Virgin, and all the Saints to descend from the skies to bring souls to her, so that she might pour into their hearts the torrents of love that spring from her own; to bring her simple childish hearts, and souls eager for confession, adoration, and prayer. She prayed our Lord to grant her some visible manifestation of His mercies. . . .

The same day there was a grand fête at Petscheski, a convent and place of pilgrimage amongst the Russians, where the contemplative life is practised. A few days later, between the days of Pentecost in the old and the new styles, a large number of Letts assembled at Kosse, urged by a longing for confession and the forgiveness of sins. My mother-in-law had felt for a long time that she ought to make a public confession of all the sins of her past life in the presence of her people. She did so whilst praying with the Letts, and, moved by the Holy Spirit, she confessed her own sins and received the confessions of the people. Not a day passes without a number of Letts arriving here. The confessions are general and public when the finger of Providence points that way; they are private and personal when circumstances demand it. Thus, in the gardens at Kosse, a living confessional is established, from which streams of blessings seem to flow; not a day passes but the part of the garden in which the Letts assemble is watered with their tears. A faithful sheep, my mother-in-law is to be found spending the greater part of the day in the midst of the lambs with which Providence has entrusted her.

In the early days she used to spend eight or nine hours on her knees, praying, pleading, interceding, receiving and making confessions, and begging of the Great High Priest absolution for her sins and for those of a penitent people.

A Lett said to her one day that it was very hard to humble oneself before a man who had been one's enemy for a long time. My mother-in-law showed him the Holy Sacrifice, and the Lett went and asked forgiveness of the man who had been his enemy.

The Lett peasantry who are connected with the Moravian Brothers are at the head of this nation of penitents; they are urged to visit Kosse by internal voices, visions, and intense spiritual yearnings. These people make public confession of their secret faults to those they have offended. The words of the Scripture, "Confess your sins one to another" are real to them. They rise up after confession and prayer, and kiss the ground and the trees which have been witnesses of their great reconciliation through the blood of Christ. Pious chants rise from their hearts and resound through the garden, and as they depart, with one accord they sing the praises of the Almighty. They carry away with them a profound inward sense of union with the Blessed Virgin and the Saints, with the inward and victorious Church that descends from heaven with the Lion of Judah at its head, to overthrow the powers of the enemy, and establish on earth the worship of adoration, in spirit and in truth.

It has been revealed to my mother-in-law that the time has come when the various mysteries of the Christian Church, of the ancient and inward Catholic Church, are to appear in a more living and active form. These words, "Ye are the temple of God" are to be accomplished in the sight of all men, and the Church will rise up from her bed of suffering, palpitating with life.

Again, a few months later, we read :—

Juliette is going to start with her brother for Kosse, where she will spend two or three months with her mother; I shall go and rejoin her, that I may bring her back to St. Petersburg, if the Lord sends me the means. My mother-in-law is in a very profound state of prayer and recollection in the midst of a simple people, in whom a spirit of reasoning has not diminished the capacity for faith. The occupants of her property are Esthonians, and the Brothers had already prepared their hearts to receive the good seed. She is surrounded by Letts, who come in great crowds to Kosse, to make confession of their sins with tears and true contrition. In answer to the prayers of my mother and of Kellner, the Almighty permits the most miraculous cures, to testify to this simple and childlike people that their Heavenly Father is in the midst of them when they invoke Him. Kellner is in the most profound state of internal recollection ; he is in an advanced condition, according to Mme. Guyon. His external behaviour is only the result of obedience, and does not in any way, as in the past, foster a spirit of property.

CHAPTER XVIII

1820-1824

IN the month of November 1820 M. de Berckheim,
who, at the time, was staying with his wife at the
house of the Princess Anna Galitzin, near St. Petersburg, was seized with some severe and sudden
malady, so that for many days his life was despaired
of.   Mme. de Krudener, whose affection for her son-
in-law quite equalled her love for her own children,
felt deeply her separation from the De Berckheims
in this time of sorrow, and her letters to her daughter,
written in her most ecstatic and mystical vein, bear
pathetic evidence of the struggle that was going on
within her, between her natural maternal anxiety and
her customary submission to the will of God.   Thus
she writes from Kosse (24th November) :—

. . . What can I say to you, my angel,—what can a miserable
creature say who is a greater sinner than any?   A great and peaceful
calm is added to the profound sorrow of my soul ; I do not suffer,
but I love.   I lay you at the feet of Him who is all things, and whose
inexpressible love you know well ; I lay there also the object of
my most tender affections, our much-loved Francis.   I long to
hurry to you, to embrace our dear invalid, and draw him to the
foot of that Cross which is his refuge and mine, only that I

know those who are round him are doing so already. . . . Why
should I weep when I see you prepared for eternity? If I draw
back in the face of sorrow, it is because I am a coward ; but grief
is none the less rich in treasures when it brings us nearer to our
God. . . .

And again, a fortnight later :—

Oh, my child, what an agonising letter we received from you
yesterday! May the merciful God who lends His powerful aid
to my children be adored and glorified! Let us prostrate ourselves; let us only see His glory—the glory of the God who became
man, who, in each one of us, performs His miracles of love, who,
according to His wisdom, causes all things to advance His reign
in our hearts. May His Heavenly Father behold us through
Him, the loving Jesus ; may the Holy Ghost enlighten, guide, and
fortify us! One secret hope sustains me : I believe our Francis
still breathes, that the God of miracles has preserved him for
us. . . .

An association for prayer for the recovery of the
invalid was established at Kosse, and the hopes of
the members were sustained by the prophetic visions
promising the ultimate restoration of the Baron to
health, with which several amongst them claimed to
have been favoured. In the meanwhile Mme. de
Krudener applied to the Emperor for permission to
take up her residence in St. Petersburg. The
absence of Alexander at the Congress of Troppau
somewhat delayed the reply, and it was not till
February (1821) that the anxious mother was enabled
to clasp her children once more in her arms. She
found her son-in-law able to leave his bed, but with
no hope of an ultimate recovery. The sequel must
be told in the words of the gentle and tender-hearted

Juliette, who had scarcely left her husband's bedside during the whole course of his illness.

> They (her mother and husband) passed many hours alone together, either in prayer, or in conversation and confession. My husband had desired to go to confession to my mother, according to the injunction of the Apostle, "Confess your sins one to another." From that time the invalid was no longer the same, but visibly gained strength. I am writing to you of facts which are deeply graven in my heart, and I can only exclaim with David: "Bless the Lord, O my soul: and all that is within me, bless His holy name."

Mme. de Krudener's reappearance at St. Petersburg was the signal for an outburst of enthusiasm on her behalf, and the salon of the Princess Anna Galitzin, at whose house she had taken up her abode, was daily besieged by a crowd of the most distinguished and elegant people in Russian court circles. This sudden demonstration must be attributed to the fact that a considerable religious ferment was in operation at this time amongst the educated classes of the Empire. The religious toleration practised for many years by the Emperor, under the judicious guidance of Prince Alexander Galitzin, his Minister of Public Worship, the impulse given to the study of the Scriptures by the establishment of Bible Societies, and the introduction into Russia of the works of Swedenborg, Saint Martin, Boehme, and other mystics, had all combined to turn the thoughts of the more earnest-minded men and women of the Empire towards the spiritual problems of existence. To all such Mme. de Krudener, with her sufferings, her strange experiences, her touching self-abnegation,

appeared in the light of a religious leader, and the
eloquent exhortations to Love and Charity, which fell
from her lips, were listened to with rapt attention.

Such was the situation at St. Petersburg when
the Emperor of Russia returned home from the
Congress of Laybach in the spring of 1821. We
have already indicated in previous chapters how, by
the force of circumstances reacting on his impressionable nature, the Tsar's feelings of love and
veneration for his spiritual directress had given
place to sentiments of coldness, and even of suspicion. Hence it was, no doubt, with a feeling of
annoyance that he found her playing once more a
prominent *rôle* in his own capital. There apparently exists no record of the first meeting at St.
Petersburg between Alexander and Mme. de
Krudener — a meeting which must have been
fraught with much sorrowful recollection for them
both ; but though it is impossible to believe that
no personal intercourse of any kind took place, it
is certain, in spite of the assertions of various writers
to the contrary, that there was not even an attempt
at a renewal of their previous confidential relations,
and that Mme. de Krudener's influence at Court
was at an end.

In truth, Alexander's political convictions had
undergone alterations in many important particulars
since the summer of 1815. In foreign affairs the
revolutionary spirit which was abroad throughout
Europe, and which kept cropping up in various
places in a manner highly inconvenient to reigning

monarchs, was craftily turned by Metternich to the furtherance of his own schemes, by disenchanting the Tsar with the liberal ideas of his youth ; whilst the bond of Christian unity amongst nations, which was to have been initiated by the Holy Alliance, was transformed by the same skilful agency into a chain of iron, which fettered the Emperor at every turn. In home affairs matters were even worse. The enormous difficulties of introducing radical reforms into the administration of so vast an empire, the sullen opposition of the bulk of the Orthodox priesthood to his policy of religious toleration, the special troubles and disorders inseparable from a lengthened period of war and national destitution, all combined to damp the ardour for social amelioration with which the Emperor had been inflamed on his return to Russia in the autumn of 1815. Under the weight of disappointment, and the growing sense of his own incapacity to deal with the gigantic task before him, Alexander grew morose, gloomy, and suspicious even of his best friends, harboured designs of relinquishing his throne to one of his brothers, and allowed the management of affairs to slip more and more into the cruel and capable hands of General Arakchéïeff.

To the Russian patriot the name of Arakchéïeff will always recall one of the worst periods of oppression and despotism through which his unhappy country has been condemned to pass in recent times—a period all the more crushing as following immediately on an interval of comparative freedom and social development. A man of iron will, ferocious cruelty, limited education, and dissolute morals, Arakchéïeff was inspired by an unbounded devotion to the person of his sovereign, and a proportionate determination to uphold the prerogatives of the throne against all encroachment. As Prince Galitzin represents the enlightened, religious, moderate side of Alexander's reign, so the General represents the narrow, bigoted, reactionary side. Between the two ministers there was, of course, open war, and Arakchéïeff[1] did not rest until at length (1824) he brought about the dismissal from office of his master's former confidant. In this task he was assisted by the monk Photius, archimandrite of the great monastery of St. George, near Novgorod, a man of fiery eloquence and a great reputation for sanctity, who obtained much influence over the vacillating mind of the Emperor in the latter years of his reign, and to whose zealous upholding of the paramount claims of the Orthodox Church on the consideration of its Supreme Head was mainly due the reversal of Alexander's cherished policy of religious toleration.

But the question which above all others absorbed the attention of St. Petersburg at the moment of Mme. de Krudener's advent in the capital, and which was beginning to attract the attention of the whole of Europe, was the insurrection of the Greeks

---

[1] General Arakchéïeff was disgraced in his turn shortly after the accession of Nicolas I. He died in 1834 at his country house at Gronsino, having preserved to the last moment of his life the most enthusiastic veneration for his former master.

against Turkey. The instinctive sympathies of Alexander for all oppressed nationalities, strengthened in the present instance by his almost lifelong friendship for the Greek patriot, Count Capo d'Istria, seemed to point him out as the natural ally of the courageous Hellenes in their struggle against Moslem tyranny. Indeed the eyes of the Greek leaders were all turned for help towards Russia. Austria, on the other hand, was determined to counteract any policy which would increase the prestige of her ally in South-eastern Europe, and Metternich put forth all the arts of his diplomacy to dissuade Alexander from any acts of open encouragement towards Greece. Distracted by these conflicting influences, urged on by his conscience to hasten to the assistance of a patriotic Christian people, and restrained by the suspicions and objections of his allies, the Emperor's attitude on the Greek question was one of pitiable weakness and vacillation, ending in complete inaction. How thoroughly the insinuations of diplomacy had gained the mastery over the natural impulses of his generous heart, may be gathered by the explanation he vouchsafed to M. de Chateaubriand at the Congress of Verona: "I seemed to see revolutionary symptoms in the troubles of the Peloponnesus, and therefore I abstained from interference."

It is almost needless to say that from the very first rumours of impending trouble in the far south, Mme. de Krudener's heart had gone out in enthusiastic sympathy to her struggling co-religionists.

From the depths of her retirement at Kosse she had penned a mystical prophetic hymn in honour of the Greek patriots, in which she preached, as it were, a new Crusade of the Cross against the Crescent. On her arrival at St. Petersburg she did not hesitate to speak out boldly and eloquently on the subject in the salon of the Princess Galitzin, and appealed openly to the Tsar to fulfil his obligations as a Christian monarch. Her words, inspired no doubt more by religious enthusiasm than by worldly prudence, were constantly repeated to Alexander, and served to embitter his heart yet more against her. Determined at length to put an end to the practical inconvenience of seeing his policy of inaction denounced in his own capital, but anxious to do so with every possible consideration for one for whom he had entertained feelings of the very warmest friendship, the Tsar resolved on writing a letter to Mme. de Krudener, in which he set forth clearly the reasons of his abstention, and the insuperable difficulties in the way of a more active policy. After blaming the liberty with which she had censured the acts of his government, the Emperor gave her to understand in friendly but unmistakable language that in fermenting discontent around his throne she was acting contrary to her obligations both as a subject and a Christian, and that her presence in the capital could only be permitted on condition of absolute silence concerning a course of action which he was not at liberty to alter at her bidding. This communication was

entrusted by the Tsar to Count Alexander Tour-
genief, with orders to read it aloud to the lady, and
then return it to the Emperor. Mme. de Krudener
listened with respect, and subsequently begged the
messenger to convey her grateful thanks to his
Imperial master for the delicate consideration with
which he had made known to her his wishes. But
his arguments naturally failed in any way to alter
her views, and feeling oppressed by the restraint
under which she was obliged to live, Mme. de
Krudener brought her visit to St. Petersburg to a
close in the course of the following winter, and
retired once more to Kosse. It is reported that
she had resolved on leaving the capital on foot, but
that the Emperor, hearing of her intentions, sent one
of his own carriages, attended by a guard, to convey
her to her destination.

The following two years (1822-23) were spent by
Mme. de Krudener at her old home in the most
complete retirement, broken only by occasional
visits from the De Berckheims. She appears to
have relinquished the whole of her vast correspondence, devoting her days exclusively to prayer
and meditation, to performing acts of charity
amongst her beloved peasantry, and to the inflic-
tion of acts of mortification upon herself. Thus
she not only fasted continually, but in the midst
of the arctic severities of a Russian winter, with
the thermometer indicating twenty degrees of cold
(Réaumur), she would spend day after day in a
room without either stove or double windows,

apparently without suffering any discomfort. Her naturally delicate health could not long bear so severe a strain, and early in the spring of 1823 she began to suffer from acute insomnia, her lungs were seriously affected, and it was ascertained that she was also threatened with cancer. In the midst of all these physical trials Mme. de Krudener received a great shock from the death of Kellner, who for so many years had been a constant member of her household, and on whom she largely depended for spiritual consolation and encouragement. For a time at least her trust in God seems to have been almost crushed out under the weight of so many sorrows; but, cheered by the tender care of her daughter Juliette, she was soon enabled to resume her usual implicit faith in the divine mercy, and even to take an active interest in a scheme propounded by the Princess Anna Galitzin, that the whole party should transfer themselves to the lands of the Princess in the Crimea, where she was desirous of founding a Christian colony of German and Swiss immigrants. The doctors having ordered Mme. de Krudener to winter in a mild climate, immediate preparations for departure were made; but, owing to various causes, and to the vast number of arrangements necessitated by so serious an undertaking, it was not till the early spring of 1824 that the party set out in barges, which were to convey them down the Volga, and thence by way of the Don to the Sea of Azof. The journey by water, though far slower than by land, was easy and restful to an invalid, and Mme. de Krudener derived much benefit from the fresh air and ever-changing scenery. A long halt was made at Theodosia, a beautiful spot on the southern shore of the Crimea, and it was mid-September before the party finally arrived at the Galitzin property of Karasu-Basar, situated towards the centre of the peninsula, and not far distant from the present imperial palace of Livadia.

Little remains to be told of these last months. Owing, no doubt, to defective arrangements, the German and Swiss colonists suffered great hardships during this first winter in the Crimea, both from scarcity of food and from want of proper accommodation. Mme. de Krudener joyfully put up with her share of the general discomfort, and did her utmost by prayer and preaching to cheer the hearts of the little community. But as the winter advanced, both the consumption and the cancer from which she was suffering made most alarming progress, and she was soon unable to quit her own room. Feeling her end approaching, and her strength slipping from her day by day, she was anxious to die at peace with all men ; and with that object she took up her pen once more to write to her step-daughter, Mme. Ochando, between whom and herself some slight coolness had arisen several years previously, owing to some outspoken and, as the event proved, well-founded strictures, which Sophie had passed on the conduct of Frederick Fontaine. In this letter Madame de Krudener, with much humility, takes the whole blame

in the matter upon herself, and after entreating her
step-daughter to convey her sincere apologies to
Mme. Armand at Geneva for any unintentional
wrong-doing towards her friend of which she may
have been guilty, she concludes her letter with these
words—the last that have been preserved from her
prolific pen :—

Oh, my Sophie, I throw myself into your arms ; forgive me,
ill and suffering as I am, and you will be blessed ; forgive me all
my wrong-doing, and with one common impulse let us cast ourselves on that mercy which never fails us.

In a letter to her sister, written after the death
of their mother, Juliette de Berckheim relates well-
nigh all that there is to know of these last months of
physical pain and weakness, sanctified by spiritual
peace and joy.

She was always so busy at Kosse that her physical strength
became insufficient to support the life of the soul ; her bodily
weakness was also a hindrance to her spiritual repose. By leaving
Kosse, it has been our Lord's will that mamma should enjoy
absolute solitude ; our journey had already helped to deprive her
of all worldly preoccupations, as well as of all the objects which
might have reminded her of her former splendid activity. How
often, on seeing mamma thus torn away from the religious sphere,
where she had enjoyed such great blessings, my soul was grieved
at not being able to replace her in it, but it was not long before
I recognised the will of God. The time had come when Jesus,
and Jesus alone, was to fill that heart, as loving as that of Mary.
She herself had a presentiment of this ; glancing backwards, in
order to note what she was leaving, and reviewing in her soul her
rapid course, she had nothing to offer save tears, and the blood
of our Saviour to wash away the stains of sin. She saw nothing
but her own worthlessness in the sight of God ; at the entrance
to the sanctuary she perceived herself to be clothed in rags, and,

like David, she cried day and night : "Who can understand my secret offences ? Oh that I had wings like a dove ! "

If my heart had not longed so ardently to keep her with us, I should have realised that it was the last great preparation. In this last terrible conflict, she had a strong desire to see her own people once more. She would often say to me : "When you write, let me put in a few lines." But I had not the courage to remind her, when I saw at last what an effort every word, or gesture, or movement, cost her. It was a great grief to her not to see you again, although she frequently said to me that she thanked God that she was here, where she was surrounded and tended by friends ; but her sympathetic soul nevertheless pined for intercourse with all whom she loved. However, she made a sacrifice of everything. . . . Six letters from Kosse were lost, so that I could not even give her news of that much-loved spot.

Unable to humble herself sufficiently in her own eyes, she often distressed me by asking pardon of me, who would gladly have kissed her feet. Frequently in the morning I would find her bathed in tears, and in the evening she would still be weeping, conversing with God and reproaching herself for the possession of even the smallest objects. . . . It is wonderful how the Lord released her from all bonds and all possessions ! He made use of her illness for that object, though he spared her any very acute pain ; but she frequently prayed for patience with tears. Her nerves were so delicate that she could hardly bear the irritation of exhaustion, and her weakness was so great that it took half the day to change her bed. Nearly every evening she had an attack of fever, followed by nervous prostration, which made us fear that she would expire. Thus, although we had prayed and longed for her preservation, the Lord taught us to regard her death as the end of her own sufferings.

On our first arrival at Karasu-Basar, she still had a little strength left, and it was then that she wrote to you ; then, cutting herself off from everything that could have hindered her, she abandoned everything to the will of God ; her suffering body insisted on its rights. Day and night she required constant care. She consented at length to take rather better food, and I prepared it all for her myself over her bedroom fire.

In November we celebrated her birthday, and she was as

happy as a child on receiving a few flowers and cakes and sweet-meats for distribution.

She had a positive craving for food, and constantly reproached herself for thinking too much about it. Towards evening she used to fall asleep. Latterly she tried to resist the temptation, saying that the feeling of reawakening was so painful, it was like the beginning of death. A young Livonian girl used to nurse her day and night, with the help of two girls, who belong to a German family here. One of them was called Emily; she had been brought up among the Moravians, and mamma regarded her with special affection. It was a treat whenever it was her turn to be in the room; mamma used to make her talk about the community life, and read her the hymns of Terstegen that we were so fond of, or something else of the same sort. When Emily left, Berckheim took her place beside the bed, but towards the end he could only read a few lines at a time. Mamma suffered from not being able to rise for prayer, and that was one of the reasons why we did not send for the minister, who had offered to come and pray with her. The state of her health required such constant attention.

May the Lord make my heart like hers! I have never seen a person with such a sense of her own weakness, such gentleness, and such resignation. No one would have imagined that there was an invalid in the house. The pain she suffered often arose from her extreme delicacy, which made her hesitate to ask for any painful services. She liked to have Berckheim with her, and she used to keep him for several hours every night and ask him to pray aloud for her. You remember the sweetness of her disposition; in her good moments she would laugh and be as bright as a child; but, as a rule, her illness appeared to have destroyed, or at least veiled, the expression of love and of charity which she possessed in so marked a degree.

It was on Christmas morning (1824), after retaining her full consciousness to the last, that Mme. de Krudener passed quietly away. She was only in her sixty-second year, but her fragile health was completely broken and worn out by the exces-

sive labour and manifold privations of her life.
Her body was deposited in the vault of the
Armenian Church at Karasu-Basar, to await the
completion of the Greek edifice, which the Princess
Galitzin was having constructed at Koreïs, and to
which the remains of her friend were transferred at
a later date. It was doubtless in their temporary
resting-place that, according to local tradition, the
Emperor Alexander, in the following November,
knelt in solitary prayer before all that was mortal of
his saintly friend, having turned aside for that purpose whilst on a tour of inspection through the
peninsula. This visit was to prove a final act of
respect, and possibly of remorse, for past coldness and
suspicion ; for already Alexander carried within him
the fatal germs of the disease which, only a few days
later, struck him down at Taganrog, and brought
his life to a premature close in the very prime of his
manhood (1st December 1825). Thus, by some
curious fatality, the friends were reunited in death,
after having drifted so far apart in the closing years
of their life.

Judged, as some of Mme. de Krudener's Protestant biographers have elected to judge her, as
a regenerator of Christianity throughout the continent of Europe, the weaknesses and feminine
inconsistencies of her character cannot be passed
over. For ourselves, we prefer to place her on a
somewhat lower pedestal, in order to offer her without reservation our most profound sympathy and
admiration. Let it be granted, at once, that she was

neither a St. Catherine, nor a St. Theresa, nor even a Mme. Guyon, by whose writings she had been so frequently inspired; but let us none the less honour her as a tender-hearted, loving woman, who, having passed through fire herself, stepped down bravely from her social eminence in order to extend a warm hand of help and sympathy to those of her brothers and sisters who were groping blindly along the stony path of life; who sacrificed much in her great love for her Divine Master, and who, in her humility, felt herself rewarded far beyond her deserts by the peace and joy which illuminated her soul throughout the years of her self-imposed apostolate.

THE END

Printed by R. & R. CLARK, *Edinburgh*.